WARRIOR'S KISS

"I do not go around kissing men, Lord MacLeod, if that's what you are implying. I'm not that sort of woman," she said tightly.

He brushed a soft curl from the curve of her heated cheek. "'Tis no' what I meant. I ken what kind of woman ye are, lass."

"What . . . what do you mean?" she stammered, raising amber eyes flecked with gold to his.

Cupping her chin in his hands, he rubbed his thumb over her full bottom lip. "I mean ye're innocent. No man has ever kissed ye, have they?"

"No," she whispered, her lips slightly parted.

"'Tis a shame that. Ye have a bonny mouth, ripe fer kissin'." Desire overrode caution and he lowered his head to claim her. He only meant for it to be one brief kiss, but the moment he touched her soft, pliant lips, he was lost . . .

Books by Debbie Mazzuca

LORD OF THE ISLES

WARRIOR OF THE ISLES

Published by Kensington Publishing Corporation

Warrior
of the Isles

Debbie Mazzuca

ZEBRA BOOKS
KENSINGTON PUBLISHING CORP.
http://www.kensingtonbooks.com

ZEBRA BOOKS are published by

Kensington Publishing Corp.
119 West 40th Street
New York, NY 10018

All Kensington titles, imprints, and distributed lines are
available at special quantity discounts for bulk purchases for
sales promotion, premiums, fund-raising, educational, or
institutional use.

Special book excerpts or customized printings can also be created to fit specific needs. For details, write or phone the office
of the Kensington Special Sales Manager: Attn. Special Sales
Department. Kensington Publishing Corp., 119 West 40th
Street, New York, NY 10018. Phone: 1-800-221-2647.

Zebra and the Z logo Reg. U.S. Pat. & TM Off.

ISBN-13: 978-1-4201-1006-7
ISBN-10: 1-4201-1006-3

First Printing: May 2011
10 9 8 7 6 5 4 3 2 1

Printed in the United States of America

To my husband, Perry, my real-life hero.
I wouldn't want to be on this journey
with anyone else but you.
I love you.

ACKNOWLEDGMENTS

To my wonderful children, April, Jess, Nic, and Shariffe. Thank you for supporting me in doing what I love to do, even though it means I don't cook and clean like I used to. I adore you guys.

Thanks to my amazingly supportive family—the LeClairs and the Mazzucas. I am truly blessed. I love you all!

To my book club gals, Carolyn, Joanne, Kathleen, Lynn, and Peggy. I wouldn't miss our Thursday nights together. Thanks for your friendship and support.

Thanks to Ludvica, Lucy, Coreene, Vanessa, and Teresa for taking the time to read for me. I so appreciate your insights, support, and friendship!

To my wonderful editor, John Scognamiglio. Thanks for your support and for always being there to answer my questions.

Thanks to my fabulous agent, Pamela Harty, for continuing to encourage and believe in me. You're the best!

To the readers who took the time to let me know how much they enjoyed Rory and Aileanna's story. I loved hearing from you. Thank you!

Prologue

Seated at a table in the back of the crowded alehouse, Aidan MacLeod attempted to slough off the burden of his responsibilities and enjoy the carefree companionship of his friends, and the voluptuous redhead in his lap.

"See what ye've been missin', MacLeod?" Gavin grinned at him from across the table, hauling a buxom blonde into his arms.

Aidan shook his head with a laugh and returned his attention to the greedy wench, who attempted to smother him in her bountiful charms.

"Ah, MacLeod, we've got company."

Aidan drew his mouth from the lass's rosy-tipped breast. Ignoring her throaty groan of protest, he followed Gavin's gaze to the front of the alehouse. Torquil, his father's man-at-arms, stood in the entryway.

As he noted Torquil's grim expression, Aidan's lust was replaced with a heavy sense of foreboding. He eased the woman from his lap and came to his feet. Without taking his eyes from the silver-haired man-at-arms, he tossed her some coin and motioned for her to take her leave.

She sidled up to him, her heavy scent cloying. "I'll take

yer coin, laddie, but I'd much rather ye give me this." To the amusement of his companions, she groped the front of his trews.

He shot her an impatient look and brushed her hand aside. "My father's back?" he asked the thickset man, who now stood before him.

"Aye, I had no chance to warn ye, lad. We left—"

Before Torquil could finish his explanation, Aidan grabbed his woolen cloak off the bench and headed for the door. His companion's entreaty to remain fell on deaf ears. His wee brother was alone and unprotected.

Thunder rumbled overhead as Aidan strode across the rain-soaked yard to the stables. Cursing every moment of delay, he kicked off the mud that caked his boots against the edge of the door. The stable hand, who had been lolling against a bale of hay, leapt to his feet.

"Bring me my mount, and his," Aidan added, sensing Torquil's presence behind him.

"Dougal will keep the lad out of the laird's way. He'll come to no harm," Torquil said as he attempted to reassure him.

Aidan swept droplets of rain from his face and focused on the man-at-arms. "Are ye tellin' me my da is no' drunk, then?" If that were the case, it would do much to allay the fear icing Aidan's veins.

Sober, his father would do nothing more to his young brother than ignore him, and although hurtful to the bairn, it would do little more than wound his heart. But if his father was in his cups, that was another matter entirely.

His question was met with tight-lipped silence and Aidan cursed. He accepted Fin's reins with a muttered thanks and leapt onto the stallion's back, turning him toward home.

Moments later, Torquil's big bay caught up to him. Despite the fading light, Aidan could see the man was holding something back. "What havena ye told me?"

Torquil raised his voice to be heard above the thunder of

the horses' hooves. "'Tis the day of the lad's birth is all, and ye ken how yer father—"

Aidan's disgusted bellow was lost in the wind. Of all the days to leave his brother alone, he'd chosen this one. With his father away at court, he'd taken the opportunity to join his friends in the hunt and a night of pleasure. At eighteen, he was more of a father to Lachlan than a brother, and lately he'd chafed at the responsibility. But never had he expected his actions would put his brother in danger.

The memory of Lachlan's birth eight years past escaped from where he'd locked it away. He tried to shove it back, but the words the old crone had uttered reverberated in his head, words that damned both his mother and his brother.

He has the mark of the Fae.

His mother's anguished cry of denial echoed in his head alongside his father's bellow of rage. Aidan squeezed his eyes closed to shut out the image of the bloody white linens shrouding his mother, the sound of his bare feet slapping against the cold stone as he ran from the room.

He wrapped his cloak tighter to ward off the bitter winds and memories. Bent low over Fin, he tore across the narrow wooden bridge, leaving Torquil far behind. Lights flickered in the distance as the tower came into view through a misty curtain of rain. Aidan's heart raced as he closed in on his home. His chest was so tight he could barely shout out his brother's name when Dougal met him in the deserted courtyard.

The old man's gnarled fingers clutched at Aidan's trews. "I canna find the lad or the laird." He jerked his whiskered chin toward the keep. "All within are searchin' now, but—"

Aidan met Dougal's worried gaze. No words needed to be exchanged. They both knew what had happened. His father had taken his brother to the cliffs. He'd uttered the threat often enough, only Aidan had never believed the man he once loved and admired would attempt such a heinous act. Even now, with every pained breath he took, he prayed he was wrong.

"Be careful, lad, I fear he's gone mad. I doona ken what set him off. Mayhap 'twas somethin' yer uncle said, but 'tis worse than before."

Aidan gave a tight nod, blinking hard to keep his tears at bay. He was a man, and this was no time for a woman's emotion. With a sharp tug on Fin's reins, he brought the horse around and headed back into the night.

As the granite cliffs came into view, he called out his brother's name, but the words were lost on the plaintive howl of the wind. His eyes burned from straining to see through the gloaming, and the rain. A flash of lightning illuminated the rugged landscape. A hulking shadow dragged a struggling white bundle toward the rocks.

An agonized cry ripped from his throat. "Nay, Da, nay." He leapt from Fin. His fear making him clumsy, he stumbled toward them.

"Ye canna stop me, Aidan. This day I will ken the truth." Alexander MacLeod's words were thick and slurred. He jerked Lachlan's arm, and the bairn cried in anguish.

Aidan slammed down his anger and his fear. He needed to keep his wits about him. With his gaze trained on his father, he searched for an opportunity to get his brother out of harm's way. Inching closer, he heard the waves crash against the rocks below, smelled the salty tang of the sea air, and his senses reeled.

Lachlan whimpered. His eyes were wide with terror, golden curls plastered to his angelic face.

"Da, doona do this. Give him to me, please," Aidan begged.

With a fierce shake of his head, Alexander snaked an arm around Lachlan, whose wee body convulsed with fear. Soaked to the skin, the white nightshirt clung to his brother's slight frame, and his bare feet dangled high above the ground. His father's blue eyes looked black—wild and glazed. In that moment Aidan knew nothing he could say would stop his father. He had to act.

"I'm givin' him back to the Fae and ye canna stop me." Alexander lost his footing on the rain-slicked turf and his hand shot out. Trying to regain his balance, he loosened his hold on Lachlan.

In his mindless state, his father's movements were slow and exaggerated. Aidan, seeing his advantage, threw himself forward. Grabbing his brother's outstretched arm, he wrenched Lachlan free from his father's hold. Aidan cradled Lan's trembling body to his chest and rolled a safe distance from the ledge. Alexander stumbled backward, his eyes widened, and his arms flailed. With a harrowing cry, he disappeared over the sheer rock face.

"Da!" Shoving Lachlan behind him, Aidan lunged to where his father clung to the rocky outcropping. He twined his fingers through Alexander's bony ones. The muscles in Aidan's arms quaked as he struggled to hold on. He tried to dig the toes of his boots into the wet earth, but found no purchase. The jagged rock scoured his chest as inch by inch Alexander's weight dragged Aidan over the edge of the cliff.

Their eyes held for a brief moment, and Aidan panicked at the grim resolve he saw in his father's watery blue gaze. "Nay, Da!" he cried as Alexander wrenched his fingers from Aidan's grasp. He squeezed his eyes shut, unable to witness his father falling into the churning black water below. Burying his head in his arms to drown out the last of Alexander's dying scream, he could no longer contain his heartbroken sob.

A warm breath whispered in his ear. "I can call the faeries, Aidan. She'll save him."

White-hot rage flared to life inside him and he staggered to his feet, dragging his brother from the edge of the cliff. His fingers bit into Lan's narrow shoulders, and he shook him so hard his brother's head snapped back. "Never again, Lachlan, never again will ye speak of the Fae. Do ye hear me?"

Tears streamed down his brother's wee face and his lower lip quivered. "Aye, Aidan," he whispered. "Aye."

He sensed movement behind him and turned from Lan. Torquil and Dougal stood in silence by their mounts, then Dougal took a hesitant step toward him. "Give us the bairn. We'll see him home."

The blinding haze of Aidan's anger dissipated. Looking down at Lachlan, he saw clearly the fear he'd put in his young brother's eyes. Aidan's chest tightened, and he swallowed past the suffocating knot in his throat. "Nay, I'll take him."

He swung Lachlan into his arms and gave him a fierce hug before wrapping him in the blanket Torquil handed him. "I'd no' harm ye, brother. And I'll let no other put ye in harm's way. I'll protect ye always. Ye ken that, doona ye?"

Lachlan wrapped his thin arms around Aidan's neck and buried his face in his chest. "I ken, Aidan. I love ye."

"I love ye, too, Lan." Aidan vowed, if ever he had the chance, he'd make the Fae pay for what they'd done to his family.

Chapter 1

The Enchanted Isles, 1603

Princess Syrena, astride her white-winged steed Bowen, glided over the Enchanted Isles. Far below, the placid azure pools twinkled in the noonday sun, and the thick verdant forest of ancient oaks met the tall swaying grasses of meadow's dotted with purple and white flowers.

Syrena surveyed her kingdom—her father's kingdom, she corrected—with pride. Surely no other realm was as beautiful, although those who remembered the stories of their forbearers claimed the heavens were. Since the Fae race had descended from six angels tossed from the celestial heights for interfering with the Mortals, Syrena supposed there must be some truth to their claims. But it mattered not. To her, nothing was as lovely as the Enchanted Isles.

Tapping Bowen's sleek, muscular hindquarters with her pink satin slippers, she directed him toward home. She couldn't put it off any longer. At this very moment her father was ensconced in his throne room, choosing his successor. After a bloody battle in the Fae realm of the Far North over succession, the wizard Uscias insisted her father name the next in line.

There were four in the running: Lord Bana and Lord Erwn,

her father's cousins and closest advisors; her stepmother, Queen Morgana; and at Uscias's insistence, Syrena. King Arwan hadn't cared that Syrena as his only heir should have been named without hesitation. No matter how hard she tried, she failed to measure up to both his and the Fae's expectations. If only they would give her a chance, she would show them her worth.

As she and Bowen flew alongside the razor-sharp peaks of granite, the crystal palace, nestled high atop the mountain, came into view. Noting the palatial mansions of the aristocracy cast in shadows at its base, Lord Bana's and Lord Erwn's among them, she wondered if even now one of them celebrated. One of the two was clearly her father's choice.

It didn't matter, not really, she comforted herself. King Arwan's successor would never get the chance to rule. The only way her father would willingly cede his authority was through death. And since the Fae were immortal—could only be killed by the juice of the Rowan berry, a wound from a magickal weapon, or fade if they so chose—her powerful father would reign forever.

"Well, Bowen, time to land." She patted the neck of her beloved steed, a gift from her mother the week before she faded. With a firm tug on his mane, she banked to the left. "No!" she cried, realizing too late that she'd forgotten his deformed wing.

They tumbled from the cloudless sky.

The pressure from the whistling wind pulled at her cheeks and whipped the crown from her head. Her long hair wrapped around her face, muffling her warbled scream.

She dangled helplessly in midair, struggling to tangle her hands in Bowen's mane to keep from falling. Her foot found purchase on his stunted wing, and she flung herself over the top of him. Hooves kicking wildly, Bowen fought to right himself. As he flapped his one, powerful, full-sized wing, the frightening free fall was over as quickly as it had begun.

She clung to him, her heart returning to its rightful place

behind her rib cage. "I'm sorry, Bowen," she said once she'd recovered. "If I ever do something so foolish again, ignore my command." He nickered and nodded as though he agreed.

Distracted with thoughts of her mother, she'd banked to the left without thinking. Deformed since birth, Bowen's left wing was half the size of his right. Syrena and her steed had learned to compensate for his shortcomings. But obviously his tendency to comply with her commands, no matter how foolish, was something they had to work on. Although there had been other incidents, no one as yet had found them out. Syrena only hoped it would be the same today.

Her hope was short-lived. As soon as Bowen's hooves hit the cobblestones, Rainer, one of the stable hands, crossed the courtyard to greet them. He twirled Syrena's jeweled crown on his finger.

"Interesting maneuvers, princess." His thin upper lip curled in contempt. "Too bad you didn't think to use your magick."

And risk turning Bowen into a bird?

But no, she couldn't say that. None of the Fae knew Syrena couldn't do magick. Well, she could, she just wasn't very good at it. And there was a time when that inability almost cost Syrena her life. But her mother had protected, just as Evangeline, her handmaiden and friend, did now.

She slid from Bowen's back. Her legs wobbly, she leaned against her steed for support. "A trick, that's all it was, and a very good one if I do say so myself."

Rainer raised a dark brow, towering over her as most of the Fae did. "That's not how it looked to me or to anyone else. As we speak, the head of the royal guard is reporting the incident to your father. It's about time, if you ask me, wasting our energy on this pathetic excuse for a steed. He's better off dead."

Overcome by a frantic pounding in her chest, she struggled to project a confident demeanor. Tears and begging would make no difference to Rainer. If anything, they would increase the pleasure he took in tormenting her. The stable hands looked for an excuse to put Bowen down. They were intolerant of any disability, any imperfection. Power was the only thing they understood.

She swallowed her fear and snatched her crown from his finger. She shoved it on her head and pushed a hank of golden hair from her eyes. "You forget yourself, Rainer. Bowen is mine. He's under my protection. No one touches him."

With an insolent look, he tracked his gaze from the top of her head to the tips of her toes. "Your protection," he scoffed. "I guess he's as good as dead, then."

Syrena tried to push past him, but he wouldn't budge. She took a step to the left and he did the same. She moved to the right and he followed suit, laughing at her futile attempt to outmaneuver him. Bowen nudged him out of the way and Rainer turned on her steed. "You'll pay for that," he snarled at Bowen, balling his big hand into a fist. Her only thought to protect her steed, Syrena lunged and knocked him off balance before he could hit Bowen.

His angular face contorted in rage, and he drew back to strike her. With no time to get out of his way, she squeezed her eyes closed and steeled herself to receive the blow. He wasn't as big as her father. It wouldn't be as painful, she reassured herself. There was a gush of air, a strangled squeal, and then a splash.

Cracking an eye open, she noted Rainer, sitting in a cement trough, spurting water from his mouth.

"You're lucky it is only your pride that has been wounded, Rainer. The penalty for striking royalty is death," Uscias informed him equitably, then turned to Syrena, his blue eyes intent beneath thick silver brows. "Although, your highness, the decision ultimately rests with you."

"No . . . no, your punishment was more than adequate, Uscias, thank you."

The wizard waved his gnarled fingers, and Rainer stood pale and dripping before them. "Take Princess Syrena's steed to the stables. And remember, if anything should happen to Bowen, your fate rests in her highness's hands."

As Uscias led her away, she took one last worried look over her shoulder. He patted her arm. "I will keep an eye on him, but right now our presence has been requested by the king."

Her jaw dropped and she clutched his arm. "Mine? You're certain, Uscias? He wants me?"

"Yes, my dear, that is what I was told."

She blinked back tears. "Oh, I cannot tell you how happy this makes me. They will have to address my concerns now, don't you think?" Too excited to wait for his response, she went on, "You may not be aware, Uscias, but our laws are unfairly slanted to the benefit of men. And truly, our approach to the other realms is severely outdated. Diplomacy, Uscias, diplomacy is the an—"

"Princess," he interrupted gently. "I'm afraid you misunderstood me. I am not at all certain your father has chosen you as his successor. The presence of all candidates was requested."

A heated flush prickled beneath her skin. How could she have thought anything had changed? Her father would never name her as his successor and she might as well accept it now. Years spent memorizing the dusty tomes, documenting her arguments against antiquated laws, were all for naught.

"I'm sorry, Uscias, you must think me a fool to believe my father would see past . . ." The tears that welled in her eyes threatened to overflow, and she couldn't go on.

"No, my dear, you are far from foolish. It is the ones that do not see you for who you truly are who deserve to be called such. Now, I'm afraid we must go."

As Uscias and Syrena entered the palace, an ear-piercing scream shattered the quiet hum of activity. Queen Morgana, her stepmother, stumbled from the throne room.

"The king, King Arwan has faded!" she cried while Nessa, her handmaiden, reached out to steady her.

Servants stopped what they were doing, frozen in their disbelief. Syrena's heart skittered in her chest and her legs went weak. *No, not her father, there must be some mistake. He wouldn't fade. He loved his kingdom. He loved the Isles. He loved her.* But no, even in a state of shock, she knew the last was not true. He didn't love her. He never had.

Lord Bana and Lord Erwn came out of the grand hall, shouldering their way through the gathering crowd, their perfect faces lined with confusion. They joined Syrena and Uscias. "What is it? What's happened?"

"The king, Morgana says he's faded." Uscias informed them before he strode purposefully toward the throne room. His sapphire robes billowing behind him.

"Your highness," Evangeline's melodious voice came from beside her, and she wrapped a supportive arm around Syrena's shoulders. "You should sit."

"No, I can't," she said, watching as Lord Bana, Lord Erwn, then Morgana and Nessa followed after Uscias. "I really must . . . I have to understand. I have to know . . . Why, Evangeline, why would he fade?"

"I don't know, my lady, perhaps Uscias will be able to explain it." Holding her close, her friend guided her to the throne room.

Uscias, no bigger than Syrena, was dwarfed by the two lords and Morgana as they pummeled him with their frantic questions. He pinched the bridge of his nose. "I cannot think with all the shouting. Give me a moment."

Syrena, coming to stand beside him, followed his gaze to King Arwan's golden throne. A pile of ashes on the red satin cushion was all that remained of her father. The sight triggered a memory of the day her mother faded. Memories she'd buried clawed their way to the surface. An image of her running into the room to give her mother a carefully chosen bouquet of pink and white flowers, only to have her father rip them from her hands and crush them beneath his boot. He'd forced Syrena to her knees in front of the throne, making certain she knew she was to blame for her mother's decision. All that remained of the beautiful, loving Helyna was a tidy pile of ashes on a red satin pillow.

She bowed her head and focused on the gold veins that ran through the white marble floor, shutting away the painful memories.

"Morgana, where is the Sword of Nuada?" Uscias asked.

Her stepmother's mouth formed a pinched line. "I don't know."

"The parchment for succession that I delivered the other day, do you at least know where that is?"

Morgana shared a surreptitious look with Nessa, who stood at the back of the room with Evangeline, and Bana and Erwn's servants.

"There, beside his throne," she said as she pointed to it.

Uscias jerked his chin at the liveried guard standing at attention behind the throne. The man retrieved the rolled scroll and delivered it into the wizard's hand. Uscias unrolled it with care. Syrena looked at the bottom of the parchment where her father's name was signed with a flourish. On the line that named his successor there was one letter—the letter *L*.

The wizard passed a twisted finger over the letter and it disappeared. Syrena blinked. Uscias, looking at her from the corner of his eye, raised a bushy brow. He was right. It could have been either Erwn or Bana.

"Who is it? Who did he name?" Morgana asked, although there was something in her stance, in her tone, that said to Syrena her stepmother already knew the answer. Had her father confided in his wife? Given their strained relations, Syrena doubted he would. Morgana had as much chance of holding the throne as she did.

"No one," the wizard said blandly. "And since he did not have the opportunity to name his successor, or hand over the Sword of Nuada, the four of you will have to compete for the honor. In the Books of Fae, the parameters of the test are clearly set out for circumstances such as these."

Having all but memorized the five ancient tomes, Syrena

knew exactly what the test entailed and her heart sank. The first segment, knowledge of the laws, she knew she could easily win. The test of courage and strength, she didn't even try to fool herself that she had a chance at. And the third, a test of the competitor's magickal abilities, would have been laughable if not for the danger it posed to her.

The Fae were tested three times, once at the age of four, again at the age of twelve, and on their twenty-first birthday, the last and most difficult of the tests. The highest level to be awarded was a five. Syrena had yet to see anyone other than a wizard achieve the designation. Her own level was a dismal two, and that accomplished only with the help of her mother and then Evangeline.

Her mother had died a month after Syrena passed the second test. And she didn't know what she would have done if three years ago her handmaiden hadn't arrived in the En- chanted Isles, a week before Syrena's twenty-first birthday. To this day, how Evangeline had come to be in the Isles re- mained a mystery. Noting her handmaiden's distress when- ever Syrena questioned her as to who she was and where she'd come from, she had learned to temper her natural cu- riosity. She hadn't wanted to hurt or alienate the only friend she'd ever known.

While Uscias lay out the parameters of the test to the other three, Syrena hazarded a glance at Evangeline. *Don't worry*, her handmaiden's confident violet gaze seemed to say.

Uscias, his attention focused on Syrena, announced, "The test is set for one week from today."

A snidely confident smile on his aristocratic face, Lord Erwn said, "Perhaps it would be best for the princess and Queen to concede at this point."

Morgana's emerald eyes flashed, and her scarlet painted lips twisted. "How dare you, Erwn! This test is a travesty and well you know it. As Arwan's Queen, I should retain my crown and lead the kingdom."

"I don't see your name on the succession document,

Morgana, nor do I see the Sword of Nuada in your hand. If anyone has a *right* to the throne, it would be Princess Syrena." Bana's condescending bark of laughter grated on Syrena's nerves, and she longed to put him in his place, but if she tried, he'd only laugh at her as he did now.

He was as arrogant as his brother, but he frightened her more than Lord Erwn. Both men had vied for her hand in marriage. As brutally dismissive of women as King Arwan, she'd been thankful that, seeking a more powerful match, her father had denied both their suits.

Erwn had never hidden the fact that he still wanted her, even though they were second cousins, but, unlike his brother, he'd never tried to force himself upon her. If not for Evangeline's timely intervention two weeks past, she wouldn't have escaped Bana's unwanted attention.

Suppressing a shudder of unease at the memory, she met her stepmother's sharp-eyed gaze. Within that moment of silent exchange, Syrena knew Morgana realized neither of them stood a chance. She felt a pang of sympathy for her stepmother. The title of Queen meant more to her than it did to Syrena. The only consolation, Morgana would no longer have to suffer her father's brutality. She'd been the one to take the brunt of his anger, but it hadn't stopped her from protecting Syrena from his wrath. She'd intervened on her stepdaughter's behalf on more than one occasion, and for that Syrena would always be grateful.

Uscias raised his hand. "Enough. As Wizard of the Enchanted Isles, my decision stands."

Morgana, obviously unwilling to concede, tossed her long ebony tresses in a supremely confident manner. "For the interim, Uscias, I believe I should retain my role as sovereign. We cannot afford King Rohan to sense any weakness on our part. He has too much power as it is. Given the opportunity, I have no doubt he'd seize the Isles."

Syrena wasn't certain having King Rohan take over the Isles would be such a terrible fate. Unlike her father, her uncle was a fair and considerate leader. He'd always been kind to her, and she thought he would protect her from Bana and Erwn, but perhaps he had changed. She hadn't seen him in a very long time, not since the day her mother had faded. Syrena had remembered thinking he grieved more for Helyna than her father did. But the brothers had fought, and that was the last she'd seen of her uncle.

"That will be unnecessary, Morgana," Uscias said. "King Rohan has no desire to take over the Isles. His only concern will be that a strong leader is in place. Until such time, I will see to the needs of the kingdom. As to the four of you, I suggest you take the opportunity to prepare yourselves for the contest."

While the others took their leave, Syrena stayed back to ask Uscias, "Do you think my uncle knows?" Since word traveled quickly in the Fae realm, Syrena didn't wish her uncle to receive word of his brother's death from a servant.

"No, I—" Uscias came to an abrupt halt. His gaze drifted and his lips moved as though he was talking to himself, then he nodded. "Princess, do not worry about King Rohan, I'm on my way to the Seelie court now. I know how difficult this has been for you, my dear. Why don't you go down to your sanctuary in the woods?"

Since Uscias's stone cottage was not far from Syrena's secret hideaway, it was understandable he would know where it was, but nonetheless disconcerting.

She nodded.

"You will see, princess, things have a way of turning out for the best."

Uscias was a wizard, but Syrena didn't think he had the gift of second sight. If he did, he'd know, at least where she was concerned, that things would not turn out well. In fact, they were bound to get worse.

"Are you certain you do not wish me to remain with you, your highness?" Evangeline asked once she had transported Syrena from the palace to her refuge in the woods.

It was no different than anytime before, but today Syrena's inability to transport herself from place to place with the same ease as the other Fae left her feeling more inept than usual. "No, I will be fine," she assured her handmaiden.

Once Evangeline had departed, Syrena sat upon the sun-warmed moss at the base of the old oak and let the beauty and familiarity of her secret place soothe her. It was here she came to escape ridicule, to hide her sorrow, and dream of the day the Fae would hold her in high regard. It didn't look like that would happen anytime soon.

Trying to alleviate her fears of what would transpire in a week's time, she inhaled the sweet fragrance of bell flowers and gazed out over the azure waters lapping gently along the rocky shore. She allowed the rhythmic ebb and flow to lull her turbulent emotions, hoping in the quiet of her mind to discover an answer to her problems.

A dark shadow loomed over her, blocking the warmth of the sun, causing her to shiver.

"Hiding, you're always hiding."

She blinked, then blinked again.

It couldn't be.

She rubbed her eyes with the backs of her hands. The vision didn't disappear. King Arwan shimmered before her in a golden light so bright it hurt her eyes.

"Father . . . but how? They . . . they said you faded."

"Faded," he bellowed, his voice a blast of hot air that shook the leaves from the trees. "And you believed them, you foolish chit? Only the weak fade. I was murdered."

Syrena came unsteadily to her feet. "Murdered, but how? Who would do such a thing?" Using the oak for support, she tried to control the trembling that began at the top of her head and moved to the tips her toes, but it did no good.

"Juice from the Rowan tree." He spat out the words as if they were the poison he'd swallowed. "The angels forbid me from telling you who did the deed, but my death will be avenged, of that I am assured."

Syrena didn't know what shocked her more. The fact her

father appeared to be in the company of angels, or that he had been murdered. Her fierce and powerful father brought down by the juice of a berry.

She swallowed before she made her heartfelt offer. "I will avenge you, Father."

He gave a contemptuous snort. "You . . . avenge me?"

Her cheeks heated. "If not me, then whom?"

His gaze softened, a faraway look in his eyes. "My son."

"But . . . but you have no son," Syrena protested quietly, afraid to draw his wrath.

"Ah, but I do. The angels have shown him to me." His handsome face crumpled. "If only I had known whilst I lived, but no, even that they took from me, hiding his essence so I would not learn of his existence."

Never before had Syrena seen her father grieve, but it was obvious he did so now—for his son. Her chest ached. How could a child he'd never known hold a place of honor in his heart? What was wrong with her that she could not?

"Hold out your hands," he demanded.

Startled, Syrena looked up at him. She rubbed her damp palms against her pale pink robes then complied with his wishes. She commanded her hands to remain steady, but they trembled nonetheless.

Her father shook his head and cursed. "I cannot think why they chose *you* for this task," his tone scathing as his gaze raked her from head to toe. "Hardly bigger than a sprite, and afraid of your own shadow." It wasn't true. Only her father frightened her, her father and the Fae men, but she had good reason to be afraid.

"Fools, that's what they are." He stumbled as though pushed.

Syrena gritted her teeth to keep her chin from quivering and blinked away the moisture that gathered in her eyes. If the angels had chosen her for the task, he had no right to deny her.

King Arwan lifted the Sword of Nuada. She gasped as sunlight glinted off the precious stones embedded in the hilt, sending out a rainbow of light.

He placed the golden sword in her hands and she staggered

under its weight. It took every ounce of her strength to hold it steady. A warm glow seeped through her hands and up her arms. It was as though the sword was alive, imbuing her with its magick. For the first time in Syrena's life she felt powerful, fearless.

She stood tall and lifted her gaze to her father. "What is it you would have me do?" she asked with a confidence she didn't know she possessed, at least in her father's presence. King Arwan appeared as surprised as she was. Syrena knew then that she would never give up the golden sword.

He narrowed his eyes on her before he spoke. "You will seek out your brother and bring him back to the Enchanted Isles, where he will take his rightful place as king."

She stiffened. "But I hold the sword. You gave it to me. I'm as much your heir as he is," she protested.

"A woman cannot lead, especially one as weak as you. My choice is made. You will find your brother and relinquish the sword."

No, not the sword, she wanted to cry out, but instead asked, "How? I don't know who or where he is?"

Her father's massive warrior's body shimmered then faded. Particles of gold dust danced in the sunlight. The deep rumble of his voice echoed through the trees. "His name is Lachlan MacLeod. He lives in the Mortal realm on the Isle of Lewis. Find him, Syrena, and bring him home."

The unfairness of his edict was painful and she vowed to prove to her father that she, too, was worthy of his love. To find Lachlan, a brother who would assuage the loneliness she'd endured since the loss of her mother. They were family. They would love and protect each other. A sense of purpose surged through her at the thought, and she raised the sword high above her head. This was her destiny.

She would not falter.

She would not fail.

She would retrieve her brother, and *together* they would rule the Isles.

Chapter 2

No one could deny her the right to rule now, Syrena thought, shifting the weight of the golden blade as she strode along the well-worn path through the forest. There would be no humiliating tests, no aspersions cast against her strength or her abilities. She would be Queen of the Isles.

A niggling of guilt slipped inside the bubble of her happiness that her life-long dream had come about as a result of her father's death. She still had a hard time believing he had been murdered. Not that someone had wanted him dead—her father was a brutal dictator—but that they'd succeeded. She had come up with a long list of suspects, but her duty was to find Lachlan MacLeod, the brother she never knew existed. And until her quest was complete, the mystery of her father's murder must wait to be solved.

She shuddered at the thought her journey would take her to the Mortal realm. But no matter how difficult, she would find a way to complete the task her father had set out before her. Her father and the angels, she reminded herself, still uncertain why the heavenly beings had chosen to get involved.

Standing at the base of the mountain, she looked up at the palace gleaming in the late afternoon sun, a shimmer of white light nestled among the highest peaks. Her gaze tracked the long, winding steps carved into granite. A steep and treacherous path to her home—one the Fae men used often to keep their powerful physiques battle-ready.

Anxious to test her newfound strength, she began the trek up the mountain. Stunned by the strength in her limbs and her stamina, Syrena couldn't help but wonder if her magick had improved as well. Deciding to find out, she widened her stance and prepared to transport herself. She closed her eyes and pictured her chambers as Evangeline had instructed a hundred times before, murmuring the appropriate words.

Crash. Crack. Thud.

"Ouch." She rubbed her bottom, and with a defeated sigh crawled from beneath the overgrown prickly bush just below the castle walls. It seemed not even the Sword of Nuada's powerful magick had the force to overcome her disability.

Wide-eyed, two of the royal guardsmen watched as she pulled a branch from her hair and straightened her crown. "Princess, is something amiss?" the younger of the two asked.

"No, of course not, just checking our defenses," she informed them airily.

The older guardsman, one well acquainted with Syrena, was about to laugh until he spied the Sword of Nuada. "Your highness." He bowed low, his tone respectful, and the younger man followed suit. "Allow us to escort you, my lady."

"No, thank you, I do not wish to take you from your duties." She smiled, her disappointment over her failed magick subsiding somewhat at their show of respect.

As she crossed the courtyard on her way to the palace, she heard Rainer's voice raised in anger. "If I see you in my stables again, I'll send you to the Fae of the Far North, where they eat children such as you for breakfast. Now, get out of my sight!"

A small child in a mud brown robe was shoved through the door. The little girl tripped and fell to her knees before Syrena could reach her. Tear-filled blue eyes peered through a cloud of blond curls.

She recognized the angelic face immediately. As the Fae did

not conceive easily, the Isles were not overrun with children, so it was not a difficult task. And Syrena made it a point to know them all. "Aurora, are you hurt?"

A tear slid down the little girl's cheek and the anger simmering inside Syrena erupted. "Rainer, come here!"

The door to the stable crashed open and he slammed out. "What do you—" Catching sight of her sword, he came to an abrupt halt. Color leeched from his long, angular face. "Your . . . your highness," he stuttered, bowing low.

Aurora scooted behind Syrena, and she reached down to give the silky head a reassuring pat. "If you ever touch a child in that manner again, I will see you charged."

His jaw dropped. "She's a servant's whelp. I can't be charged with anything."

He was right, but it was a law she meant to change.

"She's a child, Rainer, an innocent child who deserves to be treated with kindness, who deserves to be protected." Syrena was disgusted by his behavior, but not entirely surprised. Fae men treated both women and children abominably, her father was a perfect example. She often wondered if the men of the Enchanted Isles simply followed King Arwan's lead, or if their cruelty was an inherent flaw in their makeup. "Children are a gift to be cherished." And she was determined to protect each and every one of them, noble and lowborn alike.

Rainer kept a watchful eye on her blade. The sword shimmered with the fiery glow of the setting sun. Gritting his teeth, he said, "I'm sorry."

Satisfied with his apology for now, Syrena waved him off. "That will be all. Come, Aurora, let us check on Bowen," she said, slanting a pointed look at Rainer before he fled to his companions, who had been watching the entire exchange. He wouldn't dare harm Bowen now, not with her elevated status.

As she took Aurora's small hand in hers, she caught a glimpse of Rainer. "Oh," she gasped. The stable hand now sported a long white tail. She glanced at the little girl, her baby finger crooked in the air. "Did you do that?"

Aurora grinned and nodded.

Syrena sighed. Even at the tender age of four, the child—a servant's child at that—surpassed Syrena's level of magick. "Perhaps you should undo the spell, little one. I think he's learned his lesson." He *was* a horse's ass, but since she had taken him to task in front of his friends, it might not be wise to embarrass him further.

Confused by his companions' burst of laughter, Rainer glanced behind him, but Aurora had already reversed the spell.

Once Syrena had assured herself Bowen had been well groomed and fed, she insisted the little girl leave the stable with her.

It was obvious the child had no fear, but Syrena could not rid herself of her own concern.

"Aurora, I need you to promise me you won't come to the stables by yourself."

The little girl's bottom lip quivered. "But I have no one to bring me. Mama is always busy at the palace, and . . . and my grandmama faded."

She crouched beside Aurora. "I'm sorry to hear about your grandmother. Who looks after you now?"

Aurora shrugged.

Syrena schooled her features to hide her pity. All children deserved the same love and protection she'd received from Helyna. "Why don't we find your mother and see if we can work something out?"

Several years ago, two of the servants' children had stepped into the path of Arwan's lethal blade and died on the training field. From that point on, Syrena had been consumed with the desire to make certain it never happened again. But when she approached her father with her suggestions, he had simply laughed at her and held her up to the council for ridicule. A council made up of noblemen who had fathered most of the children she was trying to protect.

When a few months later a child went missing, Syrena, despite her father's promise of punishment if she disobeyed him, spent her days caring for the children. Her father had found out and beaten her, keeping her under guard until he was certain of her submission. But now, thanks to her sword, she could make the changes she wished to.

As Syrena came to her feet, she caught Aurora eyeing the golden blade with interest and smiled. "It's pretty, isn't it?"

The little girl tentatively touched the jeweled hilt. "What's his name?"

"Ah, the Sword of Nuada."

Aurora giggled. "You can't call him that."

"No?"

Aurora adamantly shook her head, flaxen curls bouncing. "No, he needs a real name."

Syrena tapped a finger to her lips, pretending to mull over the child's suggestion. "Hmm, I'm having a hard time coming up with one. Why don't you give it a try?"

Aurora nodded and closed her eyes for a moment. "Nuie. He wants you to call him Nuie."

"He does, does he?" Syrena chuckled. "All right, Nuie it is."

As they approached the doors to the palace, Morgana burst through them. Her stepmother's eyes widened. "So it's true." She jerked her shocked gaze to Syrena's. "Come, we have much to discuss. We'll go to my anteroom."

"Morgana, I need to speak with Aurora's mother first and—"

"Who is Aurora?" Noting the child's presence, she waved her bejeweled fingers. "Nessa will see to her."

Nessa was the last person Syrena would have see to a child's care. The woman had been her mother's handmaiden. Her devotion to Helyna had been undeniable, but she'd never hidden her dislike of Syrena, a dislike that had intensified upon her mother's death.

"I'd rather do it myself. I will meet you—" Before she

could finish, her stepmother had grabbed hold of Aurora and dragged her across the marble floor.

The servants hurrying about their duties came to an abrupt halt. They gaped at Syrena then bowed low. She imagined they were more than just shocked she held the sword, they were afraid. Afraid she would not be up to the task. She didn't blame them.

Now that she was within the palace walls, the enormity of what she faced weighed heavily upon her. She reminded herself of all the good she could do, and thanks to the Sword of Nuada, she was no longer the fearful weakling they thought her to be.

Two of the servants pushed Anna, Aurora's mother, toward Morgana, who in turn shoved Aurora at the woman. Syrena rushed forward. "Really, Morgana. I'm sorry," she apologized to Anna.

"What . . . what has she done?" Anna asked, her delicate features strained.

"Nothing, she's done nothing wrong. I'm concerned for her welfare is all. I understand your mother has faded and you have no one to look after her while you're at the palace."

"I'm sorry, your highness, I have been unable to make arrangements as yet."

"I'd like you to take leave of your duties for one month. If in that time you are unsuccessful in finding a solution, come to me and together we will work something out."

"I appreciate your concern, my lady, but if I did as you ask I—"

"Anna, I will take care of it." The lowborn were branded at birth, their powers muted. They were contracted to a life of servitude. Failure to fulfill their contract resulted in death.

Syrena crouched beside the little girl. "There now, Aurora, you and your mother can spend some time together."

The child placed her hands on either side of Syrena's face and looked deep into her eyes. Aurora's blue eyes swirled with a multitude of vibrant colors. Mesmerized, Syrena could not draw her gaze away. The little girl leaned into her. A lyrical voice—not the child's—whispered, "Darkness awaits you in a realm not of your own. Carry the light with you or all will be doomed."

Taken aback by the foreboding message, Syrena took a moment before she registered Anna's panicked cry, "No, Aurora, stop!"

Anna jerked her daughter away from Syrena. "I'm . . . I'm sorry, your highness."

"No, it's . . . it's all right." Shaken from the experience, Syrena came slowly to her feet. Aurora smiled up at her as though nothing was amiss. Her eyes had returned to their normal color.

Before she could question Anna, Morgana tugged impatiently at her arm. "Syrena, we cannot afford to waste any more time. Come!"

She released an exasperated sigh. "All right, I'm coming. Anna—" She turned from her stepmother to speak to the servant, but the woman and her child were nowhere in sight. Syrena would deal first with Morgana then go in search of Anna. She needed to know if it was the first time Aurora had exhibited such behavior. Considering her mother's reaction, she thought not.

"I understand you have questions, Morgana, but—" Syrena began when her stepmother closed the door to her anteroom behind them.

Morgana cut her off, "We have to come to some form of agreement before Erwn and Bana learn you have the sword." She gestured to a purple velvet settee decorated with jewel-toned pillows. The room was as vibrantly alive with color as her stepmother.

"What kind of agreement?" Syrena frowned, sinking into the sumptuous cushions.

Fixing her with a hard, uncompromising look, Morgana said, "Do you really think you can rule on your own?"

A part of her wanted to protest her stepmother's audacity

to ask such a question, but how could she when she wondered the same thing?

"Syrena, please, your intelligence will only take you so far. And the sword, while I'm certain it will add much to your standing with the Fae, it's not enough. I propose we rule the Isles together."

She raised her hand before Syrena could refute her statement about the sword. It did much more than simply add to her standing. "Before you refuse, I think you should consider what would happen if the Fae were to learn how limited your magick truly is."

She nearly dropped the cup Morgana handed her. Syrena's fingers trembled and tea sloshed over the rim. She gripped the fragile porcelain with both hands in an attempt to hide her panic. Her stepmother didn't know the truth. She couldn't. "Why do you say that?"

"Please, Syrena, a level two." She arched a perfect brow. "As Queen, you will be required to use your magick—often."

If her stepmother thought being a level two made her unfit to rule, what would she think if she knew Syrena had only achieved the score with help? A lot of help. And now, even though she carried the Sword of Nuada, her magick had not improved. Morgana was right. She would endanger both the Fae and herself. "What do you have in mind?"

With a triumphant smile, Morgana sat beside her. "I have become accustomed to wearing the mantle of Queen, Syrena, and do not wish to give up the crown. But all decisions will be made by the two of us. Besides, I know the title is of little interest to you. Your concerns lie in the changes you can make, do they not?"

She nodded. "Yes, I wish to make a difference in the lives of the women and children of the realm, Morgana." She held her stepmother's emerald gaze. "And if you are not in agreement with that, then I'm afraid, no matter the level of my magickal abilities, I will assume the crown."

Morgana patted her hand. "We desire the same thing, my

dear. Tonight, at the tribute to your father, we will make the announcement."

Although painful to admit, Syrena had no choice but to agree to the compact with Morgana. She would not put the Fae at risk, and her search for her brother would take her from the Enchanted realm. At the thought of Lachlan, the dull ache in the back of her skull eased. Soon her brother would be with her. No longer would she battle the petty machinations of the court alone. Coming to her feet, she said, "I will see you, then."

"Syrena," her stepmother called out as she reached the door. "It will be better, you know, now that he's gone."

She nodded, but didn't turn around. It would be, but what kind of daughter did that make her to admit as much?

"And, my dear, don't think to cross me. I will let no one stand between me and the throne, not even you."

Startled by her stepmother's virulent tone, she glanced over her shoulder. Morgana, the rim of the porcelain teacup at her lips, smiled sweetly. Syrena might have thought she imagined the threat in her stepmother's words if she didn't know her so well. She suppressed a shiver of unease. She'd have to be careful to keep her quest from Morgana.

A servant met her outside the Queen's chambers. "Your highness, Uscias awaits you in the crystal room."

"Thank you," Syrena said with a weary sigh.

She closed the door to the crystal room behind her. Uscias, hands clasped behind his back, turned from where he'd been looking out the floor-to-ceiling window. "I see you've been given the sword, princess. I thought as much." He gestured to the white velvet divan covered in overstuffed pillows. "Sit with me for a moment. We have much to discuss."

The ache in Syrena's head returned, but she stifled a groan and took her place beside him. Stroking his silver beard, he focused his attention on the sword she laid across her lap.

She bowed her head. "You don't think I deserve to carry the sword, do you?"

He placed his gnarled fingers beneath her chin and forced

her to meet his gaze. "Of course I do. But the Sword of Nuada is a powerful weapon, we—"

Her shoulders sagged. "I was right. You don't think I'm worthy. You want me to give him up, don't you?"

He clicked his tongue. "You are worthy, my dear, just not ready. I only wish to keep the sword until you have spent time with me in training."

"But my father, the angels, they gave me the weapon to aid in my quest. I am to bring my brother home."

"I know, and you shall, but for that you do not need the sword."

"But I do. You don't understand, Uscias. He makes me strong, powerful. Without him, I don't think I'm up to the task." Her cheeks heated at the admission.

"Nonsense." He placed her hand over her heart and tapped it. "It comes from here and here, your head and your heart. It's always been there. Look for it." He tapped her head. "You already have everything you require inside you. It simply awaits your discovery."

"But my brother, how will I find him without my sword?"

"Your father told you where he is. You will find him and he will know you when you do."

"How? We've never met. I didn't know he existed until today."

"Think, Syrena. Do you not remember the child who talked to you in your mind all those years ago?"

Her gaze flew to his, shocked by his revelation. How did Uscias know? She'd only ever told Evangeline about the little boy. *He's a wizard, Syrena*, she chided herself.

The memory of the child's voice echoed in her mind. She'd spent many a sleepless night worrying about him when he'd stopped communicating with her. Even after all these years, she'd been unable to forget him. Now that she knew the little boy she'd come to love was her brother, she'd let nothing stop her from finding him.

"You have a long, difficult road to travel before your quest is complete."

"It would not be as difficult if I had my sword," she said, unable to keep the querulous tone from her voice.

"Yes, it would, in more ways than you know. The responsibility of wielding a weapon of destruction is not to be taken lightly." Uscias waved off her protest. "Please, your highness, it is for the best. Trust me." He held out his hand for the sword.

She trusted him, but she didn't want to give up the sword or the power it imbued her with. "Wait. What shall I tell Morgana? She will be furious with me for giving him up."

He gave her a long, considering look. "I see. Morgana has convinced you that you should rule together, has she?"

"Yes. Do you think I should have refused?"

"Not necessarily. Time will tell. You haven't told her of your quest, have you?"

"No."

"I suggest you don't. I will be at the tribute for your father this evening, sanctifying the arrangement you and Morgana have come to. At that time I will inform the Queen and the Fae that the sword is in need of repair. It is all they need to know. As the sword was my gift to the Fae, to the heir to the throne, no one will dispute my claim. When you have returned from the Mortal realm, we will begin your training." Uscias gestured for the blade.

When Syrena handed over the sword, she felt empty inside, as though a part of her was missing, a strong powerful piece that hadn't existed until today. "Good-bye, Nuie," she murmured.

"Soon," a voice whispered near her ear. She blinked and her gaze shot to Uscias, but he was busy wrapping her sword in a thick black cloth. She pressed her fingers to her temples. It must be the ache in her head causing her to hear things.

Uscias looked at her over his shoulder. "Did you call the sword Nuie?"

She flushed. "Yes, Aurora named him for me."

"Ah, I see."

"Uscias, she gave me a warning earlier. I can't explain how, but it was given in the voice of an older woman, and her eyes swirled with different colors. I think it had to do with my quest to the Mortal realm. She said something about darkness and light."

"The child is special, princess. Heed her warning. I will see you at the tribute." With a wave of his hand, he disappeared into a brilliant shower of colorful light.

"Princess, wake up."

Evangeline's insistent tone drew her from her sleep. Syrena lifted heavy lids to glance out the window. The rising sun painted the sky a delicate pink with thin ribbons of mauve, and she shuddered. Whatever had possessed Evangeline to awaken her at such an hour?

Pulling the blankets over her head, she groused, "Why must I leave so early?"

Evangeline tugged the covers down and rolled her eyes. "Because, my lady, like you, most of the Fae hate to rise before midday. If you leave now, no one will know you travel to the Mortal realm. Did you not wish to keep your quest a secret?"

"Yes . . . yes," Syrena grumbled, throwing off the blankets. The book of the Mortal realm she had studied before she went to sleep fell to the floor with a heavy thud. She leaned over and picked it up, flipping to the page she wanted to show Evangeline. She pointed to an illustration. "As I must blend in with the Mortals, I suppose I will need a gown such as this."

Her handmaiden grimaced.

"I know, everything about them is strange. The more I read, the more determined I am to retrieve my brother from that horrible place. Speaking of Lachlan, I meant to ask you last night if you had ever heard mention of his mother?" The servants were privy to the kingdoms goings-on, more so than the nobility, and Evangeline had been a font of information through the years.

Two bright pink spots appeared on her handmaiden's cheeks. "Tell me."

"I cannot be certain it is your brother's mother they spoke of, but they say there was once a Mortal woman who entranced your father to the point of distraction. I think she captured the Fae's imagination because at first she refused him, not something that happened to King Arwan. She was said to be very beautiful and your father, unwilling to be denied what he wanted, took her. He didn't care that she was married or Mortal." Anger reverberated in Evangeline's voice.

Syrena swallowed. "Against her will?"

"He enchanted her. His magick was stronger than her will." Her lips thinned, her low opinion of King Arwan's behavior obvious.

"But that's against Fae law."

"He was the king, princess. Who would punish him?" Evangeline said it as though she wished she could have.

"Maybe someone found a way," Syrena murmured, thinking of the ashes on the pillow.

Evangeline's gaze jerked to hers. "What do you mean?"

Syrena waved off her question. "Nothing." She'd told no one her father had been murdered, and she didn't plan to, not even Evangeline. If the murderer knew their treachery had been discovered, neither Syrena nor her handmaiden would be safe. "And you've heard no mention of my brother?"

"No, not ever, and your secret is safe with me. You know that, don't you?"

She smiled. "I do. Now we have no time to waste." Her brother needed her.

Evangeline joined her by the foot of the bed and murmured the incantation.

The tightly fitted emerald silk gown her handmaiden clothed her in caused Syrena to stumble and suck in a pained breath.

"I can't breathe, Evangeline, loosen the ties," she pleaded, tugging frantically at the bodice that plumped her breasts. Why couldn't the women of the Mortal realm wear the loose robes the Fae favored?

"Princess, if I do that, the gown will not fit as it is meant to."

With an exasperated sigh, Syrena yanked one last time on the gown and said, "Fine, I'm ready." Not really, but maybe if she pretended she was, she would be.

Evangeline transported her to a clearing not far from Syrena's hideaway. Standing within a cluster of stones, her handmaiden said, "Now remember, princess, you must use the standing stones to transport you between worlds. And be careful, the Mortals must never know you are Fae or they will try and steal your magick."

Syrena arched a brow. "Then I will not be in much danger."

The standing stones spat Syrena into the Mortal realm with such force, she landed with a hard thunk on her bottom. Sitting within the circle of granite monoliths, she swiped her hair from her eyes and glared at the gray rock towering over her. She came to her feet and rubbed her behind while she took in the barren land that seemed to go on forever. A black, angry sea crashed below the hill on which she stood, a stark contrast to the placid, azure pools of the Enchanted Isles.

Syrena wrinkled her nose. The Mortal realm was ugly and unwelcoming. And cold, she thought, when a brisk wind whipped her gown about her ankles. She lifted the hem of her skirts and wiggled her shoeless feet. Muttering beneath her breath, she searched through the long, razor-sharp blades of grass for her slippers.

Her toe connected with a rock, sending a jolt of pain up her foot.

Grumbling, she retrieved one shoe from the base of the standing stone, and slipped it over her throbbing toe. Among a clump of yellow flowers, she caught a glint of gold and gingerly tugged her other slipper free.

"Ouch!" She sucked a pinprick of blood from her finger and glared at the thorny bush. She was tempted to return home until she thought of her brother alone in this Fae-forsaken place.

Hands on her hips, Syrena surveyed the dreary landscape. Then with a determined stride, she set off in the direction she'd mapped out earlier. Maps were not her forte so she could only hope she hadn't turned herself around.

Several hours later, she'd tromped through so many clumps of purple she grew tired of the color. She examined her mud-soaked slippers, wishing Bowen could've come with her. The bitter winds cut through her silk gown, and her feet ached. Beyond weary, but determined to find Lachlan as quickly as possible, she wrapped her arms around herself to keep warm and continued on.

When she came to a stand of trees, she took comfort in the somewhat familiar landscape. Birds, smaller and less color-ful than the ones from the Enchanted Isles, flitted through the branches overhead. Their sweet song was music to her ears, and for the first time that day, she smiled. Perhaps all would be well.

Something swooshed past, lifting her hair to strike the tree at her back. She swallowed, and glanced over her shoulder.

An arrow.

She froze in place, her heart drumming in her ears. Had someone seen her come through the stones and now hunted her?

An animal, she recognized as a deer from her perusal of the book of Mortals, darted out from behind the tree. Her fear turned to anger. They didn't hunt her, they hunted this poor defenseless creature! The deer looked to be on its own and Syrena was searching for its family when another arrow whizzed past her head.

"This way," she called. The doe turned terrified brown eyes

upon her. Something crashed through the trees and she ran back to pat the animal's flank. "Come, I'll protect you." Sensing she'd gained the doe's trust, Syrena sprinted deeper into the woods where the trees were thick and the foliage full.

"Over—" Syrena turned to cajole the deer just as another arrow whistled past. Its legs buckled and it crumpled in a heap on the ground.

"No," she cried and rushed to the animal's side. An arrow protruded from the thick muscle of its hindquarters, blood leeching from the wound. She stroked the soft, reddish-brown coat and attempted a calming spell. As she uttered the last word of the incantation, she wrapped her hands around the shaft and tugged.

The animal bucked and its hoof slammed into her knee. Pain exploded inside her leg and she gritted her teeth. Why couldn't her magick work, just once, she fumed. She glared at the arrow and flung it to the ground, outraged someone would seek to harm the helpless creature. Her hand shook as she tore the hem of her gown then wadded the fabric against the wound.

Branches crackled beneath heavy footfalls as someone approached from the woods behind her. She flung herself on top of the animal, intent on protecting it from the beast out to deprive it of its life.

"Bloody hell," a deep voice cursed.

She refused to be afraid. She was power . . . well . . . she had her magick. *Oh, Hades!* Then she remembered, he was merely a Mortal. What harm could he do her?

"Lass, are ye hurt?"

She peeked through the thick curtain of her hair. A pair of very large, dirt-encrusted black boots filled her vision.

He crouched at her side, and a big hand as gentle as his voice brushed the hair from her cheek. Her breath caught in her throat. Silvery-gray eyes framed with long, black lashes locked on to hers. She couldn't tear her gaze from his, ensnared not only by their brilliance, but by the concern she saw there. Men did not look at her in that way. In their eyes she'd seen lust, anger, and frustration, but never concern.

The idea he worried over her well-being caused a flutter in her belly, a warmth that chased the chill from her limbs. She barely resisted the urge to bury her face in his palm and let his masculine scent of wind, leather, and sunshine comfort her.

"I saw ye blink so I ken ye're no' dead. Mayhap ye'd give me an answer now." He looked at her from beneath hooded eyes as he scanned her length.

She heard the hint of amusement in the low rumble of his voice and her gaze dropped to his mouth. His full lips curved to reveal straight, white teeth and a tiny indent in his cheek.

He patted her face. "Come on, my wee beauty, snap out of it."

The admiration in his gaze was unmistakable. She'd misread his concern. He was no different than the Fae. Her eyes darted to the animal squirming beneath her, and she shook off the man's mesmerizing effect. He was a beast. He'd shot a defenseless creature.

Rolling onto her back, she spread her arms wide. No matter what the consequences were, she would protect her deer.

The man stood to tower over her and Syrena's eyes widened. He was huge. She did not expect Mortals to be as big as the Fae. His shoulders were as broad as Lord Bana's. And the fabric of his white shirt did little to conceal the powerful muscles beneath. A heated flush rose to her face at the form-fitting material that encased his narrow hips, his thick thighs and . . . She snapped her eyes shut.

He snorted a laugh and a warm hand enveloped hers. "Up ye come. I've mouths to feed and that deer ye're lyin' on is our dinner."

She gasped, and her eyes shot open. "Eat her? You mean to eat her?" Outraged, she struggled to free herself. "You most certainly will not. She's mine."

Brow arched, he tugged her to her feet.

Her weight landed on the leg the deer had kicked and she groaned. Being Fae, by morning there would be no sign of the injury, but it did nothing to alleviate her pain at the moment.

He frowned. "Ye're injured. Why didna ye say so when I asked?" He pulled her closer as though to offer support.

She placed a palm on his broad chest to keep some distance between them, but it didn't have the desired effect. Not when she could feel the heat of his skin beneath her fingers, the hard, well-honed muscles. His heartbeat was strong and steady, unlike the rapid, staccato beat of hers. His warm breath caressed her cheek, and she jerked away, overcome by a strange, tingly sensation.

She met his gaze full on and her step faltered. Her mouth went dry. The man was beautiful. Not the classic, refined beauty of the Fae, his was rugged and intimidating. Hair the color of a moonless night fell in loose waves to his shoulders, and a dark shadow lined his firm jaw. A dent in his chin matched the one in his cheek. Sun-bronzed skin stretched over high, chiseled cheekbones, and a slightly crooked nose.

"I'm not hurt. I'm fine," she croaked. What was wrong with her that this Mortal had such an effect on her?

At the rustle of leaves, she turned to see the deer struggling to get up. The man moved away and Syrena looked back at him. Her mouth dropped as he removed an arrow from his quiver.

"No," she cried, throwing herself at him.

He stumbled and shot her an irritated look. "Are ye daft, lass? What do ye think ye're doin'?"

She rubbed her forehead where she'd knocked it against his shoulder and scowled at him. "I will not allow you to harm her."

"I'm puttin' her out of her misery is what I'm doin'," he growled, raising his bow.

She reached out and snagged the string. Yanking the bow from his grasp, she flung it to the ground and stomped on it for good measure. "She's not miserable. Now go away and leave us be," she commanded, dropping down beside the deer.

"I'm no' leavin' without our dinner."

She folded her arms across her chest and tipped her chin. "Yes, you are, because I will not let you have her."

Hands on his hips, he narrowed his stormy gaze on her. "And how do ye plan on stoppin' me?"

If she had Nuie, she would know how, but she didn't, so Syrena did the only thing she could think of. She wrapped her arms around the animal's neck, and said, "Go away."

"Ye're daft, do ye ken that? Makin' a pet of a wee beastie," he grumbled, a note of disgust in his tone. He threw up his hands and turned to walk away, muttering something about her stealing food from children.

Her eyes widened, astonished by his response. A Fae man would take what he wanted, and the woman who stood up to him would pay the price. She fought back a surge of admiration for the Mortal, watching as he strode toward the big, black steed that appeared when he whistled.

Good, he's leaving.

Her pet would be safe, and so would she.

Although he had not harmed her, he'd stirred something unfamiliar within her. And it was not something she wanted stirred. The feelings he aroused were dangerous. They had to be. What other than danger would cause her knees to go weak, or the wild fluttering in her belly when he looked at her, touched her?

"Aidan." A man's voice called from the edge of the woods. "MacLeod, where did ye get to?"

She started at the name.

"Oh, no," she groaned. *The beast is related to my brother.* She had to call him back.

Chapter 3

Of all the fool things Aidan had ever witnessed, this day trumped them all. Imagine, a wee lass protecting a beastie and him being the idiot who allowed it.

He shook his head in disgust. "I'm comin'," he shouted over his shoulder as he swiped his battered bow from the forest floor, refusing to give in to the temptation to look at her.

The image of the bonny lass lying on her back taunted him. Her arms spread wide, hair the color of burnished gold tumbling over the tops of full creamy breasts encased in a rich green fabric.

The place where she'd torn her gown revealed the delicate turn of her ankle, a tantalizing glimpse that had caused his trews to tighten, as had the innocent flush that pinked her bonny face when her topaz gaze traveled his length.

Aidan's grin turned to a frown. Bloody hell, what was he thinking? He couldn't leave her alone in the woods, injured and unprotected. He pivoted on his heel, his forward motion brought to an abrupt halt by her wide-eyed gaze. Her luscious pink lips parted as though she meant to call him back.

He focused on the tree above her head before his trews grew any tighter. He cleared his throat, but the words came out on a low rasp. "I canna leave ye here, lass. I'll take ye to yer kin."

She peeked at him through the long, thick fringe of her lashes. "No, I can't go back, not without—" She caught her full bottom lip between pearly white teeth before offering him a tentative smile. "But I will go home with you."

He arched a brow. Many a lass had offered to go home with him, but not in the quiet, beseeching way she did. He'd been prepared for her to protest since only moments ago, in no uncertain terms, she'd sent him on his way.

Warily, he approached and crouched at her side. "I doona think yer family would approve. Now where is it ye hail from?"

With a defiant tilt of her chin, she folded her arms over her chest. "It doesn't matter. I'm coming home with you."

"Ye are, are ye?" His cock twitched, responding to her bold statement. Aye, a part of him was more than ready to take the lush, wee beauty home with him, to feel her beneath him. But despite what her words implied, he was certain she was an innocent. He should know; he'd had enough experience with women who weren't. And that's how he meant to keep it. Women like this one were meant to be admired from a distance, like the Minch in a storm.

The stubborn chit gave a jerky nod.

Getting his thoughts back to where they belonged, he rose to his feet. "All right then, but ye'll tell me who yer kin are before the day is out. 'Tis no' right leavin' them to worry over ye."

"They won't," she assured him, placing a dainty hand in his.

He pulled her to her feet and swept her into his arms before she could put any weight on her injured leg.

"What . . . what do you think you're doing?" she sputtered.

Ignoring her, he strode to where Fin waited and placed her on the stallion's back.

"Oh." She smoothed her skirts into place, averting her gaze from his.

With one foot already in the stirrup, he was about to swing

his other leg over when she gave him a hard shove. If he hadn't had a good grip on the saddle, he would've landed on his arse. "Bloody hell, what was that for?"

"You forgot my deer. I'm not leaving without her." She rolled onto her belly in an attempt to slide off Fin.

"Stay put." His hand grazed her rounded behind as he grasped her narrow waist and placed her firmly upright. He didn't miss her startled gasp, and if she happened to look down, he doubted she'd miss what that innocent touch had done to him.

Leaves scattered beneath his angry strides. *Fool*, that's what he was for catering to her daft notions. He bent down and lifted the struggling animal into his arms, turning in time to see his men, Donald and Gavin, come crashing through the underbrush on horseback. Aidan scowled at their amused expressions, about to tell them what they could do with the comments they were bound to make. But they were too busy ogling the lass sitting astride Fin to bother with him.

He fought back a wave of possessiveness, the urge to plant his fist in their ugly mugs. Out of the corner of his eye, he spotted a fine pair of antlers sticking out from behind Gavin and winced.

"Donald." He tried to gain the other man's attention, intent on sending them on their way before the lass spotted the big buck strapped across the horse's back. Never comfortable dealing with emotional women, he had every intention of avoiding a scene. With her head bowed, her fingers twisting in Fin's mane, she'd yet to notice.

"Are ye no' goin' to introduce us to yer bonny wee *friend?*" Donald's green eyes glinted with mischief.

"Later. Here, take her." He placed the deer in front of Donald.

"Have ye lost yer mind? In case ye havena noticed, Aidan, she's still alive, and," he cried out, "kickin'."

At a feminine cry, Aidan turned in time to see the lass scramble off Fin.

"I will not have her ride with those . . . those murderers."
Her furious gaze locked on the buck, she limped to his side.

He sighed and placed his hands firmly upon her shoulders.
"No harm will come to yer pet. Ye have my word on it."

He thought a man could be burned from the fiery glint in
the topaz eyes she raised to his. "But they . . . he . . ."

"Provided food for our clan, somethin' ye denied me the
satisfaction of doin'." He brought his face within inches of
hers. "Somethin' ye'd best no' be remindin' me of if ye ken
what's good fer ye."

"Ye canna be serious, Aidan? I thought ye merely wished
us to kill the beastie when we were out of the lass's sight,"
Donald protested as he struggled to keep the deer on his lap.

The lass let out an ear-piercing screech and lunged at
Donald. Aidan grabbed her. With an arm around her waist, he
anchored her to his chest.

"Let me go you . . . you, big ogre." She stomped on his foot
then yelped.

"Fiery wee thing, isna she?" Gavin observed.

"Aye," Aidan muttered, waving them off. "Head fer home.
I'll be there shortly. Enough," he growled in the delicate shell
of her ear as she struggled to get away from him, the movement of her behind against his groin nearly more than he
could bear.

Gavin caught his eye, his smirk letting Aidan know he saw
he struggled with more than the lass. "Mayhap I should take
her, and ye the buck. She doesna' appear to like ye verra
much." He chuckled at the dark look Aidan shot him. "We're
leavin', but doona take long or we'll come back fer ye."

Aidan swung her under his arm and stomped to his horse.
"Mind where ye're hittin'." He grunted when her wee fists
pounding on his thighs came too close for comfort.

None-too-gently, he set her on top of Fin. As he attempted
to mount, the lass swung her foot, hitting the stallion instead
of her intended target—him. Fin reared with an angry
whinny, sending Aidan on his arse. Muttering his opinion of

the troublesome wench under his breath, he stood to brush himself off. He glared at the termagant, but she was too busy comforting his horse to notice. Burying her face in Fin's mane, she stroked his shiny black coat, murmuring her apology.

He raised a brow, surprised to see his temperamental mount respond to her gentle touch. Settling himself on top of Fin, he wrapped an arm around her waist and tugged her toward him. "No more of yer kickin'," he muttered against her ear.

She stiffened in his embrace then straightened as though to put some space between them. Tapping his heel to Fin's flank, the horse took off at a gallop.

"Oh," she gasped when the movement pressed her body tight to his.

The wind whipped her long, golden locks against Aidan's face. He transferred the reins to the hand that held her in place while he brushed her hair away with the other. He tucked the tresses between them, unable to resist winding the silken strands around his fingers.

"What are you . . . ouch," she cried when she turned to look at him. Putting a hand to the back of her head, she glared at him. "That hurt."

Her warm breath caressed his cheek. Sweet with a tantalizing hint of honey, it reminded him of the cakes Cook made for him and he fought the urge to taste her soft pink lips— explore the temptation of her bonny mouth. Her eyes widened and her lips parted as though she sensed the direction of his thoughts. She whipped her head around and tried to angle her body away from his.

Aidan chuckled and tugged her back into his protective embrace. "Ye're cold, ye need my warmth." He ran his hand down her arm, his roughened palm catching on her sleeve. He frowned, rubbing the rich material between his thumb and forefinger. Both the cut of the gown and the quality of its fabric bespoke wealth.

"Who are ye, lass, and where are ye from?"

"Pr . . . Syrena. My name is Syrena. Who are you?" She glanced at him over her shoulder.

"Syrena," he murmured, finding her name as beautiful as she was. "I'm Aidan MacLeod." Losing himself in the shimmering depths of her enchanting eyes, he nearly forgot the intent of his questions. He cleared his throat. "I ken I havena' seen ye in these parts. I would've remembered." It was the truth. She was not someone he'd easily forget. "Where is it ye're from?" he repeated his question.

Nibbling on her bottom lip, she looked out over the moors as though she were lost. "I don't know."

He frowned. Cupping her cheek in his palm, he forced her to look at him. "What do ye mean, ye doona ken? Did ye hit yer head earlier?"

She lifted her shoulder, eyes downcast. "Maybe."

He ran his fingers through her hair and over her scalp, but found no bumps, no sign of injury. Growing suspicious, he asked, "Ye're no' a Lowlander, are ye?"

The Lowlanders were his sworn enemies, ravaging scavengers who bled his people dry at King James VI's behest. If she was one of them, he'd have no choice but to hold her for ransom. His coffers were nearly empty, and coin for her safe return would go a long way in replenishing them. But he didn't want to think she had anything in common with that rabble, or that she shared the Lowlander's contempt for him and his people.

"What is a Lowlander?"

"A bunch of lowlife from the borders."

"No, I'm certainly not one of them." She gave a firm shake of her head.

His lips twitched. "Well, I canna think ye're from around these parts. Like I said, I would remember ye, and the way ye speak 'tis str . . . unusual."

"Is it? And here I thought your speech str . . . unusual." Her lips curved in a smile that took his breath away, and right then and there Aidan decided he didn't care who she was, she was his.

Now where the bloody hell had that come from?

The last thing Aidan wanted was to saddle himself with a woman, especially a woman of means who would expect marriage. His circumstances were too badly compromised to consider making such an offer. What with the constant fighting and raiding of the Lowlanders over the last few years, his coin was depleted, and the keep barely fit to live in.

But that was beside the point. He'd witnessed how destructive marriage could be. Women were not to be trusted, which was why he never stayed long enough with one to get attached.

After what his mother's betrayal had done to his father, you'd think he would have learned his lesson, but nay, he had to find out the hard way. And find out he did. Lady Davina Scott, the one woman he thought he could trust, a woman he gave his heart to, had betrayed him with another.

Syrena rubbed her arms, and shivered. He gathered her to his chest and this time she didn't protest. Instead, she turned toward him and snuggled close, folding her hands beneath her cheek. With a soft contented sigh, her eyes fluttered closed. The quiet sound caused Aidan to harden in his trews, and his mind turned to another way he'd like to keep her warm. The soft cries she'd make when he had her naked beneath him, when he was deep inside her.

Enough. This is madness.

He'd been too long without a woman was all. And he planned to rectify the matter as soon as he delivered the lass safely to her kin. Someone would claim her. As beautiful as she was, who would not? He ignored the tightening in his chest at the thought she belonged to another. He dug his heels into Fin's flanks and urged the stallion to quicken his pace, determined to seek out the Widow Blackmore as soon as he saw the lass settled.

Fin trotted into the courtyard and Aidan viewed the overgrown grounds and ramshackle dwellings with a familiar surge of frustration. Their troubles with the Lowlanders were lessening, and he would soon have the time to begin the repairs required to set Lewes to rights. Aye, he knew he needed coin to do so, but somehow he'd find a way to deal with that as well. Turning his attention to the sleeping lass in his arms, he tried to wake her. The gentle shake to her shoulder failed to rouse her, and he shook her a little harder.

"Stop it, Evangeline," she grumbled, slapping his hand away. She nudged her head against his chest as though she meant to burrow beneath his tunic. Her breath warmed his skin, fanning the flame of awareness that already burned deep in his belly.

"So, ye tamed the wee lass have ye, Aidan? I thought she might take longer than she did," Donald remarked as he and Gavin sauntered toward him.

Aidan hesitated before he said, "I canna wake her, come give me a hand." He gestured Donald over, better him than the lecherous Gavin.

"Ah, so that's how ye did it. Knocked her out, did ye?" Gavin nodded his head as though he thought it a grand idea.

"Are ye daft, mon? She's asleep is all. Have a care with her, Donald," he admonished the gangly sandy-haired man. Barely had he placed her in his friend's arms before he had her back in his. He ignored the knowing look the two men exchanged. "Did ye put her deer in the stables?"

"Aye, but old Tom is none too happy about it."

Aidan adjusted her weight in his arms. "I'll see the lass settled then have a word with him." He shouldered his way through the doors of the keep with Donald and Gavin at his heels.

"Ye're certain there's nothing wrong with her, Aidan? I doona ken when I've seen a lass sleep like that."

Gavin gave Donald a hardy slap to his shoulder. "Then ye're doin' it all wrong, mon."

Donald rolled his eyes. "Nay, I'm more careful than ye is all. I doona ram their heads into the wall."

"We did no more than ride home," Aidan protested. He wouldn't allow them to think he'd compromised Syrena's innocence. "I think she may have hit her head."

Donald's brows bunched together. "'Twould explain her wantin' to keep the beastie fer a pet."

"Mayhap," Aidan said, looking down at the angel in his arms. She was innocent and vulnerable, he had no business thinking the thoughts he'd been thinking. He took a quick look into the grand hall, hoping to catch a glimpse of Beth or one of the other maidservants. But there was no one about. The hall was deserted.

"Where's Lachlan?"

"A bunch of them left to raid the Lowlanders." Gavin eyed him. "Was it no' on yer orders?"

Aidan clenched his jaw so tight his teeth ached. His brother grew more rebellious by the day. He'd learned to accept as the day of Lachlan's birth drew near he became reckless. But his behavior of late grew dangerous, and Aidan knew he had to put a stop to it before someone got hurt. "Ye ken full well I didna. Lachlan goes too far this time," he grated out.

The lass stirred, drawing his attention. She yawned and rubbed her eyes, giving him a sleepy smile. "Is Lachlan here?"

Aidan stiffened. "How do ye ken my brother?" He didn't keep the censure from his voice, not liking the tender look in her eyes when she asked after Lan.

Syrena's eyes widened. *Oh for the love of Fae*. If his steely gaze was anything to go by, she'd given herself away. Taking refuge in the excuse he'd provided earlier, she pressed the back of her hand to her forehead. "Do you have to be so loud? My head aches."

He narrowed his gaze, setting her on her feet. "I asked ye a question, Syrena. How do ye ken, my brother?" he repeated. A muscle twitched in the hard edge of his jaw.

"Aye, we'd be interestin' in learnin' that as well." The tall sandy-haired man and his redheaded companion from the woods eyed her suspiciously.

She paid them no mind, knowing it was Aidan who held her fate in his hands. "I knew someone named Lachlan, when I was younger." She pretended nonchalance. Evangeline had warned her not to give away her identity, and Syrena planned on heeding her advice. She peeked at him through her lashes. "I would like to see my doe."

He took hold of her arm. With a jerk of his chin, he sent the two men on their way, ignoring their grumbled protest. "Yer pet is bein' seen to. Now answer me."

She chewed on her bottom lip. "I did. Like I said, Lachlan was someone I met a long time ago." If only she hadn't woken to the mention of her brother's name. Despite her apprehension, she felt a spurt of relief that she'd followed her instincts and let Aidan take her to his home. She just wouldn't think about the disturbing reaction she had to the man—a reaction that had only intensified when he held her in his protective embrace.

She averted her gaze from his, taking in the stone wall leading down a dark, dank corridor that listed dangerously inward. Her eyes widened. Several doors were hanging off their hinges and deep gouges marred the slate floor beneath her feet. The Fae's stables were more habitable than this place. "Is . . . is this your home?" She hoped he didn't take note of the horrified shudder that accompanied her question.

"Aye." He arched a brow. "Is it no' to yer likin'?"

"It . . . it's very . . . big." She curled her toes when a draught of damp air swirled about her feet. And ugly. And cold. The only time she'd been warm in this realm was in his arms. Unbidden, her eyes went to his broad chest and muscular arms. She barely caught the wistful sigh before it escaped from her lips.

His sensuous mouth quirked at the corner. "I should be offended."

Her cheeks heated. "I'm sorry. I didn't mean to be rude."

"No apologies necessary, lass. I'm no' blind to how the keep appears to others. 'Twill take time, but I'll have it back to the way it once was." He looked about him before he returned his gaze to hers. "This Lachlan ye referred to, where was it exactly that ye met?"

In my mind. She swallowed a giggle as she pictured what his reaction would be if she said the words out loud.

He crossed his arms over his chest, his expression grim. "It seems you have fond memories of the mon."

"I do, but he was only a boy when I knew him." A memory of Lachlan sounding scared and alone echoed in her mind, and she wondered if Aidan had been the cause of her brother's anguish. Her temper flared on Lachlan's behalf. She matched Aidan's stance and pinned him with an indignant look of her own. "You were angry at your brother. Why?"

He frowned. "'Tis no concern of yers."

She opened her mouth to protest then closed it. She couldn't tell him the truth, and without it, to argue would be pointless.

"I have much to do, lass, before the gatherin'. So it would be best if ye tell me who yer kin are and I can have ye back to them before nightfall."

"You're having a gathering—here." She couldn't help it, her nose wrinkled.

"Aye, in a few days' time, but ye needn't worry. Most of my guests' expectations are lower than what yers appear to be."

Once more heat flooded her cheeks. "I'm sorry." She looked toward the grand hall. "I could help you tidy things up while we wait for . . . I mean, until I recall my kin."

He angled his head to study her. "Ye still canna recall them?"

"No." She shook her head firmly. "I can't." Syrena stepped into the hall. "Oh my," she murmured. The sight that greeted her horrified her Fae sensibilities. There were buckets scattered everywhere. The tables and chairs that remained intact were coated with grime. A far wall with a large hole in it looked as though it might crumble into a heap right before her eyes.

"Lord MacLeod, do you not have servants to help you with . . ." Unable to think of a word that would not offend him, she waved her hand.

He grinned. "Are ye takin' back yer offer to help, Syrena?"

"No, of course not, but I . . . I think perhaps you should hold your gathering out of doors." Her poor brother, to see the squalor in which he lived pained Syrena. The sooner she got him away from this place, the better.

Aidan rubbed his hand along his jaw. "'Tis no' a bad idea, lass, if the weather holds."

She smiled. No one had ever taken one of her suggestions seriously before, and the thought Aidan did ignited a happy glow inside her.

He took her hands in his and turned her palms up. She watched, mesmerized, as his thumbs traced her sensitive skin. His hands dwarfed hers, and his touch caused a flutter low in her belly. She drew her gaze to his and their eyes held.

"I doona think these hands have ever seen a day's work, have they, Syrena?" Her name rolled off his tongue as though he caressed her, a heated caress that warmed her in places never before touched.

Forgetting everything but how she'd felt in his arms, she stepped closer. He watched her as he stroked her palms, and she trembled with the intensity of his gaze.

"Aidan, old Tom is beside him . . . oh." The man named Gavin grinned. "Sorry, I didna mean to interrupt ye."

Aidan released her hands. "Ye didna. Now what was that ye were sayin'?"

"'Tis Tom, he says . . ." He waggled his brows.

"Mayhap 'twould be best if I speak with him now. Syrena, make yerself comfortable while I—"

"I'm coming with you," she said, certain there was a problem with her deer.

"Nay, let me calm old Tom before ye have a visit with yer pet."

She placed a hand on his arm. "You promise no one will harm her?"

"I promise, now be a good lass and let me be on my way." Aidan looked over his shoulder when a tall, auburn-haired woman pushed past Gavin. "Beth, I was wonderin' where ye got to. Lady Syrena has offered to give ye a hand with the cleanin'. Mayhap ye can fetch her a bucket and some rags."

The woman's mouth dropped. "Ye canna be serious, my—"

"Ah, but I am." He grinned and winked at Syrena before he followed Gavin from the castle.

The woman rolled her eyes. "I must apologize fer our laird. He likes to tease."

"I did offer," she assured the woman with a smile. "And by the looks of things, you could use my help." She clapped a hand to her mouth. "I'm sorry. I shouldn't—"

Beth waved off her apology. "No offense taken, my lady. There've been a fair number of lasses hurt of late on account of the keep's disrepair. And 'tis a lot fer only four bodies to manage."

Syrena, wanting to let the woman know she was serious, rolled up her sleeves in the manner in which the servants at the palace did.

With a shake of her head, Beth said, "I'll be back with yer rags." Chuckling, she left the hall.

Over the last hour, Syrena had developed an appreciation for all the servants accomplished in the Enchanted Isles. Although she was certain they had never dealt with filth such as this. She wrinkled her nose as she wrung out the blackened cloth, her arms aching from the constant scrubbing. But when she looked at the long wooden table she'd cleaned, she stood taller. Pleased with her accomplishment.

A low drawn-out hiss came from behind her and she turned. Her eyes widened. *What in the name of Fae is that?*

An animal, as black as night, slunk across the room toward

her, its yellow eyes gleaming. It hissed again and bared its
pointed teeth. She thought back to the book she'd read the
night before, sorting through her memory. A cat, it was a cat.
A tingle of nerves prickled beneath her skin. There was something important she was forgetting, something about cats and
the Fae. "Go away," she pleaded as it prowled toward her.

She whimpered, sensing the evil intent that pulsed from the
creature. Her hip bumped the table and she squealed. The
animal arched its back, hair standing on end. Syrena whirled
around and clambered on top of the table, tugging her gown
from where it caught on the splintered wood.

The creature lunged, its teeth bared, long extended claws
glittered white against its shiny black coat and latched onto
her gown. She screamed, shaking her skirt, trying to dislodge
the animal. And in the midst of her terror, she remembered—
cats suck the very essence from a faery. Her panicked cries
echoed in the grand hall as the animal slithered its way up
her body.

Chapter 4

Syrena's high-pitched shriek greeted Aidan as soon as he entered the keep. He raced into the hall, laughter rumbling in his chest at the sight of her standing in the middle of the table with a wee cat attached to her gown. His laughter faded when he noted the look of terror in her eyes, and the pallor of her skin. The woman was beside herself with fear.

He strode to the table. "He'll no' harm ye, Syrena," he tried to reassure her while he pried the animal from her gown. He cursed the wee beastie when it got in one last swipe and raked the delicate skin of her chest with its claws, leaving a fiery red welt in its wake.

"Beth," he bellowed.

"I'm here, my laird, no need to make me deef," Beth remarked from behind him.

He shoved the hissing animal into her arms. "Take the cat and lock it away. It appears to have gone mad." As though to make a mockery of his statement, the wee beastie purred loudly as it left the hall in Beth's arms.

Aidan turned back to Syrena. Placing his hands on either side of her tiny waist, he lifted her easily from the table and into his arms. Wrapping her arms around his neck, she released a shuddered breath and hiccupped on a sob.

"Shh, angel, ye're all right," he murmured into her hair, inhaling her now familiar sweet scent.

"I . . . I know. It's just a little . . . a little scratch."

Aidan bit back a smile at her attempt to hide how frightened she'd been, and lowered himself on a chair, settling her on his lap.

He placed his finger beneath her chin and tilted her face upward. "The cat willna bother ye again," he promised, entranced by the shimmering depths of her topaz eyes.

She drew her arms from his neck and plucked at the laces of his tunic. "Thank you for saving me," she murmured.

He chuckled. "'Twas only a wee cat. Yer life was never in danger, Syrena."

She lifted her wide-eyed gaze to his. "But it was. You don't understand. Cats will suck the essence from a . . ." She caught her full bottom lip between her teeth and dipped her head while absently stroking the flesh at the opening of his tunic.

The action seemed to comfort her, but it was wreaking havoc on his self-control. Glad of the voluminous amount of fabric between them, he hoped it was enough that she wouldn't feel him harden beneath her. He wrapped his fingers around hers, and brought them to his lips. "I ken the beastie appeared mad, but ye calmed Fin, and befriended a deer. I canna imagine why ye're afraid of a wee cat."

"I told you . . ." She clamped her mouth closed. Bringing her hand to her chest, she touched the raised, reddened mark that marred her creamy white skin.

His eyes were drawn to the dark valley between her breasts, and he cleared his throat, jerking his chin to the scratch. "Does it hurt?"

Watching the tip of her finger trail the length of the welt, he had to tamp down the temptation to press his lips to her satiny smooth skin. To soothe her heated flesh.

"It burns." She let her hand fall away.

Aidan couldn't help himself. He pressed his palm to the mark.

"Oh," she gasped. Her gaze went to his, and instead of the

rebuke he expected, she rewarded him with a soft smile. "Your hand is cool. It's soothing." She rested her head on his shoulder.

The gentle rise and fall of her chest beneath his palm caused him to swallow a groan. The tips of his fingers inadvertently stroked the full swell of her breast and he felt her squirm in his lap. Unable to resist the temptation any longer, he lowered his head, about to press his lips to her wound when the clamor of male voices drew his attention. He jerked his hand away.

"Ouch," she cried, bringing her hand to where his had been.

He winced. "I'm sorry, Syrena."

She followed his gaze. "Who is that?"

"My brother. Mayhap ye should have that visit with yer pet now." He nudged her from his lap, then thought it may not have been the wisest move on his part—his desire for her plain for all to see. He turned his mind to his brother and his blatant disregard of his orders, relieved when the action had the desired effect.

Lachlan swaggered into the hall with the men trailing behind him. "And what have we here?" his brother asked. Coming toward them, he eyed Syrena with appreciation. The others glanced their way before gathering by the hearth and bellowing at the maidservants for ale.

Aidan nudged Syrena, but she paid him no mind. "See to yer pet." His tone gruff, angry at how his brother looked at her, and at himself that it irked him as much as it did.

She shook her head. Her gaze riveted on Lachlan. Her pink lips parted as though entranced by what she saw.

His brother grinned, well used to his effect on women. "'Twould appear the lass wishes to remain, Aidan." Lan took her hand in his and brought it to his lips. "'Tis a pleasure to meet ye, my lady. Doona mind my brother. My men and I would welcome yer bonny company."

Aidan barely contained the urge to shake him. "Yer men, brother? Nay, ye're mistaken, they're my men, and 'tis the last time ye'll risk their lives fer some foolhardy scheme ye've concocted." He yanked the lass's hand from Lachlan's.

"Syrena," he snapped. "If ye doona go to that wee beastie of yers and see to her care, we'll be havin' her fer our dinner."

His threat was enough to draw her attention, she whirled to face him. "How can you say that to me? You promised you would not harm her. I just wanted to spend some time with—"

"I doona care what ye wanted. I mean to have words with my brother and I can promise ye they'll no' be fit fer a lady's ears. Now be on yer way." He gave her a light shove in the direction of the hall's entrance. Between his brother, and her reaction to him, Aidan's patience wore thin.

She glared at him, and jabbed her finger into his chest. "I thought you were different, but you're not." She rose up on the tips of her golden slippers in an effort to look him in the eye. "I intend to . . . I intend to come right back here once I'm finished seeing to my deer and you . . . you can't stop me."

He lowered his face to hers. "I can, and I will. And until I say ye may return, I doona want to see yer bonny face anywhere near here. Do ye understand me?"

With a haughty toss of her head, and one last look at his brother, she limped from the room. He heard the heavy doors to the keep shut once, and then again. Despite himself, he chuckled at her futile attempt to slam them.

Lachlan eyed him with interest. "I apologize, brother, I didna ken ye wanted the lass fer yerself."

"I doona." He did, but it was not something his brother needed to know. Especially since nothing could come of it. "Stay away from her, Lan."

Lachlan held up his hands. "Whatever ye say. All I want is some ale and to celebrate with the men. 'Twas a verra successful raid, wasna it, lads?"

"Aye," several of the men shouted. At Aidan's quelling look, the celebratory cheers ended. They sheepishly averted their gazes from his.

He returned his attention to his brother. "On whose authority did ye make this raid?"

"Mine," Lachlan said belligerently. "Ye were no' here."

"Aye, I wasna. And ye ken well enough I wouldna given it to ye in the first place. I grow tired of this, Lan. 'Tis time to rebuild and no' take part in these petty skirmishes that put the men at risk. The Lowlanders are done for. Given time they'll realize it. And besides that, our uncle has been appointed agent to King James and means to put in a good word for us. So—"

Lachlan gave a derisive snort. "That should go over well with John Henry."

Aidan didn't want to talk about his cousin. At one time they'd been close, but since John Henry had married Davina, the woman that had been promised to Aidan, there relations were strained. "As I was sayin,' I'll no' have ye puttin' our chance fer peace at risk. No more, Lachlan, or ye'll suffer the same consequences as anyone else who goes against my orders. I am laird and my word is law, best ye remember it."

"How can I no', brother? 'Tis all I ever hear and I grow tired of it. Am I never to be given any responsibility?"

Aidan ran his hand through his hair, weary of the never-ending battle of wills with his brother. "Ye have much to learn, Lan. Ye're only nineteen, time enough fer ye to bear the burden of responsibility."

"We return with two cows and no one injured." Lan glanced over his shoulder. "No' bad at least, and ye canna even congratulate us on a job well done. All ye do is make me feel foolish, as worthless as a bairn." He pushed aside Aidan's restraining hand and strode from the hall.

Syrena sat on the hard, mud-packed floor strewn with hay, the deer's head in her lap. "Who does he think he is ordering me about like that?" she said, casting a surreptitious glance around the interior of the stable to be sure she was alone. Relieved when she saw no sign of the cantankerous old man who had confronted her at the entrance to the barn.

She patted the soft muzzle of the deer and released a heartfelt sigh. She'd found her brother, and he was as beautiful as the most handsome of the Fae men with his golden hair and eyes. As beautiful as his brother.

Syrena frowned as soon as the thought entered her head. She wished she could deny it, but she couldn't. Aidan was beautiful, powerful yet gentle with an underlying kindness. She snorted at her fanciful musings. Gentle . . . hah, kind . . . hah, the man was an overbearing beast.

Her hand went to her chest as she remembered how his palm had cooled the scratch that ravaged her skin. The memory of his fingers stroking the tops of her breasts and her body's reaction to his touch caused a shiver of trepidation to ripple down her spine. She'd wanted him to keep touching her, to kiss her. Never before had she had feelings such as those. She groaned. She'd been right from the beginning. Aidan MacLeod was dangerous, and the sooner she and Lachlan were away from there, the better.

The door to the stables flung open and her brother stormed into the dimly lit room, cursing loudly. He came to an abrupt halt upon seeing her. "I'm sorry, my lady, I didna ken ye were about." He rubbed the darkened stubble along his jaw in a manner similar to his brother. "What have we here?" he asked, lowering himself onto the ground beside her.

The deer sent Syrena a pained look and she realized that in her excitement her fingers dug into its fur. She grimaced, and gentled her touch. "She's my pet. Your brother shot her, but I think she will soon recover." She smiled at him, finding it hard to believe her brother sat beside her. The little boy she'd come to love had grown up, and he was her family. The only family she had left.

His brows shot up. "Ye've made a pet of the beastie and my brother allowed it?" At her nod, he let out a low whistle. "Aidan must be more taken with ye than I first imagined."

Heat suffused her cheeks. "He's not taken with me, and I'm not taken with him," she felt the need to add. She didn't want to talk about Aidan, or think about him for that matter. Her only interest lay in her brother.

A crooked grin creased his beautiful face. "Nay? Then mayhap ye and I should get to ken each other a bit better." He raked her from head to toe with a bold look, then reached out and wrapped a strand of her hair around his finger.

She let out a horrified gasp and slapped his hand away. "Stop that, Lachlan. I'm your sister," she blurted out.

He frowned, slowly unfurling her hair from his finger. "Are ye daft? I have no sister."

She hadn't meant for it come out that way. Now she had no choice but to tell him the truth. "Yes, you do. We share the same father and he's asked that I bring you home to the Enchanted realm."

He leapt to his feet and backed away from her, stumbling over a clump of earth. "Who . . . who are ye?"

Syrena lifted the deer's head from her lap and gently placed it on a pillow of hay. She came to her feet, but didn't try to close the gap between them. "I told you, I'm your sister. Don't you remember me, Lachlan? When you were a little boy, you came to me in my mind."

A look of panic darkened his chiseled features. "Go. Leave here, now!"

"It's the truth, Lachlan. You are my brother, and I can't leave you. I've come to take you home with me."

"I said leave here. I don't want ye anywhere near me." He grabbed her by the shoulders and shook her hard before pushing her away from him. "I want nothin' to do with ye."

Her breath came in painful gasps, his rejection a tight fist closing around her heart. But she couldn't let it end, not like this. "Please, Lachlan, I understand your shock, but we must talk. We're family."

He shook his head vehemently from side to side. "No' another word. Get away from here before I can no longer control myself. Yer kind has brought nothin' but sorrow to my family. If my brother finds out what ye are, he'll kill ye with his bare hands."

The force of his anger caused her to take a step back. His face was a terrifying mask of fury, and well-honed muscles bunched in his big arms. She swallowed past her fear to plead with him, "But you're part Fae. You're a part of me. How can you hate me? I never forgot you. I always remembered that scared little boy you once were." He kept his gaze averted from hers, but she continued, hoping to reach him, to somehow make him understand. "I loved you then, even though I didn't yet know you were my brother."

He covered his ears with his hands. "Stop it. I willna listen to ye. I'm no' like ye. I'll never be like ye. I doona want to be."

She pressed her hand to her mouth. How could he hate her? She'd never done anything to hurt him. All she wanted was for him to love her.

He leaned against the wall and slid to the floor, burying his face in his knees. Syrena swallowed what little pride she had left and crouched by his side. She laid her hand on his shoulder. She would leave. She never meant to cause him pain. "I'm sorry, Lachlan. I didn't mean to hurt you. I . . . I thought you'd be as happy to find me as I was to find you."

He lifted his tearstained face and wiped away the moisture with the back of his hand. His gaze searched hers. "Please, go."

She came slowly to her feet. "I will, but all I ask is that you let me come back and check on my deer. I won't bother you or your brother. I promise."

He glanced from her to the animal asleep in the hay. "And ye give yer word never to mention this again?"

"I do," she whispered.

"Ye may come back to check on yer pet, but that is all."

"Thank you," she said as she pushed open the stable door. "Good-bye, Lachlan."

"I do remember ye. I could never forget ye," he said so quietly she almost didn't hear him.

Syrena turned her face to the fading light streaming through the open door so he would not see the hope his simple acknowledgment ignited in her. Afraid if he did, he would find the words to take it away from her, just like her father always had.

"Princess, princess." An urgent whisper came from the side of the stable.

Syrena peeked around the corner and Evangeline grabbed her hand, jerking her to her side. "Evangeline, what in the name of Fae are you doing here? How—"

"We must hurry, princess. The Queen is searching for you."

"But how—"

"There's no time."

Syrena opened her mouth to protest, but before she had a chance to utter a word, Evangeline had transported them to the ring of standing stones.

"Come . . . come." Evangeline dragged her toward the largest of the stones.

Syrena stubbed her shoeless foot on a rock. "Ouch! Oh, look, Evangeline, you've made me lose my slipper."

Her handmaiden lifted her eyes to the heavens and shook her head. Murmuring an incantation, she replaced Syrena's shoe. "Princess, what happened?" Her gaze was fastened on the raised welt on Syrena's chest.

"A cat."

Her handmaiden shuddered then murmured another incantation.

Syrena breathed a sigh of relief when she found herself clad in shimmering robes of white shot through with gold threads that concealed her wound. "Thank you."

Evangeline tugged on her hand, dragging her into the stone. No sooner had they come through to the other side, than her handmaiden transported them to her quarters.

Syrena pressed her fingers to her temples, dizzy from the

speed of Evangeline's transportations. "Some warning would have been appreciated," she remarked dryly.

"There's no time." As she uttered the words, Morgana screeched in the outer hall. The door to Syrena's chambers flew open and her stepmother flounced inside.

"Oh, there you are, my dear. I've been looking all over for you. Your handmaiden has been no help at all," she said, casting a look of pure malice in Evangeline's direction.

The look didn't surprise Syrena. Morgana had never made an attempt to conceal her hatred of Evangeline. Syrena could not be sure, but thought perhaps her father's admiration of her handmaiden the cause. The king had been enchanted by Evangeline's long dark tresses and sultry beauty, and had made no secret of it. But as far as Syrena knew, he had never acted on his attraction. If he had, she was certain Evangeline would have told her.

"I'm sorry, Morgana, I fell asleep by the lake."

"You're forgiven." Her stepmother patted her cheek. "You do look a bit peaked. Are you certain you're all right?"

"I'm fine." Although truthfully, she'd never felt worse, her heart battered by Lachlan's rejection. "What is it you wanted me for?"

"I've formed a new council. We are set to meet within the hour. It is only right you sit at my side, with the Sword of Nuada, of course."

Syrena sighed. "Don't you remember, Morgana, the sword is with Uscias for repair?"

Her stepmother's gaze narrowed. "Do you question my authority, Syrena?"

A chill raced down her spine. What had she gotten herself into? She couldn't take a stand against her stepmother. The Fae were not behind her, she had no magick, and at the moment, she had no sword.

"I simply state a fact. You can rest assured, Morgana, when the time comes I will have my sword."

"There is no call for impudence, Syrena."

Syrena just barely refrained from rolling her eyes. "Perhaps you are right. I'm not feeling my best."

Her stepmother clicked her tongue sympathetically. "Then return to your slumber, my dear. I have decided your presence is unnecessary."

"Your highness, I'm certain Princess Syrena does not wish to disappoint you. If you give her a few moments, she'll be ready."

Syrena gaped at her handmaiden, and her stepmother glared at her. Fearing, this time, her handmaiden would not escape Morgana's wrath. Syrena stepped in to fill the breach. "Evangeline is right. I will be with you momentarily."

The Queen muttered something under her breath, her crimson robes billowing behind her as she swept from the room.

"Evangeline, whatever has come over you?" Syrena asked once they were alone.

Her handmaiden wrung her hands, two bright spots appearing on her high cheekbones. "I know it's not my place to say, my lady, but you have to take a stand. Let everyone know she does not rule alone. Mark my words, if you don't, we shall all pay the price."

Chapter 5

Aidan crossed the courtyard in search of Syrena. She'd yet to return to the hall and he imagined he'd find her with her wee pet nursing a fit of pique. He supposed he owed her an apology for his earlier behavior. She'd been none too pleased when he'd unceremoniously sent her on her way. Mayhap he'd been a little rough on her, but his brother had enflamed his temper and she'd only added to it with her obvious admiration of Lachlan.

With a resigned sigh, he entered the stables, the doors squeaking open on their rusted hinges. Slivers of the setting sun penetrated the shadows, and he noted Syrena's pet, struggling to stand.

"Nay, ye're no' quite ready, girl. Down ye get." He crouched beside the deer and held her in place until she settled back on a bed of sweet-smelling hay—obviously Syrena's handiwork, since it would not be Tom's. If the old man had his way, the doe would be gracing their tables this night.

Aidan sat back on his heels, scanning the empty stalls. *Where is she?* A shuffling sound drew his attention. He looked to the opposite end of the stables to see his brother dragging himself to his feet.

"Lan, I didna see ye there." He frowned at the expression on his brother's face. The lad looked like he'd lost his best friend. "What's wrong with ye? I ken ye were no' happy with what I had to say, but—" A sense of unease crawled up his spine as he looked from the deer to Lan. "What happened? What did ye do to her? I swear, Lan, if ye—"

His brother's gaze jerked from the stable doors, and he held up his hands. "Nay . . . nay, I didna do anythin' to her. She left is all."

Aidan shot to his feet and strode toward Lan. "What do ye mean, left? She doesna' even ken who she is. Where the bloody hell do ye think she would go?"

"I doona ken." His brother dragged his fingers through his hair then shot him a beseeching look. "Let her go, Aidan, just let her go. She's no' what . . . she's no' fer ye."

"What are ye babblin' about? She's injured, Lan, and she's here under my protection. So help me, if ye—"

"Nay, I wouldna hurt her. I couldna . . ." His brother's voice trailed off. Lan rubbed his eyes with the backs of his grimy hands, reminding Aidan of the scared and lonely child his brother had once been.

He squeezed Lachlan's shoulder in an attempt to comfort him. "I ken somethin' is troublin' ye, lad, and after I've found Syrena, I think 'tis time we have a talk."

Lan lifted his gaze to his, shaking his head. "Nay, I doona think ye'd want to hear what I have to say. I'm sorry I disappointed ye, Aidan. I'll no' do so again."

Aidan didn't suffer his brother's rebellious arrogance easily, but at the moment, he'd prefer it to the defeated demeanor he now displayed.

He threw a companionable arm over Lan's shoulders. "Come, help me find Syrena, and when we do, we'll have an ale together and ye can listen to her berate me fer my insufferable behavior." He thought to garner at least a smile from his brother, but all Lan did was nod and walk stiffly by his side.

"I doona ken where she's at, Aidan, but I think she'll be

back on account of the deer," Lan said, although to Aidan it sounded suspiciously like his brother hoped she wouldn't be.

"Aye." Lachlan was right. She wouldn't leave her pet.

From outside the stables, Aidan scanned the empty courtyard and the wooded grounds bordering the keep. He released an exasperated sigh. *Where the bloody hell had she gone and why?* He rounded the side of the stables, and a shimmer of golden light caught his eye. He bent down and tugged a delicate slipper from the overgrown bush. It was Syrena's.

He slapped the shoe against his thigh, searching the woodlands for some sign of her. "Syrena," he yelled, hoping for a response, frustrated when he received none. Something was wrong. She wouldn't go traipsin' about on her own, or would she? She'd been nothing but trouble since the moment he'd laid eyes on her. And he was too busy trying to set castle and clan to rights to be spending time chasing after a wayward lass.

He clenched the ridiculous excuse for a shoe in his hand. It was flimsy and delicate, not meant for the out of doors. Just like her. "I'm goin' to look fer her. Tell Gavin and Donald to meet me here."

"Let her go, Aidan," Lan said, his voice thick with emotion.

"I canna do that. She's under my protection. And I doona understand why ye'd want me to." He searched his brother's face, trying to gain some insight into what was going on inside that head of his.

Lan looked away then shrugged. "She left of her own accord is all I'm sayin'."

"Nay, I doona think so. There's more to it than that."

Color leeched from Lachlan's sun-darkened face. "Why . . . why would ye think that?"

Aidan narrowed his gaze on him, disturbed by his brother's reaction until a wave of insight slapped him upside the head. *The Lowlanders.* Lachlan thought the Lowlanders had taken her in retaliation for the raid. Aidan wanted to shake him. Yell at him about the consequences of his actions, but he couldn't do it. Not when it was so obvious how badly his brother felt. At the thought of Syrena in the hands of his enemies, anger and fear raged within him, squeezing the air from his lungs. Bloody hell, if they held her for ransom, how was he supposed to meet their demands?

Syrena shifted from one foot to the other while Evangeline fussed with her hair, and the emerald green gown she'd worn the day before. She wished she could wear another, but she didn't know how she'd explain the change of clothing to Aidan. Actually, that was the least of her worries. She'd yet to invent an excuse for where she'd been.

Evangeline tucked a strand of hair behind Syrena's ear, eyeing her with trepidation. "Are you certain about this, your highness?"

"I just can't leave him there, Evangeline. I can't. I won't. It's a horrible place." She shuddered at the memory of the bitter winds, the dreary landscape, and the hovel her brother lived in. "And truly, I don't think he is happy there. Besides, I have no choice but to fulfill my quest. You know that as well as I."

"Of course, my lady." Her dark head bent, she chewed on her lower lip, smoothing the fabric at Syrena's waist.

She stilled Evangeline's hand. "Is there something you're keeping from me? I know you're worried about some of the changes Morgana is making. And I admit banishing Lord Bana and Lord Erwn may not have been the smartest move on her part, but they attempted to turn the men against her when all she has tried to do is improve the lot of the women."

For the most part Syrena had been pleased with the council meeting. Her motion to have the servants' children cared for while their mothers worked had been readily accepted. The laws she wished to change were being taken into consideration, although she imagined part of her success was due to the fact the council was now made up entirely of women. But like Evangeline, she was somewhat concerned how the Fae men would fare under Morgana's rule.

"It was not Queen Morgana's actions I referred to, my lady, but since you bring it up, I must tell you I . . ." Evangeline dipped her head. "I beg your pardon, your highness, it's not my place."

She reached for Evangeline's hand. "You must always feel free to speak your mind with me. Truly, you are the only one I trust. I think of you as my friend."

Evangeline smiled. "Thank you, my lady, but my real concern lies in your return to the Mortal realm. I don't wish to upset you, but I'm anxious for your safety. I worry what your brother will do to you."

Syrena tugged at her sleeve, trying to banish her brother's words from her head. "He did agree that I could come and check on my deer, and honestly, I can't believe he doesn't harbor some feelings for me. Maybe if he gets to know me, he'll come to lo . . . like me." She averted her gaze from her handmaiden's knowing look.

Evangeline took her hands within hers. "I'm certain you're right, but what of *his* brother?"

Her cheeks heated. Surely she hadn't said anything to make Evangeline question her feelings for Aidan. Of course she hadn't, she reassured herself. *Why would she?* The man was an ogre, and most likely the cause of her brother's unhappiness. It was of no consequence that his gentle touch made her knees weak and her heart flutter, or that the warmth of his powerful arms made her feel safe and protected, something no Fae man had ever made her feel before. She cleared her throat. "He doesn't matter. He is of no consequence."

Evangeline arched an elegantly shaped brow. "No? Did Lachlan not say his brother would kill you with his bare hands if he found out who you were?"

Syrena shuddered. She had tried to banish the words her brother yelled, pretend he hadn't said them. But now, hearing Evangeline repeat them, she admitted to herself that it bothered her more than it should. Aidan had held her in his arms, quietened her fears, and to know he would wish to harm her if he learned that she was Fae was difficult to hear. Waving off her handmaiden's question as though it were inconsequential, Syrena said, "We both know he can't kill me, at least not with his bare hands."

"No, but he could hurt you."

"Yes . . . yes, he could." In some ways, simply knowing he would hate her if he knew the truth about her had already accomplished that. She pushed the thought aside and hardened her resolve. "But it's a risk I'm willing to take in hopes I can win over my brother. Trust me, Evangeline, I'll be careful. I might not be brave, as you well know, but I am not stupid either."

"You are brave, princess, you just don't choose to see it."

Syrena snorted. "You sound like Uscias, and speaking of him, if my stepmother questions you about my whereabouts, tell her I'm staying at his cottage. And that he's teaching me all I need to know about my sword. Hopefully that will appease her."

"If I can't dissuade you from remaining in the Mortal realm, then the least I can do is circumvent the Queen from discovering what it is you are up to."

She nibbled her finger. The last thing she wanted to dwell upon was what her stepmother would do if she discovered what she was up to. She couldn't help but think Morgana was striking back at the men for all she had suffered at her father's hand. So how would she react when Syrena returned with her brother, a man her father expected to rule the Enchanted Isles? She pushed the thought to the far recesses of her mind. She had enough to contend with without worrying about that.

"Actually, there is something else you can do for me, Evangeline. I've been thinking if I were to bring a gift to my brother, I might stand a better chance of winning him over."

Evangeline pursed her lips, a sure sign of her disapproval. "You're a wonderful person, my lady. I should hope you don't need to bribe your brother to gain his affection. If you do, his love is not worth having."

Syrena had the distinct impression her friend didn't particularly care for her brother. "Thank you, that is sweet of you to say, but if there's anything I can do to make this easier, I shall." She tapped a finger against her cheek, smiling when an idea came to mind. "I know exactly what I need to put my plan into action, a bag of coin."

Evangeline arched a brow. "Coin, my lady?"

She gave a decisive nod. "Yes, coin. Gold and silver coins are what they use in the Mortal realm. At least that's what it said in my book. We must have some in the treasury."

"I would imagine so, but as you well know, you require the Queen's permission to enter the vault."

"You're right, although as I rule alongside the Queen, I shouldn't." At the look of consternation on Evangeline's face, she sighed. "Yes, yes, I know it was only a ruse on her part and the guards will not let me in without her say-so. I can't rightly go to her with my request, but your magick is very powerful, Evangeline, you must be able to get in and out without their knowledge." Her handmaiden's magick grew more powerful with each passing year and it was something Syrena wished to talk to her about, but now was not the time.

"I can, but I would rather not. If I am caught, Morgana will banish me."

The thought of losing Evangeline terrified Syrena. She would be all alone. "You're right, she would. There is no love lost between the two of you." She studied her handmaiden. "Is there a reason for her animosity, something you haven't told me?" It was a question she'd been meaning to ask since the confrontation with Morgana the day before.

Evangeline's expression shuttered. "Not that I am aware of, your highness. And if you mean for me to break into the treasury, I'd best do it now before the palace awakens."

She gave her handmaiden an impetuous hug. "Thank you. I don't know what I'd do without you."

* * *

Hours had passed since Syrena came through the standing stones. The sun, hidden as it was behind surly gray clouds, did little to warm her. She'd found the woods where she'd first met Aidan easily enough. But upon leaving the shelter of the pines, she could only guess at the direction he had taken her and hope she'd chosen the right one.

As a way to pass the time as she trudged over the boggy ground, Syrena tried to come up with a plausible explanation for where she had been. Lost in her thoughts, she was startled when the earth trembled beneath her feet. She looked up to see Aidan on his great black steed bearing down upon her, with Donald and Gavin bringing up the rear.

With the wind blowing Aidan's blue-black hair from his face, he was even more beautiful than she remembered. His mesmerizing eyes mirrored the relief she herself felt, until she remembered her brother's proclamation. Her stomach churned and she worriedly searched his face. But there was no sign of anger upon his handsome visage when he looked at her. If anything, he appeared happy to see her. His mouth curved in a smile that set her heart aflutter.

He didn't know she was Fae—not yet.

He leapt from his mount and came swiftly to her side, standing so close the heat from his powerful body enveloped her in warmth. Placing his fingers beneath her chin, he raised her face to search her eyes. "Are ye all right, lass? They did ye no harm?"

She nodded. His gentle touch, the concern in his slate gray eyes, rendered her speechless.

He raised his gaze from hers and scanned the woods at her back. "Where are they?" he asked.

Syrena roused herself from his spell. *Whom did he speak of?* Afraid if she asked the question aloud she would give herself away, she decided to follow his lead as best she could. "I don't know."

He frowned, then jerking his chin in the direction of the woods, he said to Donald and Gavin, "Have a look around."

"Do ye ken how many there were, Syrena? Did ye get a good look at them?" he asked after his companions took their leave.

Tension banded her chest, making it difficult to breathe. "No," she answered, her voice little more than a whisper. She chewed on her bottom lip, wishing she had the ability to read minds. His interrogation grew painful, and he appeared to grow frustrated with her. Remembering what her father's response had been when she frustrated him, she took a wary step back.

Emotion flared in his eyes, and he muttered something under his breath. He gathered her in his arms. "I'm sorry, lass, this can wait. All that matters is ye're safe now."

The words rumbled deep in his chest soothed her fears and warmed her heart. She tipped her head back, unable to keep a smile from her lips. "You were worried about me?"

"Aye." He returned her smile, and stroked her cheek with his knuckles. "We've been searchin' fer ye ever since I found yer wee shoe."

Syrena sucked in an alarmed breath. As carefully as she could, without drawing his attention, she slid her foot from her slipper and tried to squish it into the soft, wet earth.

"I'll get it fer ye." He released her and strode toward Fin, rummaging through his saddlebag.

Syrena squeezed her eyes closed and murmured the words she prayed would make her slipper disappear. An odd sensation prickled from her foot to her knee, but she had no time to discover if her magick had been successful. Aidan stood before her, slipper in hand.

He bent down on one knee and carefully lifted the hem of her gown. She scrambled for some explanation, but her mind went blank, panic scattering her thoughts.

Aidan raised a quizzical brow.

Syrena looked down to see she wore an oversized black

boot. *Oh, for the love of Fae.* "I . . . I found it over there."
She pointed in the direction of the woods.

He removed the boot and tossed it aside, holding her bare
foot in the palm of his hand. Syrena grabbed hold of his broad
shoulders to keep from falling over while he warmed her foot
in his hand. He blew a heated breath across her icy cold skin
and she gasped inwardly at the sensation. Warmth unfurled
deep in her belly then spread to the core of her femininity.
She curled her fingers into the soft fabric of his brown jacket,
resisting the urge to run them through the dark waves on his
bent head.

He lifted his gaze, watching her as he slid her slipper onto
her foot. He slowly came to his feet and, without a word,
lifted her into his arms. Syrena clutched the back of his neck,
inhaling his masculine scent, trying to understand the emotions he awakened in her. No one had ever made her feel as
protected as he did, or aroused a desire for their touch. She
shivered, afraid if she spent too much time with this man
she'd leave a piece of her heart behind when she returned to
the Enchanted Isles.

Aidan settled her carefully on top of Fin, treating her as
though she were a fragile piece of crystal. He swung into the
saddle behind her, tugging her against his chest. She snuggled
into him. He leaned over and pulled a blanket from his pack.

She wrinkled her nose at the smell of damp wool and
horses, but swallowed her complaint once Aidan had tucked
her within its heavy warmth.

At the sound of Donald and Gavin's return, he twisted in
the saddle. "Any sign of them?"

"Nay, they're long gone," Donald said as he brought his
horse alongside them. "How's the lass?"

Syrena was about to tell him she was fine, but then thought
better of it. She didn't have the answers to the questions that
would surely follow. She wriggled deeper beneath the blanket.

"As good as can be expected after what she's been through."

"Ye doona think they—"

"Nay," Aidan said gruffly, tightening his hold on her. "Nay, but I'll question her further once she's rested."

"She's verra lucky. Remember what happened to wee Tess? When the Lowlanders were through with the lass, she was never the same."

"Enough, Gavin. Ride on ahead and have Beth prepare a bath fer her."

Once she heard the horses ride off, Syrena pushed the gray wool from her head. "What happened to Tess?" At least she knew now they thought the Lowlanders had been involved in her disappearance. If she asked some pertinent questions, she hoped to come up with a believable response when Aidan interrogated her later.

He curled a big hand around her neck and stroked her cheek with his thumb. "'Tis no' somethin' ye need to ken, Syrena. I'll no' let those bloody Lowlanders near ye again."

She nuzzled her cheek against the coarse fabric of his shirt, smoothing her palm over the muscular planes of his chest. "Thank you," she murmured.

"Yer thanks isna necessary. Ye're under my protection until we find yer kin."

Unwilling to get caught in a lie, she decided to probe further. "Why did they take me?"

He shrugged then looked down at her. "I suspect it was in retaliation for Lachlan's raid. If ye hadna gotten away, they would've held ye fer ransom."

She plucked at the laces on his shirt, lowering her eyes from the intensity in his. "Would you have paid?"

He tipped her chin, bringing her gaze back to his. "Aye, and if I didna have the coin they demanded, I would've found a way to steal ye back from them."

Considering the state of his home, she knew he did not have much coin. The thought he would use whatever he had to rescue her touched her heart. She wanted to show him the depth of her gratitude and decided to gift him with a portion of the coin she'd brought for Lachlan. She reached inside her gown, about to pull the black velvet bag from her bodice.

Aidan frowned, pushing her hand aside. "Where is yer wound?" He traced his fingers along her chest.

She tried to form some reasonable explanation, willing her brain to work, but desire, warm and liquid, coursed through her veins, leaving her thoughts scattered, and her body boneless.

"Syrena?" The censure in his deep voice penetrated her muddled senses.

"I don't know," she managed to say. "Perhaps the sun has colored my skin as it has yours. And the mark has simply—"

"Nay." He hooked a finger in the neckline of her gown and lowered it, exposing the tops of her breasts.

"Aidan!" she gasped, but he ignored her.

"Nay, ye're the same milky white here where the sun's rays do not reach." His voice was low and husky, and he trailed a calloused finger over her heated flesh.

She shivered, the look in his eyes searing her as deeply as his touch.

Under the scrutiny of his gaze, she attempted an unconcerned shrug. "It must not have been as deep as it first appeared."

His hand stilled and he frowned, then he dipped his fingers between the valley of her breasts. "What is this?" he asked, removing the velvet bag. The coin clinked when he swung the pouch from the tips of his fingers. The disapproval in his tone robbed her of her good intentions.

"It's mine. You can't have it." She tried to retrieve the coin, but he held it out of her reach.

He shifted her weight in his arms and opened the bag. His eyes widened. "Bloody hell, Syrena, who are ye?"

Chapter 6

"Enough," Aidan grated out when Syrena struggled to adjust the front of her gown. Her rounded behind rubbed against his straining erection, causing the dull throb in his trews to rival the ache in his head. An ache caused by the discovery of enough coin to ransom a king.

He rubbed his hand over his eyes in order to gain some semblance of control over his burgeoning lust for the woman in his arms. The sight of her full breasts when he lowered her gown, and the memory of how warm and satiny smooth she felt beneath his fingers, didn't help.

He lifted the bag and shook it in front of her bonny face. "Answer my question."

She stopped squirming and regarded him with a haughty look. "I told you who I am. My name is Syrena, and as yet I have no memory of my family. But what does *that* have to do with the coin?"

"It would go a long way in tellin' me who I'm dealin' with, now wouldna it? Ye're either a thief or the daughter of someone with incredible wealth, and from where I'm sittin', either one will bring down their wrath on my clan. Now, which is it?"

"Give it back. I'm no thief." She lunged for the bag, but he jerked it high above her head. "The coin is mine, all treasure belongs to . . ." She scowled at him. Clamping her mouth shut, she crossed her arms over her heaving chest.

"Where, Syrena? Where did ye come by the coin?"

Her expression shuttered. She nibbled on her finger then pointed in the direction of the woods. "I found it with the boot. I was going to share it with you if only you'd given me a chance."

He didn't know whether to believe her or not. He prayed she told the truth. He had no desire to battle the sheriff on her behalf, or a clan hell-bent on revenge. But looking down into her wide, innocent eyes and a face as bonny as an angel, he doubted she had it in her to lie.

The heavy weight in the bag regained his attention, and he pushed aside the niggling of doubt that so much didn't add up where she was concerned. In his hands lay the answer to his prayers. The coin would go a long way in putting the keep and his clan to rights.

Fin pawed at the ground, snorting puffs of mist. "All right, boy, we'll head fer home," he said, giving the horse his lead. With one last look toward the wood, he asked her. "So, ye're tellin' me ye didna see whose boot ye wore or coin ye took?"

She released an exasperated sigh and looked up at him, her topaz eyes flashing. "I'm not a thief. I told you I planned on giving you the coin, but if you don't want it, give it back to me."

He bit back a grin. "Ye were, were ye? And why might that be?"

Her long lashes fanned cheeks flushed a becoming pink. "Because . . . because you offered me your protection and you need it more than I do."

"Aye, that'd be the truth, but I'll have no part of ill-gotten goods. Ye must swear to me, Syrena, ye didna steal the coin."

She glared at him. "Why won't you listen to me? I told you, I didn't steal it. The coin is mine."

The angry rise and fall of her chest captured his attention and he battled an overwhelming urge to touch her. Unable to resist the temptation, using the coin as an excuse, he balanced the weight of the bag in his hand and then, taking his time, tucked the black velvet between the valley of her breasts. His finger's brushed her full heated curves, the satiny softness of her skin.

At her startled intake of breath, he slowly withdrew his hand. He cleared his throat, shifting uncomfortably beneath her. "'Tis as good a place as any to hide the coin. It would be best if we tell no one of our good fortune, at least fer now."

She sat stiffly in his lap. "Syrena?" He waited until she met his eyes. "Thank ye fer sharin' yer coin with me."

Her gaze searched his, and then she smiled. "You're welcome. And thank you for your offer of protection."

His hard-won defenses were useless against her.

Achingly sweet and gentle, the lass drew him to her like no other. And now, she gifted him with gold and silver beyond his wildest imaginings. He wrapped her in the blanket and brought Syrena against his chest, brushing the top of her silky head with his lips. "I promise ye, Syrena, I'll let no one harm ye."

She snuggled close. "I know."

This time, upon their arrival at the keep, Syrena required only a slight nudge to come fully awake. The courtyard was crowded with his men. Gavin stepped forward to take Fin's reins while Aidan dismounted. He reached for Syrena, frowning when he noted the fearful expression that shadowed her delicate features. He glanced over his shoulder to see what had prompted her reaction, only to meet his brother's angry gaze full on.

Lifting her from Fin, Aidan tucked her to his side. Noting the tremble that shook her slight frame, he glared at Lachlan. "Ye're scarin' the lass with yer fierce looks, brother. What is the matter with ye?" From the corner of his eye, he noted his men take their leave, obviously not eager to get in the middle of one of his and Lan's all too frequent battles.

"Nothin'," his brother snarled, then turned and stomped toward the keep.

Aidan wearily shook his head, too tired to wonder at Lachlan's reaction to the lass. He'd spent the better part of the day and night searching for Syrena, and he wanted nothing more than a tankard of ale and the comfort of his bed.

"I'd like to check on my deer if you don't mind."

Before he had a chance to respond, she'd pivoted on her heel and headed in the direction of the stables.

Gavin caught his eye. "Lan doesna' appear to like the lass overmuch. I never saw him be anythin' but charmin' to the lassies, especially one as bonny as Lady Syrena." He shrugged, about to lead Fin to the stables.

"Nay, I'll take him." Aidan retrieved the reins from Gavin. "Mayhap ye and Donald can see what ails the lad," he suggested. At times like these he felt the loss of his father's menat-arms, Torquil and Dougal. They had been a steadying influence on Lan. Their deaths two years past had been a devastating blow to the both of them.

"Are ye goin' to the lass?"

"Aye, I need to ken if my brother was the cause of her leavin' the stables before the Lowlanders got a hold of her."

"Did she say any more about her capture?"

"Nay, and I didna want to upset her."

"I'm sure ye didna. Ye looked mighty cozy when ye rode in." Gavin grinned, whistling as he went on his way.

Aidan scowled after his friend. The man had only one thing on his mind, and Aidan didn't need reminding of what that one thing was. He was doing his best not to think about it.

When he entered the stables, Syrena looked up from where she sat on a bed of hay beside her pet. Her eyes were red-rimmed, and he cursed his brother. The animal, as though sensing her distress, licked her hand. Aidan hesitated before breaking the strained silence. "The wee beastie appears glad to see ye."

She offered him a woebegone smile and nodded, then went back to stroking her pet without saying a word.

He clenched Fin's reins in his fist and walked him into the stall behind Syrena. Unable to keep his gaze from her bent head and her long, golden locks, he jerked the saddle from his mount and tossed it over the wooden slats. Resting a boot on the lower rung, he leaned over the rail. "Ye ken, Syrena, my brother's foul temper has naught to do with ye."

She glanced up at him with a hopeful light in her eyes. "No?"

"Nay," he managed to say despite the sharp stab of jealousy that his brother's opinion mattered so much to her. He shoved off the wall. Latching the door to Fin's stall, he came around and lowered himself to the ground beside her. He petted the doe's downy soft head, biding his time. But no matter how much he wished to put it off, he couldn't. He needed an answer to his question.

"Syrena, did somethin' go on between my brother and ye the other day?"

Her fingers stilled. She kept her eyes focused on her pet. "What . . . what do you mean?"

"'Tis a simple enough question." Yet he had a hard time asking it. "Did ye . . . did he . . . ?"

Her eyes flew to his. "No . . . no, how could you think such a thing?"

Relief thrummed through his body at her response. "Ye didna let me finish. I—"

"I didn't have to. I could see it in your eyes. You thought he and I . . . well that . . . ." Her dainty hands fluttered in front of her and she wrinkled her turned-up nose in what looked to be disgust. "I wouldn't do that. He's . . . well, I couldn't do that."

"So, is it just my brother ye would no' kiss?"

"I do not go around kissing men, Lord MacLeod, if that's

what you are implying. I'm not that sort of woman," she said tightly.

He brushed a soft curl from the curve of her heated cheek. "'Tis no' what I meant. I ken what kind of woman ye are, lass."

"What . . . what do you mean?" she stammered, raising amber eyes flecked with gold to his.

Cupping her chin in his hands, he rubbed his thumb over her full bottom lip. "I mean ye're innocent. No man has ever kissed ye, have they?"

"No," she whispered, her lips slightly parted.

"'Tis a shame that. Ye have a bonny mouth, ripe fer kissin'." Desire overrode caution, and he lowered his head to claim her. He only meant for it to be one brief kiss, but the moment he touched her soft, pliant lips, he was lost. Sliding his lips in a slow, sensuous motion, back and forth over hers, the gentle friction stoked the flame of his passion. His heart pounded at her tentative response and it took all the control he could muster to take it slow.

She leaned into him, her lips parted, and he deepened the kiss, touching his tongue to hers, tasting her honeyed sweetness. The kiss grew hotter, wetter, and he had to cup her face with both his hands to stop himself from stroking her milky white breasts pressed to his chest.

A soft mewling sound from low in her throat caused him to groan in frustration. He couldn't do it. He couldn't let it go any further. He'd gone far enough. *Innocent, she's innocent and wealthy*, Aidan reminded himself. A combination that would have his neck in the proverbial noose if he wasn't careful. An irate father would have just cause in demanding he wed her. And no matter how attracted he was, no woman was worth the trouble, the pain. He brought his hands to her shoulders and gently broke their connection.

She blinked, a look of bemusement in her topaz eyes. He pressed his lips to her smooth forehead. "Thank ye fer allowin' me the honor of yer first kiss." He tried to keep his voice light, but it was no use. It came out in a strangled rasp, but it was enough to keep him from saying the words he wanted to say. That she was his and his alone, that no other would kiss that rosebud mouth, swollen and slick from the fervor of his kiss. He didn't know what he damned most at that moment, his mother and Davina's betrayal, or his deep-seated sense of honor.

He set her aside and came to his feet. He held out his hand. "Come, yer bath will have cooled. Beth will have to prepare ye another."

She cast him a troubled look then shook her head. "No, I think it best if I remain here."

"Are ye plannin' on beddin' down with yer pet, then?"

She nodded, appearing as unhappy with the idea as he was.

He crouched beside her. "Did I frighten ye with my kiss, is that what this is about?"

She looked at him as though he were daft. "No, of course not."

Growing frustrated now, he said, "Then ye'd best explain to me what the trouble is."

"M . . . your brother doesn't want me here."

"'Tis no' the lad's decision, 'tis mine. Besides, I've told ye his temper has no' to do with ye." Seeing the doubt in her eyes, he tried to reassure her, "Lachlan's day of birth is almost upon us. Somethin' happened a long time ago that he, both of us fer that matter, havena gotten past. No matter how much we'd like to think we have. So ye see, 'tis no' ye, but the memories that have him in a temper. 'Twill pass, I promise ye. Now come, I'm weary and in need of some ale. And ye're in need of a soft place to lay yer head."

"A soft bed," she murmured in a wistful voice. "And warm, it is warm, isn't it?"

The corner of his mouth quirked. "Aye, a soft, warm bed." He looked down at her beautiful face, her luscious curves, and thought how he'd like to be the one to keep her warm.

After a quick hug to her doe, she rose to her feet. He

reached out a hand to steady her. She narrowed her gaze on him. "It doesn't have holes in the wall like your hall, does it?"

"Nay, and with the coin I'll right that soon enough. Mayhap 'twould be best if ye give me the treasure, Syrena, and I'll put it away fer safekeepin'." Resisting the urge to retrieve the bag himself, he watched as she dipped her hand into her bodice and handed him the bag still warm from the heat of her flesh.

He took the coin, frowning at her outstretched hand. "Ye want it back?"

"No, but I said I'd share it with you, not give you all of it."

He arched a brow. "If I remember correctly, ye said ye had no need of the coin."

"Well, I do." She wiggled her fingers.

Aidan figured he could hardly begrudge her a few coins since he'd have none if not for her. He untied the bag and dug inside, lining her palm in silver and gold.

"Thank you," she said, closing her fingers over the coin, a wide smile curving her lips.

"Do ye mind tellin' me what ye plan on doin' with yer share?" he asked as they left the barn.

"It's a present for Lachlan's day of birth." Her hand tightened into a fist, and she glanced at him through a fan of long lashes.

He groaned. "Nay, lass, 'tis too much. The lad will use it to . . . 'Tis no' a good idea is all."

"But it's what I want to do. It will make him happy and then he won't . . ." She shrugged. "I just want to make him happy."

Even though he knew what his brother would do with the coin, Aidan couldn't disillusion her. He sensed she meant to win his brother's friendship. Why it was so important to her, he'd yet to discover, but it was, and at that moment it was all that mattered. As sweet as Syrena was, Aidan imagined she was unused to being on the receiving end of someone's anger.

"Ye give him yer gift, angel, and I'm certain ye'll have gained a friend fer life."

"Do you really think so?" she asked hopefully.

He entwined his fingers with hers. "Aye, I do."

Syrena awoke to the sound of Beth clomping along the hall outside her chambers and pulled the blankets over her head, even though she knew it wouldn't do her any good. Despite spending several days at Lewes, she'd been unable to break the woman's annoying habit of dragging her from her bed in the early morning hours.

The heavy door creaked open and Syrena heard Beth chuckle. "Och, ye ken it will do ye no good hidin' on me." Beth clicked her tongue. "Never did I see a body require as much sleep as ye do, my lady. Come now, we have much to do on account of the gatherin' bein' this day."

Syrena groaned, lowering the blanket. "Don't tell me you want me to help in the kitchens again."

"Och, nay. The laird left strict orders no' to let ye anywhere near them."

She rolled her eyes. "It's not as though I set the kitchen ablaze, only the cakes."

"Aye, but we didna ken that until the smoke cleared."

Her cheeks heated. In her panic, she'd used her magick to put out the burning cakes and instead filled the room with thick, billowing black smoke.

"Ye were quite the sight covered from head to toe in soot. I doona ken when I've seen the laird laugh so hard."

Oh yes, Aidan had found her very funny indeed. Despite herself, Syrena smiled at the memory and a happy glow enveloped her. But her smile faded, if she wasn't careful, the warm glow of contentment would grow into something more, if it hadn't already.

From the moment she met Aidan, she'd responded to him in a way she'd never responded to another. She touched her lips at the memory of his kiss. Although they hadn't shared another since that day in the barn, she could still feel his firm mouth pressed to hers. At first gentle and then more demanding, awakening in her a desire so strong it seared her to her very soul.

He spoke the truth when he said she was innocent, untouched, but that didn't mean she was ignorant of the ways between a man and a woman. The Fae were sensual beings, carrying on freely, no matter who their audience was. She shuddered, remembering Lord Bana's aggressive attempt to initiate her in sexual play, groping hands, and slobbering lips she barely managed to escape.

The memory of her first kiss would be one she cherished, but she knew it was because of the man she shared it with. Certain no other would make her feel as Aidan did.

She pushed aside a heavy sense of regret. They had no future. She belonged in the Fae realm. And if Lachlan told the truth, if ever Aidan learned who she was, he would want nothing to do with her. Worse, he would despise her.

"Are ye all right, my lady? Ye've lost all the color in yer wee face," Beth said, her brow furrowed in concern.

Pushing the troubling thoughts aside, Syrena flipped back the covers and came to her feet. "Yes, I'm fine. Now, what can I do to help?"

Angling her head to study her, Beth said, "Ye ken, my lady, no' many of yer station would do as ye've done fer us. Ye should ken the lasses and I are verra grateful fer all yer help."

"Even after the mess I made of the kitchens?" she asked in an attempt to lighten the moment. Afraid if she didn't, Beth would see how much her kind words meant to her.

"Aye." The woman chuckled then her expression grew serious. "Ye've made a difference, Lady Syrena, no' only fer us but fer Laird Aidan. It may be bold of me to say so, but 'tis our hope ye will remain here at Lewes, that ye and our laird will—"

"Listen to that, Beth. It sounds as if the men are already

at work below," she cut off the older woman abruptly and hurried over to the window. Turning her back, she gripped the sill and tried to gather control of her emotions. She cleared her throat. "It looks as though they're moving out the tables. You should probably go and be certain they don't damage them. You know how careless men can be."

"Aye, I do, my lady. I found a gown fer ye to wear to the gatherin'. I'll bring it by later," Beth said quietly and patted Syrena's shoulder before she left the room.

Syrena wiped the moisture from her eyes. No matter what Beth said, there was no place for Aidan in her life. And it didn't matter how much she wished there were.

She blew out a resigned sigh and began to dress in the ugly brown gown Beth had brought to her after she'd ruined her own the day before. They had much to do to prepare for the gathering, for Lachlan's day of birth celebration. Syrena held out hope that somehow her gift would turn the tide in their relationship. Her time spent in Lewes certainly hadn't. Lachlan had avoided her at every turn, but today, today she somehow had to convince him he belonged with her in the Enchanted Isles. She just wouldn't think of the pain she would cause Aidan by taking him. But the thought that the two men did little more than fight alleviated some of her guilt.

Striding toward the heavy oak door, she came to an abrupt halt. Shaking her head at her absentmindedness, she returned to retrieve the coins from beneath her pillow. She folded her gift in a dull white handkerchief and tucked the treasure into the front of her bodice.

Walking along the dingy corridor, she batted at a silken web that floated above her head. Unable to contain her squeak of dismay when a black creature with long legs landed on the tip of her nose, she slapped it away, managing to throw herself off-kilter. The sole of her threadbare shoe slid on the top step and she lunged for the wooden banister, releasing a relieved breath when she managed to regain her balance.

She started down the long staircase, keeping a firm grip on the banister. Once her rattled nerves had calmed, she became aware of the low timbre of male voices coming from the hall. Her body responded instantly to Aidan's deep baritone—calling orders to his men in his thick, delicious brogue—a quickening of her pulse, a frisson of excitement racing along her spine.

She took a steadying breath and stiffened her resolve, vowing not to react to him. And then she saw him coming through the doors of the hall. Bare-chested, he carried a long trestle table with the help of another man. She couldn't take her eyes from him, mesmerized by the power and beauty of his glistening, sun-bronzed warrior's body, the bulging muscles in his arms and chest as they rippled and flexed. Clamping a hand over her mouth to contain a groan, she dug her fingers into the banister.

As he drew near the bottom of the staircase, she tried to tear her eyes away, afraid he would recognize the emotions thrumming through her. Just as she was about to lower her gaze, he raised his.

Their eyes met. An instant awareness crackled between them, and then Aidan cursed. Startled, she jumped. He dropped his end of the table and took a step forward, a hand raised in warning.

"Syrena, move away from the—"

An ominous groan filled the air.

Chapter 7

The banister broke free of its moorings, dragging Syrena along with it. Her strangled cry was drowned out by his men shouting directions. "Quiet," Aidan yelled and ran to position himself beneath her. He held up his arms. "Jump, lass, I'll catch ye."

She clung to the wood, hanging high above him, her eyes wide with alarm.

"Let go, angel. Do it now," he commanded in a voice that revealed none of his desperate concern. "Trust me."

With a jerky nod, she squeezed her eyes closed, then let go. She landed with a whoosh in his arms. Crushing her to his chest, he stumbled backward just as a horrendous crash rattled the keep. A cloud of dust billowed around the rotted timber that lay on the floor, inches from his feet.

He drew in a shuddered breath, managing a smile for the trembling bundle in his arms. "Ye're wee, but ye're no lightweight," he said, in an attempt to make light of what had happened.

Stepping away from the fallen timber, he tried not to think what would have become of her had she not trusted him enough to let go. "I'm sorry. I should've warned ye about that," he said, angling his chin in the direction of the stairs. Like everything else in the bloody keep, the timber had shown signs of wear, he just hadn't had the time or coin to do anything about it.

She shook her head. Her long silken tresses tickled his bare chest, causing his taut muscles to twitch in response. "No, I should have realized it was unstable." Uncurling her fist, she smoothed her palm over his heated flesh. The pads of her fingers moved in a slow rhythmic motion, up and down, up and down, as though she comforted herself.

"Good catch." Gavin chuckled, drawing Aidan's attention from the havoc she wreaked on his overly responsive body. Several of the men came forward to inspect the damage before getting back to the job at hand. Wood scraped over the slate as they dragged the tables across the floor.

He looked down at Syrena and glanced pointedly at her hand. "I think it best ye stop, lass. We have an audience and I canna be held accountable fer my actions if ye doona."

"Oh," she gasped, jerking her hand away. As she peeked at him from beneath her lashes, her cheeks pinked.

He grinned and kissed the tip of her nose. "I'm teasin'. Steady now," he said as he set her on her feet and she swayed against him. Her gown slid down her arm to reveal the delicate slope of her shoulder and enough of her breast to cause him to harden in his trews.

"I think Beth might have found ye somethin' more suitable to wear." The cool calm of his voice belied his heated awareness of her. His fingers trailed over her satiny smooth skin as he drew the gown into place. Holding the excess fabric in his hand, he reached back and pulled the leather thong from his hair. "Turn around," he said, his voice gruff.

She cast him an uncertain look then complied with his demand. Hair the color of burnished gold slid through his fingers as he moved the heavy tangle of curls aside. He inhaled deeply, determined not to give in to the desire to press his lips to the creamy skin at the nape of her neck. Afraid he'd be unable to stop at just a kiss. With unsteady fingers, he wrapped the piece of leather around the coarse fabric and tied it in place. She glanced warily over her shoulder.

He lifted a brow. "Better?"

She nibbled on her bottom lip and nodded. "Much. Thank you, and thank you for saving me, Aidan. Again."

"Ye're welcome." He drew his attention from her and kicked at the wooden remains on the floor. Glancing at the stairs, he dragged his hand through his hair. "'Tis just one more thing to add to my list of repairs and now it takes priority over the hall." He gave an irritated shake of his head. "Bloody hell, this place is falling down around us."

With a hand resting on the seductive curve of her hip, she looked around the keep in much the same manner as he had. "You're right, it is."

He laughed. He couldn't take offense from her comment, not when it was the truth. And she looked so adorable saying it with her hair a tumbled mass of golden curls, eyes wide and earnest in her heart-shaped face.

She leaned into him, stretching up on the tips of her toes. "But you have coin enough to help you now," she whispered conspiratorially.

He grinned. "Aye, I do, thanks to you."

"Aidan," his brother snapped, glaring at him over Syrena's head. "The men need to ken how many more tables ye'll be needin'."

Entranced by the woman before him, Aidan hadn't noted his brother's approach. He shot Lan a quelling look before returning his attention to Syrena. "Ye're certain ye'll be all right, lass?"

"Yes, I'm fine," she murmured. But as Aidan went to move away from her, she laid a hand upon his arm. "Since I've been banned from the kitchens, I thought I may be of some help to you with the tables."

He smiled and ran his knuckles gently over her cheek. "Only because I feared fer yer safety."

"Uhmm, mine and your cakes." Her eyes sparkled with

amusement and he wished his brother wasn't standing nearby glowering at them.

"Mayhap, and as fer the tables, I'm certain we have all we'll be needin'. Besides, 'tis no' a job fer a lady."

"No, I meant I could clean the tables and have them ready for the linens and flowers."

"Linens . . . flowers?" he asked over Lan's derisive snort. "I wasna plannin' on makin' it a fancy affair, lass." They hadn't dined on anything other than scarred wood since his mother's death. All life's niceties had died with her.

"Oh, but you must make it special. It's the day of your brother's birth." She cast a shy smile in Lan's direction.

His brother's expression darkened, and he all but shouted at Syrena, "How did ye ken that?"

"Your brother told me." She edged closer to Aidan.

Bloody hell, he wanted to shake the lad for upsetting her. Aidan gave her shoulder a reassuring squeeze. "Aye, do as ye wish, Syrena." He left his hand on her shoulder and skewered his brother with a look he'd be familiar with. "I ken this day reminds ye of things ye'd rather forget, but I'll no' have ye takin' out yer foul humor on Syrena." Aidan wondered if the lass's gift would lessen his brother's anger. He hoped so. He didn't relish the idea of pummeling him on his day of birth. But if he continued to treat Syrena as he did, Aidan would be sorely tempted to do just that. He bent his head and said quietly, "Why doona ye give him yer gift?"

At his nod of encouragement, she took a hesitant step in Lan's direction. Slipping her fingers into her gown, she withdrew the wee bundle and tentatively offered it to his brother.

Lan looked as though she had offered him a newt and took a horrified step back. "What . . . what's that?"

She glanced over her shoulder at Aidan, small, perfect white teeth worrying her bottom lip before she answered, "Your present," and once more offered him her gift.

Lan snarled, "Nay, I want nothin' from ye, nothin'!" With a violent sweep of his hand, he knocked the bundle from

Syrena's fingers and sent the coin flying. Gold and silver bounced on the slate, a dull clinking sound echoing in the deafening silence.

Syrena let out a startled gasp and sank to the floor. Her head bent, she picked up the scattered pieces with trembling fingers.

Aidan strode to his brother's side. Fisting his hand in the front of Lachlan's tunic, he shook him. "Ye go too far, brother. Apologize to her. Now!" His voice was strangled with barely controlled rage.

Lan shoved him away. "Nay, I willna do it. I want nothing from her, do ye hear me? Ye're a fool, brother. Ye doona—"

"Aidan, please, it doesn't matter." Syrena came to his side, covering his fist with icy fingers. "Please, don't," she begged him. Her topaz eyes glistened, brimming with unshed tears.

Aidan released his pent-up frustration on a heavy sigh. Unclenching his fist, he covered her hand with his. Behind him, the door to the keep slammed. He shook his head, disgusted with his brother. "I doona ken what to say to ye, lass." A tear trickled down her pale face. With his thumb, he brushed it away. "Ye doona deserve his anger. When he calms down, I'll speak to him."

She swallowed hard and shook her head. "No, please, let it be." The anguished look on her sweet face drew an emotion from him so strong it caught him off guard. He pulled her into his arms and held her as though he'd never let her go, and at that moment, he didn't want to.

He stroked her back. "There's much to do on account of the gatherin' and I need yer help. 'Tis no' only my brother we celebrate this day but a lessenin' of our troubles," he said, trying to distract her.

She lifted her head to look up at him. "You really want my help?"

"Aye, I do." He kissed the reddened tip of her upturned nose just as the door to the keep creaked open.

"See, didna I tell ye where he'd be. Ye owe me two shillings, Donald."

Donald snorted. "'Twas said in jest, Gavin. I doona have a penny to me name and well ye ken it."

Aidan looked down at Syrena and arched a brow, receiving the ghost of a smile in return. She handed him two gold coins, and he tossed one to each of them. "Ye can thank the lass fer it, and no' a word to anyone else." If it was friends she was after, he was determined she'd have them.

Donald sketched her a bow that would do a mother proud. And before Aidan could stop him, Gavin was on his knees at her feet, kissin' her hands. At the sound of her soft giggle, Aidan knew he'd do whatever it took to ensure her happiness.

With a cautious glance over her shoulder, Syrena crept unseen from the bush she hid behind. Not an easy task considering Gavin and Donald had remained attached to her hip, and Aidan had kept a very close eye on her. Every time she'd looked up from setting the tables, she'd met his gaze, the gentle concern in his mesmerizing eyes a soothing balm to the bitter hurt of Lachlan's rejection. Donald and Gavin had lightened her mood, too, with their steadfast devotion and playful flirtations. But she was worn out from all of the attention and longed for the quiet companionship of her deer.

Syrena hurried across the deserted courtyard to the stables. She stepped within the dimly lit barn, and fingers closed over her wrist and jerked her inside. The doors banged closed behind her. The panicked scream that gurgled in her throat dissolved the moment she recognized her captor.

Recovering her voice, she cried, "Evangeline, what in the name of Fae are you doing here?" But she was immediately distracted by the notable absence of her deer. "My pet, she's gone!" She tugged on Evangeline's arm. "We must find her. Give us some light."

"Calm yourself, my lady. She seemed lonely so I put her in

with him. Look." With a wave of her hand a lantern appeared on the post by Fin's stall. The light cast the stables in a soft amber glow. Syrena blew out a relieved breath. Her pet was happily cozened up to the big, black stallion.

Her handmaiden's violet eyes widened. "My lady, whatever are you wearing?" Before she had a chance to respond, Evangeline began to murmur an incantation.

Syrena tugged on the sleeve of her handmaiden's amethyst robes. "No, no. I don't want you to change my gown. I want to know what you're doing here."

"You're right. We have no time to waste. Come, princess, we must go."

Knowing the close confines of the stable would make transportation difficult for her handmaiden, Syrena dug in her heels. Dust billowed up from the dirt floor as Evangeline dragged her toward the door. At the sound of muffled grunts coming from the far end of the stables, Syrena jerked back in alarm. Noting Evangeline's furious glare in the direction of the sound, she slowly turned.

Her eyes widened and her mouth dropped. "What have you done?" she groaned. Her gaze darting from her brother, who hung upside down from the rafters, a rag stuffed in his mouth, to Evangeline, who simply shrugged.

Evangeline shot Lachlan a look of pure loathing. A look Syrena had never before seen in her handmaiden's eyes, and it shocked her into silence.

"He attacked me. But don't worry, I'll wipe his mind of the memory and release him once we're safely away from here."

Lachlan fought his restraints. Returning Evangeline's hostile glare, his grunts grew louder.

Syrena tugged her hand free. "I told you, I'm not going anywhere, and"—she pointed at Lachlan—"you can't wipe his mind. He has Fae blood." Anger at both her brother and Evangeline boiled in the pit of her stomach. Lachlan had hurt her badly, but she still had hopes—small though they might be— of changing his mind about her. But now, after Evangeline's antics, she doubted there was much chance of that. "He's my brother!"

"Him?" Evangeline's lips pulled back in a menacing sneer.

"Evangeline, release him," Syrena growled.

"I will not. The Mortal is an arrogant, disgusting, overbearing lout, with the sensitivity of a rock. He made you cry!"

Lachlan appeared ready to strangle her handmaiden if he could but break free from the ropes that held him in place.

Syrena blew out an exasperated breath. The two of them sorely tried her temper. "Please, Evangeline, for me."

A mutinous expression hardened Evangeline's fine-boned features. She crossed her arms over her chest and snarled, "No."

Syrena stamped her foot in frustration. "You have to obey me, I'm your princess."

"You are, and it is my duty to protect you from the likes of him." She jerked her head in Lachlan's direction. "Princess, it is urgent you return home. I promise, I'll release the . . . him, when we're at the stones."

"The council isn't set to meet again for a fortnight. How urgent can the matter be?"

Evangeline grimaced. "Queen Morgana has sent a missive to Uscias demanding the Sword of Nuada."

Syrena stiffened. "She can't do that, there is no precedent for such an act."

"No, but she is arguing that because of the agreement between the two of you, the point is moot."

"The sword is mine. Besides, the council would never agree to such a request."

Evangeline lowered her eyes from hers.

"Tell me the council didn't give her their consent?"

"I'm sorry, your highness, they did," Evangeline said quietly.

Syrena tamped down a growing sense of unease. "It doesn't matter, even if the council has given their support to her, the vote would never pass. She would have to prove I'm incompetent. She can't win."

"I'm sorry, I don't wish to wound you, princess, but she has already begun a campaign against you. She is reminding everyone of your inexperience, but more damaging than that she's reminding them of your test scores."

Syrena buried her face in her hands. What had possessed Morgana to put their agreement at risk? She knew her stepmother had been unhappy when Syrena voiced her concern over the actions Morgana had taken against the Fae men, but surely that couldn't be the reason. But whether Morgana wanted to admit it or not, Syrena had the upper hand. The Sword of Nuada was hers.

Dropping her hands to her sides, she looked at Evangeline. "Uscias will not hand over the sword, I'm certain of it. He knows of my . . ." She chewed on her bottom lip, unable to continue in Lachlan's presence, certain he would do anything to have her gone from his life, from his brother's life.

Her stomach knotted at the thought of Aidan, and the memory of his tenderness, of how he made her feel. She glanced up to see Lachlan watching her. She couldn't leave, not yet. Winning her brother's love was as important to her as completing her quest, maybe more so. And considering Morgana's actions, having Lachlan rule beside her just might be what was required to circumvent her stepmother.

She would return to the Enchanted Isles in triumph, her quest complete. Uscias would give her Nuie, and then all would see she was the one to lead them. "What of Lord Bana and Lord Erwn, surely they would not cast their lot with Morgana?"

"It is said she seeks to disallow the men's votes."

"On what grounds?"

"I don't know. She and Nessa pour over the Books of Fae for hours on end searching for some old ruling that will justify the edict."

Syrena felt somewhat more hopeful, since no one knew the Books of Fae better than she did. "There is no such ruling. You must seek out Uscias. He knows why I'm here and will advise you. If he thinks I should return, then I shall, but until then I will remain here."

"I cannot change your mind?"

"No." She gave Evangeline's arm a reassuring squeeze, grateful for her friend's loyalty and protection.

"All right." Muttering something beneath her breath, Evangeline waved her hand and Lachlan crashed to the mud-packed floor. Still bound by the ropes, he lay on his back, groaning.

"Oh, Evangeline, you could have at least let him down gently," she protested, hurrying to her brother's side.

"Yes. I could have." Evangeline moved to stand over Lachlan and snarled, "You hurt her again and you'll answer to me. Do you hear me?" She prodded him with the toe of her embroidered black slipper. "Nod if you do, you big oaf."

"Evangeline!" Syrena cried out, but her handmaiden ignored her.

Lachlan growled beneath the dirty rag, his eyes flashing. Evangeline nudged him again, and he nodded.

Turning to Syrena, Evangeline took her hand in hers. "He's a fool if he rejects your love, princess, as are the Fae if they listen to Morgana."

She blinked back tears and embraced Evangeline. "No one has ever had a friend as loyal as you. Thank you."

A rosy hue tinted her handmaiden's porcelain complexion, and she dipped her head. "You deserve no less. Take care, my lady." With one last glare in Lachlan's direction, Evangeline left the stables.

Syrena dropped to her knees at her brother's side. "I'm sorry, Lachlan. At times she can be a little overprotective is all," she apologized while removing the gag from his mouth, praying he didn't yell once she did.

"Just get these bloody ropes off of me," he rasped.

"Yes, of course." She dug her fingers into the knots and tried to loosen them, but they were too tight. The thick twine scraped and burned her tender skin. Unwilling to give up, she moved to his feet and tried to pull the rope over his boots.

He blew out an impatient breath. "Can ye no' do magick like her?"

She grimaced. "No, I wish I could. If I tried, I'm just as likely to tighten the knots as loosen them."

His amber eyes widened in alarm. "Nay, doona do it then. Ye'll squeeze the life out of me if ye do."

She once more bent over her task. Moisture beaded on her forehead as she struggled with the bindings. Crouching to gain momentum, she rocked back on her heels, tugging as she did, and landed with a thud on her bottom. She heard a low rumble and looked up to see Lachlan laughing at her. The chiseled lines of his handsome face softened.

"At this rate, I'll be two and twenty before ye have me free." He jerked his chin. "There's a dagger in my boot, Syrena. See if you can reach it."

A warmth filled her chest and her heart swelled with hope. Syrena couldn't have wiped the smile from her face even if she wanted to. She leaned over, digging inside the soft leather of his calf-length brown boot. Finding the dagger, she carefully withdrew it.

"Have a care. 'Tis sharp," he warned, craning his neck to watch her work it beneath the rope.

Gripping the shaft with two hands, she sawed through the thick twine. "I did it," she cried triumphantly when the rope fell apart. Setting the knife aside, she unwound the coils that ensnared her brother. He raised himself up in order to help her.

Free of the rope, Lachlan shook out his limbs then rubbed his long legs. "That woman is a menace. Mad as old Tom on a bender, she is."

Syrena handed him his knife then sat quietly at his side, her knees pulled to her chest. "I'm sorry for what she did to you, Lachlan. As I said before, she's very protective of me."

He cast her a sidelong glance as he slid his dagger into his boot. "Aye, 'tis obvious." He dragged his hand over his face. "To be fair, I shouldna tussled with her like I did."

Her eyes widened. "You fought with Evangeline?"

"Nay, well, aye, but 'twas dark in here and I mistook her for a lass I was plannin' to meet up with before the gatherin'. I kissed her." He flushed under Syrena's scrutiny. "Before I had a chance to apologize, she had me strung up from the rafters."

"You're lucky that's all she did to you," she commented dryly, remembering one of the royal guards who ended up chained in iron and hanging from a mountain peak after attempting to kiss Evangeline.

"And ye canna do that? Do magick like she does?"

"No, not like Evangeline. Her magick is very powerful. In truth, I don't know of many with her abilities. She's tried to teach me, but I seem to be unteachable."

"She called ye princess. Are ye?"

"Yes, our . . . I mean, my father was king," she corrected herself so as not to anger him.

"Was?" His voice had gone very quiet.

"Yes, he's dead. He was murdered."

"How? I didna think faeries could die."

"Not easily, but we can. Weapons such as my sword and the juice from Rowan berries will kill us, and then there are some who simply grow weary and choose to fade."

"Fade?"

"They ask for their life to end, say the incantation, and then that's it, poof, they're gone. Nothing remains but faery dust. As for my father, someone poisoned him with Rowan berry juice."

His brow furrowed, and then he asked, "Do ye ken who?"

"No." She shook her head. Her father said it was her brother who would one day avenge his death. She didn't think that possible given how Lachlan felt about the Fae. But she had enough to worry about without adding that to her list.

"Who is this Morgana, the one who wants the sword?"

"My stepmother. She wants to rule the Isles, but when my father gifted me with the Sword of Nuada, it became my right." She didn't tell him she was supposed to hand over Nuie and cede the throne to him. She didn't want to ruin their time together.

"Is there none in yer clan to protect ye?"

"Evangeline, and Uscias would help me if I asked. As for the others, I never lived up to the Fae's expectations. I can't do magick like they do, and I'm not very brave, and as you can see, I'm little."

"Aye." Lachlan grinned. "Ye are wee. But yer father, he would've protected ye, demanded his clan be loyal to ye."

"No, I was a disappointment to my father, and he made certain all were well aware of the fact."

An uncomfortable silence ensued and Syrena was afraid she'd said too much. Outside the barn, people shouted out their greetings to one another. Lachlan came slowly to his feet and offered her his hand. "Come, I hear the others arrivin' to celebrate."

"You . . . you want me to celebrate with you?" She held her breath, afraid to hold out hope. Afraid she'd misunderstood him.

"Aye, I do. I'm sorry fer earlier. I ken I hurt ye. I—"

"It's all right. I made you a promise and I broke it."

He tightened his hold on her hand and searched her face. "Ye didna tell Aidan who ye are, did ye?"

"No, I—"

"Syrena, I ken there is somethin' between ye and my brother and I will keep yer secret, but trust me when I tell ye he must never learn ye're Fae."

"There is nothing between us," she protested half-heartedly.

He arched a brow. "I'm no' daft, Syrena. I've seen the two of ye together. But I fear 'twill end badly, and one or both of ye will be hurt."

Chapter 8

Flames from the open pits licked the chill from the crisp, spring air. The roasted deer and pig had been removed from the spits to be carved for the guests who stood quaffing ale by the warmth of the fires. Aidan rolled his eyes when Gavin, well in his cups, tossed some of the brew into the flames. At least he had the sense to jump back when the blaze hissed, spitting its bright orange sparks into the clear night sky.

"I see Gavin hasna changed since last we met," his cousin observed dryly.

"Nay, and I doubt he ever will." Aidan turned to clap Iain on the back. "'Tis good to see ye, cousin. I didna ken ye meant to visit."

Iain shrugged. "I wanted to see how you fared in yer battle with the Lowlanders, and truth be told, I had need of an excuse to leave Dunvegan and the Isle of Skye fer a spell."

He grinned at his cousin's disgruntled expression. "The bairns drivin' ye mad, are they?"

"Nay, 'tis my brother and Aileanna seein' to that. Nauseatin' is what the two of them are. Never did I think to see my brother laid low by a woman. Has him by the ballocks, she does." He shook his head in disgust. "They canna keep their hands off one another, and I tell you, they doona care who's about to see them."

Aidan laughed. "Ye're jealous." He nudged his cousin with his elbow. "But think, mon, ye wouldna want to be tied to one lass, now would ye?"

Iain cast an appreciative eye over a handful of lasses giggling to the right of them, his gaze coming to rest on the beauteous Widow Blackmore with her flaming red hair. A woman who had castigated Aidan earlier for his failure to visit her, but of late, her bountiful charms had little effect on him, and he was afraid he knew the reason why.

With his thoughts turned to Syrena, he searched the crowd. He didn't know where she'd disappeared to earlier, but he decided if she didn't make an appearance soon, he would go in search of her. Aidan drew his attention back to his cousin, trying not to allow his concern to get the best of him.

Iain shrugged. "I doona ken. If I found someone like Aileanna, I might consider it. But what about you? Ye're older than me, 'tis about time you settled down and had yerself a bairn or two. Now that yer feud with the Lowlanders is dyin' down, you have no excuse."

"Nay, I have enough . . ." Speech abandoned him at the sight of Lachlan, with Syrena on his arm, entering the grounds. Illuminated in the fiery glow from the flames, she laughed up at his brother. Her long unbound hair dazzled the eye as did the lavender velvet gown that clung to her lush curves. A gown, if memory served him, that had once belonged to his mother.

The clamor of voices faded to hushed whispers as those gathered observed the golden couple in their midst. Obviously uncomfortable with the attention, Syrena hung back. Lan whispered something in her ear then nudged her in Aidan and Iain's direction.

Aidan's fingers tightened on the silver goblet in his hand, reminding himself his brother had simply showed the lass a kindness. And wasn't that what he had wanted all along? Just as he assured himself the knot of tension tightening his belly had naught to do with the soft smile she bestowed upon his brother, but was in response to the salacious gleam in every man's eye that looked upon her.

His cousin followed his gaze and sighed. "Leave it to Lan to find the woman of my dreams before I did. The lad has the luck of the Irish when it comes to the lasses."

"He didna find her, I did," Aidan grated out. Tipping his head back, he took a deep swallow of ale.

Iain clapped him on the back with a hearty laugh. "Ah, so that's the way of it, is it? 'Twill be like the old days, only I'll be the one comin' between the two of you instead of you comin' between Rory and me."

With Syrena and his brother almost upon them, Aidan chose not to respond. What would he say if he did? Blurt out the whole sordid tale of his mother and Davina? Tell his cousin that though he wanted Syrena more than any woman he'd ever known, he couldn't have her? He wouldn't leave himself open to the certainty of betrayal. Now if only he could make his heart and his body listen.

Lachlan, acknowledging the crowd's good wishes, had yet to note his cousin's presence. When he did, he moved away from Syrena to grab hold of Iain. "'Tis good to see ye, cousin. It's been too long."

"Aye, it has. You've grown again. You'll soon be towerin' over the lot of us."

Lan grinned, looking more like the lighthearted lad Aidan remembered. It had taken years after their father's death for the withdrawn, frightened child to become the fun-loving, adventurous lad of recent memory. Giving their cousin a playful shove, Lan said, "Stronger, too."

Iain grimaced. Rubbing his shoulder, his gaze came to rest on Syrena, who stood quietly behind Lachlan. "Are you no' goin' to introduce me to yer bonny friend?"

Sensing her unease, Aidan drew her toward him and laid a proprietary hand at the small of her back. His fingers warmed from the heat beneath the soft fabric. With a concerted effort, he fought the urge to let his hand drift to the delectable curve of her behind. "Lady Syrena, I'd like ye to meet our cousin, Sir Iain MacLeod of Dunvegan on the Isle of Skye."

Iain gave her a courtly bow and pressed a kiss to her hand. "'Tis an honor to meet you, my lady. And please, call me Iain."

Syrena's brow furrowed, then after a slight hesitation, she made the poorest excuse for a curtsy Aidan had ever witnessed. "I'm pleased to meet you, Iain."

Aidan frowned. A lass of her station must have been to court a time or two. Unless, he reasoned, the knock on her wee head had stolen more than the memory of her kin. As though sensing his surprise, she lifted her shoulder, offering him a wry smile.

Noting the serving girls weave their way among the crowd with platters of roasted meats held high above their heads, Aidan said, "It appears the meal is about to be served, Syrena." He offered her his arm. She glanced up, and her fingers tightened on his sleeve. He covered her hand. With a reassuring squeeze, he led her to the table and placed her in the chair at his right. Iain took the seat to his left while Lan commandeered the one beside Syrena.

Aidan remained standing and raised his goblet. "Thank ye all fer comin'. I ask ye to join me in a toast to my brother, Lachlan, who turns nineteen this day, and to our latest battle with the Lowlanders. May it be our last." He waited for the cheers to die down before continuing, "And I'd like ye all to welcome my cousin, Sir Iain MacLeod of Dunvegan, who has battled alongside us a time or two, and the beautiful Lady Syrena." He lifted his goblet once more, smiling down at Syrena, whose cheeks pinked.

"Are you no' goin' to smile at me like that?" Iain chuckled, laughing harder at the look Aidan shot him.

"Aye, aye, to Lady Syrena, fairest of them all," Gavin cried. Standing on the bench, he swayed precariously. Donald had the foresight to grab him by the back of his plaid and tug him down. Gavin glared at his friend and staggered back to his feet, raising his mug in Syrena's direction. "And doona ye worry, my lady. 'Tis no' yer wee pet we're eatin' this night."

Syrena's mouth dropped open.

The serving girl placed a platter piled high with venison in front of Aidan, and Syrena blanched. He grabbed the pitcher of mead and poured some in a goblet. "Here." He held the rim to her lips. "Drink," he ordered.

Lan caught his eye then motioned for the girl to come back for the platter. He spoke quietly to the lass, who frowned at Syrena, then shrugged.

"Did I miss somethin'?" Iain inquired, brow quirked.

"Nay, but I hope ye didna have a cravin' fer venison this night, cousin, as all we'll be eatin' at this table is pork."

Syrena muttered something about murderous beasts under her breath then downed her mead. She placed the empty goblet on the table and nudged it toward him.

Aidan tilted his head, narrowing his gaze on her. "Syrena, ye best eat somethin' if ye're goin' to be consumin' mead in that fashion."

"I'm . . . I'm not going to eat *that*."

"Here then, have some of this, Syrena." His brother placed a hunk of bread in her trencher.

"Thank you," she said, rewarding Lachlan with a smile before turning a contemptuous look upon Aidan, making it obvious she held him accountable for all the dead animals gracing their table this night.

"The lass looks none too happy with you, Aidan," his cousin observed.

"Aye, and she's made her displeasure rather well known," he said loud enough for her to hear. If he expected her to apologize for her behavior, he was mistaken. She kept as much distance between them as she could, giving all her attention to his brother.

Iain managed to provide ample distraction from her censure, regaling him with news from court. With word of Queen Elizabeth I's death, it appeared King James VI would soon rule from the English throne as James I of England. Aidan wondered how that would affect the MacLeods of both Lewis and Skye. His musings were brought to an abrupt halt when he heard Syrena's quiet cry of delight.

Her countenance lightened now that the main course had been cleared and the pastries served. She fairly hummed when Lachlan placed a slice of fruit pie and some honey cakes in front of her.

Her soft sounds of pleasure brought an image of her in his bed, writhing beneath him as he plundered her honeyed lips. He barely stifled a groan when she brought her fingers to her mouth and delicately licked the sugar coating from each one.

His restraint in tatters, he shot to his feet. "Music," he barked at the men tuning their instruments.

Iain caught his eye, his shoulders shaking with unrestrained mirth. "I doona ken if I should tell you this, cousin, but you have the same look my brother gets when he doesna' ken whether to strangle Aileanna, or kiss her senseless." He laughed all the harder at Aidan's muttered denial.

Syrena looked down at the fingers she'd licked clean. She didn't think she'd done anything wrong. Everyone else had eaten the little cakes in the same manner—she'd made certain before she did. The dainty delicacies had tasted so wonderful she couldn't resist getting the last of the crystallized drops. The honeyed cakes were so delicious she'd almost been willing to forgive Aidan for butchering the helpless creatures that had graced the table earlier. Not that he was the only one to eat heartedly of their meat. Her brother had done so as well.

She cast a sidelong glance at Aidan, who was obviously annoyed by something his cousin had said. Jumping to his feet, he jolted the table, and wine spilled from her goblet onto the pristine white linens. She tried unsuccessfully to sop up the bright red puddle with a piece of linen.

"Leave it be, Syrena," he said brusquely.

She stilled, startled by the smoldering gleam in his smoky gray eyes.

"Did you enjoy the pastries, my lady?" his cousin inquired with a smile, interrupting their silent exchange.

She dragged her gaze from Aidan, trying to ignore the heated tingle pulsating through her limbs to settle beween her thighs. She leaned forward in an attempt to see past his brawny physique.

"Oh, yes," she said, managing to keep her voice even though the position brought her closer to Aidan. So close his plaid brushed her arm, and the warmth, and his clean masculine scent, scattered her senses. She shifted in her chair, putting some distance between them. However small, it helped. "They were wonderful. Did you?"

Iain grinned, his amber eyes warm with amusement, and Syrena decided she liked this man with the laughing eyes and handsome face. "Verra much, although I think you liked them a wee bit more than I did. Wouldna you agree, cousin?"

She glanced at Aidan, his gaze fixated on her mouth. Certain crumbs remained, she swiped her tongue over her lips in an attempt to remove them.

With a groan, Aidan dropped to the chair at her side and tilted his head back, closing his eyes. "Go dance with the lasses, Iain," he muttered.

"You may no' have noticed, cousin, but it appears they mean to put on a wee show."

Beneath the table, Syrena tapped her feet to the music, watching as the women took to the open area, the fires dancing at their backs. Swaying in time to the music, the varying hues of their gowns created a kaleidoscope of color.

Four of them focused their attention solely on the three men at Syrena's table. The women, one blonde, two with dark hair, and the other a vibrant redhead, sauntered toward them. They tossed their long, unbound hair, flirtatious smiles upon their lips. Syrena couldn't blame them—the MacLeod men were beautiful—although she didn't care for the auburn-haired beauty, who made no secret of the fact she performed for Aidan alone.

The woman's movements were practiced and seductive. Bending low at the waist, her long fiery locks did little to conceal the generous expanse of creamy white flesh she so boldly displayed.

Hands on her lap, Syrena's nails bit into her palms. From the corner of her eye, she snuck a peek at Aidan to gauge his reaction. She was tempted to hit him when she noted the lazy smile that played across his full, sensuous mouth. *Mortal or Fae, men are all alike*, she thought scornfully.

A light tap on her shoulder stopped Syrena from contemplating a more violent action than a simple knock on his head. "My lady, come join us," Beth invited, tugging her from her chair.

Syrena was tempted to demur, but her feet would have none of it. She caught the look of surprise in Aidan's eyes before she followed Beth into the midst of swirling gowns. After a self-conscious moment, she closed her eyes and allowed the sound of the music to take over, to envelop her in its seductive rhythm. The crackle of the fire, its warm amber glow, and its smoky scent were an intoxicating mix that fueled her excitement.

Her body mimicked the movements of the woman who performed for Aidan. But then her own natural instincts took over, her love of dancing. Although, when she danced in the Enchanted Isles, it had never been like this. She'd been afraid of what the others would say, afraid of their contempt, their laughter. But tonight, she didn't care, there was no one to impress. Like her, the other women simply loved to dance. Caught within the heated, spinning vortex of bodies, she gave herself up to the music.

She kicked off her slippers and felt the cool dampness of the grass beneath her feet. Laughing, she tossed her head back and twirled. The heavy weight of her gown caressed her bare legs, sending shivers of delight over her heated flesh. Her hips swaying to the music, she drew her hands over her curves to raise them in the air, the movements slow and sensual. She danced like a woman—a woman who wanted a man, and not just any man. She wanted Aidan.

She stumbled at the thought, and it took her a moment to regain the rhythm. But no matter how hard she tried, she couldn't deny her feelings for him. And wouldn't the Fae delight in her folly—falling in love with a Mortal. A Mortal, if her brother was right, who would hold her in the same contempt as the Fae were he to learn her secret.

But tonight she was Lady Syrena, a woman, who despite her innocence sensed Aidan's attraction to her. He wanted her as much as she wanted him. It was apparent in the way he treated her, the way he touched her with his big hands and his warm skillful lips.

And just this once, for this one magickal night, she wanted to forget the Fae and Morgana, and be the woman he thought her to be.

The sound of clapping broke the spell. Syrena's arms fell to her sides, her toes curled in the grass, and she slowly opened her eyes, afraid she'd made a fool of herself. Heat suffused her cheeks. But the warmth in the smiling faces and laughing eyes of the women and men that now surrounded her belied the thought. They applauded her performance, and she beamed, happier than she thought she could be. Never had she felt so accepted, and not even the voluptuous redhead pinning her with a malevolent stare could take that away from her.

The music started up again, a raucous tune, and the men joined the women. Gavin popped up, swaying in front of her. Laughing, she tugged her hand from his. The man was too inebriated to stand let alone dance. To prove her point, he landed at her feet in a heap.

"Oh, Gavin." She nudged him with her toe. He slapped her foot away then curled on his side, snoring.

She shook her head and sighed. Placing her hands beneath his arms, she tried to drag him to his feet, but he was deadweight. She searched the dancing couples for some sign of

Donald, but found Aidan instead, weaving his way toward her. His rugged, masculine beauty stole her breath away. Then she noticed the harsh lines bracketing his mouth and felt a moment of trepidation, wondering if his anger was directed at her. The redhead attempted to waylay him, as did several others, but his long powerful strides didn't slow until he stood before her.

She chewed on her bottom lip, raising her eyes from the colorful plaid belted at his waist and slung carelessly over his shoulder. The marble white shirt that he wore clung to his broad chest, accentuating the bronzed column of his thick neck.

All sound and movement faded when she met his eyes. His gaze, a shimmer of heated silver, raked her from head to toe, searing her with its intensity, with his desire.

"Doona move," he ordered in a low rasp. He cursed Gavin then, muscles flexing, tossed him over his shoulder and strode through the laughing crowd.

She stood frozen in place, her emotions in turmoil, unsure what it was Aidan was feeling. Had she embarrassed him with her wanton behavior? By Fae standards her dancing would be considered modest, and she didn't think her movements had been any more provocative than the woman who had danced for him earlier.

A giant of a man swung a giggling woman high in the air and Syrena managed to jump out of their way. But not far enough that his big foot missed hers.

She waved off the man's apology with a pained smile and searched the ground, hoping for a glimpse of her slippers. She didn't notice Aidan until he grabbed hold of her hand, tugging her after him. She stumbled. "Aidan, stop. My slippers, I need my slippers," she said breathlessly.

He turned to look at her, and she lifted the hem of her gown to show him her bare feet. With a muttered oath, he swung her into his arms, ignoring the ribald comments their audience called out after them.

Syrena buried her burning face in his plaid, her arms

wrapped around his neck. She felt the rhythmic beat of his heart against her chest and tipped her head back to look at him. His expression harsh, inscrutable, he stared off in the distance.

He slowed then stopped beside an ancient oak, far from the revelry. The heat of the fires a distant memory. A cool breeze lifted her hair, and she shivered, drawing his attention.

"Ye'll no' be cold fer long," he murmured into her hair, pressing her back against the tree, her feet dangling above the ground. Placing his heavily muscled thigh between her legs, he anchored her to the trunk.

She swallowed a moan of pleasure as his heat seeped into her sensitive skin and pulsated to her very core. He cupped her cheeks with his big hands. Shafts of moonlight danced across his beautiful face. And his eyes, dark and fathomless, glittered like the stars above them.

"Tell me, Syrena, who were ye dancin' fer?" His voice was a deep rumble in his chest.

"Me," she managed, her voice little more than a whisper. And then, tangling his silky, midnight-black curls between her fingers, she told him the truth, casting caution aside with one word, "You."

He groaned, and capturing her lips with his, devoured her. His kiss, possessive and demanding, enthralled her. Creating a desire so strong she squirmed against his rock-hard thigh, needing release from the aching throb between her legs. "Aidan," she whimpered against his mouth.

He pulled back, his breathing harsh, his eyes searching hers. "From now on, ye dance fer me alone."

Her cheeks flushed, and she dipped her head. "You didn't like it?"

He tilted her chin with his thumbs. "Oh, aye, angel, I liked it all right." His warm breath caressed her cheek. "Verra, verra much," he murmured against her mouth.

Chapter 9

"I doona ken what has ye so riled, Aidan, the gatherin' was a grand success."

Aidan glanced from his mug of ale to his brother's head. His fingers itched with the urge to douse the grinning fool.

"Aye, and the Lady Syrena seemed to enjoy herself, dancin' the night away as she did." He caught the laughter in his cousin's voice and shot him an irritated look.

"Aye, 'twas a good thing the Widow Blackmore found her wee slippers," his brother said, looking up from shoveling porridge into his mouth to frown at Aidan. "I canna imagine ye thought to find them so far from the celebration. I wouldna found ye if no' fer the widow."

Aidan shoved a spoonful of porridge in his mouth before he said something he'd regret. Damning Lachlan and that blasted woman to Hades for interrupting him last night. He'd spent the entire evening in a state of frustration thanks to the two of them. And Syrena hadn't helped matters—flitting from one man to the next, her bonny face alight with pleasure. Every time he'd heard her husky laugh, he'd downed a mug of ale. And if he could go by the pounding in his head, she'd laughed too bloody often.

"Aidan, ye have the look of a man sufferin' the effects of too much ale. 'Tis a shame I canna make you the concoction

Aileanna is always forcin' down our throats when we've done the same." Iain shuddered. "'Tis vile, but it works."

"Aye, a real shame," Aidan muttered, wishing the timber that appeared ready to fall from the ceiling would land on top of his cousin's irritating head.

"'Tis no' like ye to imbibe as ye did last night. Is somethin' amiss, brother?"

Aye, something was amiss all right. They'd interrupted him before he'd satisfied one iota of his desire for Syrena. One small taste was all he'd managed before the bumbling idiots had stumbled upon them. A taste that had enflamed his desire to a raging inferno, only to have his brother lead a blushing Syrena back to the gathering. And Aidan to drown his lust in ale and wonder at the fool he was making of himself over a woman.

"Nay. Now do ye think the two of ye could just break yer fast instead of babblin' like a couple of old maids?"

"Ye are . . . Syrena." His brother's voice boomed across the hall. A broad grin creased his face as he waved over the object of Aidan's frustration.

In a demure, pink gown, she looked the picture of innocence—a far cry from the alluring, provocative wench of last night. Aidan was thankful it had only been during the first dance she'd displayed a wantonness that fired his blood, or else he never would have been able to restrain himself. Bloody hell, he pinched the bridge of his nose. She was driving him mad.

Several members of the clan called out to her, and she stopped to have a wee chat before making her way toward them.

"Ye look about as happy as my brother, Syrena. What's the matter, lass?" Lan asked, holding out the chair between them.

"Thank you," she murmured, giving Aidan a sidelong glance before taking her seat.

"Come now, what's troublin' ye?" his brother cajoled.

"Beth," Syrena muttered. "She is very irritating so early in the morning. I wasn't even awake and she drew the draperies, crashing and banging about in my chambers. How is anyone supposed to sleep with the amount of noise she makes?" She thanked the serving girl who placed a bowl of porridge in front of her.

"'Tis no' what most would call early, Syrena," Aidan commented dryly. She scowled at him, then flashed a smile at Iain, who passed her a pot of honey.

He met his cousin's amused gaze over her bent head. "Is it no' time fer ye to be headin' back to Dunvegan?"

"Tired of my company, cousin?" Iain drawled.

"Nay, no' at all, I'm just thinkin' Rory will have need of ye."

Iain snorted. "Nay, I willna be headin' back to Dunvegan as yet. I'm headin' fer court. I'm thinkin' I'm due fer some adventure. Remember when we were lads, Aidan, how we talked about sailin' to distant lands, makin' our fortunes at sea?"

"Aye," Aidan said quietly. He remembered it well. All his dreams had ended that night long ago on the cliffs when at eighteen he'd assumed responsibility for the clan. But truth be told, he never would have left Lan, not until he was old enough to protect himself.

His brother watched him closely as though he knew what it was he was feeling. Aidan cleared his throat. "Ye have somethin' in mind?"

"Aye, I've been talkin' with the McNeils. I'm thinkin' of investin' in their next venture."

"What does Rory think?"

Iain shrugged. "I havena' discussed it with him, no' as yet."

"I wonder . . ."

Syrena's quiet hum drew Aidan's attention. She savored her honey-drenched porridge with her eyes closed. His gaze tracked her pink tongue as it glided over her moist lips.

Lan chuckled. "At the rate ye eat that stuff, Syrena, we'll need a cartload to keep ye content."

Her husky giggle shot straight to Aidan's loins. "I can't help myself. It tastes so good."

Before he could stop himself, he reached over and wiped the golden droplet from her chin onto his finger. "Ye missed some." His voice was a deep rumble.

Lan and Iain guffawed.

Syrena arched a brow, and Aidan shrugged, sliding his finger into his mouth. "Ye're right, 'tis verra good." He could only think how much better it would be if he could lean over and lick it from her glistening lips.

Iain grinned then leaned back in his chair. "Well, lads, 'tis time I took my leave. My thanks fer the grand time. Syrena." He took her hand in his. "A pleasure to meet you, and I shall tell my sister-by-marriage all about you. I'm certain she'll be verra interested, won't she, Aidan?" His amused expression turned serious. "I'll make yer inquiries while I'm at court, cousin. Doona worry, Syrena. Sooner or later we'll manage to find yer kin."

Aidan didn't miss the surreptitious glance the lass sent his brother. Nor the reassuring one Lan offered in return. "Is there somethin' I should be made aware of, Syrena? Lachlan?"

Her cheeks flushed. "I . . . I'm . . . well . . ."

"What she means to say, Aidan, is every time she thinks on her kin, she gets an ache in her head and feels ill. I suggested fer the time being she doesna' worry on it, and that she's welcome to remain with us."

"Is this true, Syrena?"

With her spoon, she moved the oats around in the bowl. "Uhmm, yes, if that's all right with you. I promise not to be any trouble."

Not bloody likely. Having her under his roof these past few days had already overtaxed his restraint. Although if he were honest, he'd admit he didn't want her to leave, would have a difficult time letting her go. And if her kin finally came to claim her, he wasn't so sure he'd be able to. He'd claim her as his and marry the troublesome wench just so he could kiss her honeyed lips anytime he damned well pleased. Look upon her bonny face from sunrise to sunset. And bask in the laughter and warmth she'd brought to his home.

"Aidan?" His brother gave him an odd look, jerking his head in Syrena's direction.

He shoved his hand through his hair. "Aye, doona fash yerself, Syrena, we'll . . ."

A commotion at the other end of the hall drew his attention. Gavin, waving off the comments of the men who held their noses, strode toward them.

When he came to stand beside their table, Aidan gagged, and his eyes watered. "Bloody hell, mon, ye smell like ye rolled around in a pile of . . ." Catching himself, Aidan glanced at Syrena, who looked ready to retch, her sleeve pressed to her nose. "Go on, get yerself to the stable and have someone . . ."

Gavin glared at him, his eyes bloodshot. "'Tis where I have been—some fool thought it amusin' to leave me there fer the night. Only they didna bother to check what they were layin' me down in." He turned to walk away, the remains of what he'd been sleeping on clearly evident on his back, saying, "And ye may wish to get yerself to the stables if yer of a mind to save Lady Syrena's wee pet."

Syrena gasped, but before he could stop her, she'd shot from her chair.

Aidan groaned. His head pounded as he ran after her with Lan and Iain close on his heels. She might be wee, but she was fast, and he had a devil of a time catching up to her. He finally managed to snag her arm several feet from the stables.

Wrapping his arms around her waist, he held her to his chest. "Bloody hell, quit yer squirmin'." He tried to ignore the curve of her rounded behind pressed against him, the slight waist he embraced, and the heavy weight of her breasts brushing his forearms.

"Enough." He grimaced when her heel hit him in the shins. "I'll no' let ye go until ye settle down. Tom's liable to hurt ye."

She tilted her head, her amber eyes flashing. "You promise you won't let him harm my deer?"

"Aye. Lan, hold on to . . ." Nay, no one would hold her but him. "Watch her." He turned Syrena to face him. "And ye, doona move."

He held his breath when Gavin came up alongside him.

His friend rolled his eyes. "Careful, he's armed."

With a muttered oath, Aidan shoved the doors open. Old Tom, his white hair standing on end, was backed against the wall of Fin's stall, jabbing a pitchfork in the direction of the black stallion, who shielded Syrena's wee pet.

"Drop it, Tom, and get yer arse over here."

"Are ye mad? That beast attacked me."

"The deer?"

The old man scowled at him. "Nay, Fin. He bit me."

Aidan rubbed the stubble along his jaw. Fin had a temper, but it did not usually show itself unless he'd been provoked. "And just what were ye doin' to make him react in such a manner?"

"Gettin' that creature out of his stall is what I was doin'. I doona ken who . . . her, it must've been her," he shouted, pointing a trembling finger at someone behind Aidan.

He glanced over his shoulder. "I told ye to keep Syrena outside, Lan."

"He tried," his cousin said dryly.

"And I ken she's the one who knocked me on the heed, makin' me miss the gatherin'. Took me out with a tankard of ale, wastin' all my lovely brew," he whined.

Aidan arched a brow in Syrena's direction.

"I did no such thing," she protested, but the corner of her mouth twitched.

His brother coughed to smother a laugh, and Aidan narrowed his gaze on the two of them. Lachlan was notorious for his antics, and God help Aidan if he now had a partner in crime. He shook his head, trying not to smile at how hard the two of them attempted not to laugh.

He moved toward Fin, patting his hindquarters. "Protectin' the wee beastie, were ye? Ah, ye're a good lad." He took the rusted pitchfork from Tom and nudged the grumbling old man from the stall.

Aidan glanced at Lan and Syrena, who were giggling like a pair of fools—a pair of fools who looked as though they were kin. He rubbed his eyes. Nay, 'twas only on account of their similar coloring that made them appear so, he assured himself, a trick of the shaft of light penetrating the shadows.

"Take yer pet out of doors, Syrena. She looks well enough, and a walk will do her good." The lass seemed happy to comply with his wishes. Making a wide circle of Tom, she came alongside Fin and gave him a quick cuddle. The big stallion nickered against her neck.

Aidan scrubbed his hand over his face. Aye, 'twas time for a ride, a good long one. "Lan, we'll see Iain off at the docks and then we'll take a ride down Harris way."

He couldn't put it off any longer. He had to search for her kin. Mayhap if he was lucky, they would force his hand and he'd have no choice but to marry the wee beauty. Aye, she was making him daft, turning his long-standing objection to marriage on its head, working her way past his distrust with her sweet and gentle nature.

Syrena lifted a hand in farewell as Aidan, Iain, and her brother rode off. She wrinkled her nose when Gavin came to stand beside her.

"I doona smell *that* bad."

"Yes . . . you do," she muttered into her palm.

"Ah, well, I'll take myself off then. Doona wander too far afield. We wouldna want the Lowlanders to get a hold of ye again. The laird would have my head."

Their concern for her, especially Aidan's, warmed Syrena with a sense of belonging. "I won't go far, Gavin, maybe just beyond the stables." She pointed out the path she intended to take.

Guttural curses and a resounding crash came from within the barn and he winced. "Aye, 'tis a good idea." Turning on his heel, he strode away, leaving behind a trail of hay and whatever it was that made him smell so bad.

Her deer nudged the backs of her legs as though urging her on. Syrena chuckled—if the smell bothered an animal, it was indeed as putrid as she thought. She unfastened the pink ribbon from her hair and tied it around the deer's neck, leaving a long enough piece for her to hold on to.

Watching the animal frolic among the white-tipped grass, Syrena realized she would soon have to set it free. Her heart pinched at the thought. It didn't belong here, and even more painful to admit, neither did she. Even though she was beginning to feel like she did.

For the first time in her life she'd been able to be herself, and she hadn't been castigated for it. No one laughed at her. She'd been accepted for who she was. No one cared that she was small, that her magickal abilities were lacking.

But you're not Mortal, you're Fae.

How long could she keep her secret from Aidan?

The fluffy white clouds scuttling across the sky darkened. An ominous rumble shattered the slumberous quiet as though the Isles were reacting to Syrena's tumultuous emotions.

Why couldn't she have fallen in love with a Fae man? Her life would be so much simpler. But no, as always, she had to be different. And it was not as if she'd fallen in love with Aidan on purpose. If anything, she'd tried not to.

While she fought her inner battles, the ribbon slipped through her fingers, jerking Syrena's attention to her deer, who bounded toward a small copse of trees. She sprinted after her pet, skidding to a halt when in the center of the verdant shadows a cluster of colorful lights sparked and sputtered to life. From the smoky aftermath stepped a man. He filled the space with his omnipotent presence. Her legs trembled, and she wanted to run, but knew she wouldn't get far, not if he wanted her.

He was Fae.

He flicked an errant spark from robes as golden as his hair, then raised a gaze as blue as the Isles skies to hers. His mouth curved in a predatory smile. "So good of you to come and meet me, princess. I would hate to spend any longer in this dung heap than is necessary."

Before she could think of what to do, a brilliant burst of yellow exploded, and Evangeline appeared. Syrena's trepidation eased somewhat at her handmaiden's appearance.

"I'm sorry, my lady, I did not tell him you were here. Morgana did. I tried to stop him." Fear interlaced with anger knitted her handmaiden's expression.

Syrena sucked in a shocked gasp. Morgana knew. And if her stepmother knew she was in the Mortal realm, here at Lewes, she knew about Lachlan. The realization filled her with panic, but she fought against it. She had to, or she wouldn't be able to deal with the intimidating Fae man standing before her.

He shot Evangeline an irritated look. "As if *you* could stop me. But even if you could, why would you? I come to claim what is rightfully mine." Ignoring Evangeline, who'd moved to Syrena's side, he raked Syrena with a proprietary look and held out his hand. "Come, our wedding takes place this day."

Her heart leapt to her throat. "I don't even know you." There had to be some mistake. This couldn't be happening, not now.

He quirked an arrogant brow. "You wound me, princess. I didn't think I was so easily forgotten. But then again, when last we met, I had yet to assume the throne. I was Prince Magnus from the land of the Far North. Lucky for you I am now king, else you'd be betrothed to my father. And I can't imagine you would have survived him." In one long stride he closed the short distance between them and jerked Syrena from Evangeline's hold.

"Let me go." She slammed her palm into his cast-iron chest, kicking her feet as he held her above the forest floor.

He laughed at her. "I'll enjoy taming you, little one." Her foot made contact with the bulge between his legs. He grunted, and his amusement evaporated. His arm banded her chest in a vice-like grip, leaving her gasping for air.

"Stop, you're hurting her. Put her down," Evangeline demanded.

"You try my patience, wench." Magnus raised his hand and a bolt of white light arched toward Evangeline. Palm up, she deflected it back at him. He cried out. Staggering, he fought to remain upright, and let go of Syrena in the effort.

A tingling, pulsating sensation surged through Syrena's veins, and she dropped to her knees.

Evangeline, keeping an eye on Magnus, hurried to her side. "I'm sorry, your highness. I should have realized you'd feel the effects as well."

Rising to her feet, she leaned against her handmaiden. "No, it's all right, I'm fine. Thank you."

The king rubbed his arm, narrowing his gaze on Evangeline. "Interfere again, and I take the matter before your Queen."

"No . . . no, she seeks to protect me, that is all," Syrena protested, knowing Morgana needed little excuse to punish her friend. And word of Evangeline's magick, more magick than a servant should possess, would have dire consequences.

Magnus studied her. "You will accompany me without complaint?"

It was the last thing she wanted to do, but the matter needed to be settled. She would not allow Evangeline to be punished because of her. And Magnus, well, he would learn a mistake had been made. A shiver of dread slithered along her spine at the thought Morgana knew Magnus meant to marry her. She tamped it down, determined to make everything right. Surely she and Morgana could come to an agreement. Syrena only hoped they could do so before Aidan and her brother realized she was gone.

Something cold and damp nudged her hand and she looked into the trusting brown eyes of her pet. "Evangeline, would you return her before we leave?"

"To the stables?"

"Yes, and this time do not knock the old man out, I—"

The ground trembled beneath her feet, the pounding of horses' hooves drawing near. *Please, no, not Aidan, don't let it be him.* Evangeline stood behind Magnus. Her apprehensive gaze met Syrena's and she knew then that it was.

"Now what have we here?" Magnus purred. Grabbing Syrena's hand, he tugged her into his arms. "Have you been playing with the Mortals, my love?"

She struggled in his arms and attempted to call out a warning to Aidan but Magnus curled his big hand around her neck. Cutting off her breath, he pressed her face into his chest.

"It seems you have been. Lucky for you, I prefer a woman with some experience to a maiden." His fingers dug into her throat. Pinpricks of light flashed before her eyes. "But that doesn't mean he won't pay for the privilege with his life."

Chapter 10

Aidan's heart pounded in tandem with Fin's hooves thundering across the boggy terrain. Instinct, battle-honed, warned him Syrena was in danger. She stood in the center of the woods with her deer, a woman with long, dark hair, and a man—an impossibly large man in golden robes.

"Bloody hell, who are they?" he asked Lan, who rode alongside him. His brother wouldn't look at him, he stared straight ahead, the color leeching from his face.

Aidan jerked his gaze to Syrena, cursing when the tawny-haired stranger pulled her against him. Putting his heels to Fin, he raced toward the small copse of trees.

"Aidan, no!" his brother shouted after him.

Aidan ducked below a low-hanging branch to be swallowed up in the cool, damp shadows. When he lifted his eyes, he met the cold, lethal gaze of the stranger head-on. A warning flared to life inside him.

Fae.

The man was Fae, and he wanted Syrena.

Red hazed his vision; a raw, all-consuming blood lust overriding his apprehension. He would do whatever he had to. No Fae man would take someone he loved—not again. With a jerk of the reins, he brought Fin to a halt and swung from his saddle, reaching for his claymore before his feet touched the ground.

"No, please, don't hurt him," Syrena pleaded, grabbing hold of her captor's arm. The man pushed her aside to prowl toward Aidan.

Meeting her frantic gaze, Aidan tried to reassure her, "Doona worry, lass, 'twill be all right."

A malevolent laugh raised the hair on the back of his neck. The man's thin upper lip curled in contempt. "I wouldn't be so sure of that, Mortal." With a wave of his hand, he replaced his glittering robes with form-fitting trews. Muscle rippled beneath his golden skin.

"Who are ye?"

His opponent arched a brow then shrugged. "I suppose it is only right for you to know the name of the one who is about to kill you—King Magnus. Now shall we begin?"

Syrena and Lan's panicked cries reverberated through the woods. Blowing out an exasperated breath, Magnus said, "Such dramatics."

Leaves and branches rustled behind Aidan, and Magnus looked over Aidan's shoulder. Brow lifted, he glanced at Syrena, who was being held back by the dark-haired woman.

"Interesting," he murmured. Returning his attention to Aidan, he said, "I'd advise you to tell him not to interfere. No need for you both to die when my battle is with you alone."

"Stay back, Lan," Aidan warned, not taking his eyes from Magnus, who armed himself with a sword. "Why bother with the blade when ye mean to use magick?"

Magnus sneered. "Has no one ever told you, Mortal, it's against Fae law to use magick when dealing with your race? Not that I need to against the likes of you." He added with a maniacal grin.

They circled one another. His opponent delivered the first blow, and pain shot through Aidan's arm. He tightened his grip on his claymore and steeled himself against the tremor of unease that this was one battle he could not win. For Syrena's sake, for his own, he cast the thought aside.

The forest filled with the sound of metal scraping metal. Their swords locked, caught in a fight for supremacy. The muscles in Aidan's arms shook and sweat burned his eyes, hazing his vision. A blurred image of Syrena, white-faced with fear, drew from him a cold, hard resolve. He allowed his sword to slip, ducked, and spun to his right. Raising his foot, he delivered a blow to Magnus's ballocks that brought the man to his knees.

Centering his energy, Aidan smashed the sword from his opponent's hand. The blade skittered across the forest floor. But there was no chance to savor his victory. Recovering quickly, Magnus wrenched the sword from Aidan's hand, and flung it against a tree with such force it bent the blade in half. Seemingly unfazed by the blood pumping from his hand, Magnus said, "It's only fair, don't you think?"

Before Aidan could respond, a ham-sized fist caught him on his chin and his head snapped back. Refocusing in time to block Magnus's next punch, the battle raged on. They landed blow after punishing blow on each other.

In the distance, thunder rumbled and lightning stemmed the approach of encroaching shadows. Aidan welcomed the cool droplets that splattered his sweat-soaked tunic, mingling with his blood. Every inch of his body protested, but he couldn't give up. He wouldn't let the Fae have her.

The thought fueled his rage, reviving his flagging strength. With a roar, he barreled into his opponent, taking him to the ground. Magnus grunted as his head hit the forest floor. He grabbed Aidan's arms. Locked in a warrior's embrace, they rolled, pine needles, branches, rocks digging into Aidan's bruised back. The winds picked up and the driving rain pelted them with stinging intensity. Aidan gained control, rising to his knees. He prepared to go with the advantage, and then his foot slipped, throwing him off balance. It was all the leverage Magnus needed. He surged up and tossed Aidan on his back, planting his forearm across Aidan's throat. Inch by inch, he squeezed the breath from him. Spots dotted his vision, swallowing the light. And then the pressure lifted. Hand to his throat, he struggled to sit up, gasping for air. Only to be slammed to the ground once more, a foot planted on his chest.

"You fight well for a Mortal. And for that reason alone I shall let you live." Slowly Magnus lifted his boot and turned to stride away.

Syrena's cry pierced Aidan's oxygen-depleted brain. Wincing, he rolled to his side. Magnus, again clad in his golden robes, dragged Syrena to her feet.

Aidan's bruised throat constricted. He had to find some way to stop the bastard. With bloodied fingers, he dug inside his boot for his dagger. Every muscle in his body ached as he struggled to his knees. At the sight of Syrena's tearstained face, it felt as though Magnus had ripped Aidan's heart from his chest.

"Say a last good-bye, my bride. For you'll never see him again."

"No." His plea was a tortured whisper. He rubbed his eyes to clear the blood and sweat that clouded his vision. A pained, white-knuckled grip on his dagger, he drew his hand back. With Syrena struggling in the grip of Magnus's right arm, Aidan aimed for his left thigh. The dagger whistled through the air, straight and true to its mark. And then they were gone, disappearing in a cascade of light.

He threw his head back and let loose a strangled bellow, "No . . . no." A dull thud penetrated his anguish, and he looked in the direction of the sound. "Sweet Christ, what have I done?"

Staggering to his feet, he made his way to the side of Syrena's wee pet, and dropped to his knees, his dagger buried to the hilt in her chest. Blood soaked through the pink ribbon tied at her neck, pooling in an ever-widening puddle beneath her. Aidan buried his face in his hands, aware of his brother's presence at his side, his ragged breathing.

"She'll never forgive me." Lowering his hands, he closed the doe's unseeing eyes and drew his dagger from her chest.

Lan gently squeezed his shoulder. "'Twas an accident."

Aidan came unsteadily to his feet. "You have to talk to the Fae, Lan. Like when ye were a bairn. I ken I told ye never to do it again, but just this once, for Syrena. Ye have to. 'Tis the only way to get her back."

His brother shook his head, an unreadable emotion in his eyes.

Frantic with the need to convince Lachlan, he grabbed him by the shoulders. "Lan, I can't lose her. He means to take her fer his wife. Ye're the only one who can save her. I've never asked anythin' of ye before, but I ask ye fer this. I'm beggin' ye, brother. I'll go down on my knees if need be."

Lan bowed his head. "I canna do it, Aidan, I'm sorry," he murmured.

"Bloody hell, ye canna mean to leave her to the Fae." A torrent of grief and rage surged through him at his brother's refusal. Without Lan, he had no way of finding her, no way to get her back. The ache in his chest intensified. With a brutality conceived of frustrated anguish, he closed his fingers over his brother's shoulders, ignoring Lachlan's pain-filled gasp.

"Do it now," Aidan grated through clenched teeth.

Lan raised eyes filled with pity. "Syrena's Fae, Aidan. She's a Fae princess. No harm will come to her."

Aidan shoved his brother away from him with such force he stumbled. His stomach churned, and his heart pounded as though it would explode. Nay, it couldn't be true. He tried to ignore the doubt, the voice inside him that said it was so.

He flexed his hands, his knuckles cracked. "How do ye ken?" he grated out.

"She told me, that day in the barn. She's my sister, Aidan. It was Syrena I talked to—"

He slammed his fist in Lan's gut, and his brother doubled over, gasping for air.

Aidan paced the forest floor, shaking off the pain in his hand. His rage suffocated him, and he barely managed to restrain himself from beating his brother senseless.

"Why . . . why did she come here?"

"I doona ken. Her father was murdered, mayhap she was afraid, lonely. She wanted me to go back with her."

Aidan shoved his hand through his damp hair and inhaled deeply of the pine-scented air in an attempt to tame the inferno raging inside him. He needed to get some control over his emotions before the pain of her betrayal brought him to his knees.

His brother came to stand beside him, laying a tentative hand on his shoulder. "Aidan, I'm sorry I didna tell ye. I ken ye felt somethin' fer her, and—"

With a bitter laugh, Aidan jerked away from him. "Is that what ye thought? Nay, I felt nothin' more fer her than any other bonny lass I lusted after." After the grief the Fae had caused his family, he'd been fool enough to let one into his home, his heart. She'd manipulated him, used him to get to his brother.

He shoved the image of her tearstained face from his mind. Never again would he allow his heart, his loins, to ignore the lessons in betrayal his mother, Davina, and now Syrena had taught him. "I doona ever want to hear her name mentioned again, Lan, do ye understand me?"

His brother gave a jerky nod. "Aye, I'll speak of her no more."

Syrena stumbled blindly through the standing stones. If not for Magnus's arm around her waist, she'd be unable to move. Her stomach lurched as visions of Aidan, bloodied and bruised, replayed in her mind. A dagger clenched in his fist as he struggled to his knees and the look of horror on her brother's face were the last things she remembered. She choked back a sob—Aidan now knew her secret. An overwhelming need to go to him, to soothe the wounds he'd suffered on account of her and to explain everything, flared to life inside her. She struggled in Magnus's grasp. "Please, I have to go back. Let me go."

With a rough jerk on her arm, they reappeared in the Enchanted realm, not far from Syrena's hideaway.

Magnus looked down at her, irritation sparked in his eyes. "You try my patience, princess," he drawled. "I let your lover live, for that you owe me your gratitude. Ask more of me and you will be on the receiving end of my anger, and believe me, that is the last place you wish to be." His fingers bit into the flesh of her upper arm.

"But I—"

He slammed her against a tree. The back of her head cracked sharply against the wood. Pinpricks of light flickered before her eyes. The weight of his body suffocated her, and the bark pierced the fabric of her gown to scratch her flesh.

"I think you need a lesson in obedience, little one," he rasped. Imprisoning her wrists in a punishing grip, he pinned her hands above her head.

Through a panic-filled haze she heard Evangeline cry, "Stop, you're hurting her."

Her captor slowly turned his head, his profile hard as he pinned her handmaiden with a lethal stare. "Interfere and you'll regret it. Leave us be." He jerked his chin in the direction of the palace. The heat of his anger pulsated from him, burning Syrena with its intensity.

His attention returned to her, and he lowered his huge hand to her neck. The pulse at the base of her throat beat frantically beneath the pressure of his thumb. "Frightened, princess?"

She was, she was terrified, and the big hand skimming over her breast, her waist, was a catalyst to act. To get away from him before it was too late. She pushed against his barrel chest, squirming in an effort to free herself.

"If you're trying to enflame my desire, you're doing a fine job of it." He ground his thick bulge against her belly.

She froze, her breath coming in painful gasps. A panicked

whimper escaped when his free hand worked its way beneath the hem of her gown. "No, please, don't."

He nuzzled her neck, his beard-roughened chin abrading her skin. He forced his knee between her legs, kneading her inner thigh. "I begin to wonder if you're an innocent, after all," he murmured.

She turned her head, the bark scraped her cheek, and tears blurred her vision.

Evangeline hovered nearby, wringing her hands.

"I think I shall claim you as mine right here, right now."

Syrena squeezed her eyes shut. There had to be something she could do, but she was powerless against his strength.

Magick.

Think, think, she commanded her fear-addled brain. In her mind she shouted the first words to come to her, not knowing whether they were right or wrong. A moment later, his weight lifted and a light breeze caressed her face. A relieved sob escaped her bruised throat.

Forcing her eyes open, she scanned the wood for some sign of him. He was nowhere to be found. But before she could revel in her freedom, the fact her magick finally worked, the branches overhead shook. Her gaze followed the path of the leaves fluttering to the ground at her feet, and her relieved smile turned to a frown.

Magnus hung upside down, struggling against the iron chains that bound him. An ominous crack reverberated through the forest as the branch protested his weight.

She turned to Evangeline. Her maid gave an imperceptible shrug of her shoulder then held out her hand. "Come, my lady, he won't remain confined for long."

She should have known it was her handmaiden's magick that had worked, not her own. She hurried to Evangeline's side, risking one last glance at the king, who attempted to spit the rag from his mouth.

"Matteus, Andras," he bellowed as they transported to Syrena's chambers.

Standing beside her bed, she hugged Evangeline. "Thank you. I don't know what I'd do without you. At first I thought my magick had worked. I wonder—"

She followed Evangeline's pointed stare and looked down. A heated flush suffused her cheeks. Her spell hadn't removed Magnus, it had removed her gown. Once more proving her stepmother right. She buried her face in her hands and shook her head. "What am I going to do?"

In the midst of clothing her in sapphire blue robes dotted with crystals, Evangeline said, "You have to come up with a reason not to go through with the betrothal. He's powerful, princess, and his word carries some weight now that he holds all the lands in the Far North."

Evangeline misunderstood. Syrena referred to Aidan and her brother, but her handmaiden was right. She had to deal with King Magnus, and if he was as powerful as Evangeline insinuated, it did not bode well for her. Tucking an errant curl into place, she took a steadying breath. "I have to confront Morgana. I only wish I understood why she agreed to the match in the first place."

Evangeline adjusted the crown on Syrena's head. "It's an easy way to have you gone from the Enchanted Isles, but knowing the Queen, I suspect there's something more behind her decision."

"Of course there is. As Queen of the Far North, I would lose the Sword of Nuada. But still, I find it hard to believe knowing how she feels about men that she would turn me over to someone like Magnus."

Evangeline gave her shoulder a reassuring squeeze. "I'm sorry, princess. I understand how difficult this is for you. Be strong, you cannot let her get away with this. The Fae need you."

"I don't know. What if my father and the angels were mistaken? I'm no closer to returning my brother to the Isles. In fact, I'm almost certain that after today I never will." Her chest felt so tight she could barely breathe. How had everything gone so wrong?

"It will all work out," Evangeline said as though she knew how close Syrena was to breaking down.

"Come with me, please. I can't do this alone."

Evangeline hesitated then nodded. As they walked from her chambers, they were greeted by the sounds of angry voices reverberating off the vaulted glass ceiling. Syrena groaned.

"This is your home, your kingdom, princess. Fight for it." The fierceness in Evangeline's tone startled Syrena, but she was right. For now, Lachlan and Aidan would have to wait. She could not let her stepmother usurp her place.

Lifting her chin, she strengthened her resolve, hiding her fear behind a mask of haughty disdain.

Magnus stood in the center of the hall, flanked by two men, her stepmother and her handmaiden Nessa to his right. Arms crossed over his chest, he raked Syrena with a bone-chilling look. One of his companions, a younger version of the king, took a menacing step toward her.

"Hold." Magnus waved him back.

"She insulted you, brother. She should be made to pay for the slight."

"She will." The threat in Magnus's tone was implicit.

She faltered, her foot slipping off the last step.

Morgana came forward, her magenta robes swishing across the marble floor. "Syrena, what is the meaning of this? King Magnus has—"

"I wish to speak with you in private, Morgana. The crystal room, if you please."

Her stepmother's eyes widened and she exchanged an uncertain look with Nessa. Intent on retaining the façade of cool confidence—despite the frantic beating of her heart—Syrena had no time to wonder at the exchange.

Praying her stepmother would follow, she walked toward the heavy, gilt-framed doors. But Morgana didn't follow her.

Instead she stood in front of Evangeline and waved over three of the royal guards. "See that she remains here until I'm ready to deal with her."

At Syrena's outraged gasp, Morgana leveled her with an implacable stare. "She has much to answer for."

Evangeline stared straight ahead as though Morgana's words did not affect her, but Syrena saw her lips pinch and bright spots of color appear on her cheeks.

"What . . . what are you talking about?" She ignored Magnus, who leaned against the white marble column, a look of amusement glinting in his gaze.

Her stepmother waved a dismissive hand. "You seemed anxious to speak with me—shall we?" She whirled on Syrena as soon as the door's closed behind them. "Now what is the meaning of this? You may be a princess, but I am Queen, and I will not be ordered about like that again, do you understand me?" Her eyes flashed, an angry flush working its way up her long, elegant neck.

Syrena fought the urge to flinch in the face of Morgana's wrath. If she had any hope of saving herself from an unwanted marriage and protecting Evangeline, she had to take a stand now. Crossing her arms, she hid her trembling hands from her stepmother. "Have I missed something, Morgana? I didn't realize you were now in possession of the Sword of Nuada."

"I will have . . ." Her stepmother raised her chin and eyed Syrena with what appeared to be interest. "It is unlike you to show backbone, Syrena. Is it because I agreed to your betrothal with King Magnus?"

"I will not marry him, Morgana. You had no right to make the arrangement behind my back."

"*I* went behind *your* back? No, that would be what you have done. And as far as your marriage is concerned, it was an alliance your father negotiated just days before his death. I don't understand why you're so upset, you must have known. I knew, as did Bana and Erwn, although I can tell you neither of them was pleased with your father's decision."

"My father and the angels bequeathed the sword to me with all that encompasses. So it matters not what arrangements he made prior to his death."

Her stepmother appeared unruffled, but Syrena noted the tell-a-tale twitch in her eye, her long fingernails curling into her palms. "Maybe not, but you lack the level of magick required to lead, Syrena. You are too young, too inexperienced to rule on your own, and you know it as well as I. That's why we decided we would rule together."

"We did, but as you seem intent on ruling without me, I consider the arrangement null and void from this point on."

"You think to overthrow me, usurp my position as Queen?" Drawing herself to her full height, Morgana made Syrena feel small and inept. Reminding her just what she was up against. Many of the Fae already had aligned themselves with her stepmother. Before she managed a response, Morgana tapped a finger to her painted lips. "Perhaps there is something you should see before you give me your answer."

With a flick of her wrist, the black scrying mirror appeared in her stepmother's hand. "I think it best if you sit for this, my dear." A feral smile curled her lips, and she nudged Syrena toward the white velvet chaise.

Syrena sat on the edge of the divan, tension coiling low in her belly. Sweeping her gown from beneath her, Morgana took her place beside Syrena, holding the mirror in the palm of her hands. "Look."

She forced her gaze to the black agate. Tendrils of gray smoke slithered over its polished surface. When the mist lifted, her brother and Aidan came into sharp relief. "Oh," she gasped, touching Aidan's bruised face.

"Tsk, tsk, a Mortal? Really, Syrena, what would the Fae think?"

She jerked her hand away. She should have known what Morgana was up to.

"I . . ." When Aidan came to his feet, she saw her deer, lying on the forest floor in a pool of blood, a dagger protruding from her chest. She clapped a hand over her mouth, holding back the nauseous waves that leapt to her throat. He'd killed her deer. He'd killed that poor, helpless creature, and all because of her. She closed her eyes to shut out the sickening sight.

"He killed the animal, but does he mean to kill your brother as well?" Morgana trilled.

The question ripped through the heavy weight of Syrena's grief, and her eyes shot open.

Lachlan was bent over, clutching his stomach. "A shame, he only hit him." Her stepmother's pitiless laugh filled her with revulsion.

"You knew. You knew all along."

Morgana arched a brow then shrugged. "No, not all along." She patted Syrena's knee as though nothing were amiss. "Now shall I tell you what they are saying about you? I'm adept at reading lips, you know." She didn't wait for a response from Syrena, as if she would be able to give one.

"Hmm, oh my, the man, Aidan, isn't it? Well, I'm afraid now that he knows your true identity, he doesn't want anything to do with you, nor, it seems, does your brother. They really do despise you. I suppose that will make it rather difficult to bring your brother back to the Isles. That was your plan, wasn't it?"

Morgana smiled pleasantly, as though she hadn't just crushed Syrena's hopes and dreams. Torn her heart from her chest and ground it beneath the heel of her purple slippers. Syrena pressed her palm to her mouth to contain her anguished sob, but it was as useless as trying to contain the tears that spilled from her eyes.

"There, there." Her stepmother patted her shoulder awkwardly. "It must be clear to you now, Syrena, that you need me and, I suppose, I need you. So let's put this unpleasantness behind us and rule as we agreed." She sighed. "Enough, you'll make yourself sick. You must learn to control your emotions, child. Men are not worth the pain they cause. I thought you'd learned that lesson with your father."

Laying the scrying mirror on the chaise, Morgana rose to her feet, tugging Syrena along with her. "Dry your eyes, we have much to do. Our first order of business is to get rid of his majesty. I suppose it was unfair of me to push for the marriage, but really, you left me no choice going behind my back as you did. Well, that's over with now, isn't it?" She pressed a cool kiss to Syrena's cheek. "We'll get back to how we once were, mother and daughter. Oh, the plans I have for us."

Syrena stood in stunned silence while Morgana dried her tears and straightened her crown. "There, you are somewhat presentable. Now, leave the talking to me."

A hysterical laugh bubbled up inside her, and she barely managed to swallow it before Morgana dragged her from the room to face Magnus. Her mind bombarded with visions of her deer, Aidan, and Lachlan, she didn't hear a word her stepmother said to him.

Magnus loomed over her, startling her from her stupor, his gaze as threatening as the anger that radiated from him. "One day you'll pay for this. You all will."

He stormed from the palace, his men trailing behind him. The doors shuddered and all held their breath, prepared for them to fall from their moorings.

"Syrena, pull yourself together. You can retire to your chambers after we deal with your handmaiden."

"What are you talking about, Morgana? Evangeline has done nothing wrong."

"Most would disagree. She's being charged with the murder of your father."

"No!" Syrena cried out.

Morgana merely raised a hand to silence her, and continued, "She has been in your uncle's employ since the day she arrived. The evidence is conclusive. It's my belief King

Rohan wanted your father dead to further his ambitions. The trial is set for—"

"No, it can't be true." She pushed aside the guards. "Evangeline?"

"Of course it isn't, my lady. The accusations are false."

Syrena heard the tremor in her friend's voice. Evangeline's face devoid of color, she held herself erect, her expression defiant.

Morgana elbowed Syrena out of the way. "Did you think that one day I would not recognize you, Evangeline? That one day I would not see my cousin's face in yours. Did you not wonder at her magick, Syrena—a magick more powerful than anyone else's? Her father's your uncle's wizard. And her mother, my cousin, was responsible for the deaths of Tatianna and her brethren. Andora was evil and that same evil thrives in you." Her stepmother viciously spat the words at Evangeline.

She grabbed her friend's hand. "Evangeline?" she croaked.

A tear slid down Evangeline's porcelain white cheek. "I'm sorry, princess."

In a burst of light, she disappeared.

Chapter 11

Power can be intoxicating. Use it wisely. Don't become enslaved by it.

Uscias's warning resonated as strongly with Syrena now as it had on that day a year ago when she'd gone to reclaim the Sword of Nuada. Devastated by Evangeline's abandonment and the knowledge her brother and Aidan wanted nothing to do with her, she sought out Nuie. Vowing never again would she be at someone's mercy.

The wizard had persuaded Syrena to remain with him, using their time together to teach her everything she needed to know about Nuie and healing her heart in the process. Although there was nothing he could say that would ease the pain of losing Aidan and Lachlan, his insights into why Evangeline left had helped.

Evangeline's mother, Andora, had destroyed Tatianna and the Fae of the Enchanted Isles. She'd been responsible for releasing the dark lords, and because of that, Uscias assured Syrena her friend would never do anything to bring harm to their world, including murdering King Arwan. Evangeline had lived in fear of anyone finding out who her mother was, and thanks to Morgana, the secret she'd tried desperately to hide had been revealed.

Once Syrena's sorrow had eased, Uscias taught her to wield a sword with deadly accuracy, pitting her against first one royal guard, then two. Until at the end of her training, she fought three easily. She battled them from sunrise to sunset, and when they begged for a day's reprieve, she built her stamina and strength by running from the base of the mountain to the top. At night, no matter how exhausted she might be, Uscias taught her the strategies of war. Soon their efforts had paid off, and she had become a warrior worthy of carrying the magickal weapon.

Syrena sat astride Bowen with her sword across her lap and rubbed her thumb over the precious stones embedded in gold. "I think Uscias would agree, Nuie, I have used my power wisely indeed." Her heart swelled with pride as she watched the women train in a meadow dotted with purple and pink flowers. Shayla trained five of them in the use of bow and arrow while four others rode alongside Riana. The women watched as Riana leaned over the side of her black steed and struck the stuffed target with brutal efficiency.

Fallyn, and Riana, Shayla's youngest sister, galloped up the grassy knoll, reining in her mount alongside Syrena. The rays from the midmorning sun glinted in the long, curly mass of her chestnut hair. "Good morning, your highness. You're up early. Is something amiss?" Fallyn's emerald eyes sparkled with amusement.

Syrena smiled at the woman who over the last year had become a dear friend, helping to fill the void left by Evangeline. Fallyn had fled from her betrothed, King Broderick of the Welsh Fae, on the eve of their nuptials. Catching him with another woman was only one of the reasons she'd chosen to forgo the arrangement.

Shayla and Riana had followed their sister to the Enchanted Isles. The three women had proven invaluable to

Syrena, not only on the battlefield, but in the friendship they so readily offered.

"I wanted to check on our new recruits before I have to meet with Morgana."

Fallyn winced. "Not the scrying mirror again?"

"No, I've hidden it. I won't let her torment me any longer." Syrena chewed on her bottom lip. She'd said more than she intended to. She didn't want anyone to know how seeing Aidan take his pleasure with other women still had the power to affect her, to twist her insides into knots that didn't unravel for days. But her stepmother seemed to have a sixth sense when it came to Syrena and her feelings for Aidan and her brother.

Whenever the urge to visit the Mortal realm tempted her, Morgana took great pleasure in using the scrying mirror to show her just how little she'd meant to them. Taking advantage of the opportunity to expound on the failings of men—both Mortal and Fae alike.

Fallyn gave Syrena's shoulder a reassuring squeeze. "Good for you. I don't know how you've put up with her torture for as long as you have. If I had to see Broderick cavorting with his many mistresses, I think I'd go mad."

"Do you still love him?"

Fallyn grimaced then nodded. "Silly, isn't it? After all this time you would think I'd be over the man."

How could she think Fallyn a fool when she still found herself thinking of Aidan, a Mortal who not only didn't return her feelings, but despised her for who she was.

Syrena sighed. "Maybe we should be more like Morgana."

Fallyn looked horrified. "Surely you jest. The woman has no heart. She thinks of no one but herself and her desires. She goes through lovers faster than most men."

Syrena wrinkled her nose. "You're right, but for many women, the Isles have become a sanctuary. And without Morgana's vision, it never would have happened."

"I suppose, but don't diminish your part in it all, Syrena.

Without you leading our army, protecting the Enchanted realm, none of this would be possible. Lord Bana and Erwn's rebellion wouldn't have been put down, and the battle you fought against Magnus and his army has become legendary."

Syrena waved a dismissive hand. "I didn't do it alone. None of it would have been possible without you and your sisters, or the other women who fight with us."

"I know, but it's you who lead us."

"And I thank Uscias every day for his guidance." A flash of red shot between her fingers and Syrena laughed, patting her sword. "And you, too, Nuie, I haven't forgotten about you." The red glow turned golden, indicating Nuie's pleasure at her praise.

"How is Uscias?"

"I don't know. He's been busy seeing to Aurora's training. It seems like forever since I last saw him, but I hope to spend a few days with him once the new recruits are settled."

"You should go now. We can—" Fallyn's lips pursed in a grim line as she looked over Syrena's shoulder.

Syrena shifted in the saddle to see what had drawn her friend's attention.

"Nessa." She acknowledged the older woman while tightening her hold on Nuie. Morgana's handmaiden did little to disguise the fact that she disliked her. Not that it had ever been any different, but it seemed to Syrena that Nessa's dislike of her had intensified of late. She thought her growing influence over the Fae most likely the cause.

Nessa sneered then thrust a rolled parchment bearing King Rohan's red seal toward Syrena. A flicker of unease stirred to life inside her. They had been skirting her uncle's authority for some time now and it seemed he meant to take them to task over the matter.

"Why didn't Morgana open this?"

"Because your uncle chose to send it to *you*, instead of to the rightful Queen."

Syrena ignored her comment and carefully unraveled the

scroll. She scanned King Rohan's missive. Looking up to meet Fallyn's questioning gaze, she said, "We've been called before the Seelie court and this time my uncle will not tolerate our absence." She turned her attention to Nessa. "You'd best tell my stepmother to make the necessary preparations. We depart within the hour."

"My Queen answers to no one. She will call her council together and decide how to respond after they have considered the matter."

Syrena leaned over Bowen's flank. "You will tell my stepmother to prepare herself now. I will not risk my warriors in a battle with King Rohan, King Broderick, and King Gabriel simply because of some petty machinations on Morgana's part."

"How dare you think to dictate—"

"You go too far, Nessa. See to your mistress. We leave on the hour."

Fallyn shuddered after Nessa departed in a bluster of smoke and light. "That woman turns my blood cold."

Syrena absently stroked Nuie. "She does the same to me."

"You did well. I wouldn't have guessed," Fallyn reassured her. "So, you can't put your uncle off any longer?"

"No, to do so would be pure folly. We are a formidable opponent, but not if the three of them join forces against us as they appear ready to."

Fallyn looked past her to the line of oaks swaying in the gentle breeze. "Broderick will be there?"

"Yes, I'm certain he will be. Is there anything you'd like me to say to him? I can deliver a missive if you'd rather."

Fallyn's gaze met hers, and Syrena noted the sadness in her eyes. "No, I've been here close to a year and he hasn't cared enough to inquire into my well-being."

"He's a fool for letting you go without a fight. You're an incredible woman, Fallyn, and if he's too stupid to realize that, you're well rid of him."

"Thank you, you're a good friend." She gave Syrena a hug. "Good luck."

"I think I'll need more than luck unless you'd like to render my stepmother speechless for the duration of our visit."

"Morgana." Syrena nudged her stepmother toward the massive gilded doors leading into the chambers where her uncle and the Seelie court awaited them. "Stop stalling. We're already late and I doubt the grand entrance you hope to make will have the desired effect. And please, could you at least try to be civil to the servants."

Syrena smiled at the royal guardsmen, who bowed low as a measure of their respect.

Morgana whirled to face her, her ice blue robes swirling about her ankles. "Why should I? Princess Syrena this, Princess Syrena that, all of them bowing and scraping in your presence as if I, the Queen, were nothing more then your minion."

Syrena suppressed a smile. "You're exaggerating. They offered you the same courtesies they extended to me."

Morgana narrowed her gaze, then tossing her glossy black mane, barked a command for the guards to announce them.

Syrena took a steadying breath and smoothed her hand over the creamy satin robes threaded with gold. Riana, Fallyn's youngest sister, had outdone herself. By mutual agreement, the three women had taken over for Evangeline, and Syrena didn't know how she would have managed without them. Determined to make sure Morgana would never learn just how limited Syrena's magick truly was, they readily participated in the subterfuge. So much so, that her stepmother had begun to believe Syrena's abilities were no less than anyone else's.

Not that Morgana could use her lack of magick against her—not any longer. As far as the rest of the Fae from the Enchanted realm were concerned, Syrena was their true Queen. She knew she had Uscias and Nuie to thank for their acceptance.

Her dream of claiming a place in her people's hearts had come to pass. But there was an emptiness inside her, a deep void she seemed unable to fill. She did her best to ignore the dull ache, putting it down to her inability to fulfill her father's last wish—her quest, a quest that had been doomed from the very beginning. Lachlan, like his brother, wanted nothing to do with the Fae. She reasoned it was for the best. The last thing she wanted to do was hand over Nuie.

"Syrena," her stepmother hissed, her silver bracelets clinking as she motioned for her to enter. Syrena knew Morgana only wanted her to go first in case of an assassination attempt. She would be the first to fall, and her stepmother would be able to make her escape.

Pausing beneath the intertwined branches of white ash trees, Syrena withdrew Nuie from the silken sheath strapped to her back. Her eyes adjusted to a hall awash in a crystal clear light. Sprites, with lanterns in hand, flitted from the branches that formed a high ceiling. Her uncle sat at the head of a marble table on an intricately carved throne of white ash.

A hush fell over the room, the only sound the gentle burble of water spurting from the iridescent blue fountains that fed the waterways lining the outer edges of the chambers. Pink and purple flowers floated peacefully on the turquoise waters. But the men and women surrounding the marble table looked anything but peaceful. They looked furious—with her.

Her uncle's topaz eyes gleamed as brilliantly as the jewels on Nuie's hilt. He rose from his throne, waving off the caustic muttering directed at Syrena. Two of the guards he motioned for hesitated before coming to her side, their expressions apprehensive.

"It has been a long time, my dear, and as you have never before graced us with your presence, I will not take offense that you have broken an ordinance by carrying your weapon within our hallowed hall. Please, give your sword to my men."

"As if we would hand over our greatest treasure to you, Rohan." Her stepmother's voice was frosty enough to coat the branches in ice. Leaving Syrena to deal with their transgression, Morgana pushed past the guards to take her place at the far end of the table. The gilded legs of her chair scraped across the marble floor, punctuating the glacial silence.

"I'm sorry, Uncle, but Morgana does have a point. I'm afraid I must refuse your request. But you have my word I will not use my sword." With that said, she sheathed Nuie.

Her uncle regarded her for a long moment. "You've changed, Syrena." He bestowed a kiss on her cheek and waved off the Welsh King's angry objection. While he led Syrena to a chair beside Morgana, he said, "Enough, Broderick, I trust my niece to keep her word. Besides, we have no time to waste."

Fallyn's betrothed slouched in his chair and eyed Syrena with unmitigated rage. His black gaze glittered like polished agate.

A deep rumble of laughter to Syrena's left drew her attention. "Do you really think your evil looks will have any effect on the woman, Broderick? It is said she eats men such as us for breakfast." The rakish smile King Gabriel of England's Fae sent Syrena was lethal when combined with his beauty. He had the look of an angel, which considering how long he'd been king of England's Fae, was not surprising.

"Don't waste your time trying to charm her, Gabriel. She's not referred to as the Ice Queen for no reason."

From the corner of her eye, Syrena noted the angry flush staining Morgana's cheeks. Certain her stepmother was about to explode, she quickly interceded, "As interesting as your observations may be, I thought it was a matter of grave importance for which we have been called before you."

"You're right, Syrena, it is. We—"

"Want our women back!" Broderick slammed his fist on the table and it rattled with the force of his rage. The servant who filled the heavy gold chalices with wine gave a startled yelp and jumped back, spilling the contents onto Broderick. His hair and black leather jerkin saturated with the thick, syrupy liquid, he shook his head in disgust. "This is what happens when men are forced into the roles of women. Now make our demands, Rohan."

No wonder Fallyn left him, Syrena thought.

"I was about to, Broderick. Morgana, Syrena, the exodus of our women to the Enchanted Isles must cease. We—"

"Cease . . . cease!" the raven-haired king bellowed. "No, they must be returned posthaste." Broderick shot to his feet, his chair clattering to the floor.

"Syrena, no," her uncle ordered as she was about to withdraw Nuie. "Broderick, sit, I will make this one last allowance to your conduct on account of Fallyn, but it will be the last."

Slowly Syrena removed her hand from Nuie's hilt and focused on her uncle. "The women come to us because they've been mistreated. I think I can speak for both Morgana and myself when I say we will not force them to return simply because you find yourself in need of servants."

The last thing Syrena wanted to do was turn the women away, but even she had to admit they grew overcrowded. And some of the women, if she was honest, quite a few, had left for no other reason than they felt unappreciated. While a part of her understood the sentiment, even sympathized, they couldn't go to war on account of it.

She raised her hand when once more Broderick shot to his feet. "To show our good intentions, from this day forward we will attempt to ascertain if a woman has just cause to seek sanctuary. If you would be patient, I am certain most of the women will return to their homes of their own free will."

Morgana grabbed her sleeve and hissed, "What are you doing?"

Her stepmother had agreed to let Syrena do the talking while they were at court, but obviously she'd reached her limit. Syrena lowered her voice. "We cannot continue to go on as we are, Morgana. Our numbers are such that we can barely sustain those we have."

"Princess Syrena is right—over the last several weeks

many of our women have returned. I say we wait. We cannot afford to allow this to come between us, not with the threat of war hanging over our heads," Gabriel said reasonably.

"Who threatens us?" Morgana demanded.

"We have heard rumors that King Magnus and King Dmitri seek to join forces. Magnus because of his defeat at Syrena's hands, and Dmitri on account of Broderick stealing his wife."

"Stole his wife?" Broderick snorted. "She was more slave than wife. He nearly killed her. You wouldn't treat an ogre as badly as he treated Shayla."

Syrena glanced at the harsh lines of Broderick's profile. For all that he had hurt her friend, Fallyn never forgot how her betrothed had gone to her sister's rescue.

"I believe those incidents are little more than an excuse to come after our Hallows, and if not our treasures, the wizards who created them. Uscias, Morfessa, Esras, and Murias are in danger as well." Rohan's gaze came to rest on Syrena. "The reputations of you and your women warriors precede you, my dear. We ask that if the time comes, you will join forces with us."

Her uncle's request was testament to how far Syrena had risen in the Fae's esteem. She smiled. "Of course."

Broderick's fingers curled around the chalice in a white-knuckled grip, and he lifted his gaze to Syrena. "But only if Fallyn does not ride with you. I will not see her harmed."

"I'm pleased that you're concerned for Fallyn's welfare, King Broderick, but perhaps it would be best if you took the matter up with her. Although I doubt you will meet with much success. She's one of my finest warriors if that helps alleviate some of your worry."

Her uncle silenced Broderick's dark mutterings with a firm shake of his head. "Thank you, Syrena. Now with that settled, there is another matter of grave import we must deal with. Gabriel, perhaps it would be best for you to explain it."

The man's easygoing, flirtatious manner changed instantly, his sublime features drawn into a cold, expressionless mask. "Over the last month, five of my men have disappeared in the

Mortal realm. There are rumors circulating that black magick is involved. I've used every means at my disposal to recover them, but as yet have been unsuccessful." He stared darkly into his chalice.

Her uncle reached over and patted his arm. "We'll get to the bottom of it, Gabriel." He nodded to two of the royal guards and they quietly left the room. "As a precautionary measure, the portals to the Mortal realm will be closed until further notice."

"You may wish to give our people some notice, Rohan. Since our women are in short supply, my men have been taking their pleasure with the Mortals," Broderick informed her uncle.

Syrena pressed a hand to her stomach to settle the nause-ating roil. Were she and Morgana responsible for other Mortal women being at the mercy of Fae men intent on assuaging their lust? Even if they had to use magick to do so, as her father had done to Aidan and Lachlan's mother?

"You know my feelings on that, Broderick. If I find any of the Fae have used magick to seduce the Mortals, they will suffer the consequences."

Her uncle was an honorable man, and he made Syrena proud to be his niece. She couldn't help but wonder how two brothers could be so different. Her uncle would have made a wonderful father, and she thought it sad he never married.

Broderick rolled his eyes. "As if they need magick to seduce the Mortals. The women cannot resist them."

Syrena gritted her teeth. She'd had ample opportunity to witness Mortal women throwing themselves at a man simply because he was beautiful. Aidan and Lachlan were perfect ex-amples. Remembering her own response to Aidan, Syrena thought she should refrain from passing judgment.

Her uncle withdrew his stern gaze from Broderick when the doors to the hall opened. He motioned for someone to enter. Morgana looked over her shoulder and released a horrified shriek. "What is *she* doing here? You harbor a viper in your midst, Rohan." Her face mottled with rage, Morgana's nails dug into Syrena's arm. "Do something! She killed your father."

Her uncle, a hand to his brow, shook his head. "Evangeline did not kill my brother, Morgana. She is guilty of nothing. She looked after my niece's welfare at my behest, that is all. I have asked her here to share her insights into the matter before us. We must ascertain what we are dealing with in the Mortal realm. We need to learn if someone has one of the Grimoires and attempts to release the dark lord using the spells contained within the book. Although we can account for three of them, two are missing."

Evangeline stood between Gabriel and Rohan. With her head bowed, her long, mahogany tresses shielded her expression from Syrena. She wouldn't look in their direction, and a wave of grief welled within Syrena. She missed her friend. Seeing her now brought back the depths of despair she'd felt when Evangeline abandoned her.

But Syrena understood how it felt to be the subject of the Fae's derision, and wished she could comfort Evangeline as she had so often comforted her.

"Then certainly Andora's daughter would be the one to ask since her mother stole a Grimoire to release the dark lords against Tatianna!" Morgana snarled low in her throat. "You may be fool enough to trust her, Rohan, but I'm not and I demand she stand trial!"

On the day her stepmother had first confronted Evangeline, Syrena had been helpless to do anything. She'd been overcome with grief, her mind in emotional turmoil. But she could do something now. Determined to protect her friend, she said, "Stop, Morgana. Evangeline did not kill my father. He named his murderer on the day he gave me the Sword of Nuada."

Evangeline lifted her violet-blue gaze to Syrena. Her stepmother and uncle stared at her, open-mouthed.

Chapter 12

The hand at the back of Aidan's head shoved him beneath the blue-green water. Suffocated in its icy embrace, he twisted and turned in an attempt to break free. His lungs burned as though they were about to explode. He dug his fingers into the wood railing, and with a gurgled roar pushed off the side, sending the fool who attempted to drown him sprawling across the deck.

Aidan leaned against the rail and gasped for air. His breathing eased, and he shook his head like an overgrown seal. Shoving his hair from his face, he glared at Gavin.

"Bloody hell, have ye gone mad?" He lowered himself to the wooden planks. "Nay, doona answer, I already ken ye are."

"Ha, ha, our laird makes an attempt at humor, Donald. Mayhap we should have tried to drown him a ways back. To be sure, he'd have been easier to live with." Gavin pushed to his feet, his boots sliding through the puddles of water on the deck, and he landed with a thud on his arse. He scowled at Aidan. "And just so ye ken, ye were the color of the greens Beth is always tryin' to shove down our throats. I wasna about to have ye toss up yer accounts on board. Ye smell bad enough as 'tis."

Aidan surreptitiously brought his soiled shirt to his nose

and sniffed. 'Twas the truth, he was ripe. "Mayhap if ye allowed me to bathe before kidnappin' me, I wouldna offend yer delicate sensibilities."

Gavin crawled over to Aidan and sat beside him. "Aye, and if we did, ye would have refused to come. Like ye did when we asked ye a fortnight ago, and the time before that." He turned to Aidan, his expression pensive. "He's been gone too long. Somethin' is amiss. I ken things havena' been the same between the two of ye, no' since . . ." He shoved his hand through his hair. "Ye need to find him, Aidan. If anythin' happened to Lan, ye'd never forgive yerself."

Aidan breathed in the salty sea air and looked out across the sparkling turquoise waters the midmorning sun danced upon. Gavin was right. Lan had been gone too long. He should have listened to his men when they first suggested he head to Dunvegan.

He scrubbed his hands over his face, his fingers snagging in his beard. Bloody hell, he hadn't realized how long it had been since he'd taken a blade to his face.

Gavin crossed his arms over his chest. "Aye, ye're a shaggy beast. 'Tis my hope yer cousin's wife will take ye in hand."

"While the two of ye are yammerin', I'm doin' all the work. We're comin' in to shallow waters," Donald informed them in a disgruntled voice.

Aidan pulled himself to his feet and leaned over the rail. Dunvegan was now visible to the right of the bow, perched above the loch, gleaming golden in the noonday sun. In the crystal clear waters below them, a trout wove its way through the rocks. "Sweet Christ, Donald, ye'll run us aground fer sure."

Gavin, leaning over alongside him, nodded his head. "Over ye go, then."

"What?" Aidan bellowed. "Are ye daft? The water is freezin' and we're almost a league from shore."

Gavin shrugged. "Ye swim like a fish. Ye'll be fine. Besides, ye need a bath."

"I'm no'—"

Splash.

The weight of his clothes dragged Aidan beneath the water. With a violent kick of his feet, he exploded above the surface. He treaded water and glared up at Gavin and Donald. "Ye wait until I get home. The two of ye will pay fer that."

Gavin sniggered, wiggling his scrawny legs. "We're shakin' in our boots. Ye havena' trained in ages. We'd beat ye with one hand tied behind our backs."

The icy waters caused Aidan's muscles to tighten. He couldn't waste his energy exchanging insults with the two fools hanging over the rails laughing at him. He cursed while he struggled to remove his boots, thinking the least they could've done was let him strip down to his braies before they tossed him overboard.

It took him longer than it should have to reach the shore. Gavin was right. They could beat him with *both* hands tied behind their backs. Dragging himself onto the rocks, he rolled onto his back. His heart hammered in his chest and his breath came in harsh gasps. Exhaustion turned his arms and legs to jelly, and he closed his eyes. He needed a wee rest was all. A brief respite before he faced his cousin Rory and his family.

Aidan awoke with a start. He opened his eyes, his vision obscured by a heavy clump of rusty brown water weeds. Cursing, he pulled them off his face, spitting the stringy remains from his mouth. Two wee demons, one dark, one fair, stared down at him, their mouths agape.

Ewwhh. Their terrified screams rent the air, and Aidan's ears.

"He's no' dead, Jamie. The creature lives," the dark-haired one cried out.

"I'm no' a creature," he growled, struggling to sit up. The piles of pebbles and sand he'd been buried beneath cascaded from his chest and arms.

"Jamie, he's gettin' up. He's goin' to eat us."

"Nay, I'll no' let him, Alex." The fair-haired demon whacked Aidan on the head with a long, blackened stick.

"Ouch! Stop that, ye little monster." He lifted an arm to protect himself while trying to grab hold of his attacker's weapon with the other, but he was too fast for him. Aidan wrapped his arms about his head when the dark-haired one joined in.

Certain he heard a man and woman laughing not far in the distance, Aidan called out, "Help!"

"What the . . . Jamie, Alex, stop beatin' on yer Uncle Aidan." He heard the distinctive rumble of laughter in his cousin's deep voice.

Aidan slowly lowered his arms, and glared up at Rory. "I should've kent the wee demons were yers." He rose to his feet, shaking off the last of the rocks and sand. "And I'm no' their uncle. I'm their cousin," he muttered.

Rory shrugged, the corner of his mouth twitching. "They only have Iain, so we made you an honorary one." His cousin turned his attention to the wee demons, who whispered to one another. Crossing his arms over his chest, he said, "Now, apologize to yer uncle fer beatin' on him."

Rory's wife, Aileanna, scrambled over the rocks. She frowned, then her eyes widened. "Aidan?" Looking from him to her sons, she asked, "Jamie, Alex, what did you do?"

"We didna ken he was our uncle, Mama. Right, Alex?"

"Nay, we thought he was a monster. He was goin' like this." The wee brat mimicked a loud snoring sound.

"Aye . . . aye, and then he growled."

No longer able to contain his mirth, his cousin howled with laughter.

"Rory!" Aileanna elbowed her husband in the side. But Aidan didn't miss the fact she bit the inside of her cheek and her bonny blue eyes sparkled with amusement. "I'm . . . I'm sorry, Aidan. Boys, apologize."

Heads bowed, the two of them moved the stones in the sand with the toes of their boots. "Sorry," they mumbled, peeking at him from beneath their long lashes as though they were a couple of wee angels.

The dark-haired one's eyes widened and he tugged on the sleeve of Aileanna's violet gown. "Mama, he looks like he's goin' to eat us," he whimpered.

Rory angled his head. "You do look kinda fierce, cousin. Mayhap you can give them a wee smile."

"Oh, fer the love of God."

Aileanna slanted him an unamused look, her lips pursed.

"All right," he grumbled and bared his teeth.

Their mouths dropped open. Squealing, they turned on their heels and ran.

"Alex, Jamie, be careful," their mother shouted after them.

Shaking her head, Aileanna approached Aidan, reaching up on the tips of her toes to press a kiss to his cheek. "Oh, dear Lord, what did the boys douse you with?" She waved a hand in front of her nose. "I'll have a bath prepared for you, Aidan."

Before she walked away, his cousin grabbed her hand and pulled her into his arms. "'Tis a shame our sons interrupted us. Mayhap later we'll take up where we left off," he murmured.

Sweet Christ, now he knew why Iain chose to spend as little time at Dunvegan as he did.

Aileanna smiled up at her husband. "You may have missed your chance, darling." She patted Rory's chest while stepping away from him. "My father and aunt have promised to come for a visit and I have much to do to prepare for their arrival."

"Aileanna," Rory called to her retreating back. "Aileanna, that's no' funny. Tell me yer jokin'. Aileanna!"

They heard her husky laugh over the gentle lap of the waves along the shore.

"She'd best be jokin'. The old goat was here only a fortnight ago," his cousin grumbled.

"Ye and the MacDonald are as close as ever, I see."

"Aye, 'tis lucky fer him I adore my wife and would do anythin' to make her happy. If I had my way, he'd be visitin' but once a year." Rory drew his gaze from Aileanna and clapped

Aidan on the back. "It's been too long, cousin. I almost didna recognize you."

Aidan rubbed his bearded jaw as they walked along the beach toward Dunvegan. "Aye, it has."

Rory glanced down at Aidan's bare feet then out over the loch. "Gavin and Donald throw you overboard?"

He grunted.

Rory laid a hand on his arm, forcing him to stop. "Somethin' is amiss. What is it?"

"Lan." He lifted his gaze to the white, fluffy clouds scuttling above the verdant green of the treetops, unable to meet the concern in Rory's eyes. "He hasna' come home. 'Tis close to two months since he's been gone."

Rory shook his head slowly. "I didna realize that much time had passed since he'd paid us a visit. He seemed fine to me, but Aileanna didna think so. She thought he appeared troubled."

"Aye, well, we've had our differences of late. And I ken ye heard about the Lamonts."

With a reassuring squeeze to Aidan's shoulder, Rory said, "Aye, a nasty business that, but doona ye worry, we'll find him. Once you've cleaned up, you, Fergus, and I will put our heads together."

"Iain's no' about?"

"Nay, he and the McNeils put out to sea around the same time Lan stopped by."

"He's doin' well, then?" Aidan asked as they neared the keep.

"Aye, better than well. The lad has made a small fortune in the venture."

Mrs. Mac, his cousin's housekeeper, and Aileanna turned when they walked through the doors. "Och, I see what you mean." The older woman wrinkled her nose and Rory's wife's cheeks pinked. "Come with me, Laird MacLeod, we'll have you good as new in no time."

Aidan groaned at the determined look in Mrs. Mac's eyes.

* * *

Hours later, outfitted in a pair of his cousin's trews and a clean white tunic, Aidan entered the grand hall. He felt more like himself than he had in a long while. Mrs. Mac had rubbed his skin raw, but not entirely satisfied, she'd shoved him in a chair and went to work on his hair and beard. The woman was as stubborn as Fin on a bad day, and Aidan considered taking her back with him once he found Lan. 'Twould serve Donald and Gavin right.

Dunvegan was much changed. Evidence of Aileanna's feminine touch was everywhere; in the rich tapestries hanging from the walls, to the flowers gracing the delicate furnishings she'd added throughout. She'd turned the once austere keep into a home—a stark contrast to Lewes. His grand plans for his own keep had never come to fruition. Repairs took coin, coin he did not have. Oh, aye, he still had the gold and silver *she'd* given him, but knowing it had come from the Fae, he refused to touch it.

Rory waved him over from his place on the dais. Aidan frowned upon seeing the two wee demons sitting on either side of their mother and father. Had his cousin gone daft? Bairns were to eat in the nursery, no' with the adults. As he wound his way through the tables, he greeted several men who had fought the Lowlanders with them. Reaching the dais, he shared a word with Fergus then warily sat himself down beside the dark-haired demon. Alex, if he remembered correctly.

"See, lads, he's no' a monster." His cousin grinned, and took a swallow of his mead.

Aidan narrowed his gaze on him then looked over at Aileanna. "I thought yer da was to join us, Aileanna? I hope nothin's amiss. I was lookin' forward to seein' him again." He stifled a groan when Rory kicked him beneath the table.

"Nay, a messenger arrived a short time ago. He's been delayed for a day or two." Jamie demanded her attention and she turned to assist her son, ignoring her husband muttering beside her.

"Rory tells me Lan is missin'. Any idea where he was headed?" Fergus who sat beside him asked.

The knot of guilt riding low in his belly tightened. "Aye, a couple of the lads thought he might have been on his way to London. He's been restless of late."

Restless. His brother had been like a whirlpool in the loch, spinning out of control, sucking everyone down with him. And Aidan had done nothing. He'd stood back and watched as if naught were amiss. Too busy battling his own demons to deal with his brother's. Too afraid if he peeled back the scab from the wound, anger and blame would ooze to the surface, and he'd say things he could never take back.

"Aye, I thought I heard mention of that when last he was here. I wouldna fret, he's a braw lad. He can handle himself."

Drawing comfort from Fergus's assertion, a man Aidan greatly respected, he allowed himself to relax. As he brought the goblet of mead to his lips, the wee demon shook his arm and the ruby red liquid sloshed onto his tunic. "What?" he growled.

Innocent blue eyes blinked up at him, and the lad pointed to the slab of beef on his platter. Aidan glanced at his cousin, who was deep in conversation with his wife. With a disgruntled sigh, he took out his dirk and cut off a piece of meat for the bairn.

"Thank you," Alex mumbled.

"Ye're welcome," Aidan said, dabbing at the stain with the linen. Something hit him on the head then dropped into his goblet with a splash. More of the sticky liquid splattered his tunic.

Rory looked over at him, brow arched. "I doona remember you bein' such a messy eater."

Aidan glared at Alex and Jamie, who snickered behind their wee hands. "'Twas no' me."

Aileanna pinned her sons with a withering glare. "I'm

sorry, Aidan." Rising from her chair, she gathered the protesting Jamie under her arm. "Nay, if you throw your food, you'll eat in the nursery. You, too, Alex."

"But, Mama, I didna—"

"I know, pet, but your brother will not stay put without you. And Mama's too tired to be running up and down after him."

His cousin shot his wife a worried look. "Are you no' feelin' well, love?"

Aileanna smiled. With the backs of her fingers, she stroked her husband's cheek. They shared an intimate look, and Rory pressed her fingers to his lips.

Sweet Christ, Iain was right. 'Twas enough to make a man gag.

"I'm fine. Come along, Alex," she said as she walked away.

Alex held out his arms to Aidan.

"What?"

"I canna get off." He wiggled in his chair and Aidan noted the extra padding that kept him tucked in place.

"Fer the love of God," he grumbled, lifting the lad into his arms. His baby soft hair tickled Aidan's nose. When the bairn wrapped his arms tightly around Aidan's neck, a memory of Lan at a similar age came over him. He closed his eyes at the surge of emotion that threatened to overwhelm him.

"Mama, Uncle Aidan cursed," Alex said, scampering after Aileanna.

"I did no'," he muttered. Returning to his chair, he stabbed his meat.

Rory chuckled. "You have a way with the bairns, cousin. Mayhap Aileanna and I should take ourselves off fer a wee while and leave you to mind them."

"Doona even think about it. I'll no' be here fer long, I have to find my brother."

Rory's amusement faded. "Aye. If he was in the area, I'm certain we would've heard about it. Mayhap he decided to stay in London fer a while. Isna yer uncle—"

"Aye, I sent him a missive and await his reply."

Rory leaned back and nursed his mead. "Why doona we give it a week or so? He's probably makin' his way back. In the meantime, I'll write to some of my acquaintances and see what comes of it."

Aidan nodded, but he couldn't rid himself of the feeling that Laclan was in trouble.

A week later, they received two missives from his cousin's acquaintances and sequestered themselves in Rory's study to review the contents.

Aidan threw down the letter his cousin had grimly passed to him, and cursed. "We canna deny it any longer, Rory, something's amiss. We've searched everywhere within a two days' journey of Dunvegan and still there's no sign of him."

Rory blew out a frustrated breath. "'Tis like he's disappeared into thin air."

At his cousin's words, a horrifying revelation came to Aidan. The memory of Syrena disappearing before his very eyes caused him to jump to his feet. The chair clattered to the floor. "The Fae! I should've kent it. Bloody hell, I'll kill her if I ever get my hands on her."

"Aidan, calm yerself. Sit down. What do you mean the Fae? You canna tell me you actually believe in faeries. They doona exist, no' in our time. 'Tis simply the imaginin's of the old ones and bairns."

Aidan slumped in his chair and met his cousin's incredulous stare. "Believe me, I wish that was all it was, but 'tis no'." He scrubbed his hands over his face, ashamed of revealing his family's secret. But seeing no way around it, he told the sorry tale to the two men he'd trust with his life, leaving out as much about Syrena as he could.

An uncomfortable silence ensued then Rory asked, "Why did you never tell us this before?"

Aidan's harsh bark of laughter contained every ounce of bitterness reliving the tale had caused him. "'Tis no' somethin' one wants people to ken, Rory. My mother had an affair with a faery, my brother's half-Fae and talked to them when he was a bairn, and my father died trying to kill him. Nay, 'tis fodder fer the gossipmongers I'd rather they no' have."

"I understand that, Aidan, but ye're like a brother to me and Iain. You didna have to go through this alone."

Aidan met Fergus's sympathetic gaze. The older man laid a heavy hand on his shoulder. "The lad is right. You should've come to us."

"Well, now ye ken it all."

"Iain mentioned meeting a woman last year by the name of Syrena. Is she, by chance, the one you referred to as Lan's sister?"

Aidan lowered his gaze from his cousin's penetrating green eyes.

"I see," Rory murmured as though he saw far more than Aidan wanted him to.

His cousin and Fergus shared an assessing look. "There's only one thing we can do. We'll raise the faery flag. We have one wish left and we'll use it to get Lan back."

Aidan slammed his fist on the desk. "Nay, Rory, nay, I'll no' touch anythin' belongin' to them. I want nothin' to do with the Fae." He hung his head between his hands. Sweet Christ, the last thing he wanted to do was call upon the Fae for help. But if they had Lan, how else would he get his brother back?

Rory circled the desk. Removing several dusty tomes from the bookshelf, he opened a concealed compartment. He glanced at Fergus, then handed Aidan a piece of faded silk.

Aidan closed his hand around the fabric and nodded. "Aye." Rory was right. There were no other options available to him. He had to call on a people he reviled. A race that had destroyed his family and now was attempting to steal his brother from him. Would his suffering at the hands of the Fae never end?

With a heavy heart he followed the two men up the narrow

stone steps to the tower. A strong gust of wind ripped the latch from Rory's hand and the door slammed against the stone wall. A spattering of icy rain fell upon them. Lightning crackled in the night sky followed by a blast of thunder so fierce it rattled the stone beneath their feet. The lantern Fergus held swung back and forth, squeaking on its rusted hinges, its amber light cutting a swath through the inky blackness.

"Mayhap we should wait fer the weather to clear."

"Nay, you canna put it off, Aidan. Here, I'll help you," his cousin offered quietly.

The flag snapped in the wind, once, twice, three times. There was an explosive clap. Bright blues, yellows, and greens sparked and sputtered to life then a cloud of smoke engulfed them. The three of them choked, coughing on the thick acrid air. Aidan's eyes burned, and he rubbed them. When his vision cleared, the woman he thought never to see again stood before him.

"Syrena."

Chapter 13

Syrena rubbed her eyes. Only moments ago she'd fled the Seelie court. In her attempt to escape the barrage of questions from her stepmother and uncle, had she unwittingly used her magick? She had sought a moment of solitude to come up with answers that would incriminate no one but leave no doubt as to Evangeline's innocence.

If she had used her magick, she thought as a bitter wind pushed her against a hard surface, what Fae-forsaken place had she sent herself? Syrena batted at the smoky haze. One day, she vowed, her magick would work the way it was supposed to.

"Syrena." The deep, raspy voice with the thick brogue was unmistakable. A voice from her past, one she'd desperately tried to forget, but never could.

"Aidan," she whispered, helpless to still the excited beat of her heart.

The haze lifted. Amber light danced across the harsh planes of his beautiful face. A face that had haunted her dreams, but this was no dream. They stared at each other across the windblown parapet. The first to shake free from the shock, Aidan took a menacing step toward her, a feral grin slashing across his face.

There was no mistaking his intent. Every muscle coiled to pounce; he was like a creature stalking his prey. And from the way he looked at her, she had little doubt his intended prey was her. The images from the scrying mirror came quickly to mind, and she reached behind her to unsheathe Nuie.

The man she thought she loved no longer existed. In his place stood a stranger—a stranger who wanted her dead. The images her stepmother had once tormented her with came back to taunt her, but this time Syrena embraced them. She was a warrior. No longer would a man, Mortal or Fae, make her feel vulnerable.

"Don't come any closer," she warned. The wind whipped a lock of hair across her face, and she shoved it away.

Aidan barked a harsh laugh. "Do ye think to frighten me with yer wee sword?"

Nuie hummed. Shards of red emitted from between her fingers. Syrena heard a startled oath and for the first time noted the presence of two more men. The one standing directly behind Aidan was as big and dark as he was, with the same fierce expression upon his face. But the older man who stood a little to their right looked more curious than angry. She wondered if he at least could be made to see reason.

Despite the pain Aidan had caused her in the past, she didn't wish to kill him or his friends. She did her best, even in battle, to preserve life. Nuie could kill both Mortal and Fae with a single blow. But Uscias had taught her how to command him so the magick emitted at lower doses would wound, not kill.

The wind howled and rain lashed her gown to her body. Intent on remaining upright, her stance defensive, she barely made out the words Aidan yelled at her. "Where is he? Where is my brother?"

They moved closer, crowding her, towering above her. Their handsome faces carved into seething masks of rage.

She glanced at the older man. "If you value your friends' lives, call them back." But he made no move to stop them. With little more than a foot between them, Syrena acted quickly, commanding Nuie to full force. She gripped the rain-slicked hilt with both hands and swung at the base of the pole. There was a loud clang as metal met metal and sparks blistered the air. Nuie vibrated in her hand with the force of the blow. The pole smashed to the ground between them.

Aidan and his friend jumped back, their jaws dropped. She met the older man's startled gaze. "That was a warning. See they don't threaten me again."

A door creaked open and a sliver of light escaped before a beautiful woman with long, flaxen hair stepped onto the parapet. "Rory, what's going on out here? Oh . . ." She frowned upon seeing Syrena.

"Aileanna, get back inside. Now!" the man beside Aidan yelled.

The woman scowled. "I'm not going anywhere until you tell me what's going on. And don't you dare yell at me, Rory MacLeod."

The man heaved an exasperated sigh. "Aileanna, *mo chridhe,* 'tis dangerous. Go back inside. *Please.*"

She narrowed her gaze on him. "Nay, I'm not going anywhere. Not until you tell me where this woman came from and why you have her backed into a corner in the pouring rain?"

"Fer the love of God, woman, do you have to be so bloody stubborn? Get yer arse in the keep, now!"

The woman skirted his attempt to reach for her. Lifting her gown, she leaped over the pole. Syrena quickly muted Nuie's power when the woman placed herself between Syrena and the men.

"I don't know what's going on here, but I'm not going to stand by while the three of you threaten a defenseless woman."

"Defenseless? She's the one with the sword!"

Ignoring the man she called Rory, she looked over her shoulder at Syrena.

"I'm Aileanna MacLeod, and I apologize for my husband and his cousin's behavior."

Syrena couldn't help but smile at the woman who attempted to defend her. She reminded her of Fallyn. Aileanna

MacLeod would make a good warrior. "I'm Princess Syrena. And please, don't worry about me, I can look after myself. Besides, you're getting wet."

"So are you." She tilted her head. "Syrena, I wonder . . . Iain mentioned someone—"

"Enough! Aileanna, she's Fae and she's taken Lachlan. Now do as your husband says so I can deal with her," Aidan bellowed.

Syrena nudged Aileanna aside. "What are you talking about? I haven't taken Lachlan. I haven't seen him since—"

"Doona think ye can feed me yer lies. He's disappeared and I want him back."

She flinched in the face of his fury. If she had any doubts about his opinion of her, he'd just made his feelings abundantly clear. Rory placed a restraining hand on his shoulder.

Syrena ignored the ache in her heart. She didn't care how he felt about her—whatever feelings she once had for him no longer existed. Her stepmother was right. He was no different than Fae men. But her brother was another matter, and the fact he seemed to have disappeared worried her. She thought back to what King Gabriel had said about his missing men. But surely they had nothing to do with Lachlan; no one knew he was Fae. At least she didn't think anyone did.

Before Syrena had a chance to respond, Aileanna took matters into her own hands. Pushing her wet hair from her face, she said, "I'm freezing. We'll continue this inside." She took hold of Syrena's hand. "We'll get you into some dry clothing before you catch a chill."

"Aileanna, I doona think—"

"I'm well aware of that, Rory MacLeod. Now, go." She motioned them away with her hand. "Fergus, take Aidan with you. We'll meet in my solar shortly."

Aidan muttered something about Iain being right before he shot Syrena a malevolent glare. The older man none-too-gently ushered him to the door.

Syrena looked from Nuie to the broad backs of the three

men who tromped down the stone steps in front of them. They stood head and shoulders above her, and at least two of them looked like they wanted to strangle her. But she had a feeling the woman at her side wouldn't allow it and reached back to resheathe her sword. She didn't want to hurt anyone, although a part of her may have been tempted to maim Aidan, just a little. Let him feel a smidgen of what she'd felt when she'd seen her deer lying dead on the forest floor with his dagger buried to the hilt in her blood-stained fur. To have him suffer a portion of the devastating ache she'd endured every time Morgana forced her to look in the scrying mirror. To experience a single iota of the pain she'd suffered knowing how much he despised her for simply being Fae.

She hadn't realized she'd stopped walking until she felt Aileanna's intent gaze upon her. "Is something the matter?" Syrena asked.

"Nay." She tilted her head. "You're not what I expected."

Syrena quirked a brow.

"I mean . . . I thought a faery would be . . . well, taller, ethereal with . . . wings," she finished with a grimace.

Syrena barely managed to restrain her laughter. "No wings, but you're right, I am smaller then any of the Fae I know." She didn't feel the need to list her many other shortcomings in the eyes of the Fae, although these days none of her brethren seemed inclined to point them out.

"And the story that you steal babies isn't true either, is it?"

Syrena's eyes widened. "No, is that what they say about us?"

"Among other things, but don't worry, I prefer to form my own opinions. I consider myself a fairly good judge of people and you seem like a nice person, Syrena."

"Thank you, so do you." She smiled, relieved that Aileanna wasn't as judgmental as *some* members of her family. "You're very open-minded."

Aileanna laughed. "Well, if you knew anything about my past, you'd understand why." At her questioning look, she said, "I'll tell you some other time."

The men turned and glared at Aileanna. "Don't worry, I won't let them harm you," she said, a stubborn set to her chin.

"Thank you," Syrena murmured, descending the final step to the small enclosed landing.

The three men stood several feet ahead of them, about to descend another set of stairs. Aidan jerked from their hold and strode back to them with his cousin and Fergus on his heels. He filled the small dank space with his imposing bulk. Torchlight bounced off the stone walls to cast the hard lines of his face in a sinister glow. His gray eyes were glacial. As though he fought to restrain himself, his big hands balled into fists at his sides and muscles rippled beneath the wet white shirt that clung to him like a second skin.

"Doona think ye can escape. I'll get an answer from ye if it takes all night." He stood so close the heat of his breath fanned her cheek.

She lifted her chin, fighting to contain a shiver of unease. "I don't plan on going anywhere until I find out what you've done to my brother." As if she could go anywhere, the portals to the Enchanted realm would now be closed. But she told him the truth. Until she knew what had happened to Lachlan, she would not leave. "But just so you know, if I wanted to, *you* couldn't stop me."

Fury darkened his eyes, and she reached back to unsheathe Nuie. Aileanna inserted herself between them, placing her hands on his chest. "Rory, Fergus," she snapped. "Get Aidan out of here."

Rory slanted a furious look in his wife's direction before he jerked Aidan away, shoving him toward their companion. Wagging his finger at Aileanna, Rory said, "I'm no' verra happy with you at the moment. Once we have this matter taken care of, you and I have a few things to discuss."

"Aye, we do, and you'd best keep your voices down before you wake the boys."

He included Syrena in his disapproving grunt before he stomped after Aidan and Fergus.

"Men," Aileanna harrumphed. Taking Syrena by the hand, she led her along a dimly lit corridor, past the staircase the men had descended. A loud crash echoed from below, and the men's voices rose in anger. "I should've locked them in the tower until they had their tempers under control. If Jamie and Alex wake up, I'll never get them back to sleep."

"I'm sorry, Aileanna, it's my fault."

Syrena bumped into the other woman when she came to an abrupt halt. Aileanna turned to look at her, her brow furrowed. "Why? Did you take Lan?"

"No, of course not, I—"

With a relieved smile, she said, "Thank goodness. I wouldn't have wanted to hand you over to Aidan. I've never seen him so angry."

Syrena stood a little taller, a belligerent tilt to her head. "I can handle him if I have to."

Aileanna's lips twitched, and she patted her shoulder. "I'm sure you can, but it won't be necessary." She opened a heavy wooden door and nudged Syrena inside. "Don't worry, we'll get this all straightened out. We'll find Lan." While Aileanna attempted to light a fire in the stone hearth, she glanced over her shoulder at Syrena. "You said Lachlan was your brother, but I never heard mention of Aidan and Lan having a sister."

Syrena's cheeks flushed. "I'm Lan's sister, not Aidan's."

"Oh . . . oh, I see." She cleared her throat then came to her feet. "I've never been able to light a fire, and I'll be damned if I'll call Rory to light it for us. Wrap yourself up in that blanket and I'll bring you some dry clothes," she said, pointing to a thick brown woolen blanket at the foot of the large four-poster bed.

Before she left the room, Syrena asked, "Aileanna, how did I come to be here?"

The woman stopped, closing the door she'd just opened and leaning against it. "The faery flag," she murmured. After a slowly released breath, Aileanna said, "It's how I came to be at Dunvegan."

She came to sit beside Syrena on the edge of the bed. "I'm from the twenty-first century. I was a physician in my time and was here on Skye, in the castle, when Iain raised the faery flag in the year 1598. Rory was badly wounded in a battle and Iain was terrified he was going to die so the flag was their last hope. And . . . well, thanks to the faeries, here I am." She smiled.

"You didn't wish to go back to your own time?"

Aileanna laughed. "Oh, yes, I did in the beginning. But then I fell in love with Rory and got my happily ever after." She came to her feet and patted Syrena's shoulder. "Don't worry, I'm sure everything will work out for you, too. Was it your family who gave the MacLeods the flag?"

"No. I've heard it said that it was Tatianna."

"Does she live where you do?"

"No, she and her brethren were killed a long time ago." Knowing Evangeline's mother had been directly responsible for the deaths made it uncomfortable for Syrena to speak about. She felt as though she somehow betrayed her friend when she did.

"I see," Aileanna said slowly, but before she could say anything further, someone pounded on the door and she rolled her eyes. "I did say happily ever after, didn't I?"

Aidan glared across the room at his cousin's wife, who sat with a protective arm wrapped around Syrena's shoulders. If they would give him but a few minutes alone with the lying, deceitful wench, he'd get the truth from her. He didn't care how innocent she looked with her wide-eyed topaz gaze in her exquisite face, tendrils of damp hair curling provocatively over her shoulder.

No matter what she said, she couldn't be trusted. And Rory and Fergus were daft to think she could be. If they told him to calm himself one more time, he was going to beat them to a bloody pulp. Mayhap he should—at the least it would relieve some of his pent-up fury. Release some of the anger that the damn faery flag had brought *her*, the one person he'd hoped never to see again.

She raised her golden gaze to his and he silently cursed, wondering how her resemblance to his brother had escaped him. He'd been so bloody enchanted by her bonny looks and sweet nature he'd failed to note anything else but that.

"What did you do to Lachlan to make him run away?"

"Me?" he roared. "Ye have a lot of nerve tryin' to pin this on me."

"Don't you yell at her, Aidan MacLeod," Aileanna said fiercely.

Rory sighed, gesturing for his wife to calm herself. "Aidan, can you keep it down lest you wake the bairns. We seem to be goin' around in circles with the two of you blamin' each other, but 'tis no' doin' Lan a bit of good. The hour grows late, why doona we sleep on this and mayhap on the morrow things will appear clearer?"

"Nay, I doona care if we have to stay up all night. I'm goin' to get the truth from her."

"You're wasting your time. I keep trying to tell you, I haven't seen my brother in more than a year."

"And why should I believe ye? 'Tis in yer nature to lie. 'Tis what ye did from the first time I laid eyes on ye."

Her wee hands balled into fists on her lap, and not for the first time Aidan wondered how Aileanna had convinced her to part with her golden sword. "I never lied to Lachlan."

"Nay, but ye lied to me. 'I canna remember my kin,'" he mimicked. "'The Lowlanders took me.'"

"I never said that, you did," she snapped.

"But ye didna deny it. Men could've died on account of yer lie but that wouldna bothered ye. All ye Fae are a murderous bunch."

She sprang to her feet and strode toward him, her eyes flashing. "Don't cast aspersions on my race, Mortal! You don't have any idea of what you speak. The only reason I kept my identity a secret was because Lachlan told me you would want me dead."

"Aye, I would have. That's the first truthful thing to come out of yer mouth this night." He steeled himself against the wounded expression that crossed her delicate features.

She looked like he'd slapped her. He slammed down a pang of regret that he'd hurt her. Pushed aside the memory of her in his arms, the soft innocence of her lips pressed to his, the feel of her lush curves molded to his body. Reminding himself again that, if not for her, Lan wouldn't be missing. If not for her, the last words he'd spoken to his brother would not have been said in anger. His relationship with Lachlan hadn't been the same since that long-ago day in the woods, and he blamed her for that.

Rory, Fergus, and Aileanna looked at him in shocked disbelief. He scowled at Syrena. It was all her fault. They couldn't see past the innocence of her looks to who she truly was. At that moment, he realized he had to change tactics or she'd turn his family against him. Or worse, she'd disappear again, leaving him with no hope of finding his brother.

No matter what the others thought, he knew the Fae were behind Lan's disappearance. If he wanted to get his brother back, he had to use another method to find his answers. Anger and threats had little effect on the woman standing before him. But he'd turn the tables on her, lull her into complacency. Manipulation and seduction were stock in trade for women like her, like his mother, like Davina—see how she liked it when they were used against her.

His teeth clenched so tight he was surprised he managed to get the words out. "I'm sorry, Syrena, that was uncalled fer. My only excuse is I'm worried about Lan."

Rory's and Fergus's gazes narrowed with suspicion. Syrena blinked. Her eyes searched his, and then she nodded, a tentative smile touching her pink lips.

Chapter 14

Syrena opened one eye then the other. Two little boys, their chins propped on their hands, lay on the big four-poster bed regarding her with interest. With one pair of eyes as blue as the sky in the Enchanted Isles, the other's leaf green, it was easy to guess who their parents were.

"Good morning," she croaked, reaching to prop the down-filled pillows behind her back and make sure Nuie was safely concealed beneath them. Stifling a yawn, she rubbed her gritty eyes. She'd be surprised if she'd managed a solid hour of sleep, tossing and turning when her attempts to reach Lan in her mind proved futile. But it was the images of Aidan from the night before, towering above her, his beautiful face a frightening caricature of itself as he chased her through her dreams. The ferocity of his anger suffocated her beneath a heavy blanket of fear and despair.

"Good morrow," said the fair-haired boy with an impish grin. "Mama told us ye're a princess from a far-off land come to visit."

"I am, but you can call me Syrena. And who are you?"

"Jamie, I'm the biggest, and this is my brother Alex," he said, jerking his thumb at the dark-haired boy who lay quietly beside him.

"We're goin' to protect you from the monster," Alex whispered with a furtive glance over his shoulder.

Syrena bit back a smile, entranced by their sweet cherub faces. She hadn't spent much time with the children of the Enchanted Isles of late, and she'd missed them. Their sweet scent, the innocent way they looked at the world, and their willingness to give their love even when it was not deserved. She thought back to her long-ago conversations with Lachlan and swallowed a lump in her throat. Not much older than these two, his childlike prattle and innocent giggles had been overshadowed by his underlying fear and sorrow.

"Thank you. Is it a very big monster?"

They both nodded. "Aye, verra big," Jamie said. Puffing out his narrow chest, he tugged a wooden sword from beneath him and Alex did the same. "But we bested him the other day. If our da hadna come along, he'd no' be botherin' ye."

She winced when the two of them began to bang their swords together in mock battle. Rising to their feet, they bounced up and down, giggling uproariously.

"Be careful now." She managed to grab hold of Alex before he toppled to the floor. "Jamie, watch out!" she cried when he clutched the bed curtain for support, pulling it down on top of her. Tugging the swath of red velvet from her head, she looked up to see Aileanna standing at the foot of the bed, hands on her hips, lips pursed. Aileanna cleared her throat, loudly, and her sons landed with a whoosh on the bed, scrambling to hide their swords beneath the bedding.

Jamie's sword poked her sharply in the leg and she stifled a groan.

Aileanna wiggled her fingers. "Give me your wee swords."

"But, Mam . . ." Jamie whined.

Alex glanced from his mother to his brother before quietly retrieving his sword and handing it over. Jamie scowled at him, making a grand show of searching for his. He held up his hands and shrugged. "I canna find it."

Aileanna folded her arms, her foot tapping impatiently on the slate floor.

"But, Mam, Da said we could play with them, and we promised the princess we would protect her from the monster."

His mother blew out an exasperated breath. "Jamie MacLeod, there is no monster. Besides, Syrena has her own sword. She's well able to protect herself."

Jamie giggled, shaking his blond head at his mother. "Mam, ye're silly, lasses doona carry swords. They have the men to look after them."

"You've obviously been spending too much time with your father," Aileanna commented dryly. "Show him your sword, Syrena."

She hesitated, but at Aileanna's insistent nod, she reached behind her and withdrew Nuie from beneath the mound of pillows, running her hand over the hilt to satisfy herself his power was muted. She suppressed a smile at the sight of the boys' wide-eyed wonder.

Jamie and Alex tentatively touched the shimmering stones. "A golden sword, 'tis verra pretty," Jamie said in a voice tinged with awe.

She laughed when her sword glowed red between their chubby fingers. "I don't think Nuie likes to be called pretty. He's a boy sword. Why don't you tell him he's . . . hmmm . . . magnificent."

"Ye're mag . . . magnificent," Alex said, stumbling over the word.

Shards of yellow light caused Nuie to glisten. "There, he likes that."

"He's magick!" Jamie exclaimed.

Syrena grimaced. "Sorry," she apologized to Aileanna.

"Why? My sons can keep a secret. Can't you, Jamie, Alex?"

"Aye, we willna tell anyone, especially the monster. Then you can surprise him and knock him on his arse," Jamie pronounced, bouncing excitedly on the bed.

Alex's mouth dropped and he looked at his mother.

Syrena bit the inside of her cheek to keep from laughing.

"Jamie, what have I told you about using bad language?"

"But Da—"

"Oh, don't you worry, I know what your da says, and next time I'll wash *both* of your mouths out with soap. Come, let's leave Syrena be. She'll want to get dressed and break her fast."

Jamie retrieved his sword, all the while giggling with his brother, obviously imagining their warrior father with a mouthful of bubbles.

At the children's laughter, a familiar ache bloomed in Syrena's chest. Aileanna was blessed. She had everything Syrena longed for but would never have. There had been only one man she had thought to give her heart, and her body, to— Aidan—but he didn't want anything to do with her. Not now, not ever. She assured herself it was for the best. She didn't want him either.

"Join us in the hall, whenever you're ready, Syrena. The men have gone off to train in the glen so all will be quiet. I left some gowns in the wardrobe for you to choose from."

Not sure of Aileanna's reaction, Syrena hesitated before asking, "If it's no trouble, would you have some breeches and boots I could borrow instead? I'd like to train with the men and a gown . . ."

The three of them stared at her, mouths agape. Aileanna was the first to recover. A slow smile curved her lips. "If that's what you'd like, I'm sure Connor has something that will fit you."

Syrena was determined to show Aidan she had changed and thought battling him in the field would be the best way to do so. He would see then that he could not take her for granted, use her weakness against her.

Alex and Jamie followed on Aileanna and Syrena's heels as they walked along a well-worn path through the tall grass of the meadow. "Do you do this often, Syrena, train with the men?"

"I train every day, but not with men. Only women fight in my army."

Coming to a dead stop, Aileanna grabbed her arm, causing the boys to bump into their legs. "Women . . . army, are you telling me you lead a group of women and you actually fight?"

"Yes, but we've only been in two battles to date."

"Did you win?"

"Yes."

"So you're good?"

"I suppose so." She smiled at Aileanna's gleeful expression.

"You know, Syrena, the most difficult thing I've had to overcome since coming to this time is my abhorrence of violence. But I've learned in some situations there is no other way. And right now, I have to tell you, I can't wait to see the look on those men's faces when you step onto the field. I've never met a more arrogant, chauvinistic bunch as this lot."

Syrena chuckled. "I hope I don't disappoint you."

Aileanna looked her over. "Somehow, I don't think you will."

As they passed through a stand of pines into a wide-open field, they heard the metallic clang of steel against steel. At least forty men were paired off, grunting and groaning with their exertions. Despite a cool breeze, most had shed their shirts, and seemingly of their own accord, her eyes sought Aidan. He was not difficult to spot standing head and shoulders above most of the men, except the one he battled. She tried not to stare at Aidan's sun-bronzed skin, the way his muscles rippled along his arms and back as he parried with his cousin.

"Sweet Christ, Rory, I could've sliced ye in two droppin' yer guard as ye did. And ye're tellin' me I'm no' in shape.

What are ye . . ." He followed his cousin's incredulous gaze and glanced over his shoulder.

His mouth went dry.

Syrena, dressed in form-fitting trews and a white tunic that left little to the imagination, stood in the field alongside Aileanna. The wee demons tugged on her hand to tell her something, then pointed in his direction. Whatever they said set the women off, their silvery peals of laughter drawing the attention of the other men on the field.

"Bloody hell, what are they doin' here?"

Rory bent down and grabbed his tunic from the ground. "I'll find out." He shot Aidan a warning look.

Aidan had shared with them how he planned to get the truth from Syrena. Neither his cousin nor Fergus had been overly impressed. More to the point, they'd heartily disapproved. But he knew it had nothing to do with them believing she was innocent, she'd simply enchanted them as she had him. But he was immune to her charms now. He knew who she was, what she was.

His blood boiled, and he had to school his features to ensure no one knew what was going on in his head, especially her. He tried to ignore the loudly whispered comments of the men, who'd stopped to see who interrupted their training. Their admiring perusal of Syrena was more difficult to ignore. Aidan convinced himself the urge to pummel every last one of them had naught to do with jealousy and everything to do with his anger. Anger at having to face the woman behind his brother's disappearance and pretend he didn't despise her, want to throttle her with his bare hands.

Upon reaching his wife, Rory pulled her protesting into his sweaty embrace, paying no mind to the gagging noises the wee demons were making. For the first time, Aidan found himself agreeing with the bairns. His cousin and his wife were nauseating.

Rory pulled back from Aileanna, whatever she said causing

him to glance in Aidan's direction. Shrugging, he yelled, "Aidan, Syrena's takin' my place."

He hung his head, cursing Rory under his breath. Aileanna had turned his cousin's brain to mush, 'twas the only explanation. Madness, that's what it was, expecting him to fight a woman the size of a wee lad. A woman!

Aye, and there she was, walking toward him as though she didn't have a care in the world. She reached back, capturing long golden locks that swirled around her too bonny face. The tunic molded to her full breasts as she raised her arms to confine the silky curls in a thong. Nay, there'd be no mistaking her fer a lad.

His hand tightened convulsively on the hilt of his sword. *Fae*, he reminded himself, *she's Fae*.

She came to a stop, leaving several feet between them, and withdrew her sword. He shook his head. "I doona ken what ye're playin' at, Syrena, but I'll no' fight a—"

Clang.

Her sword struck his in a powerful blow.

"I'm no' goin' to fight—"

Clang.

"Bloody hell, are ye usin' yer magick?"

She laughed. "No, even if I wanted to, I couldn't."

He didn't have the chance to consider what she said as her next blow nearly wrenched his sword from his hand.

Muscles straining, his body reacted as though they'd battled for hours. Sweat beaded on his forehead. Winded, his harsh breath burned in his chest, his throat. The bloody wench was fast. She struck with deadly accuracy, and he wondered what had happened to the wee lass who'd been afraid of a cat. Her face shone, and not with sweat. She was barely winded. Aidan glared at her. He'd had enough. No more holding back, he'd end it now.

Going after her with all he had, his sword whistled as it sliced through the crisp autumn air. He struck hard and fast. She parried each of his blows. As though sensing the battle between them had turned serious, a deathly quiet fell over the field, the only sound the thunderous clash of their swords.

He was heartened to hear her breath come out in short, harsh rasps. Her bonny face was a study in concentration, finely honed muscles taut beneath the flimsy sweat-dampened tunic that molded to her lush curves. It was all it took. That one lapse in his concentration proved his downfall.

Sweeping past his defense, her blade slashed his chest. Blood oozed from the burning wound.

Cursing, he met her gaze with his own. Color leeched from her face. She dropped her hands to her sides, leaving herself undefended, open to his retaliation.

"I'm sorry. I didn't mean to . . ." Her voice was husky, thick with regret.

He waved off her apology. "'Tis naught but a scratch, I've received worse from Connor." He jerked his chin in the direction of the lean, lanky lad standing alongside Fergus. It was a lie. No one other than Rory had ever bested him. "'Tis what I get fer no' bein' in shape. I've let my trainin' slide of late."

She gave him a tight nod before she bent down to retrieve his tunic. He wasn't sure if she believed him or not. Worrying her full bottom lip between her teeth, she handed it to him.

"You should let Aileanna see to your wound," she suggested quietly.

He sighed. "'Tis nothin'." Remembering his plan, he grudgingly added, "You handle a sword well . . . fer a woman."

She slanted him a look as they walked from the field, shaking her head. "And you fight well . . . for a man out of practice."

Before he shot back a caustic retort, his cousin slapped him on the back, grinning like a fool. "Never did I think to see the day you'd be bested by a woman." Aidan glanced at Syrena, but she was too busy accepting Aileanna and the demons' hearty congratulations to notice. "Ye tired me out, is all. Next time ye can fight her and we'll see how well ye fare."

Rory laughed. "Nay, I'm no' daft. Aileanna tells me she

leads a band of warrior women and they train daily. If they all handle a blade as well as Syrena, I don't doubt they win more than they lose."

Aidan snorted, finding it difficult to believe the Fae men allowed their women to play at war. Especially Syrena's husband, the one he'd fought that day in the woods. He dragged his hand through his damp hair. Even now, feeling about her as he did, he could not control a flare of jealousy that she was another man's wife.

He shrugged into his tunic, meeting her worried gaze over the top of the snowy white fabric. "What?" he grumbled.

She waved her hand at his chest. "Let Aileanna see to your wound," she said as she reached behind her to sheathe her sword. Aidan, unable to take his gaze from her full breasts straining against the fabric, didn't respond. His cousin nudged him.

"Don't worry, Syrena, I'll see to him when we get back to the keep whether he wants me to or not," Aileanna promised with a determined look in her eyes.

"Mama, the monst . . . Uncle Aidan has blood on his tunic. Is he goin' to die?"

Aidan scowled at Jamie. The wee demon seemed delighted at the possibility, and Syrena shot a panicked look in his direction. He'd been made enough of a fool of for one day. The last thing he needed was two women fussing over a wee scratch in front of the men. He strode toward the keep, the thought of Syrena's hands upon his heated flesh causing him to quicken his pace.

An uncomfortable certainty that the concern in her eyes had not been an act grated on his conscience, but he reminded himself she was not to be trusted. He'd made that mistake before and look where it got him.

He didn't get far before he heard someone coming up from behind him. "Aidan, hold up a moment," Syrena called to him.

Cursing under his breath, he turned to look at her. The anger that warred inside him must have shown on his face as her eyes widened and her step faltered. "What do ye want, Syrena?" He reined in his temper in an effort to keep his voice even.

"I . . . I just wanted to know when we would be leaving to look for Lan."

The woman should be on the stage. "I'm expectin' a letter from my uncle any day now. Once it arrives, I'll have a better idea as to Lan's whereabouts."

"Do you not think we should head directly to London instead of wasting our time here?" She kept pace with him, smiling when the bairns ran past screaming like a pair of banshees.

Certain no one had said anything about his brother being in London, Aidan clenched his hands, resisting the urge to shake the truth from her. He couldn't let her think he retained his suspicions. She'd slipped up, and if he remained patient, he'd soon discover where she'd taken his brother.

"Who said anything about Lachlan bein' in London?"

"I . . . I thought you did, but maybe I was mistaken and it was Aileanna." She bowed her head, and he noted her flushed cheeks.

Liar. He swallowed hard, his control unraveling with each deceitful word she uttered. "'Tis a possibility we've considered, but until we ken fer certain, 'tis best to remain at Dunvegan."

"But I think—"

"What, Syrena, what do ye think?" No matter how hard he tried, he was unable to keep the desperation from his voice.

Her eyes shot to his. "I told you, I don't know where he is. I wish I did."

Jamie tore through the trees and he jerked his gaze from hers. Tears tracked down the bairn's dirt-smudged cheeks, and his mouth worked soundlessly. "Jamie, lad." Aidan crouched in front of him. "What's the matter?"

His wee face ghostly pale, he pointed to the woods behind him. "Alex," he whimpered.

Syrena knelt beside the lad, drawing him into her arms. Her worried gaze met Aidan's. He unsheathed his sword and raced in the direction he'd last seen the bairns headed. A thunderous crash reverberated through the woods, setting off a riotous twittering from the birds as they flew from the tops of the trees to form an undulating black cloud.

Rory ran up behind him and they followed the sound. Moments later, they came upon a stag tearing the bark from a tree with its antlers. Aidan had never seen a buck as big or as enraged. And less than a foot from the beast, Alex lay on the ground.

Aidan grabbed his cousin's arm. If Rory went off half-cocked, he'd risk not only his own life, but his son's as well. Shaking his head, Aidan silently mouthed and gestured his instructions. He'd distract the stag, get it to come after him so Rory could safely retrieve Alex. Aidan shoved down the fear that they were already too late.

Rory nodded. Aidan took off in the opposite direction, making as much noise as he could. Over and over again, he slammed his sword against the base of an ancient oak. The stag tossed his massive head then swung his incensed gaze to Aidan. Pawing the ground, he charged.

"Aye, come on, ye big bastard." He lifted his sword. "That's it, just a little further, come on, come on." Intending on using the tree as a shield, Aidan took several steps to his right, cursing when his foot got tangled in the exposed roots of the tree.

Thrown off balance, he landed with a heavy thud. The ground vibrated beneath him as the beast bore down upon him. Struggling to untangle his foot, the animal was so close he could see the whites of its eyes. Cold sweat trickled down Aidan's spine. He could do little more than raise his sword and pray.

Thunk.

The rampaging beast crumpled to the ground. The tip of its antler brushed the sole of Aidan's boot. He blinked at the golden sword buried to its jeweled hilt in the stag's side.

Chapter 15

The sickly metallic scent of death permeated the air. Blood seeped in a relentless flow from the animal's ripped flesh to pool beneath it. Syrena staggered under the weight of her memories, the image of her deer lying dead at Aidan's feet. Her anguished gaze collided with his. A shadow darkened his gray eyes and she wondered if, like her, his thoughts had returned to that day in the pine-scented wood when he'd slaughtered her deer and crushed her heart.

A familiar ache tightened in her chest. Determined not to allow the moisture pooling in her eyes to escape, she squeezed them closed. Her deer and her love for Aidan had died a long time ago. This animal was nothing like her innocent pet. The enormous beast had hurt a child she cared about, and had come close to killing Aidan. Regardless of her feelings for the man, she couldn't have allowed that to happen.

"Thank ye, Syrena." The deep timbre of Aidan's voice drew her from the dark depths of her memories. Grabbing hold of a branch, he drew himself to his feet. All the while he watched her, as though concerned for her well-being, but why would he be? He had made no secret he thought she was behind Lachlan's disappearance. Despite his recent attempt to pretend otherwise, he couldn't fool her. Adept at hiding her feelings, she was well able to recognize when another attempted to do so.

At the sound of heavy footfalls coming their way, Aidan drew his gaze from hers. Fergus and the boy Connor walked toward them. They looked from Syrena and Aidan to the dead animal, and their eyes widened.

Fergus scrubbed his auburn whiskers. "Neither of you were hurt?"

"Nay. Alex?" Although Aidan pretended indifference to the children, his worry over the little boy's condition was plain to see.

"It doesna' appear as though the buck touched him. Aileanna thinks he fell and hit his head. He's awake now. They've taken him back to the keep."

Aidan released a heavy breath then nodded. "Good to hear."

"I doona think I've ever seen a buck as big as this one." Fergus thumped Connor on the back. "We've got our work cut out fer us, lad."

"Are ye goin' to butcher him here?" Aidan asked, eyeing the animal.

"Aye, I'm no' goin' to try and drag a beast the size of this one out of here."

Syrena swallowed the bile that rose in her throat. She may not feel remorse for killing the animal, but that didn't mean she wanted to stand by and see it butchered. In her hurry to get away, the soft soles of her boots slid on a mound of pine needles, and she stumbled. Aidan grabbed hold of her arm before she fell.

His gaze searched her face. "Go back to the keep, Syrena. I'll bring ye yer sword."

Considering how he felt about her, she didn't trust him with Nuie. No matter how hard it would be for her to retrieve her sword from the gaping wound, she said, "No, I will get—"

He muttered something under his breath and strode to the animal. Fergus quirked a bushy auburn brow then stepped aside. Realizing what Aidan meant to do, Syrena quickly turned away. They talked quietly behind her then Aidan returned to her side.

He placed his big hand at the small of her back. The warmth

from his palm penetrated the sheer fabric of her shirt. She was surprised he still had the power to ease her distress, make her feel protected simply by touching her. It was not a discovery that pleased her, and she stepped away from him.

"Come, I'll walk ye back."

"Thank you, but I can manage on my own." She glanced down and noted he carried both swords in his left hand. She reached for Nuie, grateful he'd thought to wipe the blade clean.

His lips set in a grim line, he handed her back her sword. "Nay, start walkin'."

She huffed an exasperated breath. She needed to put some distance between them. "You obviously don't believe me, Aidan, but I am as concerned for Lachlan's well-being as you are. I'm not going to run away."

Raising a dark brow, he looked down at her. "Run? Nay, I didna think ye'd run. Use yer magick and disappear mayhap—that I did consider."

She sighed. "I can't do magick. Well . . . I can, but I'm not very good at it."

He looked startled by her admission. Taking hold of her arm, he forced her to stop walking. "Why?"

With his body so close to hers, his familiar scent overwhelmed her senses. It took a moment before she was able to answer him, "I'm not certain. Although when I was a child, some said I had been cursed, or that an illness had stolen my powers. My mother protected me from those that feared the sickness, the ones that called for my death. She said I was simply a late bloomer, and spent hours working with me until we perfected a charade wherein she would do the magick but all would believe it was me."

She smiled at the memory. No one had ever made her feel as loved or as cherished as her mother. She slanted a sidelong glance at the man standing deep in thought beside her. That wasn't completely true. There was a time when he had.

With a dismissive shrug, as though the dull ache radiating from her heart didn't matter, she continued, "A year later, when I was called before the council to prove my abilities, no one doubted I could do magick. My mother and I continued the charade until she . . . fade . . . faded." Syrena stumbled over the word.

Even after all these years it was difficult to believe her mother had left her. Syrena's grief was as strong now as it had been on the day her father had cruelly informed her of her mother's passing, leaving little doubt he blamed her for Helyna's death. To this day, she didn't understand what she'd done wrong. Why her mother would have taken her life.

"Evangeline, my handmaiden, took my mother's place. But then she left me, too." Syrena hadn't meant for it to sound as pitiful as it did. She didn't blame Evangeline, understood why she had to abandon her, but it didn't make it any less painful.

"Who protects ye now?"

She blinked, startled by the harsh edge in his gruff voice. "My friend Fallyn and her sisters, but I really don't need protection anymore. I can take care of myself."

"Aye, I'd forgotten. Ye're a warrior now."

He mocked her with his words, yet his tone was somehow gentle and it pricked her pride. "Yes, I am."

Rubbing a hand along the dark stubble of his jaw, he said, "So, ye didna use magick when ye fought me."

"No, I already told you that. Besides, I didn't need to." Maybe that would wipe the arrogant look from his face.

"I admit ye're skilled with a sword, Syrena, but if ye canna kill a buck without near faintin', ye canna expect me to believe ye could kill a mon."

Her temper simmered just below the surface, and she glared up at him. "I don't condone violence. I avoid killing whenever I can, but that doesn't make me any less a warrior than you. But just so you know, I have killed before, and my reaction had nothing to do with killing that creature."

Rising up on the tips of her toes, she stabbed her finger in his chest. "I was thinking about my deer if you must know— a poor innocent creature that you slaughtered because she meant something to me! Because you found out who I was and hated me so much you took it out on her!" The torrent of words rushed from her. She welcomed the release, the chance to confront him.

Before she could contain them, hot tears burned a path down her cheeks. He lifted his hand then jerked it away. "Nay, 'twas an accident, Syrena. I meant to wound Magnus, to stop him from takin' ye from m . . . to stop him from takin' ye." He clenched and unclenched his hands. "I didna see the doe. She was behind ye, and then ye disappeared and . . ."

As though she were there, she remembered the shuffling sound behind her, the gentle nudge of her deer's warm wet nose against her hand just before Magnus transported her from the woods. Aidan spoke the truth, but it was difficult for her to hear. She'd used the murder of her pet as proof he wasn't worthy of her love. That a man who could harm an innocent creature out of vengeance had no place in her heart, that he wasn't the man she thought him to be. Now that she knew the truth, the walls she'd built around her heart started to crumble. Her vulnerability frightened her.

"Speakin' of yer husband, should we be expectin' him to come to yer rescue?"

"Husband? Why would you think I married Magnus?"

His brow furrowed, and an emotion she couldn't deduce flickered in his eyes. "He said ye were his betrothed."

"I refused his suit."

He quirked a brow as though he didn't believe her. "He didna appear to be someone who would take rejection well."

"He didn't. He led an army against us. It was my first battle," she admitted. They'd been lucky that in his arrogance Magnus had not felt it necessary to bring a full contingent of warriors. With the odds ten to one in Syrena's favor, the battle had not been as deadly as it might have been.

Guilt niggled at the back of her mind when she recalled the beating Aidan had received at Magnus's hand. The memory of his bruised and battered body still had the power to make her stomach turn. "I'm sorry you suffered because of me, Aidan. I never meant for you to be hurt."

Whatever warmth she'd thought she'd seen in his eyes vanished. "Ye think I suffered on account of ye, Syrena? Nay, I would've had to feel somethin' fer ye fer that to happen. Believe me, the only thing I felt was relief to have ye out of our lives fer good. Yet here ye stand." His full upper lip curled in contempt.

She willed away the sharp stab of pain that cut through her at his words. He said nothing she didn't already know. The earlier concern she thought she'd seen in his eyes must have been nothing more than pity. "Thank you, it's always best to know where one stands with one's enemy. But just so you are aware, my apology was for the beating you received at Magnus's hands, nothing more. Believe *me*, this is the last place I want to be, and the sooner we find Lachlan, the better."

"At last, something we agree upon. So why doona ye just return him to me, then?"

She gritted her teeth. "Because. I. Don't. Have. Him! How often must I repeat myself before it penetrates your thick skull?"

"Let that be a lesson to ye, Syrena, 'tis difficult to trust a liar. But I suppose ye canna help yerself. Ye're Fae, after all."

"And you are a foolish Mortal! You know nothing about my people to make such a statement. Your irrational hatred of the Fae is going to get *my* brother killed!" Furious, she pivoted on her heel, then shot contemptuously over her shoulder, "A brother, who need I remind you, is half-Fae!"

The man was infuriating. She didn't need him. She'd find Lan on her own. How could her brother bear to live with a man who so obviously hated a part of who he was? After that day in the woods, she'd given up her father's quest. But she'd never given up on Lachlan, never stopped loving him or wanting him in her life. And now she was more certain than ever he'd be happier with her than with his beast of a brother.

At the thought of bringing Lachlan back to the Enchanted Isles to live with her, she smiled. But her bubble of optimism quickly burst when a vision of her stepmother came to mind.

And it was not only Morgana she would have to contend with, but all the women of the Isles. Lachlan's presence in the Enchanted realm would not be well received. As Syrena considered the plight of the men that remained in the Isles, she realized Morgana had gone too far, and once she returned with Lan, changes would need to be made.

Aidan slowed his pace as he neared the dais. Syrena sat between the bairns, the two of them vying for her attention while their parents looked on with amusement. Bloody hell, what was wrong with his family that they embraced the woman so easily? She was Fae, and if that wasn't enough, she was behind his brother's disappearance. No one could convince him otherwise, no matter how hard they tried.

He'd questioned Fergus, Rory, and Aileanna, and none of them had made mention to Syrena of their suspicions that Lan had gone missing in London. Yet that was the exact location *she* had thought they should search for him, and it was all the proof he needed.

The accusations she'd hurled at him as she walked away still rang in his head, and he fought the urge to confront her. Who did she think she was to comment on his feelings for his brother? She wasn't the one who'd spent the better part of her life protecting him.

He winced when he pulled out the chair between Fergus and Alex, the wound in his chest protesting the movement. He greeted Fergus then turned his attention to the bairn at his left. "Ye made a quick recovery, Alex, ye're a true MacLeod." The lad was a bit peaked, but otherwise looked none the worse for wear.

"Princess Syrena saved me," the bairn sighed, regaining some of his color as he beamed at his savior. A savior who looked every inch the princess in a pale blue gown shot through with silver.

Aidan bristled. "Well, ye ken, Alex, I did play a part in yer rescue." He felt the need to point that out.

Farther down the table he heard Rory snort before his cousin added, "Aye, Alex, yer Uncle Aidan drew the buck from you. 'Twas him Syrena saved."

Oh, aye, she'd not only beat him on the field, she had to go and rescue him as well. If not for Lan, he'd have tossed her out on her bonny arse.

His nemesis brought the goblet to her lips, but Aidan didn't miss the amused smile she attempted to hide. He scowled at her, but she paid him no mind. He wished he could say the same for the bairns. Jamie, catching his expression, drew his wee sword out from under the table and waved it in Aidan's direction, gesturing for his brother to do the same. Alex hesitated before brandishing his weapon.

Aidan rolled his eyes and lightly tapped Alex's sword away from his head.

"Jamie, Alex put those down," Aileanna said, her chair scraped along the floor as she came to retrieve their weapons. "I told you I didn't want you playing with these things. Who pray tell gave them back to you?"

They pointed at their father, who glowered at them before he gave his attention to his unhappy wife. "Now, Aileanna, they're nothin' but playthings. No call fer you to get fashed." Rory's attempt to placate his wife didn't appear to be having the desired effect.

She handed the swords to Mrs. Mac, who regarded Rory with the same look of disdain as his wife. Aidan leaned back in his chair, enjoying watching his cousin squirm. 'Twas about time someone took the heat off him.

Rory threw his hands in the air. "Fine, I'll no' let them have a sword until they're eighteen. Are you satisfied now?"

"But, Da, we're protectin' the princess from the monster," Jamie whined.

With an amused glimmer in her topaz eyes, Syrena said, "Don't worry, Jamie, I think I can handle him."

Aidan tossed back his ale. *Ha, that's what she thinks!*

While the meal was being served, Aidan listened to Fergus

speak of his and Connor's troubles butchering the buck. But Aidan found his attention straying, too interested in Syrena's interactions with the bairns. He assured himself it was only because he wanted to make certain she didn't turn their heads with talk of the Fae. And it wasn't as though their parents were paying them any mind. Rory was too intent on getting back in his wife's good graces to pay attention elsewhere.

Jamie gave his side of their exploits with the buck. Every so often Alex would pipe in with his version of the day's events. Syrena gave both bairns equal attention. Aidan didn't understand it, but she seemed truly interested in what the demons had to say. Patiently, she listened to their childish prattle, a gentle smile curving her lips.

As though she sensed his attention, she raised her eyes to his. Captured in her golden gaze, he found himself responding, the burning desire he thought long since buried stirred to life.

He jerked his attention back to Fergus. "Sorry. What was that ye were sayin'?"

Fergus brows knitted with a pointed look in Syrena's direction. "Aye, you seem distracted."

"I'm thinkin' about Lan. I doona ken how much longer I can wait. My uncle has yet to respond to my inquiries and—"

Fergus lowered his voice to interrupt Aidan. "I'm glad to hear you've come to yer senses and no longer think Syrena had anythin' to do with it."

Aidan frowned. "Nay, ye're wrong. I'm more convinced than ever she kens somethin'." His grip tightened on the silver goblet. "I'll get the truth from her yet. I'm only sayin' I have to hurry and get it from her soon."

Fergus bent over his trencher to eat the last of his chicken, waving his dirk at Aidan. "Yer plan, the one you spoke of to Rory and me, 'tis no' a good idea, lad. I'm no' sayin' I doona understand where ye're comin' from, but you've lost yer objectivity where the lass is concerned. Think before you do somethin' you'll regret."

"My only regret would be no' doin' everythin' in my power

to find my brother." His appetite lost, Aidan shoved his half-eaten meal aside.

It wasn't until he heard the familiar sound of Syrena's appreciative hum that he realized the pastries had been served. He turned in time to see her slide the tip of her tongue slowly over her honey-glazed lips. Eyes half closed, she raised one finger then the other to her rosebud mouth, licking off the sugary remains.

A low groan escaped from deep in his throat before he could contain it. The twins and Syrena swiveled their heads in his direction. Bloody hell, if Mrs. Mac served honey cakes again, he'd have to kill her.

"What?" he growled.

"You made a funny noise," Jamie informed him.

"I didna. Ye're imaginin' things." He ignored Fergus laughing beside him and shoved a piece of honey cake in his mouth.

Alex shook his head. "Did, too. I heard you."

Just as Aidan was about to respond, he noticed a well-fed black cat, yellow eyes glowing, leap onto the dais. It stalked toward Syrena. Remembering her terror that day in Lewes, Aidan slowly rose from his chair, not wanting to attract her attention, hoping he could reach the cat before it reached her. She looked up at him, a question in her eyes, then slowly shifted in her chair.

The cat arched its back and hissed. Syrena snarled and hissed back. The terror-stricken animal fled the dais. Aidan knew exactly how it felt.

He stared at her. She'd changed. And then he realized she hadn't—this was who she was. The sweet, innocent beauty who snuck past his hard-won defenses, wormed her way into his heart, never existed.

Chapter 16

The castle bustled with activity and Syrena hurried from her room, certain she'd slept through the morning meal. Coming down the stairs, she noted Aileanna speaking to an older man. They turned to her.

"Father, this is Lady Syrena, Aidan's betrothed."

Syrena gaped at Aileanna. *What in the name of Fae did she just say?* Syrena gripped the baluster before she tumbled headlong down the stairs. The handsome silver-haired man turned his piercing blue eyes upon her. Aileanna, who stood slightly behind him at the foot of the grand staircase, shrugged helplessly and mouthed, "I'll explain later."

"Syrena, this is my father, Alasdair MacDonald."

Lord MacDonald's big hand swallowed Syrena's in a firm grip as he gently guided her down the last step. He glanced back at his daughter. "She has the look of Brianna, doona ye think?"

"But she's not, you know that, don't you, Father?" Aileanna asked, casting a worried look at the older man.

He waved off his daughter's concern. "Och, aye, of course I do. But 'tis certain she has both my daughters' poor taste in men." Taking Syrena's measure, he shook his head. "What is wrong with ye lasses, fallin' fer the MacLeod lads as ye do? When ye come to yer senses, which I'm certain ye will, I ken some fine gentlemen who'd be honored to meet a bonny lass such as yerself."

"Father!"

"What? A mon is entitled to his opinion, is he no'?"

"Well, I'd appreciate it if you'd keep opinions such as those to yourself."

"Why? How do ye expect a wee lass such as this to hold her own against a MacLeod? They're a bunch of overbearing, arrogant louts. Stubborn to boot, and well ye ken it."

A bubble of laughter gurgled in Syrena's throat. Aileanna might not agree with her father's opinion of the MacLeods, but she did, at least where Aidan was concerned.

Witnessing her amusement, Alasdair grinned. His blue eyes twinkling, he wrapped a companionable arm around her shoulders. "Now, where would yer parents be? I'd like to meet the ones that produced such a bonny wee lass. I have some advice they need to hear when it comes to dealin' with the MacLeods."

"I'm afraid that's impossible, Lord MacDonald." Thank the heavens. The last thing she wanted was for them to have met her father, or Morgana for that matter. "Both my parents are . . . have passed on."

"I'm sorry to hear that, my pet." Angling his head to study her, he tightened his arm around her shoulder. "Och, well, it's settled then, since ye have no kin to see to yer interests, I'll see to them fer ye. I'll no' have the MacLeods taking advantage of ye," he proclaimed, looking pleased with the prospect.

Aileanna groaned. "If you don't behave, I'm sending you home. Where's Aunt Fiona?" she asked as though the woman was her only hope in controlling the man at Syrena's side. Aileanna glanced expectantly at the entrance doors.

Lord MacDonald looked sheepish. "Ah . . . she didna wish to come."

"Why? What did you do now?" Aileanna narrowed her gaze on her father, and crossed her arms beneath her chest.

Syrena shifted from one foot to the other, thinking it would be best to take her leave.

"Ye're makin' the lass uncomfortable, Aileanna. We'll discuss yer aunt and her daft notions later."

"Daft notions, hah." Aileanna snorted then shifted her attention to Syrena. "You'll have to excuse me. As you can see, my father has a way of . . ." She breathed a sigh of relief when Mrs. Mac bustled toward them. "Mrs. Mac, will you show my father to his room, please?" She pointed a finger at Alasdair. "And don't think you're off the hook. You and I will be having ourselves a good long chat."

Her father waved aside her comment to follow Mrs. Mac. Over his shoulder, he said, "Make sure ye seat Syrena beside me at the evenin' meal, Aileanna."

"The man is impossible," Aileanna muttered as Mrs. Mac and her father disappeared from view. "I don't know why I said you were Aidan's fiancée." She buried her face in her hands and shook her head.

"Neither do I. I was hoping you'd explain it to me. Aidan's going to be furious, Aileanna. The man can barely stand to look at me."

Aileanna looked up and grinned. "Nay, he doesn't have a problem looking at you, I can attest to that. But you're right, he won't be happy about it."

Syrena winced. It didn't matter that she said it herself; it bothered her to hear someone else confirm Aidan's low opinion of her. Even though it shouldn't, it did, and the realization was unsettling.

Aileanna lifted a slender shoulder, the pale blue fabric of her gown rustling with the movement. "There's no help for it, I couldn't tell my father you're Fae, and I couldn't think of any other way to explain your presence."

"Does your father feel the same way about the Fae as Aidan does?" Syrena's voice sounded thick with pent-up emotion. She castigated herself for being foolish—why should the opinions, the prejudice of Aileanna's father, Aidan, or anyone else for that matter, bother her? She'd spent most of her life being despised for one reason or another—why should it be any different now?

"Not to . . ." Catching what must have been a woebegone expression on her face, Aileanna gave her a quick hug. "I'm sorry, Syrena. Believe me, I know how it feels to be an outsider. It took a long time before the people of Dunvegan accepted me. As for my father, he blames the faery flag for taking my mother and I from him. But if it makes you feel any better"—she grinned—"he blames the MacLeods most of all. Besides, you didn't have anything to do with the faery flag so he can't hold you accountable."

"Then maybe you should've told him the truth."

"It seemed the best option at the—" Aileanna broke off at the sound of Aidan's loud bellow.

Poised for flight, Syrena's mouth dropped when Aidan stormed through the doors of the keep with Alex under one arm, a protesting, red-faced Jamie under the other. Clutched in the boys' hands were a set of bows and red-tipped arrows just like the one sticking out of the thick, inky black waves on top of Aidan's head.

She clapped a hand over her mouth to contain her laughter, but it was no use.

He glared at her, splotches of red on his sun-bronzed cheeks. "Ye think 'tis funny, do ye? Ye wouldna if ye were the one they were shootin' at."

Lowering the boys none-too-gently to their feet, he glowered at Aileanna. "Who was the bloody fool who gave these to the wee demons?" he asked, rattling the weapons he'd swiped from the boys' hands.

"'Tis a present from our granddad," Jamie cried. His arms windmilling, he went after Aidan, who flattened his open palm against Jamie's forehead. He managed to keep Jamie at arm's length, his foot from connecting with Aidan's shin.

"Jamie, stop that right now," his mother admonished, grabbing hold of the back of his shirt.

"But 'tis our present. He canna have them."

"Your Uncle Aidan is right. It's not a suitable gift for five-year-olds, and your grandfather and I will be having a wee chat about it. One more thing on an ever-growing list," she muttered.

Thinking of the chat Aileanna was about to have with the glowering man who towered above them, Syrena knew she didn't want to be anywhere in sight, or within earshot, when she did.

"Jamie, Alex, why don't we go outside? You can show me the hiding spot you were talking about the other day."

The twins reluctantly agreed, shooting daggers at Aidan as they took her hands.

"That's a wonderful idea. You boys go and play with your Auntie Syrena, and Mama will get on with the preparations to celebrate yer da's day of birth."

Auntie? Syrena stifled a groan, hurrying the boys out the door before Aidan exploded.

Jamie frowned, struggling to keep up with Syrena as she hustled them across the courtyard. "Why did Mama call you our auntie?"

Shooting a glance over her shoulder, relieved Aidan was not in hot pursuit, Syrena said, "She . . . she thinks I'm going to marry your Uncle Aidan."

"Ye're marryin' the monster?" Jamie asked horrified.

"Ummm . . . hmmm, I . . . maybe." Her pulse quickened at the thought. At one time it had been her fondest desire. How often had she lost herself in that particular fantasy? In the magickal world she'd created where Aidan would love her even though she was Fae.

Where they would live happily ever after with Lachlan, and their children, two boys who would look just like their father, completed the idyllic world she'd imagined. She would have laughed, if it hadn't been so painful.

The beautiful Highlander who'd once looked at her with love and desire in his gray eyes now looked at her with disdain and distrust. But it didn't matter. Her illusions had been destroyed a long time ago. She wasn't meant to be loved—her father, her mother, Aidan, and even Lachlan had proven that to her. The pain of that knowledge was no longer as difficult to bear. She'd given up on the dream a year ago. Winning the Fae's admiration was enough. It had to be.

The dire consequences of Syrena being married to Aidan were volleyed back and forth between Jamie and Alex at a pace that left her dizzy. Offering the boys a reassuring smile, she said, "Don't worry, I can handle the monster." At least she hoped she could.

Their angelic faces lit up with smiles. "We ken it," Alex said.

"Aye, and we'll have our weapons to help you." Jamie added in a conspiratorial whisper, "Our da will give them back to us."

She laughed, but watching Alex and Jamie bend down to examine a small creature inch across the cobblestone, eyes filled with wonder, her amusement faded. If her life went as planned, there would be no children for her.

No little boys to play with, to look at the world through their curious and innocent eyes, to cuddle and rock to sleep. No one to give all the love she kept bottled up inside her. She rubbed the dull ache in her chest and looked down at Jamie and Alex.

Then Syrena made a decision that eased the tight band constricting her lungs. After they found Lachlan, she'd ask Aileanna if she could come back and visit. They had become friends, and she didn't think Aileanna would mind. The thought lightened her mood. She took hold of their baby-soft hands. "Come, let's take advantage of the fine day."

Head pounding, Aidan strode across the abandoned courtyard, the keep a hive of activity as everyone within prepared for his cousin's celebration. He drank in the musky sweetness of the fall air in an attempt to cool his heated blood, his anger a barely banked inferno.

After the demons had set upon him with their bows and arrows, his day had gone from bad to worse. Thinking of Aileanna, he shook his head. Why the bloody hell did she tell her father he and Syrena were betrothed? She'd left him no choice but to play along—if he didn't, he risked the Mac-Donald discovering who Syrena really was. And he wouldn't allow his family's closely guarded secret to be exposed. A secret he'd kept hidden for so long he was sometimes able to put it behind him.

But Syrena's presence forced him to deal with the emotions he'd thought he'd overcome—anger at his father, his mother, and however unfair it may be, his brother. And now he had to pretend he loved a woman whose family had plunged his own headfirst into their nightmare.

A year ago, it wouldn't have been an act. But he knew who she was now, and like Davina, she'd lied to him, played him for a fool.

He cursed, staring at the crumpled missive in his hand. He couldn't believe it; his uncle was dead, along with his hopes of finding Lachlan alive and well in the Hamiltons London town home. And now he had no choice but to deal with his cousin, John Henry, the man Davina had betrayed him for. The newly appointed Lord Hamilton, although offering his assistance, made it clear he did so unwillingly. The easy friendship they'd enjoyed in their youth had been destroyed by the love they'd shared for the same woman.

A sultry peal of laughter rippled like the light breeze rustling the leaves overhead. Aidan took a deep breath before he set off in the direction from which it came. Regardless of his feelings for Syrena, he had to find his brother, and he was certain she held the answers he sought.

He followed the bairns' giggles to the kitchens. Rounding the corner of the squat, weathered stone building, he stopped short. Dappled sunlight filtered through the boughs of an old oak to shine down on Syrena and the bairns who sat at the base of the tree. Her hair lay loose upon her shoulders, shining like a freshly minted gold coin.

He took a step back and leaned against the warm stone. Sweet Christ, he still wanted her. She drew him in, just like Jamie and Alex, he thought wryly, noting the expressions of rapture on their wee faces as they gazed up at her.

He had heard it said bairns were the best judge of character. Aidan snorted. If that were the case, it didn't say much for his, but spoke volumes of hers. She truly cared about the lads. It was obvious from the way she spoke to them, listening to their nonsensical prattle with endless patience.

Aye, so how did he reconcile this woman with the one he condemned? Was it possible she told the truth? Did she truly have no idea as to Lan's whereabouts? A part of him hoped that was the case, while the other part prayed it wasn't. If she had played no part in his brother's disappearance, how in the bloody hell would he find him?

"You promised, Auntie Syrena, now where's our present?" Jamie demanded.

Aidan sent his eyes to the clear blue sky. *Auntie.* An auntie who appeared somewhat flustered if the faint flush coloring her cheeks was anything to go by.

"Um-hmm . . . well . . . give me a moment. You're supposed to have your eyes closed, Jamie. No peeking," she admonished.

The bairns squeezed their eyes shut. Her hands fluttered behind her back. Aidan frowned, wondering what she hoped to find since there was nothing behind her. Her fingers wiggled on top of the grass. Eyes closed, she moved her pink lips silently. Aidan stiffened.

Magick.

Bloody hell, she meant to use her magick. He stepped from the shadows to stop her, but then remembered her confession of the day before and couldn't bring himself to berate her.

Hearing how she'd suffered at the hands of the Fae when she was no older than the bairns had left him shaken. It had taken everything he had not to take her in his arms and comfort her. But she'd related the tale without tears or recriminations. And he'd stood there, undeniably proud of her strength, of her ability to get past the cruelty without visible scars.

"Can we open them now?" Alex asked.

"Not yet." Her face a study in concentration, she wiggled her fingers again. Aidan's eyes widened. What looked to be a gooey, white substance dripped from her hands. A smile lit her face then she glanced over her shoulder and groaned. With a frustrated shake of her long tousled curls, she wiped the sticky mess onto the grass and prepared to try again.

Aidan's shoulders shook with silent laughter. The emotion surprised him. He hadn't felt like laughing in a long while. What was it about her that she could make him feel that way? It had been the same from the first moment he'd met her. She'd filled him with a warmth, a lightness that stole his breath away. More likely his sanity, he thought.

"Is something wrong, Auntie Syrena?" Jamie asked, cracking one eye open.

"Ah . . . no, I'm having a hard time remembering where I put your present is all. Close your eyes, Jamie."

A movement a few feet behind Syrena drew Aidan's attention. Black nose pushed to the ground, a collie pup snuffled its way toward her. Concentrating on her magick, she wasn't aware of its presence until a pink tongue darted out to lick her fingers. Syrena shrieked and scrambled to her feet. The pup yelped and the bairns squealed with delight.

"Oh, Auntie, 'tis the bestest present ever," Alex cried as he crouched beside the pup, who licked the sticky residue from the grass.

"We always wanted a puppy, Auntie, but Mama and Da would never let us have one. But they canna say nay now." Jamie whooped and flung his arms around her legs. Alex, not to be outdone, did the same. Their excitement contagious, the puppy yapped, stretching up on its hind legs to paw at Syrena's dusty rose skirts.

She went to pat the tops of their heads, then remembering the gooey substance, she let her hands drop to her sides. Aidan chuckled, looking forward to seeing the look on his cousin's face when the bairns presented him with Syrena's gift. There was not much Rory didn't like, but dogs topped the list.

As Syrena watched the bairns, a wide smile spread over her face. Aidan didn't think she'd ever looked more beautiful.

He stepped away from the wall, and their heads swiveled in his direction. Jamie, who'd picked up the shaggy ball of tawny fur, held it tight to his chest. Casting a mutinous scowl in Aidan's direction, he said, "Ye canna take him. He's our present from Auntie Syrena."

Noting the look of defiance in her golden gaze and the stubborn jut of her chin, Aidan held out his hands. "I wasna goin' to take him from ye, Jamie. After all, 'tis a present from both yer aunt and I." Aye, he thought 'twas a grand idea. If the bairns thought the present was from the both of them, they'd quit beating on him.

She shot a look of disbelief in his direction.

Jamie looked up at her. "Is that true, Auntie?" he asked doubtfully.

"Well—"

Aidan grinned. "Of course 'tis. When a man and woman are betrothed, the gift comes from the two of them."

"Oh . . . thanks," Jamie murmured with obvious reluctance.

Alex, the politer of the two, smiled shyly. "Aye, thank you, Uncle Aidan."

"Mrs. Mac is lookin' fer the two of ye." The bairns groaned. "Off ye go now," Aidan said. After giving one last hug to Syrena, the bairns tromped off in the direction of the keep, fighting over which one should hold their pet.

Aidan watched as she wiped her hands on the grass then leaned over to retrieve her slippers. An image of her barefoot, her long hair streaming down her back as she danced provocatively in the moonlight, came upon him without warning. She met his gaze. The heat of the memory must have been written upon his face, he thought, when her topaz eyes widened. The pulse at the base of her slender neck fluttered.

Aidan cleared his throat. "Ye still prefer yer bare feet to yer shoes, do ye?" He moved closer, inhaling her sweet feminine scent.

She glanced helplessly at the delicate slippers in her hand as though, like him, the memory of the passionate interlude they'd shared that moonlit night a year ago ensnared her.

"I . . . I have to go," she stammered, hopping unsteadily on one foot as she tried to put on her shoe.

"Here, let me help ye." He held out his hand. Her cheeks flushed. Reluctantly she handed him her slipper. He lowered himself to one knee. Taking her foot in his hand, he raised his gaze to hers. "We have to talk, Syrena."

Her fingers bit into his shoulders. "You can't blame me for this, Aidan. Aileanna told her father we were betrothed because she couldn't come up with any other reason for my presence."

"I ken that. 'Twas no' what I wanted to speak to ye about."

Her brow furrowed then she grimaced. "You saw me use my magick." She released a defeated sigh. "I didn't mean to, honestly, but Alex and Jamie were so sad about losing their bows and arrows I wanted to cheer them up. I don't even know what manner of animal it is that I conjured. It isn't dangerous, is it?"

Unable to help himself, Aidan laughed at the fervent concern in her eyes. "Nay, 'tis a dog. They use them to herd sheep. And, Syrena, yer magick wasna responsible fer his appearance."

Her smooth brow furrowed. "No?"

"Nay. As fer it bein' dangerous, the only one who would believe so is Rory. He canna abide dogs, big or small. He's been afraid of them since he was a lad."

She glanced in the direction of the keep. "I suppose I'd best go and apologize then."

Rising to his feet, he took hold of her arm. "No' yet. We have to talk, about Lan."

She lowered her eyes, long lashes caressing the soft curve of her cheek. Bloody hell, she was hiding something. Once again he'd allowed himself to be taken in by her bonny looks and her gentle ways with the bairns. The memory of how much he'd wanted her, and if he was honest, how much he still did.

"Tell me what ye ken, Syrena," he demanded.

"I don't know anything and you're hurting me," she accused him. With surprising strength, she peeled his fingers from her arm.

"Ye're lyin'," he gritted from between clenched teeth.

She placed a palm on his chest and attempted to push him out of her way. "No, I'm not. I didn't take Lan. I wouldn't lie about that. I'm as afraid for him as you are."

"Can ye promise me that the Fae are no' involved?" He found himself wanting to believe her.

She chewed on her bottom lip. "I don't think they are, but I can't be certain. All I know is something strange is happening in London. Over the last few months, Fae men have gone missing, five to be exact."

"Why did ye no' tell me this before?"

"Because I'm almost certain it doesn't involve Lan. They're pure-blood, Aidan. Lan is only half. And like you, he hates the Fae. I can't see him seeking them out, can you?"

What she said made sense, but it was difficult for him to let go of his suspicions. If he did, it meant he'd wasted precious time in his search for his brother.

"I doona ken. No one has learned what happened to them?"

"No, but . . . but there have been rumors of dark magick."

"Why doesna' that surprise me with the Fae involved?"

"Are you suggesting I'm evil? You'd best think long and hard on that, Aidan MacLeod, it's not me Jamie and Alex refer to as a monster!" She made a frustrated sound. "I won't put up with your suspicions or snide remarks any longer. I'm leaving for London tomorrow, with or without you—preferably without!"

Chapter 17

Syrena's slippers tapped an angry beat across the courtyard. The man was infuriating! His inability to get past his distrust of the Fae put Lachlan at risk. How would they ever find their brother if they could not work together? She'd threatened to go to London on her own, but it was an idle threat. She didn't even know where the city was let alone how to get there.

But the thought of spending any more time in his company left her uneasy. Aidan MacLeod still held a piece of her heart. If she hadn't realized it before, she did now. The warm amusement that danced in his eyes, the deepening of the crescent moon in his cheek, and the flash of his strong white teeth when he smiled shook her resolve to keep him at arm's length. It wasn't fair he could still make her feel the way she did. Turn her emotions inside out and, with a simple touch, bring back the memory of the heated moments they'd once shared.

"Syrena!" He called from behind her, his deep voice tinged with frustration.

Good! She hoped he was as frustrated as she was.

"Bloody hell, I was no' finished talkin' with ye. Get yer bonny arse back here."

She heard a snicker of laughter, and out of the corner of her eye spotted several of Dunvegan's men-at-arms sharing a laugh at her expense. She growled low in her throat. Whirling on her heel, she strode toward Aidan. Hands on her hips, she glared into his annoyingly handsome face and demanded, "What did you just say?"

He splayed his hands. "I'm sorry, it slipped out." The twitch of his lips had her ready to call him on his lie, but before she could, he said, "Syrena, we have much to discuss that I doona wish the others to overhear. With the keep filled to overflowin', we'll no' get a moment's peace." He held out his hand. "Come with me."

She hesitated, but knew he was right. They had to make plans to get her brother back, or at the very least she needed information as to where to begin her search. She ignored the hand he held out to her. She couldn't let him touch her, couldn't let him see how he affected her. "Do you promise not to make any more disparaging remarks against the Fae?"

"We'll see." When she crossed her arms over her chest, he blew out an exasperated breath. "Fine, I'll no' say another word—for now." He tugged on her hand to drag her across the courtyard.

"Aidan, slow down, your legs are longer than mine."

"Aye, most are." He chuckled, but slowed his pace.

She recognized the path he led her to as one they'd used the day before. "Are we going to the training field?"

"Nay, 'tis no' much further. Besides, ye doona have yer sword. Where is it?"

"Hidden." Afraid the twins' curiosity would cause them to seek out Nuie and they'd come to harm, she'd tucked her sword away. Using a chair to reach the top shelf of the wardrobe, she'd buried him beneath a pile of linens. She imagined Nuie was none too happy with her at the moment.

When she was home in the Enchanted Isles, her sword was either in her hand or strapped to her back. But here at Dunvegan, she didn't feel the need to be armed at all times. In an odd way, it was freeing not to have to live up to anyone's expectations, to be the warrior the Fae had come to admire, to depend upon.

Fallyn and her sisters saw the woman beneath the façade, but no one else did. They didn't want to see that the warrior they respected was still Syrena, the half-pint princess who couldn't do magick, but here in the Mortal realm it didn't matter.

"Afraid I'll steal yer wee sword from ye?" he asked as they crossed the clearing to the shelter of the pines. Dried twigs and pine needles crunched beneath their feet.

She inhaled deeply of the heady, fragrant scent before answering, "No, Nuie, wouldn't respond in the way you'd wish him to. You'd soon return him to me."

He laughed, shaking his head. "Only ye would think to name a sword."

Considering his reaction, she wasn't about to tell him Nuie was not just a sword, but her friend.

Aidan urged her to take a seat on a large slab of rock smoothed over time to provide a comfortable, albeit cold, surface. He sat beside her, scrubbing his hands over his face before he turned to study her. "First off, ye're no' goin' to London on yer own, 'tis no' safe. And though 'tis no' somethin' I want to admit, ye may be of some help findin' Lan."

She arched a brow, surprised by his admission. "You may not have noticed, Aidan, but I am not the same woman you knew a year ago. I can take care of myself. But as far as helping you find Lachlan, other than another set of eyes and a sword, I'm not certain what I can do. I'm not familiar with the city."

"I ken ye've changed, but I'm beginnin' to think no' as much as I first thought." He didn't appear happy with whatever it was he'd imagined he'd seen. "Ye may no' be familiar with London, but ye do ken Lan. Mayhap ye can reach him with yer mind. And if the Fae are involved, I'll need yer help."

"I didn't realize you knew, about Lan, about me talking to him in my mind."

"Aye, he told me that day in the woods."

Of course, her brother would've confessed all that day. "I've been unable to reach him, Aidan. I've tried every day, several times a day, and there's been nothing."

Color drained from his sun-bronzed skin. "Ye doona think . . ."

Understanding his fears, having battled them herself, she placed her hand over his. They had that in common, their love for their brother, because despite his faults, she knew Aidan loved Lan. "No, I think I'd know if he, if he was gone."

"Aye, I feel the same." His thumb stroked her palm while he spoke.

She tried to ignore the ribbons of pleasure curling in her belly at his soothing caress. Fighting the sensation, she cleared her throat. "Why did he go to London?"

His expression shuttered. "He received a missive."

"From a woman?"

He frowned, searching her face. "Why would ye ask that?"

"Oh, I don't know, maybe because anytime I've seen the two of you, you're pleasuring a woman. It's as though that's all you have to do with your time," she snapped, then realizing what she'd said, stifled a groan.

His lips tightened, eyes the color of a stormy sky narrowed. "What do ye mean whenever ye have seen us? And how in the bloody hell would ye be around when we are . . ."

Her cheeks heated. "No, that's not what I meant to say. It's just that I know you're no different from Fae men . . . and . . . that's it, that's what I meant to say."

"Doona lie to me, Syrena."

Maybe she should tell him the truth, see if he could explain why she'd meant so little to him that he bedded any woman who came his way. But that was foolish. She hadn't meant anything to him. It had only been wishful thinking on her part. What he did and whom he did it with were none of her business, but Lan was. And if a woman drew him to London, she had a right to know. "My stepmother, Morgana, anytime she thought I might be tempted to return to the Mortal realm, she would show me . . . well . . . you know. She would show me you and Lan . . ." She lifted her hands, unable to continue.

Cupping her chin between his strong fingers, he forced her gaze to his. "Were ye tempted, Syrena? Were ye tempted to come back to us?"

Seduced by his mesmerizing gaze, the feelings she'd once had for him rose to the surface, no longer content to remain a distant memory. The emotions overwhelmed her, and she told him the truth. "Yes, I . . . yes."

His gaze fastened on her mouth. She couldn't see his eyes, couldn't see how her confession made him feel. The pad of his thumb skimmed her bottom lip, and the frisson of sensation made her shiver. He dragged his heavy-lidded gaze from her mouth to her eyes, and then she saw it, desire, searing in its intensity.

"Tell me. Tell me why?"

Because I loved you. Because I loved my brother and couldn't bear to leave either of you behind. How could she tell him? She couldn't risk his rejection, not again. His lips feathered across her heated cheek to her ear. "Tell me."

He was too close. She was helpless against the memories, they made her want to tell him the truth, to lose herself in his familiar embrace, to feel protected and cherished once more. She placed her palms against the banded muscles in his chest and pushed, but no matter how much stronger she'd become, she couldn't move him.

"No, please, Aidan." A thread of panic was woven into her voice.

He framed her face with his big hands, his thumbs gently stroking along her cheekbones to her mouth. "Shall I tell ye why ye were tempted to come back, angel?"

"Yes," she breathed, her fingers wrapped around his thick wrists. "Please."

Against the corner of her mouth he smiled. "Because ye could no' forget this." He captured her lips as easily as he had captured her heart a year ago, shattering her resolve, the fragile wall she'd built around her emotions. Her body responded as though they'd never been apart. As though it had waited for this moment, urging her to take whatever he offered, enjoy the bittersweet feel of his hands on her, his mouth claiming hers.

His groan reverberated against her lips, and he slid a hand under her legs and one behind her back to sweep her onto his lap. Beneath the folds of her gown, she felt the powerful muscles in his thighs, the hard bulge of his erection, and lost herself in his kiss. Her tongue tangled with his, and she barely noticed that he'd untied the laces of her gown until the cool autumn air nipped at her breasts. Her nipples pearled into taut buds. Feeling vulnerable, fully exposed, she moaned, "Aidan."

He lifted his head as though waiting for her to object, but the time for protest had passed the moment he'd touched his lips to hers. He smoothed the hair from her face, stroking her arm, the curve of her breast, as though he sensed she was frightened by the strength of her desire and sought to soothe her.

In one lithe movement, he rose easily from the stone with her in his arms, cradling her to his chest. She experienced a tiny thrill at his show of strength, his potent masculinity. He gently laid her on the slab of rock. Cold seeped into her back, and she gasped.

Aidan followed her down, kneeling beside her. "Doona worry, angel, ye won't be cold fer long." He gazed upon Syrena, entranced. With the dappled sunlight reaching through the boughs to gild her creamy skin, to caress her full perfect breasts, she was a veritable feast laid out for his pleasure.

Her long, golden hair spread out beneath her to tumble over the side of the rock, strands curling around her dusky rose nipples, straining buds ripe for his attention. Unable to resist the lush bounty spread out before him, he cupped her breasts, and laved first one nipple and then the other, suckling until she writhed beneath him. His name upon her parted lips glistening from his wet, open-mouthed kiss gave him a possessive thrill. Her movements grew frantic, her fingers clutching his tunic, tugging it from his trews. He stroked her silken tresses, her breasts, then laid his palm on her belly, soothing her, quieting her.

"Easy, love," he murmured. The desire to savor her, taste every inch of her perfect wee body, overwhelmed him. No other woman compared to her. He realized, no matter that she was Fae, he wanted her beyond reason, as much as she seemed to want him. Whatever defenses he'd built against her had crumbled at her admission she'd wished to return to them. He wanted to claim her as his, her body as his. They may not be able to have anything else, but this they could have.

She stroked the flat plane of his belly, the muscles rippling at the exquisite torture of her touch. He lifted his mouth from her breast and dragged his shirt over his head. His laughter rumbled deep in his chest at her frustrated moan. "Patience, my greedy little angel," he said as he formed a pillow with his tunic and eased it beneath her head.

Her amber gaze devoured him, and his cock swelled at the admiration he saw there. He took her hand and placed it over his straining erection. Her startled gasp made him smile, but his amusement faded when she fondled him through his doeskin trews.

He gently manacled her wrist. "Careful, angel." He captured her other hand and brought them together over her head, restraining her with one of his own. Fear flashed in her luminous gaze, and she twisted in his grasp. He groaned, the jiggling of her breasts firing his desire to painful heights. "Nay, Syrena, I would never hurt ye. Ye ken that, doona ye?" *Sweet Christ, say ye do.* He slid his lips over hers, slowly, back and forth, exultant when she responded tentatively at first then with an impassioned insistence that had his senses reeling.

He leaned over her, and the friction of her breasts rubbing against his chest destroyed his resolve to take it slow. He tugged her gown to her waist, his mouth following the path of his hand, licking, suckling every inch of delectable flesh he exposed. She arched her hips, and greedily he shoved the gown and her silken drawers to her thighs, past her knees, to the delicate curve of her ankles. He stroked the downy softness of her curls at the juncture between her shapely legs, and she writhed, releasing a needy whimper. Hungry to touch her, all of her, he let go of her wrists to coax her legs apart. He stroked her there, widening her with his thick fingers. Then he flicked his tongue over the throbbing nub.

She let out a shocked cry and struggled to sit up, trying to push him away. "Stop, Aidan . . . I . . . stop."

"Bloody hell, Syrena, ye'll bring the entire household down upon us." He rested his palm between the hollow of her breasts. "Lie back, angel."

"But I don't want . . ." Her voice trailed off, her cheeks stained scarlet.

"Has no one ever loved ye that way?" He stroked the silky curls, inordinately pleased when she nibbled on her kiss-swollen lips and shook her head. "I promise, ye'll no' want me to stop, just let me show ye," he murmured, sliding a finger inside her hot, wet sheath. Christ, she was tight.

"I don't think . . ." Her protest died on her parted lips. Her thighs, as though in invitation, spread a little wider. She strained against his lips as her initial apprehension faded. He'd been surprised by her earlier reaction. From the stories his father and the old crone had told, the Fae were supposed to be sensual by nature, indiscriminate in their number of bed partners. Syrena didn't appear to be.

Feeling her inner muscles tighten around his two fingers, he suckled the pulsating bud until she shattered against his mouth. The expression of utter contentment, of pleasure upon her face, brought a smile to his lips.

Unable to put off his needs any longer, he freed his rock-hard erection from the tight confines of his trews. His masculine pride was rewarded by her widening gaze and startled gasp, pleased he measured up to the Fae men.

Lowering himself upon her, he nudged her hot, slick opening with the head of his cock. Entering her slowly, he savored the sensation of being inside her. He slid a hand beneath her, kneading her firm behind as he raised her hips and surged inside her, only to meet a barrier. Her eyes flew open, and she gave a strangled cry.

He groaned and dropped his forehead to hers. "Syrena," he muttered thickly, "ye should have told me ye were innocent. I thought . . ." He bit back the words. He couldn't tell her what he thought without hurting her. His heart thudded painfully in his chest. The muscles in his arms strained as he attempted to hold back when all he wanted to do was pound his cock into her, to make her fully and completely his.

"I didn't think it mattered," she said, tucking her face into the curve of his arm.

It mattered, more than she would ever know, more than he was willing to tell her. "Aye, it does." He smoothed the tangled strands of her hair from her cheek and gently kissed her as he eased his cock from her heated embrace.

"No, don't." She wrapped her legs around him and, angling her hips, drove him back inside her, burying him to the hilt. He groaned his relief at being inside her and silenced her quiet whimpers with a kiss, luxuriating in the feel of her hot sheath enveloping him, the strength of her legs holding him to her. He held himself still until she grew accustomed to him, then slowly, carefully, moved inside her. As the rhythm of his thrusts intensified, her distressed whimpers were replaced by lusty moans of want and desire that stoked the fire in his blood.

"Aye, love, aye," he encouraged her as she kept time with him in their dance of passion. Unable to hold back any longer, he slid his hand between them, determined to give her as much pleasure as she'd given him. He watched the emotions play across her exquisite features, her soft sounds of pleasure his undoing and he shuddered his release.

Breathing heavily, he lay on top of her, savoring the feel of her warm, soft, bountiful curves.

"Aidan." She struggled beneath him, pushing frantically at his chest.

"Sorry." He grinned lazily, raising himself an inch or two above her, unwilling to pull away completely.

"Get off me." She wriggled, trying to get out from under him.

"I ken ye doona have much experience, Syrena, but trust me, ye doona have to be in such a hurry to—" She pushed him again and his cock slid from her slippery heat onto the cold unyielding slab. He winced.

"Christ," he cursed when with another push he landed bare-arse on a pile of leaves and pointy sticks. Scrambling from the rock, she grabbed her clothing. Aidan's frustrated protest died in his throat, in awe of her naked body, luminescent in the fading sunlight against the backdrop of evergreens. He'd never seen anything so beautiful.

She shot him an exasperated look and shook her head. "Get dressed! You might not care if they see us like this, but I do."

He frowned in confusion until he heard the bairns calling for her. Cursing, he stood up. "They may have the look of wee angels, but I swear those two are the devil's own."

She snorted. "Just like their uncle. Now come help me since it seems I'm the only one of us to be completely naked." Her cheeks pinked as she tried to wriggle into her undergarments.

He grinned and tugged her toward him, brushing away her hands to help her dress. "Stop fussin' and let me do it." He smoothed the gown over her shoulder and nuzzled her neck while he tied the laces. "So, ye think I look like an angel, do ye?"

She batted his hands away, ignoring his question. "Thank

you. Now go! Hurry!" she said, waving her fingers in the direction of the keep.

"Ye're verra bossy." He considered teasing her further, but relented at her embarrassed expression. "All right, doona get yerself in a dither, I'm goin'." But unable to resist one last taste, he pulled her into his arms and kissed her. "We'll finish this later," he murmured against her mouth.

"I thought we were."

"Nay, we're far from finished." With one last look at her, he strode toward the clearing, shrugging his tunic over his head.

Chapter 18

Before Aidan put ten feet between them, his cousin stepped from the shadows of the towering pines. Rory's observant, emerald gaze swept over Syrena and his lips flattened. Though she couldn't hear what he said when Aidan reached him, it was obvious he was displeased. She pressed her palms to her heated cheeks, mortified that Rory knew what they'd been doing.

At the cousins' angry exchange, heaviness settled low in her belly. The last thing she wanted to do was cause tension between the two men. But it seemed it was too late for that. With his attention focused on his cousin, Aidan didn't spare her a second look. They bellowed for the twins simultaneously, and Alex and Jamie's excited chatter faded into the distance.

She considered remaining in the woods, afraid to face the men's censure. In the Enchanted Isles, a woman's virginity was valued, those of easy virtue judged harshly. However, under Morgana's rule—a woman whose reputation in the bedchambers rivaled Syrena's father's—the lines of morality had blurred.

But despite what the men might think of her, Syrena didn't regret making love with Aidan. He'd made her feel beautiful, desirable, loved. *No, Syrena, just because he made love to you doesn't mean he loves you*, she chided herself. How often had she listened to a Fae woman cry, devastated when she learned she'd given her body, her heart, to a man who wanted nothing more than a night of pleasure? She wouldn't make the same mistake. She'd be content with the memories of what they'd shared, and not expect more from Aidan than what he offered. Even though it seemed he offered more than a passionate interlude, she didn't have enough experience to know the difference.

Within the circle of the pines, the shadows deepened as the sun dipped low in the sky. Syrena shivered. The celebration for Rory would soon begin. Unwilling to disappoint Jamie and Alex, she had no choice but to attend. In her short time at Dunvegan, they'd welcomed her as family, a very different family from the one she was accustomed to. She thought of her own, of the Fae, and felt a niggling of guilt. She'd given little consideration to those dependent upon her, but with Lan's disappearance, her mind had been elsewhere. Her only consolation was that Fallyn and her sisters could easily step in and fill the breach.

She ran her palm over the smooth surface of the stone then stood. Shaking the dirt and crumpled leaves from the bottom of her gown, she walked toward the clearing.

Upon reaching the castle's entrance, she took a calming breath and pushed open the heavy doors. She ducked inside, relieved to find no one about. A quiet hum of activity filtered out from the grand hall. Several feet from Rory's study, she noted the door was ajar. She could see Fergus, about to leave, look over his shoulder. A chair scraped across the slate floor and Fergus grunted. She lifted her skirts and rushed toward the stairs before he could see her. His deep voice followed her ascent.

"We told you yer plan to seduce the lass into confessin' was unconscionable. And to think ye went ahead with it over our objections 'tis somethin' I never would have expected. I'm sorely disappointed in you, Aidan."

* * *

Aidan exited from Rory's study. "There's no getttin' through to the two of ye. I doona care what Rory's led ye to believe. Nothin' happened! I'd already decided . . ." Aidan followed Fergus's gaze to Syrena's retreating back.

"Syrena," Aidan called as she fled up the stairs. She ignored him and he turned to blast Fergus. "Now look what ye've done!"

"Me? Nay, lad, that would be all yer doin'." Fergus shook his head, a look of disgust upon his face. "Leave her be."

Aidan ignored the man's misguided advice. He couldn't leave her be. He wouldn't have her thinking what happened between them was nothing more than an attempt on his part to get the truth from her. Aye, in his fear for Lachlan, he'd considered the idea. But the more time he'd spent with her, watching her with the bairns and his family, the more he realized he'd acted the fool. Now he just had to convince her. He shoved aside the thought that her feelings meant more to him than they should. The last thing he wanted was to cause her pain. When she spoke of her life with the Fae, he sensed she'd had her share of heartache.

Standing outside her chamber door, he rattled the latch. When it wouldn't open, he rapped his knuckles sharply on the oak planks. "Syrena, let me in."

"I doona ken what it is about ye MacLeod lads." Alasdair MacDonald's gravelly voice came from behind him. "But I'm thinkin' I should give ye a lesson on how to deal with the lasses. Lord kens ye and that son-of-mine-by-marriage could use one. Now tell me what ye've gone and done to upset yer betrothed."

Aidan sent his eyes to the timbered ceiling. God help him if Alasdair put it in his head to adopt Syrena as he once had Aileanna. "'Tis nothin', but thank ye fer yer concern."

"Nothin'? I doona ken about that. I'm warnin' ye, lad, seein' as the wee lass has no one to look to her interests, I have offered my services." The MacDonald shouldered Aidan aside and knocked. "Syrena, are ye all right, lass?"

The door opened a fraction of an inch, and Syrena smiled softly at the old man. "I'm fine, Lord MacDonald." She wouldn't look at Aidan, but he thought she'd been crying and he cursed his and Fergus's stupidity.

With his finger, Alasdair tipped her chin. "Ye're no' fine. What did the fool do to upset ye?"

"'Twas a simple misunderstandin' is all. One I mean to rectify if ye'd but leave us be, MacDonald," Aidan said.

Alasdair shook his head. "I'll say it again, I doona ken what ye lasses see in these lads. Are ye certain ye wish to marry him, pet? My offer still stands. As I told ye earlier, I ken many a fine mon who would leap at the chance to wed ye."

A fierce wave of jealously swamped him and he reacted without thinking. "The only mon she'll be marryin' is me, Alasdair. And I'd thank ye to remember that."

Syrena's astonished gaze met his.

Bloody hell, he had to get rid of the meddlin' old goat. "'Tis no' my business, Alasdair, but ye may wish to have a word with Rory. He's threatenin' to lock Aileanna in her chambers fer disobeyin' him."

Alasdair's brows shot up. "MacLeod!" he bellowed as he strode away. As Aidan intended, his daughter's plight took precedence over Syrena's.

At the sound of her soft giggle, he returned his attention to her.

"That wasn't very nice. Now Rory's in trouble with Lord MacDonald, and I'm certain he doesn't deserve to be."

He shrugged with a self-satisfied smile, then wedged his foot between the door and the frame in case she remembered her anger before he had a chance to explain. "Syrena, we need to talk."

Her eyes shadowed, and the smile faded from her lips. "I heard everything I needed to." He barely managed to tear his foot free before she slammed the door in his face.

220   *Debbie Mazzuca*

"Bloody hell, Syrena, that hurt." Putting his shoulder to the door, he got it open before she set the latch. Ignoring her outraged expression, he stepped inside and shut the door behind him. Remembering Alasdair, he bolted it.

Arms crossed, she glared at him. "Be quick about it, I have to get ready for the celebration."

"Ye look fine to me." She looked more than fine. The fire of her temper glowed in her pink-tinged cheeks and sparked a flame in her topaz eyes.

"What I look like is a woman who's been bedded."

His barely banked desire sprang to life, and he dragged her protesting into his arms. "Aye, ye do." He tangled his fingers in the thick tumble of her curls, tugging gently to force her gaze to his. "A woman well loved."

For the love of God, she was drivin' him mad. Making him say things he shouldn't say, making him feel things he shouldn't feel.

"Well used." Her wee fists beat at his chest as she struggled to free herself. "Let me go!"

"Nay, Syrena." He tightened his hold until, defeated, she stilled and held herself stiffly in his arms.

He smoothed the hair from her face. "Look at me." When she finally returned her gaze to his, he explained, "I ken ye heard what Fergus said, but 'twas no' what happened. I wanted ye, Syrena, I still do." He slid his hand to the curve of her behind and pressed her against the bulge in his trews. "And it had nothin' to do with gettin' the truth from ye. I'd decided beforehand ye had naught to do with Lan's disappearance." Even though he spoke the truth, a part of him wished he'd held back. Afraid what she'd do with the knowledge of his desire for her.

"But now they know. Fergus and Rory know we were . . ." Her fingers fluttered between them, the flush on her cheeks deepening.

He took her hand and kissed her palm. "Nay, they only think they ken." Aidan had been about to ask her what did it matter, certain that if all he heard was true, the Fae would not judge her. But he began to think it was nothing more than tall tales the old ones passed down with little relevance to the truth, especially where Syrena was concerned.

"That's easy for you to say, Aidan. Men are expected to . . . to, but women are not."

She looked adorable, sweetly flustered and innocent. "Stop, Syrena, ye're gettin' yerself worked up fer nothin'. Rory and Fergus will think no less of ye. Besides, thanks to Aileanna, we're betrothed and many couples have relations before they're wed." He grinned. "Just ask Rory and Aileanna."

"But their betrothal was real, while ours is—"

An insistent pounding on the chamber door interrupted her, and a raspy voice demanded entrance. Aidan never thought he'd be happy to hear Alasdair MacDonald bellowing his name, but he was. He knew what Syrena had been about to say, and for the life of him, he didn't know how to respond. He'd be damned either way.

"Aidan MacLeod, get yer arse out of the lass's chamber. Now!"

Syrena stared wistfully at the iced cakes Alieanna had moments ago placed in front of Alex and Jamie. Mrs. Mac had time to make only three, one for Rory, the other two for the boys. "Doona worry, I'm certain they'll share with ye." Aidan grinned from where he sat beside her, his eyes glinting with amusement.

"Not if they keep feeding their puppy, they won't," she said, watching Jamie wiggle his sugar-coated fingers under the table.

"Their da will put a stop to it soon enough. Has Rory thanked ye fer the demon's present yet?"

Syrena lifted the goblet of mead to her lips and glanced at Rory, who was talking to Fergus. Rory's arm draped over the back of his wife's chair, he absently stroked Aileanna's shoulder. "Thanks would be overstating the sentiment," she said before taking a sip of the sweetened wine. She had dreaded making an appearance despite Aidan's valiant attempt to alleviate her embarrassment. But neither Rory nor Fergus had made her feel awkward. If anything, they'd put her completely at ease. Until the subject of her present to the twins came up, then Rory had gritted his teeth when Aileanna browbeat him into thanking her.

Alex nudged her. "Look, princess." He giggled, the dog lapping at his fingers.

She smiled. "Careful, he might get sick from all the sweets."

Aidan laughed and leaned across her to speak to Alex, "Doona mind yer aunt, she's afraid ye'll have no cake left to share with her is all."

"That's not true." She looked at Aidan and got tangled up in his laughing eyes, the heat of his shoulder brushing against her arm. She'd never imagined he would look at her in that way again. She didn't know what was happening between them. She was afraid to hope that they shared more than a passionate interlude, afraid to lower her defenses, although she didn't know if she had any left. Not after he'd held her in his arms and assured her he wanted her. She lowered her gaze from his and shrugged. "Maybe, just a little."

Alasdair regarded her over Alex's head. "Did the bairn call ye princess?"

Aileanna glanced up from admonishing Jamie. "Aye, he did, Da. 'Tis Aidan's pet name for her." Aileanna caught Syrena's eye and shrugged.

Her father quirked a brow. "Treats ye like a princess, does he?"

A prickly heat worked its way from her chest to her cheeks. The last thing she wanted was for Aidan to be reminded of who she was, not that he was likely to forget, but if she could avoid it, she would. Before she could respond, Aidan answered for her.

"Of course I do, doona I, princess?" The way he said "princess," in his deep raspy voice, was as much a caress as his big hand resting at the nape of her neck, his thumb stroking her fluttering pulse.

Alasdair eyed the two of them, then announced, "I think 'tis time fer ye to wed."

She felt the imperceptible tightening of Aidan's fingers and swallowed.

"I would agree with ye, Alasdair, but Syrena and I are headin' fer London," Aidan informed him. Slowly drawing his hand from her neck, he reached for his goblet. His knuckles whitened from the force of his grip.

"London? Why would ye be goin' to London? They've only recently got the plague under control."

"Plague?" Syrena asked. A tremor raced up her spine at the thought Lachlan could have contracted the scourge. Illnesses that affected the Mortals had been much debated in the Enchanted Isles, especially when they thought her inability to do magick was the result of a disease. Her pounding heart calmed when she remembered Uscias's pronouncement that the Fae were immune to illnesses the Mortals so easily succumbed to. Her brother was half-Fae. Hopefully that would be enough to protect him.

"Aye, it broke out during James's Coronation last July—"

Rory, who'd turned from his conversation with Fergus, interrupted Alasdair, "Doona fash yerself, Syrena. I've heard from my acquaintances that everythin' has calmed over the last months."

Syrena appreciated Rory's attempt to reassure her that Lachlan was safe, at least from the plague. Alex and Jamie turned mutinous expressions upon her. "We doona want you to go," Alex protested.

"Aye, let Uncle Aidan go by hisself," Jamie added.

Aidan lifted a sardonic brow and tipped his goblet at the twins. "I'll miss ye, too."

Aileanna tousled her son's fair hair. "We don't want either

Auntie Syrena or Uncle Aidan to go, but they have to find Uncle Lachlan. When they do, they'll come here before returning to Lewes."

"Ye will?" Alex asked Syrena.

Unable to resist the pleading look in his bright blue eyes, Syrena said, "Of course I will." And she realized how very much she wanted to. And just how much the MacLeod family had come to mean to her. She kept her gaze averted from Aidan's, afraid of what she might see there.

"Well, that settles it. Ye'll have to wed on the morrow," Lord MacDonald pronounced.

"Da, I—"

"Doona argue with me, Aileanna. The lass is no' leavin' Dunvegan until I see her properly wed."

Aidan cursed quietly beside her while Fergus and Rory appeared to be having difficulty containing their mirth. Obviously they would receive no help from that end of the table. "I appreciate your concerns, Laird MacDonald, but I—"

The older man reached over and patted her hand. "Ye let me take care of this, pet. 'Tis no' somethin' a lass needs to concern herself with."

"Alasdair, I appreciate the sentiments, but there's no time, we leave on the morrow," Aidan protested, a muscle pulsating in his jaw.

Lord MacDonald sighed. "There's no help fer it then, ye'll have to do as my daughter did. Ye and yer cousin Rory are two of a kind," he muttered. Obviously not a favorable comparison, at least as far as Alasdair was concerned. "The two of ye stand up," he ordered Aidan and Syrena. His tone brooked no disagreement.

He banged his goblet on the long table, the contents spilling onto the white cloth, then bellowed above the chatter of the men and women seated in the grand hall. "Good people, I need yer attention fer a moment. I'm callin' upon ye to witness the marriage between Aidan MacLeod and Syrena . . . What's yer family name, lass?"

"Rory," Aidan growled, slowly coming to his feet.

A heated wave swamped Syrena.

"Uh . . . uh . . . LaFae. Her family name is LaFae,"Aileanna chimed in, elbowing her husband when he snorted a laugh.

"LaFae, is it? I didna ken ye were French. Ah, well, so be it." He turned back to the fifty or so people gathered around the rows of tables. "The union of Aidan MacLeod and Syrena LaFae. Syrena LaFae, do ye take Aidan MacLeod fer yer husband?"

She looked at Aidan, his focus on something beyond her. She didn't know what he wanted her to do. His beautiful face was an inscrutable mask as he stood stiffly beside her. A dull ache radiated from her chest to her throat; her gown felt three sizes too small. Sensing Alasdair's growing impatience, everyone waiting for her to speak, she swallowed and said, "Yes."

Lord MacDonald nodded then regarded Aidan sternly from beneath his silvery brows. "And ye, Aidan MacLeod, do ye take Syrena LaFae to be yer wife?"

Aidan sent his gaze to the ceiling and shook his head. Syrena thought her heart would stop. Mortified, she felt like crawling beneath the table. Through a blur, she watched the men and women of Dunvegan shift uncomfortably on the benches.

Alasdair cleared his throat, drawing Aidan's attention to her. How could he do this? If the idea of marrying her was so distasteful, why could he not have told Alasdair before, instead of humiliating her now? *And why didn't you?* she asked herself. But she knew the reason. Deep down inside, her foolish hopes lived on.

She blinked back tears, her throat so tight she struggled to breathe. She wouldn't cry. Not here, not now.

Aidan's gaze softened. He brought his hand to her cheek and wiped away a tear she didn't realize had fallen. "Aye, I'll take her fer my wife. Are ye satisfied now, MacDonald?" Aidan didn't wait for Alasdair's response. He tugged Syrena into his arms and brushed her lips with his. His kiss was gentle, a soothing balm to her savaged emotions. And in that moment, held close in his powerful embrace, she almost believed her long-ago dreams might actually come true.

"Mam, will Auntie Syrena get a bairn in her belly like ye?" Jamie asked loudly.

His mother groaned. "Jamie, that was supposed to be a secret."

"Is it true, Aileanna? Are ye with child?" her father asked.

"Aye," Aileanna admitted reluctantly. "But we'll talk of it later. 'Tis time to toast Syrena and Aidan."

Aidan's hand dropped, and he set Syrena aside. His jaw was set in a hard line, his expression shuttered. "Nay, Aileanna, I apologize, but I have much to see to if Syrena and I are to leave on the morrow." That said, he strode from the dais.

Chapter 19

Syrena's hardnosed silence grated on Aidan's nerves. They were half-a-day's ride from Dunvegan, and she'd yet to say a word to him. He'd heard her sniffling after her tearful good-byes to the bairns and Aileanna, but he didn't credit her sorrow with her sullen disposition.

Nay, he was all but certain his abrupt departure from the celebration and his absence from the marriage bed were the reasons for her terse responses whenever he attempted to make conversation.

He supposed he owed her an apology, some form of expla-nation, but he couldn't bring himself to give her one. He couldn't speak to her of the panic that all but consumed him at Jamie's mention of a bairn.

When they'd made love, Aidan had been consumed by his desire for her. Lost in her perfection, drowning in a tumul-tuous sea of tenderness at the gift of her innocence, he had spilled his seed inside her. Something he'd never allowed him-self to do before. No other woman had caused him to lose con-trol like she did. And the thought she could be carrying his child—a child who would be half-Fae—filled him with dread.

A dread born of fear. Fear that he would become his father. A man Aidan had once been honored to be compared to. But all that changed on the night of Lachlan's birth, on the rain-swept cliffs of Lewes. Aidan worried one day he, too, would be helpless to fight the darkness, unable to get past his hatred of the Fae. And never would he allow an innocent child to suffer as his brother had.

Somehow he had to make Syrena understand without revealing the sordid details of his father's madness. A madness her father had unleashed, yet he found he no longer held her to blame. She was the opposite of everything Alexander and the old crone proclaimed the Fae to be.

The hulking fair-haired Callum, who brought up the rear of their small contingent alongside Aidan, asked, "Laird MacLeod, do ye wish to set up camp fer the night?"

Watching the sun's fiery descent over the Cuillins, Aidan nodded. "Aye."

"I ken gettin' away close to midmorn was no' what ye had in mind, Laird MacLeod, but we've made good progress. Yer wife, she didna hold us up. She handles a steed as well as she does a sword."

Aye, Syrena had wreaked havoc with his plans once again, and in more ways than one. No thanks to Alasdair MacDonald—the meddling old fool. But Aidan could do nothing less than agree to the union. He'd taken her innocence. Once she'd been everything he'd wanted in a wife. He couldn't deny she still was—sweet and innocent, gentle yet strong, and more beautiful than was fair.

He'd seen the vulnerability in her eyes when he'd hesitated. He hadn't meant to hurt her, but he'd been torn between the desire to claim her as his, and the need to protect himself from the woman who'd once lied to him, a woman who was Fae. A year ago, she had shattered his illusions and brought his worst fears to light. Now he had to find a way to trust her, for Lan's sake and his own.

"Nay, she hasna. I suppose I'd best break the news to my bonny wife that we'll be sleepin' out of doors this night." Knowing her as he did, he was certain she'd not be very happy with the arrangement, especially considering the temper she was in. He'd hoped to make it as far as the Mackenzies' holdings, where he could be certain of their welcome, but it was not going to happen.

Putting his heels to Fin's flank, he brought his steed alongside Syrena. Connor, who'd been keeping her company, tipped his head and took his leave, joining the three men who rode ahead.

Aidan blew out an exasperated breath when she pointedly ignored him. "I'm no' goin' anywhere, so 'twould be best if ye told me what's troublin' ye."

She looked down her nose at him. Her attempt to appear haughty failed miserably. If she had a long aristocratic nose instead of her small upturned one, it might have worked. "I'm not troubled, and we have nothing to discuss."

"Nay? So ye're no' fashed I didna come to ye last night?"

"No. Why would you think such a thing?" She focused on the leather reins gathered tightly in her hands, inspecting them as though they needed to be repaired. But he didn't miss the compressed line of her mouth.

"I doona ken, mayhap because ye havena said more than two words to me since we left Dunvegan, and ye're pricklier than a hedgehog."

"I don't know what a hedgehog is, but if I am as prickly as one, it is because you insisted I wear this silly gown instead of breeches." She squinched her upturned nose at the dark green velvet gown she wore.

He shook his head at the memory of her coming down the stairs in a pair of Connor's breeches and tunic. She'd been none too pleased when he sent her unceremoniously back to her room to change. If it hadn't been for the MacDonald's shocked expression, he knew she would have done exactly as she pleased. But her gown had nothing to do with her temper, of that he was certain.

"Ye're a lady, Syrena, 'tis no' proper to be outfitted in trews." He reached over to brush his fingers along the curve of her cheek. "And 'tis no' the reason ye're fashed with me, be honest."

She raised her eyes to his, and he felt himself drowning in pools of liquid gold. "You embarrassed me. Why didn't you just tell Lord MacDonald you didn't wish to marry me? Instead, you made a fool of me leaving the celebration as you did. And if that wasn't bad enough, this morning I was subjected to the maids whispering and tittering how my husband spent his wedding night . . . elsewhere!" Snapping the reins, she urged her mount into a gallop, leaving Aidan in a cloud of dust.

Bloody hell!

"Callum, make camp," he shouted over his shoulder as he shot past the men gaping after his wife. Callum was right, she rode as well as she fought, mayhap better. By the time he managed to catch up to her, they'd put a fair distance between them and his men.

His temper now matched hers. "Syrena," he yelled, leaning over to grab the reins from her hands. "If ye have no' regard fer yer own life, think of yer mounts."

She blinked as though awakening from a dream. Looking down at her steed, she grimaced, and snatched the reins from Aidan's hands. Easing back, she brought her horse to a halt, then slid stiffly to the ground. Aidan dismounted and reached out to steady her. She jerked her arm from his hand. Burying her face in the steed's neck, she murmured her apologies to the horse.

"Are ye no' goin' to apologize to me?" he asked from where he stood behind her.

"For what? I've done nothing wrong."

"Nay?" He tugged her into his arms, pressing her back to his chest. He rubbed his stubbled cheek against the silky tangle of her hair. "Ye could've been hurt, Syrena, ye're no' familiar with the lay of the land."

She didn't pull away, but neither did she unbend in his arms. "I ride as well as you. I wasn't in any danger."

"I'm no' disputin' yer skill in the saddle, just yer lack of common sense."

"You have no right—"

He spun her around to face him, a firm grip on her upper arms. "I have every right. Ye're my wife."

"You don't even want—"

Framing her face with his hands, he leaned in to kiss her— a deep and possessive kiss. "Aye, I want ye," he murmured against her lips and felt a slight easing of her resistance. "There was much to do to prepare for our journey. 'Twas late before I finished and I didna wish to disturb ye." Although not the complete truth, he hoped she would be satisfied with his answer. The last thing he'd meant to do was humiliate her.

She pulled back and searched his face as though she could find the truth in his eyes. "There's more to it than that. I felt you pull away after . . . after Jamie asked if I would have—"

He silenced her with a finger pressed to her soft lips. "I ken what the lad asked." He drew her into the circle of his arms and rested his chin on top of her head, stroking her back. "Let it go fer now, Syrena, please. We have enough with tryin' to find Lan."

She nodded and he breathed a sigh of relief. She lifted her head from his chest. "Where are the others? They should have caught up by now."

"They're makin' camp."

"What do you mean making camp?"

"Just what it sounds like. I imagine they'll have built the fire and set up yer tent by now." They had ridden their mounts hard, and not wanting to cause them injury, Aidan handed Syrena her steed's reins. He took her by the shoulders and set her in the direction of the camp. Her brow furrowed as she walked beside him, then she came to an abrupt halt. "Are you telling me we're sleeping out of doors . . . on the ground?"

"Aye." He nodded, trying not to laugh at her horrified expression.

"We'll freeze to death, and I'll never be able to sleep with nothing but a hard patch of earth beneath me."

"Aye, ye will. I'll tire ye out and then ye can fall asleep on top of me." Dropping a kiss on the tip of her nose, he promised, "And I'll keep ye verra, verra warm."

With a thunderous flap, the tent in which Syrena slept was ripped from its moorings. She came fully awake, blinking into the early morning light with an outraged shriek.

"Sorry, my lady, laird's orders." Connor grinned, a lock of hair falling over his laughing green eyes.

To add insult to injury, her husband yanked her from beneath the warm blankets and she shrieked again. "Aidan, you could have warned me. I might have been naked under there," she growled, keeping her voice low.

"Since ye were washed and dressed when I left the tent, 'twas no' a concern. I should've kent ye'd crawl back beneath the covers as soon as I was gone." He hauled her to her feet and gave her bottom a familiar slap.

"Ouch." Pouting, she rubbed her behind.

"Ye missed yer callin', angel. Ye should've been on the stage." He lowered his mouth to hers for a quick kiss before calling to the men, "Time's a-wastin', lads."

She stifled a groan. They were six days into their journey, each day more grueling than the last. "Aidan, how much—"

Her husband gave an exasperated shake of his head. "Do ye ken ye ask the same question every mornin'? We have a long ways to go, but we're approachin' the Lowlands and the goin' will be easier. And if ye're a good lass, I may find ye an inn with a soft bed to lay yer bonny head on."

"I'm always good," Syrena bristled. She doubted any other woman would have been as pleasant as she had been under the circumstances. Maybe she was a little difficult to awaken in the morning, and her attempts at cooking for the men had been inedible at best. But besides that, she didn't think her husband had much to complain about.

"Aye, ye are." He grinned, the crescent moon in his cheek deepening. Unable to resist him, she reached up on the tips of her toes to kiss his full lips. Deepening the kiss, he walked her backward toward the horses. Settling her onto her mount, he dug in her saddlebag and handed her a hunk of bread. "Eat, there's an apple in yer bag fer later."

"But I don't—"

"I ken," he said with exaggerated patience. She didn't like to eat until later in the day and they had the same argument every morning. "But I doona want ye gettin' skinny on me. I like ye the way ye are." He patted her thigh and the heated look in his cloud gray gaze caused her stomach to clench, and a frisson of awareness to race up her spine. She knew she would never love anyone as much as she loved this man, and over the last few days she'd begun to believe he felt the same way.

After enduring six straight days of rain, Syrena tilted her face to the sun, smiling as its warm rays caressed her cheeks. Aidan chuckled as he mounted Fin.

"Ye've missed the sun, have ye?"

"Um-hmm. I'm not accustomed to rain. In the Enchanted Isles we have only sunshine." As soon as the words were out of her mouth, she regretted them. Knowing how Aidan felt about the Fae, she did her best not to remind him she was one of them. Certain it made it easier for him to accept his feelings for her.

She peeked at him from beneath her lashes. His expression was shuttered. After a moment of painful silence, he asked, "Do ye miss yer home?"

"No," she replied honestly. She didn't, and felt a twinge of guilt at the realization. But she did wonder how they fared without her. The knowledge Fallyn was more than qualified to lead alleviated some of her worry. And at the moment, there was nothing she could do about it; the portals to the Enchanted realm were closed. What she would do when they were opened, when they found Lachlan, she couldn't think about, not now, not yet.

He reached for her hand and brought it to his lips, about to say something, when Callum galloped toward them. Aidan slowly lowered her hand and met the other man's distressed gaze.

"Eight Lamonts comin' this way, Laird MacLeod." Callum said, but she didn't miss the silent exchange between the two men.

"Be on yer guard, lads," Aidan called out, unsheathing his sword.

Gone was her teasing husband and in his place sat a warrior. His beautiful face set in hard, unyielding lines, he exuded confidence and strength. Syrena knew he would never allow anyone to harm her, but neither would she allow anyone to harm him.

She leaned over to remove Nuie from the satchel Aidan asked her to hide him in. He'd been so insistent her protest had been minimal. Her sword was a reminder to him of who she was, and she'd been willing to make the sacrifice— for him.

"Nay, Syrena, leave yer wee sword where it is," he said firmly.

"Callum, Connor." He jerked his chin in her direction as he rode to the head of their small party.

"Wee sword," she grumbled. Callum and Connor exchanged an amused look. *Men.* But her aggravation became moot when the party of eight approached.

They had the look of hardened warriors, bulging muscles visible beneath their belted plaids and long scraggly beards that did little to hide the menace of their features. Leading them was an auburn-haired man whose barrel chest puffed up with pride. He looked at Aidan and sneered, a maniacal gleam in his pale blue eyes. Syrena tensed. She'd seen the look before, on the battlefield, in the eyes of men just before they attacked.

Despite Aidan's demand, she retrieved Nuie. Shards of red flashed through her fingers as her sword made his unhappiness at being shut away known. She laid him across her lap, touching the tips of her fingers to the gleaming jewels, ensuring he was at full power.

Connor appeared ready to protest, but she shot him a look she'd perfected on the battlefield. His brows went up, and he clamped his mouth shut. If these men attacked, they would have no choice but to allow her to fight alongside them. They would need her whether they wanted to admit it or not. Having trained her own army, Syrena recognized that only Aidan and Callum would be of any use in battle. The remaining four were too young and inexperienced. She wouldn't allow the boys to die simply because the fools wouldn't acknowledge her as a warrior.

Lowering her voice, she asked Callum, "What does that man have against Aidan?" Early on, she'd learned the best way to ensure victory in battle was to know your enemy, and know him well.

"Bad blood between the MacLeods of Lewis and the Lamonts of Harris. They were kin of Angus, the one in charge."

"Were?" Syrena asked out of the side of her mouth, keeping an eye on the man Callum referred to.

"Aye, their castle burnt to the ground, none survived."

"What has that to do with Aidan?"

"'Twas rumored he or his brother ordered the fire started."

Syrena's mouth fell open. Surely it was a misunderstanding. "Why would . . ."

Callum shook his head, his attention focused on the Lamonts. He was right—it was not the time.

"Ye're a long way from Lewes, MacLeod," the leader said. He spat on the ground, missing Fin's left hoof by an inch. With the back of his hand, he wiped gobs of spittle from his mangy auburn beard. Angus Lamont took the measure of each man in their party before his gaze came to rest on her. A salacious smile revealed broken, yellow-stained teeth.

"I ken where I am and where yer lands are, Lamont, and I'm no' even close to them. What is it ye want?" Now she understood why Aidan had seemed more cautious of late.

The man had not taken his eyes from her, and Connor and Callum stiffened in their saddles. "Curiosity ye might say. 'Twas brought to my attention ye were in the area." Jerking his head in Syrena's direction, he asked. "And who might the bonny lass be?"

"My wife." No one could miss the edge of steel that sliced through Aidan's deep voice.

"Then 'tis only polite I offer her my cond . . . congratulations."

Tension rolled off Aidan. His powerful muscles flexed across his broad back and down his sword arm. Syrena almost shook her head at Lamont's misguided attempt to bring his shaggy brown mount toward her. Aidan raised his sword and held the flat of the blade inches from the man's chest. "Doona even think about it."

The disgruntled mutters rumbling through Lamont's followers caused the five men behind Aidan to straighten in the saddle, their swords at the ready.

"'Twould be best if ye move on, Lamont."

"Would it? But mayhap I should warn the lass to have a care of the company she keeps, else she'll wind up dead like my cousin Janet."

Before the man could utter another word, Aidan had fisted his hand in Angus's plaid. "If ye want to live to see another day, you'll no' threaten my wife." With a hard shove, Aidan released him. "Now get the hell out of here."

Angus rubbed his reddened neck and sneered. "Aye, we'll be leavin'." He jerked his head at his companions, but before they rode away, he looked back at Aidan. "I hear yer brother's gone missin', MacLeod. I'd wish ye well in findin' him, but 'twould be a lie. I hope the bastard rots in hell. 'Tis where he belongs. And mark my words, ye'll be joinin' him soon enough."

Chapter 20

Aidan, with a white-knuckled grip on Fin's reins, watched as the Lamonts rode into the early morning mist, furious that there wasn't a bloody thing he could do about it. Angus and his men were ruthless. Besides Callum, he had naught but four lads, and a woman—a woman who no matter how well she wielded a sword—he would not put at risk. He didn't care how many times she'd fought before. Women had no place in battle, most especially his wife.

Syrena tugged urgently on his sleeve. "What are we waiting for? They're getting away."

He drew his gaze from the valley the Lamonts had disappeared into and met her determined gaze. "I can see that, Syrena, but what would ye have me do? We're sorely outnumbered. I'll no' put the men at risk when I doona even ken if Angus has information as to Lan's whereabouts. I'll no' put ye in danger." The glint from her sword caught his eye. "I see ye chose to disobey me, again."

She narrowed her gaze on him. "You can't truly believe I would sit by like some helpless maid while you and your men defended me. I don't need safeguarding, Aidan."

"So ye keep tellin' me." He dragged a hand through his hair. "There's enough talk about my family without ye makin' a spectacle of yerself, Syrena. The last thing I need is fer

people to start questionin' who ye are and where ye're from."
The words came out more forceful than he'd intended. The
wounded look in her eyes cut deep, but before he could take
them back, she guided her horse away from him.

Although he didn't mean to hurt her, he realized there was
more truth to his statement than he cared to admit. He'd spent
a lifetime protecting Lan from censure, protecting his
family's name. If not for the fire that had claimed the Lamonts, his efforts would have been in vain. And he would let
nothing else jeopardize his family's honor or his brother's
safety, not even his feelings for Syrena.

Callum brought his steed alongside him and Aidan realized
they awaited his command.

"We're no' goin' after Angus, then?"

"Nay." Lifting a hand, he motioned for the men to move
out and noted the look of relief in Callum's gaze.

"I ken 'twas no' an easy decision fer ye to make on account
of yer brother, but 'twas the right one if ye doona mind me
sayin' it. The Lamonts are fearsome in a fight. And no' to take
away from the lads, but they're no' battle hardened."

"I'm thinkin' 'twas a good thing Angus didna ken that. He's
been waitin' fer a chance to seek his revenge." The knowledge
weighed heavy on Aidan. Why hadn't Angus taken the opportunity to avenge his cousins' deaths as he had so often
threatened? Aidan sucked in a shuddered breath—unless
they'd already been avenged, and Lachlan was dead.

"Aye, 'tis what we've been hearin' at Dunvegan. But he's
seen yer prowess on the battlefield, Laird MacLeod, and he
didna ken the lads were untried."

"Thank ye fer that," Aidan managed, praying he was wrong
and Callum right. He followed Syrena's progress over the
glen, realizing she veered toward the forest. "I'd best see to
my wife," he said.

"She seemed a mite fashed."

"Aye," he said, wishing that was all it was. He'd rather deal
with her anger than her tears any day.

By the time Aidan skirted the forest, his regret at causing Syrena pain had vanished. He wanted to shake her until her teeth rattled for riding off and leaving herself open to attack.

Warrior, my arse!

The woman couldn't tell north from south. She'd gotten herself turned around and was headin' through the woods in the wrong direction. Thankfully, he thought, in the opposite one the Lamonts had taken.

Aidan circled back, slowing his mount. He guided Fin through the dense grove of birch and oak trees. At the sight of her riderless mount, he leapt from Fin, his heart hammering in his chest. A light breeze rustled the leaves and a glimmer of gold caught his attention. He held the branches out of the way and the tightness in his chest eased. Syrena sat on a log, talking to her sword.

He folded his arms over his chest and leaned against the tree. "Are ye hopin' yer wee friend will set ye in the right direction?"

She didn't look at him. Coming slowly to her feet, she shook out her skirts. He thought she meant to ignore him until she said, "I wasn't lost." She brushed past him, absently patting Fin's nose as she walked by him to her mount.

"More like ye kent I wouldna let ye out of my sight and would come to retrieve ye."

"No." Hand on the bridle, she turned to look at him. He wished he'd kept his bloody mouth shut when he noted her red-rimmed eyes. "For all I knew, you might be glad to be rid of me. After all, no matter how much we pretend I'm not Fae, I am. Nothing's going to change that, Aidan, and the last thing I want is for you or your family to suffer on account of who I am." With her back to him, she placed her sword, glowing blue, inside the black satchel.

Although Aidan would never admit it to her, he had been deceiving himself. He'd set who she was to the far reaches of his mind—it was easier that way.

Reaching her in two strides, he placed his hands on her

shoulders to keep her from mounting her horse. "I'm sorry I hurt ye." Her slender shoulders were rigid and he knew an apology would not be enough. "'Twas no' easy lettin' the Lamonts ride away as I did. I took my frustration out on ye and ye didna deserve it."

A slight tremor shook her body and he was angry at himself for not having insisted she wear her cloak. Ignoring her protest, he scooped her into his arms and set her on top of Fin. Grabbing her mount's reins, he swung into the saddle behind her. "Doona try and deny it—ye're freezin' and I will no' have ye catchin' a chill."

"You could've just given me a blanket," she muttered, her teeth chattering.

"Nay, I'd rather have ye in my arms." Holding her close, he breathed in her sweet scent. "Besides, I doona want anyone to hear what I have to tell ye."

She glanced over her shoulder to meet his eyes. "About what?"

"Why there's bad blood between us and the Lamonts."

"I already know. Callum says they think you set fire to their cousin's castle. Did you?"

He held her gaze, disappointed she thought him capable of such a heinous act.

She blew out an exasperated breath. "Fine, I know you wouldn't do such a thing."

Riding out of the woods and into the watery sunlight, he tipped her chin and kissed the grim set of her lips. "Ye're still fashed with me."

"Yes, but I want to hear your story."

He nodded. He wanted to tell her. Besides his cousin and Fergus, he could share the tale with no one else. But he could tell Syrena, and there was a sense of relief in being able to do so. Being able to unburden his soul to someone who would understand, someone who loved his brother as much as he did. He no longer doubted her love for Lan and knew she would do everything within her power to protect him.

"It happened several months back. Lan fancied himself in love with Janet Lamont, Angus's cousin. He began courtin' the lass. I didna ken anythin' about it until it was too late."

Aidan would've warned his brother had he known. He'd met the lass a time or two; her brothers and father doted on her. 'Twas no' right to speak ill of the dead, but for all her fine looks, she led the lads on a merry chase without a care for anyone but herself. "She found herself with child. Lan meant to marry her, so he was no' overly upset. He went to her father and asked fer her hand."

"Ouch, Aidan," Syrena protested, rubbing her arm.

He shook his head and loosened his hold on her. Telling the tale brought everything back. "Sorry," he murmured. He let his gaze drift over the distant hills in an attempt to regain a semblance of his control. "Lan had never been to the Lamonts holdings, and from their surprise he didna think the lass had made mention of him or their intentions. If no' fer the old crone, it might have worked out but—"

Syrena's smooth brow furrowed. "Old crone?"

"Aye, she had been with us since Lan's birth. 'Twas her that saw the seven-pointed star on Lan's shoulder, branding him as Fae. On the night of my father's death, I tossed her from Lewes with enough coin to buy her silence. I didna ken that she'd taken up residence with the Lamonts. Once she heard who her young charge was set to wed, and that the lass carried his bairn, the old woman went mad. Breaking her oath to me, she told the laird and his sons that Lachlan was half-Fae. She pleaded with them no' to allow the marriage, offering to rid the lass of the bairn she carried."

"No," Syrena gasped, clutching his hand.

"Aye, they beat Lan and sent him home with a missive. They demanded I marry the lass in my brother's stead and banish him from Lewes."

"Did you . . . would you have married her?"

He met her searching gaze. "Aye, I didna see any way

around it. She had been an innocent, Lan admitted as much. And the bairn, I could no' allow them to—"

"But Lan . . . you would have banished him from his home? You could do that to your own brother?" Her mouth tightened, and anger sparked in her topaz gaze.

Aye, at the time he'd felt he didn't have a choice. He'd been as furious with Lan as he had been with the old crone and the Lamonts. Once again, on account of his brother and his god-forsaken bloodline, Aidan's life was turned upside down, the chance to take a bride of his own choosing destroyed.

His gaze dropped to Syrena. Not that he wanted any other, not after her. "I thought once the furor died down, Lan would be able to return home. I would've sent him to Dunvegan, but it proved unnecessary." He closed his eyes—he could still smell the acrid scent of death, of charred remains—before continuing, "'Twas that same night the castle burned. A smol-dering shell was all that remained when I rode in with my reply the next day—all within had died."

Syrena cleared her throat, leaning heavily against him. "Did Lan . . . you don't think?"

Aidan knew what she asked. He'd asked himself the same question a hundred times before. "Nay, he was badly beaten." In his heart, 'twas what Aidan believed, what he prayed to be true. But his brother never deigned to give him an answer, barely spoke to him since that day, and in all honesty, Aidan couldn't say for certain.

Despite Aidan's protective presence at her back, a cold north wind buffeted Syrena. She snuggled deeper within her woolen mantle, stumbling over the cobblestone walk. Aidan, who had been directing three of the lads to stay behind and see to the horses, took hold of her elbow. He guided her past the carriages lining the drive in front of the stately home on the Strand. The massive town house was cloaked in shadows as the sun slid behind the rooftops of London. After their long, arduous journey, they'd finally reached their destination.

Aidan released a frustrated sigh, and Syrena drew her gaze from the dark oak door of his uncle's home. With a concerted effort, she forced her legs to move and mounted the stone steps. She didn't think she'd ever been so tired. Aidan had been relentless on the last leg of the journey. He'd pushed them to the point of exhaustion. If she hadn't been as concerned for Lachlan's welfare as he was, she might have taken him to task for it.

But their meeting with the Lamonts had cast an ominous pall on the remainder of their trek. She'd tried to reach Lan in her mind. Her inability to contact him left both her and Aidan uneasy. He had insisted she discontinue her efforts, and she wasn't entirely certain of the reason—whether it was because he had witnessed firsthand the pain the effort caused her, or because in his heart he still tried to pretend she wasn't Fae.

Even though he attempted to hide it, she knew he had yet to put who she was behind him. Although neither of them had admitted their love for one another aloud, the long weeks spent together had forged a strong bond between them. She thought once Lan was safe, their differences would be something they could overcome. At least she hoped so.

She rolled her eyes when Aidan impatiently nudged her aside to rap his knuckles against the door. "You nearly knocked me off the step," she muttered, shooting him a disgruntled look.

He glanced down at her. The weary tension hardened his stormy gaze, rolling off him in waves. She thought he might have murmured an apology, but couldn't be certain. The door swung open, and once it had, nothing else mattered but the warm gush of air that rushed out to greet them. The welcome heat should have sent Syrena running over the threshold, but there was more in the air than warmth.

Like a thick blanket of fog, dark and suffocating, icy tentacles crawled over her body, freezing her to the step. Her gaze shot through the open door to the richly appointed entryway. Regardless of the beauty of the gilded tables and polished wood, she knew somewhere within these walls evil dwelt, and it chilled her to the bone.

"Bloody hell, Syrena, with yer insistent whining fer a bed and hot bath, I thought ye'd be pushin' yer way through the doors, no' keepin' the rest of us standin' out in the cold. Now get a move on." With his hand at the small of her back, he gave her a gentle shove.

But distant memories swirled in her subconscious and she couldn't move past them. She was back in the grand hall of the palace, watching her father's triumphant unveiling of an arm reputed to be that of a dark lord killed in the battle with Tatianna. The discovery of the ravaged appendage had been made in the home of three Fae women who were being investigated for dabbling in the dark arts.

Encased in a block of ice, the limb had been preserved, the pentagram clearly visible, inked on the inside of the forearm. King Arwan and his men had laughed, throwing the arm among themselves. Its gnarled, blackened fingers pointed to the assemblage, who drew back in horror. Syrena and her mother, who stood trembling at her side, were just as affected by the dark magick that seeped from the ravaged appendage. Syrena had battled the urge to expel the contents of her belly, struggling to breathe as the icy fingers strangled her, just as they did now.

The look of frustration in Aidan's eyes softened to concern. He waved Callum and Connor past with their belongings, nudging Syrena out of the way. "What is it, angel? Yer bonny eyes are about to swallow yer wee face."

He folded her in his arms, and she greedily inhaled his familiar scent. The warmth of his embrace dispelled the bone-numbing terror that iced her limbs. Protected and strengthened by his powerful presence, she once more turned her mind to that day long ago. She'd forgotten until Aidan wrapped her in his arms that her uncle, King Rohan, had been with them.

While her father and his men, unaffected by the dark magick, disregarded those who were, her uncle had not. He'd held Syrena and her mother, quieting their fears, staying with them until their trembling ceased, as Aidan did now, with her.

He kneaded her shoulders. "Tell me."

She lifted her gaze to his. "There's something here, Aidan, something evil."

He frowned, smoothing the tangled curls from her face. "Nay, angel, ye're tired is all. Once ye—"

"I wish that was all it was, Aidan, but—"

"Ye havena' changed a bit, my laird, always one fer the lassies, ye were. Come in, I canna be waitin' all night fer ye. We're heatin' the out of doors as it is." An older man, the light from the lanterns glinting off his shiny bald head, smiled warmly at Aidan.

"Samuel, 'tis good to see ye," Aidan said, stepping away from Syrena. He took hold of her hand and tugged her along behind him as the small, wiry man ushered them inside. "'Tis been a long time. I didna ken ye came to England with my uncle. Did yer wife accompany ye?"

"Aye, after the Lady Elizabeth passed and he took up with his new wife, me and Bess didna want to leave himself to his own devices. We could no' stand the idea of him bein' served by a bunch of snooty Englishmen." His light blue eyes filled. "Ye ken he passed, doona ye, my lord?"

"Aye, I received word from John Henry. I didna ken he'd been unwell." Syrena had noted the hard slash Aidan's mouth drew into every time he made mention of his cousin, but she had yet to discover the cause.

"Unwell?" Samuel scoffed. "'Twas fit as a fiddle. If ye ask me, his wife and her brother had somethin' to do with it."

A feminine peal of laughter floated down from the second floor. "Mayhap ye'd best be keepin' those thoughts to yerself, Samuel," Aidan warned.

"Aye, 'tis—" A delighted cry drew their attention to a

heavyset woman, bright auburn curls escaping from beneath her snug, white lace cap as she bustled toward them.

She clutched Aidan's hand. "Laird MacLeod, 'tis grand to see ye. Lord Hamilton mentioned we should be expectin' a visit from ye." She lowered her voice to a conspirator's whisper. "Was none too happy about it, ye ken, on account of Lady Davina. Och, ye're well rid of that one, let me tell ye, my laird."

"Bess," Samuel admonished his wife.

"What? Och, well, 'tis no secret how—"

A grim-faced Aidan cut her off. "Bess, Samuel, this is my wife, Lady Syrena." Tugging on Syrena's hand, he set her in front of the couple.

A warm smile wreathed the older woman's round face. "Och, my laird, she's a bonny wee thing. 'Tis glad we are to meet ye, my lady."

Syrena managed a weak smile. "Thank you."

"Bonny and tired, Bess, we've had a long journey. If ye doona mind, I think she could use a bath and her bed."

"I'll see to it straightaway. And what about ye?"

"Later. I'd like to speak with my cousin first."

"Ye'll be waitin' until the morrow, then. He's taken his father's place as agent to King James and is rarely home. If he was, I doona think they'd be carryin' on as they do," Samuel said darkly, jerking his thumb to the raucous laughter coming from above.

Aidan followed the older man's gaze. "I'll question his widow. She would've been around when Lachlan was here."

Samuel and his wife shared a pained look. "We were sorry to hear yer brother is missin'. John Henry questioned all the staff, but none kent anythin' of Lachlan's whereabouts. Mayhap ye'd best wait until his lordship returns. There's strange goin's on up there, my laird. And Lady Ursula and her brother"—Samuel shuddered—"trust me, ye doona want to have anythin' to do with the likes of them."

"Aye, listen to my Samuel, Laird MacLeod, and wait until the morrow."

"I'll have to take my chances, Bess. I doona have time to waste."

"Och, well, doona say we didna warn ye. And doona imbibe of the mead, I'm fairly certain 'tis laced with laudanum."

A flicker of disgust crossed Aidan's face. "I won't. Is Lady Davina up there as well?"

Bess cast Syrena a sidelong glance. "Aye, she is."

Aidan lifted Syrena's hand to his lips and pressed a kiss to her palm. "I won't be long."

She shook her head and tightened her grip on his hand. Maybe Aidan was right, and she was simply tired. Her certainty that evil dwelled in Lord Hamilton's residence had wavered as the suffocating darkness dissipated. But Bess and Samuel's silent communication had prickled a warning. Something was going on, and she wouldn't leave Aidan to face it on his own. "No, I'll go with you."

"Nay," Aidan and Samuel said as one. As though sensing Syrena meant to insist, Bess used a potent argument, appealing to her vanity. "Now, my lady, ye canna wish to attend the soiree as ye are."

Aidan shot the older woman a look of thanks, and before Syrena could argue the point, he was already halfway up the stairs.

Bess directed Callum and Connor to Syrena's assigned chambers then led her up the long, wooden staircase. A wall of darkness slammed into her as she reached the top step, and she stumbled. She struggled to breathe, fighting past the suffocating sense of doom, the tightness in her chest.

Bess took one look at her and took hold of her arm, dragging her along behind her. "Och, sorry, my lady, I should have helped ye, ye're exhausted from yer journey." With every step they took away from the dark-paneled gallery, Syrena's breathing eased. They slowed their pace once they reached the far end of the corridor. Connor and Callum had just deposited her possessions when Syrena and Bess entered the chambers.

"Samuel will show ye to yer accommodations, lads, but I think it might be best if one of ye stand guard over yer lady."

"Aye, Laird MacLeod suggested as much," Connor piped in. "I'll be outside yer chambers if ye need me, Lady Syrena."

Noting the stubborn set of his jaw, Syrena sighed. "Thank you, Connor," she said as he and Callum took their leave.

"I ken ye doona think the precaution is warranted, my lady, but ye may be glad of his protection. There are unnatural goin's-on when this lot gathers. What I've seen would have Lord Hamilton turnin' in his grave if he were to ken. God rest his soul." Her kind brown eyes glistened with unshed tears.

"His wife didn't hold the gatherings when he was alive."

Bess looked horrified. "Nay, Lady Ursula's brother was banned from the house. He's a defrocked priest and takes his anger out against the Kirk. Lord Hamilton would have none of it and, John Henry, well, he doesna' have the sense to see what's goin' on right beneath his nose. Mayhap he doesna' want to deal with it, run off his feet with the king's incessant demands as he is. And his wife, well, that's another story altogether." She sighed. "I've told my Samuel I'll no longer remain amongst these people. 'Twas why I was so glad to hear Laird MacLeod was comin'. I'm hopin' we can travel home with ye."

"I'm certain Aidan wouldn't mind, but I'm surprised you wish to leave Lord Hamilton. It sounds as though you've been with the family a very long time."

"Aye, verra long, and I canna say it will be easy to leave, but ye havena' seen what I've seen. Mark my words, my lady, there's evil afoot in this house."

Syrena shuddered. Bess had confirmed her worst fear. King Gabriel had alluded to the use of dark magick in London, and she now knew it roamed the halls of this elegant town house on the Strand. Her brother's last known residence.

Chapter 21

Syrena lay on top of the cream-colored coverlet. Her hand slipped from Nuie's hilt, and she jolted, forcing her eyes open. Determined to make Aidan believe that someone in this house was responsible for Lachlan's disappearance, she couldn't allow herself to fall asleep.

"Syrena," a man whispered.

She blinked and sat up. With only the dying embers of the fire to light the room, she strained to see who had entered her chambers. Tightening her grip on Nuie, she asked, "Who's there?"

"Syrena." The thin voice wavered, even weaker than the first time.

Lan. "Lachlan, is that you?" Her heart hammered in her chest. Pressing her palms to her temples, she searched for him in her mind.

"Aye."

She swallowed her fear. He sounded so weak, but at least he was alive. "We're here, Lan. Aidan and I are in London. Tell me, tell me where you are."

"Nay . . . nay. Danger. Leave . . . too late."

"No! We're not going anywhere without you. Be strong, we'll find you. Lachlan, stay with me," she cried, sensing the connection fading. Pressure built inside her head with the effort to reach him. She gritted her teeth and pushed past the pain, sending him her strength, her love, but he was gone.

She sprang from the bed. She had to find Aidan and tell him Lachlan had made contact with her. Rubbing her eyes to clear her misted vision, she grabbed her mantle from the end of the bed. More certain than ever that evil dwelt within the town house, she would go nowhere without her sword. She strapped the sheath to her back and tucked Nuie inside, fastening the dark woolen cloak at her neck.

Wrapping the protective weight of the material around her hand, she lifted the iron latch.

She cursed the creak of the wood and peeked around the door. Connor, leaning against the stone wall, turned.

Oh for Fae-sakes.

He straightened when he saw her. "Is somethin' amiss, my lady?" His brow furrowed as he took in her mantle.

"I must speak with Lord MacLeod? Have you seen him?"

"Nay." He tipped his chin in the direction of the grand hall. "He's no' come this way. Ye'll have to wait fer his return, my lady."

She couldn't wait. Lachlan's life depended on them. She took a step over the threshold and Connor moved in front of her. "Connor, you don't understand. It's very important I speak with him," she said, frustrated by the determined look in his eyes.

"Ye must remain here, Lady Syrena. I canna allow ye to go to the hall. The laird would have my head. And if ye'd seen what I have stumblin' along these corridors, ye would no' want to."

Desperate to reach Aidan, but certain Connor would not let her go without a fight, she had no choice but to get Connor into her room and immobilize him for at least an hour. She wrapped her mantle around her as though she was chilled. "I'm sure you are right," she said, forcing her teeth to chatter, adding a shiver for effect.

A frown furrowed his youthful brow. "Ye're cold, my lady."

He craned his neck, looking past her to the interior of her chambers. "Ah, I can see the reason from here—yer fire is out. I'll take care of it fer ye, my lady."

"Thank you, Connor," she murmured, wishing there was another option available to her, but there wasn't, and she didn't have time to waste developing one. He crouched beside the grate, chatting to her as he nudged the flame to life with a poker. While he was distracted, she slipped her cold hand to his neck.

"What—" The rest of his startled question died on his lips as her fingers found the pressure point that rendered him unconscious.

She caught him just before he hit the floor and dragged him to the bed. She quickly secured his hands and feet. Tucking him beneath the covers, she brushed a lock of hair from his face. "I'm sorry, Connor." She assuaged her guilt with the knowledge he would suffer no ill effects. He'd simply sleep for an hour or so, and truly, what choice did she have when her brother's life was at stake?

She closed the door behind her and stepped into the narrow corridor. The cacophony of voices grew louder as she hurried along the East Wing. As she approached the curved staircase, a man and a woman, both dressed in black and wearing half-masks, staggered from the wood-paneled gallery. Oblivious to her presence, they groped one another with unrestrained lust. A cloud of sweet, intoxicating fumes rolled off the pair. Syrena stepped out of their way, reminding herself to refuse refreshments if they were offered. Lengthening her stride, she hastened toward the gallery that ran the width of the house. A heavy thud sounded behind her, then several more. She winced. The couple had fallen down the stairs. Samuel's genial voice, with his thick brogue, offered his commiseration.

Before he spotted her, Syrena slipped around the corner of the paneled wall into the gallery. On the opposite side of the room, the chatter of men's and women's voices wafted from beneath the double doors that led into the grand hall.

Within inches of the doors, a dark terror choked off her breath. *Not again.* Staggering under the oppressive weight, she stumbled and lost her balance. She reached out, stretching her fingers toward the wall to break her fall. Gasping for air, she dragged herself into a dark corner. Syrena covered her mouth to contain her silent retching, the pain in her head bringing her to her knees. She pressed her heated cheek to the wall, absorbing the coolness of the wood.

Nuie.

Groping beneath her mantle, her fingers were lifeless and she barely managed to wrap her hand around her sword's hilt. She clamped her mouth shut, swallowing convulsively to keep the bile down, and used both her hands to remove him. Nuie's life force, his strength, took hold of her, filling her with his power, a shield against the dark magick. The band constricting her chest snapped, and she dragged in much-needed air. The loud buzzing in her head faded to silence, the pain subsiding as the black cloud lifted from her mind.

"Thank you, my friend," she panted.

The doors to the grand hall swung open. Too weak to stand, she huddled in the shadows. Behind the masked couple the interior glittered in the flickering glow of candlelight. Through a swirl of color, a crowd of men and women, masked and unmasked, she strained to catch a glimpse of Aidan.

The door closed and out of the darkness, the man asked, "Are you certain you don't wish to remain a bit longer, my dear?"

"Certainly not, Jasper. Lady Hamilton's soirees have gone beyond the pale. It started off as a lark, but now they go too far."

"But, sister, I overheard Lady Ursula promise a display of the dark lord's power to the followers of Jarius. I will not learn of the location if I don't remain." There was a pleading note in the man's voice.

"Dark lords, secret location," she scoffed, "honestly, Jasper, how much wine did you consume? I swear it's drugged. Did you see Lord Billingsly? If you ask me, Lady Ursula has gone mad, and that brother of hers, Jarius, is the cause. Come, I don't wish to remain a moment longer."

"But, sister . . ." Their voices faded as the woman dragged off the protesting man.

Rubbing her temples, Syrena tried to absorb what she'd heard. They must have misunderstood. They could not have been referring to the lords of the underworld. The Fae had locked the dark lords away after the battle with Tatianna. *There was no way Mortals could release them, was there?* She searched her mind for an answer, but stopped herself. There was no time to waste. She had to find Aidan, and together they would decide what to do.

Syrena held on to the wall and pulled herself to her feet. Evil pulsed around her. If she let go of Nuie, she was certain it would attack again. After suffering its effects twice in one day, she didn't plan on letting it happen again. She had to find a way to keep her hand on her sword while concealing him at the same time. Aidan wouldn't appreciate her striding into the soiree with Nuie drawn, although if he heard what she had, he might not care. Turning her back to the doors, she cut a slit in the waist of her primrose gown and slipped Nuie inside. Red shards shot through her fingers, but she couldn't afford to mute his power. She would just have to be careful.

Tugging the mantle closed, she kept her left hand on her sword and held the fabric together with her right. Syrena slipped inside the grand hall. Flattened against the back wall, she searched for Aidan. To the right, at the front of the room, a statuesque woman in a claret gown cut low to display her ample attractions held court. Several men in robes as black as the woman's hair surrounded her, hanging on her every word.

A liveried servant stepped in front of Syrena, balancing a

tray with silver-encrusted goblets. He blocked her view. "No, thank you," she said, trying to look past him.

"Lady Hamilton insists all her guests partake, my lady."

"I'm sure she does," Syrena muttered under her breath. "I'm afraid I must decline." She waved him off, frustrated when he stood his ground.

His onyx eyes flashed and his thin lips flattened. "And I'm afraid I must insist or I'll be forced to have you removed."

She'd like to see him try. No one was making her leave until she found Aidan. Allowing her mantle to slip, she gave him a good look at Nuie.

He blinked and took a step backward. "I . . . I'll just go."

"I thought you might."

While she tracked his hasty retreat, a young woman bumped into her. "Sorry," the pretty blond twittered, stumbling toward the doors. The tall man in front of Syrena nudged his companion and jerked his head in the direction of the girl. His heavyset friend turned, the upper part of his face covered in a black half-mask, a lascivious grin creased his thick lips, and he nodded to his companion. They quickly followed after the blonde. Syrena was torn between finding Aidan and protecting the girl.

She sighed and headed after them, certain she could dispatch the lecherous louts easily enough. Before the doors to the grand hall closed behind her, a narrow shaft of light illuminated the far wall of the gallery. With her head thrown back, an expression of bliss upon her face, the girl held the backs of both men's heads, pressing their faces to her bared breasts.

Disgusted, Syrena stepped back into the hall. Now it seemed in every corner she looked couples indulged their lustful cravings with no care as to who saw them. A sidelong glance revealed the servant who'd tried to force the drink upon her, speaking to the woman in the claret gown. He tipped his head in Syrena's direction. Almost certain it was Lady Ursula he spoke to, Syrena anxiously searched the crowd. Every instinct warned her to stay as far away from the woman as she could.

Drawing her hood over her hair, she wove her way through a small cluster of people. Stretching up on the tips of her toes, she looked over the shoulder of the man in front of her to see the opposite end of the hall. Near the far wall, set apart from the crowd, stood a man with his back to her, speaking to a beautiful redhead. The familiar stance, the breadth of his shoulders, caused Syrena to expel a sigh of relief.

Aidan.

She excused herself, nudging the man out of her way. Without him blocking her view, Syrena could see Aidan and the woman were deep in conversation, oblivious to those around them. There was something about their interaction that made her uncomfortable, and she hesitated before walking toward them. From where she stood, Syrena watched as the woman took Aidan's hand and placed it on her swollen belly. She appeared to plead with him. He didn't withdraw his hand, his chiseled profile softening as he seemed to offer her comfort. It was a look Syrena was familiar with, a look she'd come to love, and she tried to ignore a pinch of jealousy. There was no help for it, her interruption might not be welcomed, but Aidan needed to hear what she'd learned.

"Not very subtle, is she?" a sultry voice said.

Syrena turned. The woman in the claret gown stood beside her, a dark brow raised as she watched Aidan and his companion. "Pardon me?"

A sympathetic smile curved her reddened lips as she turned her attention to Syrena. "Judging by your reaction, I assume you're Lord MacLeod's wife, am I correct?"

Syrena shifted uncomfortably. She didn't like what the woman seemed to imply. "I, yes, I'm Syrena MacLeod. And you are?"

"Lady Hamilton, Ursula to you, my dear." She folded her arms beneath her bountiful chest, and tilted her head. "I'm afraid Davina is regretting her choice in husbands of late.

I can't say as I blame her. My stepson pays little to no attention to her. And then this evening, in walks the gorgeous Highlander she let get away. She has horrific taste if you ask me, breaking off her betrothal to Lord MacLeod to marry John Henry."

"Davina . . . Davina and Aidan were betrothed." The words were scraped from Syrena's throat.

"Oh, yes, several years ago. She broke his heart, from what I hear."

Syrena's troubled gaze sought Aidan. Davina said something to him and he nodded. Removing his hand from the curve of her belly, he wrapped his arm around her. Davina clung to him, her head resting against his broad shoulder. Together they left through a side door.

A dull ache blossomed in Syrena's chest.

Lady Hamilton patted her arm. "Don't upset yourself. Even if he does renew his relationship with Davina, for however briefly, it's you who holds the power, my dear. Nothing more can come of it. You're his wife, and in the end, that's all that matters." Ursula frowned. "You must be newly wed to have it bother you as much as it appears to."

How could he . . . how could Aidan do this to her? Syrena tried to swallow, but her mouth had gone dry, and she could barely get the words out. "If you don't mind, Ursula, I'd like to return to my room. I've had a long journey."

"You have, haven't you? I spoke to your husband earlier. I understand he's come in search of his brother." Lady Hamilton watched Syrena as a cat watches a faery.

Lachlan. She had to concentrate on her brother, not Aidan, not his obvious affection for the beautiful redhead. A woman who'd broken his heart, a woman he'd once wanted to bear his children. Like the one Davina now carried. A woman who'd left the hall in his arms.

Syrena's heart felt as though it was breaking. She couldn't do this, not now. Pushing the tortuous thoughts and images aside, she said, "Yes, Lachlan has been missing for several weeks now. Were you able to tell Aidan anything?"

Ursula tugged her gathered sleeve over her wrist. "No, as I told Lord MacLeod, my husband passed away only a month before Lachlan's arrival. The house was in mourning. We barely saw him, although he did attend a small gathering of my friends—nothing formal, you understand, given the circumstances."

Ursula's pretense of a woman in mourning rang false. Syrena didn't know how the Mortals mourned their dead, but she had her suspicions the soiree in the grand hall this evening would not be acceptable. Whether the woman grieved her husband's passing or not had little to do with Syrena. But Ursula had drawn her interest with the fact Lan had attended one of her functions.

"Do you know if he mentioned his plans to anyone?"

"Not that I'm aware of, but I did point out several of the guests who had attended to your husband. I know Lachlan had spoken to a fair number of them, the women especially. They fell all over themselves to speak to him." She gave Syrena an arch look. "Your husband is a very handsome man, a very commanding presence. Not unlike his brother, yet they are so dissimilar in coloring. Lachlan's more like a sleeping lion, with his golden hair and gaze, and the strength in his arms . . ." Ursula shivered, fairly purring over Lan's attributes.

She looked at Syrena then, as if seeing her for the first time, she reached over and pushed the hood from Syrena's head. "Has anyone ever told you how much you look like your brother by marriage?" Before she could answer, Ursula brushed the tips of her fingers over Syrena's cheek. "So beautiful, so innocent," she murmured. Her eyes glazed with a faraway look, and she slid the tip of her tongue over her painted lips. "I must introduce you to my brother. He will be very interested in meeting you."

Warning bells clanged in Syrena's head. Nuie warmed beneath her fingers. He felt it, too.

"I . . . I think—"

Ursula cut her off before she could make her excuses. "Perhaps my brother will have more information than I do about Lachlan." She dangled the tantalizing inducement before Syrena. By the triumphant gleam in Ursula's blue eyes, Syrena understood the woman was certain she'd acquiesce.

Show no fear.

You are a warrior, she reminded herself. *Lachlan needs you.*

Syrena shut out the small voice that said she needed Aidan. She had Nuie; she didn't need anyone else. Following Ursula through the masked revelers, she tightened her fingers around her sword's hilt and absorbed his power. As they approached the front of the hall, where she'd first seen Ursula, a door set within the dark paneling opened.

Without warning, the wall of darkness slammed into her. Her stomach heaved and she slowed her breathing, trying not to inhale the noxious fumes emitting from the room. Pinpricks of light dotted her vision. The darkness was suffocating, the pain in her head debilitating.

A man in black, his entire face masked, wavered in front of her in a blurry haze. He stepped from the room and closed the door. The darkness faded, and she sucked in harsh gulps of air, steadying herself. At that moment everything came into focus. What perhaps had started as an amusement for these people had turned deadly. Somehow they'd unleashed a potent magick, dark magick, and it resided in that room. Magick, yes, but it couldn't be the dark lord's, she reassured herself. They wouldn't have the resources required to open the doors of the underworld. The Mortals wouldn't even know where the doors were located. Unless . . . unless somehow they'd discovered one of the Grimoires.

No, she wouldn't even consider the thought. She had to stay focused, not court more trouble than she could deal with. Whatever was in that room was connected to Lan, and she had to admit now, the Fae that had gone missing from London.

Once she found her brother, she would know exactly what she was dealing with and how to fix it.

"Are you all right, my dear?" Ursula inquired, reaching out to steady Syrena.

"Yes, I'm . . . I'm fine," she managed. She had to be.

"Good, for a moment you looked as though you might swoon. Colin, this is Lady MacLeod. Don't you think Jarius would like to meet her?" With a suggestive smile, Ursula trailed her fingers through Syrena's hair.

"Aye, I'm certain he would," the man rasped as though his throat was damaged. His eyes glittered through the slits in his black mask as he perused Syrena, then he turned his attention to Ursula. "But he can see no one now."

"I see," Lady Hamilton murmured. "Did he agree that you should . . ." As though she only then remembered Syrena's presence, her lips compressed.

"Aye, he did." There was a sinister tone in his scratchy voice.

Syrena shifted uneasily. "I'm sorry, Ursula, but I must return to my rooms. I have yet to recover from my journey." If only that were all it was.

The man watched her from beneath his mask. "I shall escort ye to yer rooms, Lady MacLeod."

"No . . . no, thank you." She had no intention of going anywhere with him. And she had no intention of going to her rooms. Lachlan had made contact with her here, and since the dark magick was in this room, it only made sense that it was where her search must begin. She'd scour the town house from top to bottom and wouldn't stop until she found her brother.

"So be it, but have a care. One never knows what lurks behind closed doors. Beware the shadows of the night." His ghoulish laugh followed Syrena from the grand hall.

Chapter 22

Davina trembled, and Aidan tightened his hold on her, certain it was no act. His tension eased once they entered the corridor, putting some distance between them and the dissolute rabble gathered in the grand hall.

He shook his head, disgusted with what he had seen. A pack of aristocrats with nothing better to do than relieve their boredom playing at magick and making a mockery of the Kirk. And if that wasn't bad enough, they drowned their inhibitions in drugged mead, acting out their carnal fantasies with no care as to who watched—and plenty had.

Considering the sexual play, he was glad Syrena had not been there to witness their antics. He glanced down. And mayhap witness his reunion with Davina who was now snuggled against his chest. He'd spent the majority of his time avoiding the woman he once thought to marry, questioning anyone who, according to Ursula, had met his brother on the night he disappeared.

Frustrated with the futility of his task, sickened by the goings-on, he'd been about to leave when Davina cornered him. He'd been tempted to brush her off until he realized she was truly afraid. In good conscience, he couldn't ignore her panicked plea for help.

Her bewitching face and bonny red hair had little effect on

him now. The memory of how badly she'd once wounded him had seen to that. But it was the look of fear in her wide green eyes that brought him to a standstill—fear for her unborn child.

Davina's long fingers stroked him through his tunic, caressing the ridge of muscles low in his belly. Aidan muttered a curse. He may no' be attracted to the woman, but he was no' a bloody monk. Extracting himself from her hold, he set her firmly aside, and nudged her along the corridor. "Where are yer rooms, Davina?"

She jerked her gaze to his. Tears pooled in her eyes, and her mouth trembled. "I'm sorry, I didna mean to make ye angry, Aidan. Please, doona be fashed with me." Her fingers fisted in his tunic. "Doona leave me alone."

"I'll see ye to yer chambers. If ye're truly afraid, I'll have one of my men stand watch over ye. But is John Henry no' due back this eve?"

Her face crumpled. "I doona ken. He's never here. I should no' have married him. I wish . . . I wish I would have married ye. Why did ye no' fight fer me?" Though she whispered the question, he heard her well enough.

Considering her emotional state, he didn't think now was the time to tell her she hadn't been worth it. She was a woman who would choose another man over the one she professed to love simply because his prospects were better. John Henry had offered her more coin, and all the power and influence she craved to set her up in society.

The sound of men's laughter echoed along the torch-lit corridor, bouncing off the stone walls. "'Tis no' the time nor the place fer this, Davina. Where are yer bedchambers?"

She glanced over her shoulder then nodded, wiping the moisture from her cheeks. "Third door on the right."

When they stood before the door to her chambers, Aidan reached for the latch, but she stopped him, placing a fine-boned hand over his. "Won't ye come in?" she asked, her voice husky.

"Nay, I'm married, Davina, and I'm thinkin' my wife would no' appreciate me bein' in yer rooms." In truth, he wondered what Syrena's reaction would be. He suspected she would not be pleased and smiled at an image of her bonny eyes flashing with anger.

A marriage that had begun as a charade now seemed very real to him. He was almost certain Syrena loved him though she had yet to tell him so. There were matters they needed to resolve. Most, he acknowledged, were his own, but there would be time for that later.

"I doona care what she thinks. I'm askin' ye." The harshness of her tone didn't surprise him. It was more in keeping with the woman he remembered.

"I do." He removed her hand from his and opened the door.

"Do ye love her?"

He hesitated. He thought he did, but hadn't allowed himself to think about it until now. But that was not something he'd share with Davina. "Aye, I do."

She bowed her head then raised her eyes to meet his. "She's verra lucky. I'm sorry, mayhap 'tis the bairn that is causin'..."

"Mayhap." He frowned, trying to remember what had set her off in the hall. He reached for her before she stepped into the room. "Davina, what is it ye're afraid of?"

Her hand went to her swollen belly. "Now that we're away from them, it seems silly. But I was afraid fer my bairn."

"If ye're feelin' unwell, I'll send fer Bess."

She twisted her hands in her yellow gown. "Nay." She glanced down the hall, and he had to admit she looked terrified. "Please, I canna speak of it here. Someone might overhear us. I promise, I will try no' to compromise ye." A watery smile curved her lips, reminding Aidan of what had once attracted him to her.

"A few minutes, 'tis all I can give ye. I want to check on my wife," he said, following her into her chambers. He frowned. Feeling as though someone watched them, he stepped back to scan the deserted corridor. He shook his head. Syrena and her talk of evil had him on edge.

Davina walked across the woven carpet to the fire and wrapped her arms around her thickening waist, shoulders bowed.

"Tell me what's troublin' ye."

She turned, her hand covering her mouth. "I've made a horrible mistake. I only thought to make John Henry jealous. He doesna' love me, Aidan, I'm certain of it. Since we've come to London, he has no time fer me."

"Ye got what ye wanted. A man with power and coin to spare." It sounded as though he took pleasure in her pain, but he didn't. He simply stated the truth.

"I ken I hurt ye, Aidan. I was foolish and verra spoiled. I regret it more than ye'll ever ken."

He believed her. Mayhap Davina had finally grown up, but it was too late.

"The man I used in my ploy, he didn't take kindly to the deceit. When I . . . when I refused his advances, he didna listen to me. He . . . I'm no' certain, Aidan. I'm no' certain if the bairn is John Henry's."

He closed the distance between them and took hold of her shoulders. "Are ye sayin' the man forced ye, Davina? He raped ye?"

She squeezed her eyes closed. "He said I was a tease. He said I didna ken what I wanted."

"Who, Davina? Who is it ye speak of?"

"Ursula's brother, Jarius. Nay, Aidan," she cried as he headed for the door. "Nay, I canna allow John Henry to find out. Jarius is dangerous. He has some kind of hold over these people, Aidan. They listen to him."

Tears streamed down her face. "I listened to him. I believed all his talk against the Kirk, their control. His talk about a new order. His followers, they'll do anythin' fer him, even . . . kill."

"Do ye have evidence, Davina, evidence I can take to the authorities?"

"Nay, but at some of the gatherin's I've heard talk. The drink loosens their tongues. Two men that were part of the fold questioned Jarius's authority in front of the others. We never saw them again."

He closed his eyes and swallowed hard. "Lan?"

"Nay, but I think they ken what happened to him. I heard Ursula talkin' to John Henry the day yer missive arrived. She changed her story, Aidan. I think she lies."

"I appreciate yer tellin' me, Davina. And I'll keep yer confidence, but I suggest ye speak of this to yer husband. Ye're guilty of nothin' but bein' foolish. Tell him."

She stared at him. "I canna, but I thank ye fer sayin' that." She placed a frigid hand on his arm. "Aidan, doona approach Jarius at night. 'Tis when he takes the laudanum and makes contact with . . . he calls him the lord of darkness."

Aidan scoffed. "Ye canna believe such talk. The man's so far gone, he's seein' beasties in his mind. 'Tis all that is."

"Nay. There's somethin' to it. I've . . . I've seen things." She shuddered and tightened her grip on her waist. "He has a book, and he carries it with him, always. He calls it a Grimoire, the Grimoire of Honorius. They say it contains spells to call upon the evil spirits, these dark lords he's always talkin' about."

Aidan dragged his hand through his hair. "Ye canna believe this tripe?" But how could he be certain that was all it was? He had a wife who was Fae, and a brother who was half-Fae.

"Aye, I do. Ye have no' seen him. Somethin' is planned fer Samhain, somethin' big." Her hand went to her belly. "That's why I'm worried fer my bairn. They talked of sacrifice. Sacrifice of an innocent." Pale and trembling, she pleaded with him, "Please, Aidan, please help me."

"Aye." He folded her into his arms. "Aye, I'll help ye, Davina," he murmured into the top of her head before he set her aside. "Lock yerself in yer room. I'm goin' to send Callum to guard ye. He'll let ye ken when he arrives." Hand on the latch, he turned. "When is Samhain?" The days and weeks had rolled into one on their journey and he wasn't even certain of the day's date.

"On the morrow. They'll celebrate tomorrow eve when the moon is high. They say 'tis the night the veils between the realms thin. They plan to make a sacrifice in hopes of releasing the dark lord. 'Tis what I overheard Ursula tellin' the followers this night. She said she'd have enough magick in her to be considered worthy of openin' the door. But she's addicted to the laudanum, too, so I'm no' certain ye can trust what she says. There are times she sounds mad, talkin' about drinkin' the blood of faeries . . ."

Heart pounding, he strode toward her and grabbed her by the arms. "What did ye say?"

"Stop, Aidan, stop, ye're hurtin' me. I doona understand why—"

He dropped his hands, struggling to regain control. "I'm sorry. Ye need to tell me, Davina, 'tis important. The faery blood, what did she say?"

"Aidan, ye canna believe—"

"Tell me!" He balled his hands into fists to stop himself from shaking the answer out of her.

Davina backed away from him. "She . . . she said she bleeds the faeries and drinks their blood, but—"

"Lock yer dòor!" Blood pulsed through his veins, rage blinding him to anything but revenge. He slammed the door behind him, holding on to the latch, waiting for Davina to throw the bolt. Evil, Syrena had said. She'd felt it, and he hadn't listened to her. He had to go to her, be certain she was safe. And then he'd kill the bastard and his sister. Nay, first he would learn where they held his brother.

"Fancy runnin' into ye, Laird MacLeod," a voice sneered from behind him. Aidan went to turn. A heavy object smashed into the back of his skull. The explosion of pain brought him to his knees. Blackness sucked him under. His last thought was of Syrena.

* * *

Syrena bit back a frustrated oath when she realized she'd come full circle in her search and had found no evidence of her brother. She'd tried reaching him in her mind, seeking some clue, anything to help her locate him, but she was met with a chilling silence. She wondered if the state of her emotions, the pain of Aidan's rejection, had anything to do with it.

After she had made her escape from the hall, she'd seen him, watching from the shadows as he entered Davina's chambers. Her mind cried out at the injustice of his betrayal, but somewhere inside, the truth stabbed her conscience, forcing her to acknowledge they'd made no commitment to each other. He'd broken no promise; he'd made none. It was not his fault that she'd come to love him more with each passing day.

About to round the corner of the gallery, Syrena heard a heavy thud along the corridor, followed by a guttural moan. She ran partway along the hall, coming to a standstill when she saw three men bending over something on the ground. Holding her breath, she flattened herself against the stone wall. Moving silently, she ducked into a small alcove then peered around the corner. Three men tied up what appeared to be a big man lying unmoving on the slate.

One of them came to his feet and she saw their victim more clearly, a head full of dark hair and a warrior's body. *Aidan! They had Aidan!*

Her heart leapt to her throat and her limbs went weak.

A woman's muffled scream penetrated her panic, then a sharp crack, followed by silence.

"One of ye come here and get the whore. Take her to the coach. The master and Lady Ursula await ye there. We'll follow ye as soon as I've tied up the loose ends," a man rasped.

Syrena recognized his voice. It was the man Ursula referred to as Colin, the man with the full-face mask.

Heavy footfalls pounded from the other end of the corridor behind them. "She's gone, Lord Lamont. There's a lad tied up in the bed. He's unconscious."

Connor! Thank the heavens, they'd left him unharmed. It was only after releasing a relieved breath that she realized what the other man had said.

Lamont? Aidan had said they'd all died in the fire, unless this man, like Angus, was one of their cousins.

"What the hell are ye tellin' me fer? Find her! And find her fast. We're leavin' fer Glastonbury within the hour."

The name caused the fine hairs on the back of Syrena's neck to stand on end. Glastonbury was where one of the doors to the underworld lay.

"I thought we weren't leaving until tomorrow morn."

"Change of plans. It seems Jasper's sister made a few remarks to people she shouldna."

"Do ye want us to silence her?"

"Nay, 'tis too late fer that. Just find the woman so we can get the hell out of here."

"What are we to do with her?"

"Kill . . . nay, keep her alive. The master will want to have his way with her." Lamont rolled Aidan onto his back with the toe of his boot. Her white-knuckled grip on Nuie's hilt tightened. "And him. We'll let Laird MacLeod listen to his brother and his wife scream like I did mine. Aye, we'll let him watch them die in front of him the same as I did, helpless to do anything. And then I'll rip his heart out fer killin' my family."

Hearing what he planned for all of them, Syrena gritted her teeth and held herself back. He didn't have her. That was his first mistake. And she would make him suffer for all he'd set in motion. But there were six of them, and she had to be patient. If she attacked now, they would kill Aidan. Fear no longer held her prisoner; a cold, deadly rage was all that remained within her.

A rough hand clamped over Syrena's mouth. She struggled,

lifting Nuie, but powerful fingers secured her sword arm. "Nay. 'Tis me, Callum."

She nodded and the big man released her. Tugging on her hand, he pulled her silently into an empty room. He closed the door and leaned against it, his blond head bowed. The eyes he lifted to her were haunted, sorrow filled. "They killed the three lads, my lady. All three of them. Slit their throats while they slept."

"No," she cried. Heartsick, she buried her face in her hands and shook her head. "I'm sorry, Callum. I'm so sorry."

"What madness is this, my lady? What . . . Oh, Sweet Jesu, Connor—"

Syrena wiped her eyes, pushing aside her grief for the three innocent lives lost. She couldn't save them, but she could and would avenge their deaths. She placed a reassuring hand on Callum's arm. "He's safe, for now. They're holding Lachlan in Glastonbury and it is where they plan on taking Aidan, and the Lady Davina."

"Do ye ken where the place is?"

"No, we'll need Bess and Samuel's help. Find them and bring them to my chambers and stand watch over Connor."

"Aye, but what about ye and Laird MacLeod?"

"Don't worry about me. I'll get Aidan."

"But ye're only—"

She lifted Nuie, who flamed red, vibrating with blood lust. "I have my sword. I don't need anyone else."

"Aye." He swallowed, his Adam's apple bobbing in his throat. "Aye."

Syrena inched the door open. Two men ran down the corridor. A third staggered behind—over his shoulder was a body wrapped in a blanket. A strand of long red hair escaped from the gray wool. *Davina*. She quickly weighed the odds. The risk was too great. She had to put Aidan's safety first.

"Remember, meet us back at my chambers. Hurry, we don't have much time." She squeezed his hand. "Be careful, Callum."

"God go with ye, my lady."

"And with you," she said, watching him slip silently back the way he'd come. But on this day she would need no one but Nuie's strength and power to guide her. This day she would give herself over completely to his power.

She crept from the room and went back to watch from behind the stone wall.

"He's a heavy bastard," a man complained. Standing, he wiped his brow.

"Quit yer belly achin'," his partner ordered.

They went back to dragging Aidan along the corridor. Lamont walked behind them, stopping at each door to check inside. She had to time it right. Take out the two men moving Aidan while Lamont searched the room. Syrena kept her eyes off her husband. She couldn't look at him, couldn't worry about his injuries. There would be time for that later.

Dragging in a deep breath, Syrena focused her strength. The moment Lamont stepped into the second room, she lunged from her hiding place. Wide-eyed, the men dropped Aidan's arms and legs and reached for their weapons. Nuie whistled through the air, once, twice. The two men were dead before they lifted their swords.

She positioned herself in front of Aidan. Widening her stance, she gently nudged him against the wall with her heels.

"Remind me no' to make ye mad, angel." Aidan's groggy voice came from behind her.

A warm gush of relief loosened her knotted muscles, and she couldn't keep the smile from her face. He was alive. But there was no time to see to him; Lamont had stepped from the room.

He jerked his gaze to Syrena, taking in her blood-spattered gown, the dead men at her feet. Without saying a word, he turned on his heel and ran down the corridor. She couldn't go after him, not with Aidan unprotected.

At the sound of pounding feet coming their way, she shifted. A door slammed from the opposite direction, the one Lamont had taken. As she marked the place in her mind, she heard glass shatter from behind the closed door. The man was a fool. He'd die if he attempted to jump.

The footfalls drew nearer and she prepared for battle.

"Lady Syrena!"

Callum, Bess, and Samuel rounded the corner.

Syrena released a relieved breath and dropped to her knees beside Aidan, who struggled to sit up. He winced, rubbing the back of his head. "Bloody hell, who hit me?"

"Don't try and get up, not yet." She looked over at Callum, who dragged one of the dead bodies into an empty room. "I thought I told you to meet me in my chambers."

He lifted a broad shoulder. "Aye, but we heard the commotion and thought ye might be in need of our help."

Samuel and Bess joined her on the floor and removed the ropes that bound Aidan's wrists and ankles. Syrena left them to it. "I'm going after Lamont."

Aidan's gaze shot to hers and he pushed Samuel away. "Ye're no' goin' after anyone." He scrubbed his hands over his face. "And what do ye mean, Lamont?"

Syrena met Samuel's gaze and tipped her chin at Aidan. He nodded his understanding and she rose to her feet.

"What the hell is goin' on? Sweet Christ, did they get Davina?" At the desperation in Aidan's voice a suffocating ache filled Syrena's chest. She turned away. He hadn't recovered from the blow to his head, and she couldn't tell him what the madman had in store for Lan and Davina. A woman Aidan had once loved, quite possibly still did.

"Syrena!" Aidan yelled after her.

"Callum, go get Connor." Ignoring Aidan, she ran in the direction Lamont had taken.

Samuel came up behind her, sword in hand. He shrugged. "He didna want ye to go alone."

The knowledge Aidan worried over her melted a little of the ice that had frozen her heart. She pointed her sword at the room she was certain Lamont had entered. "He's in there."

Kicking the door open, she prepared for his attack. Wind whistled through the open window. The heavy green draperies snapped in the breeze.

Not taking any chances that it was a ruse and Lamont was hiding, waiting to pounce, she cautioned Samuel, "Careful." She released a frustrated breath when Samuel ignored her and strode to the window.

She protected his back, swiveling from left to right, scanning the room. Once she was certain Lamont was long gone, she joined Samuel at the window. It was no coincidence Lamont had chosen that room. With the wide balcony beneath it, he could shimmy down the columns then jump the next ten feet to the thick shrubbery below.

"The bastard got away, didna he?"

Syrena whirled, the solid wall of Aidan's broad chest the only thing she could see. She tipped her head back and looked into his stone cold gaze. "I thought I told you to—"

"Fire! Fire! Lamont's setting the staircase ablaze!" Callum bellowed from the direction of the gallery.

Chapter 23

A dull ache pounded in the back of Aidan's skull. His vision wavered, but he refused to give in to the weakness. He had to get them to safety, away from the madness in the house, a madness Lamont was a part of. He didn't understand how Colin lived, but he did, and Aidan couldn't waste valuable time piecing everything together.

He looked into Syrena's pale face and touched her cheek. Wishing there were time for him to hold her. But there wasn't. He shifted his attention from her to the man at her back. "Samuel, is there another way down?"

"Aye, the staircase the servants use is off the grand hall and leads to the kitchens."

"Good, take my wife and yours. Once you've made it below, round up anyone ye can find," he directed. Needing something to smother the flames with, he grabbed the dark green coverlet from the bed.

"Aidan, no! I'm not leaving you." Syrena's fingers dug into his forearm while she tried to shake free of Samuel. "You can't fight the fire. You have yet to recover."

He met Samuel's worried gaze over her head and nudged Syrena through the doorway. "Doona fight me on this, angel. There's no time. We have to stop the flames before they take hold up here." He wasn't about to let the fire put innocent lives at risk.

Looking back down the corridor, he remembered Davina and cursed. "Samuel, get Davina. Bess, ye and Syrena go on ahead."

Syrena watched him closely. Her voice thick with emotion, she said, "She isn't there. Lamont and his men have her. They're taking her to Glastonbury. Aidan, it's where they hold Lachlan."

He searched her face, wondering how much she knew. How much he should tell her. Remembering Davina's fear for her child's life, Aidan clenched his hands into fists. How many lives were to be lost because of the ravings of a lunatic?

Before he had a chance to question Syrena as to how she'd come by her knowledge—why the bloody hell she wasn't safe in her room—the acrid smell of smoke banished all thought but the encroaching flame.

"Go on, get out of here." Expecting Syrena to fight him, he was baffled when, without a backward glance, she disappeared into the shadows of the gallery with Bess and Samuel. He should have been grateful, but something didn't feel right, and it was more than just her fear for their brother.

Shaking off his concern, he ran toward the upper landing, ignoring the dull ache in his head. Black smoke billowed from below, and the toxic heat seared his lungs. He ripped off his tunic.

"Callum, Connor," he yelled at the two men who attempted to smother a pocket of flame between them. Sweat streaked their soot-blackened faces. "Take off your tunics and wrap them like so," Aidan commanded, tying the ends at the back of his head.

He'd battled a blaze at Lewes. They'd been lucky to escape without injury, but he knew it was the smoke that would get them before the flames.

"I doona ken if we can hold it back, my laird," Callum

shouted, stamping on a flame that flared to life inches from his foot.

Pulling his tunic over his head, Connor stumbled, and his sleeve dragged over the smoldering banister, igniting the fabric. With a startled yelp, the lad flung the burning ball and it landed on the woolen runner behind them. Connor gasped. "Sorry, my laird."

Aidan grabbed the edge of the carpet and flipped it over to contain the fire. He stamped on an errant spark and put it out before it touched the paneled walls of the gallery. If the wood ignited, their battle would be for naught. An ominous groan rippled through the air, followed by a muted crash as a lower chunk of the banister fell to the floor below them.

Between the three of them they put out one fiery eruption after another. Aidan didn't know how much longer they could keep at it before exhaustion and fumes overcame them.

The clamor of male voices drew his attention. He wiped the soot and sweat from his eyes, squinting to search past the smoke to the floor below. Directly beneath them, a handful of men in varying states of undress waved frantically for Samuel and several others who rushed in carrying buckets of water.

He searched for Syrena, but couldn't see her. The knowledge Samuel would make certain that she and Bess were safe before battling the blaze alleviated some of his concern. He heard the gush and sizzle of water as it hit the flames, and stepped back before he was engulfed in steam. He fought with renewed determination. They had a chance now.

Four panting servants ran up from behind them, water sloshing over the rims of the buckets they carried. Aidan recognized two of the men from earlier in the evening in the grand hall. Disgust roiled in his belly. Unlike Samuel and Bess, these two had appeared to take pleasure in doing Ursula's bidding.

Before he had a chance to react, Callum grabbed hold of the dark-haired servant. Quicker than Aidan thought a man of his size could move, he'd hauled the servant over an untouched segment of banister to dangle him upside down by his legs.

"Stop . . . stop!" the man screamed.

"Bloody hell, Callum, what are ye—"

"'Twas him, Laird MacLeod. 'Twas him I saw comin' from the stables. He killed the lads while they were sleepin'. Didna ye, ye snivelin' bastard? Well, now ye're goin' to pay fer it."

"Nay . . . nay. 'Twas Lamont's men. They were the ones. Please, I have a wife and young 'uns. Please don't kill me," he begged.

An image of the three lads, full of life, laughing and joking with one another in front of the campfire, haunted Aidan. If not for him, they'd be alive. He'd dragged them into this hell-hole. He should've come for Lan on his own.

The man's denial broke Aidan free of his self-flagellation and he grabbed hold of one of the servant's stick-thin legs.

"Callum, he says he didna do it. Save yer anger fer the one who did. Ye doona want the blood of an innocent man on yer hands, do ye?" They had no proof, and if there was a chance the servant was innocent, Aidan would not see a family deprived of their father.

Callum grunted. Pulling the man over the railing, he shoved him aside. The servant's legs buckled, and he fell to his knees, scrambling away from them. His companion lifted him to his feet, shooting an uneasy glance at Callum.

The landing grew crowded as others came to replace the four men. With the fire under control, Aidan motioned for Callum and Connor to follow him.

They walked in silence through the grand hall toward the back stairs. The sound of their footsteps echoed in the eerie quiet of the shadowed hall. Candles sputtered, burned down to the quick in the silver branches atop a black marble altar in front of the cavernous room.

Aidan forced himself to keep walking. He hadn't noticed the idolatrous piece of furnishing earlier. The room had been too crowded. He wondered if it would have made a difference if he had. He thought back to Syrena's comment when they'd first arrived, her belief that evil resided in the house on the Strand. He wondered if she knew how bad it really was. Christ, could it only have been hours ago? It felt like a lifetime.

"I'm sorry about the lads. The ones responsible will be punished. I can promise ye that much," he said in a dry rasp, his throat raw from inhaling the smoke.

They both offered him a jerky nod.

Aidan stood on the narrow landing at the top of the stairs. "After what ye've seen, I can understand if ye wish to return to Dunvegan. I willna hold it against ye if ye do."

"Nay, I willna rest until I see the ones responsible brought to justice." Callum's white teeth glinted in his blackened face, and he glanced at Connor. "Besides, ye need me. Yer wife is deadly with her sword and ties a fine knot, but there's too many of them fer even the two of ye."

Connor, the tips of his ears pink, glared at Callum then said, "I'll be comin' with ye as well, Laird MacLeod."

Aidan glanced from one to the other. "Am I missin' somethin'?"

"Callum here thinks 'tis amusin' that yer wife knocked me unconscious and left me hog-tied in her bed," Connor muttered.

What the bloody hell had she been up to? Instinct warned Aidan he wouldn't like the answer. "Do ye have any idea why she did so?"

The lad shrugged his shoulders, looking none too pleased. "All I ken is she was verra anxious to speak with ye."

Callum clapped Connor on the back. "Ye should be grateful, lad. In all likelihood, Lady Syrena saved yer life. Lamont's men went to her chambers to get her. If ye would've been guardin' her door instead of lyin' abed unconscious, ye would be dead."

The question of why she wanted to find him was pushed aside by the thought Lamont had been after Syrena as well.

"How do ye ken they meant to take her?"

"I heard them. We both did. Lady Syrena was searchin' fer yer brother when she came upon ye." Callum's gaze skittered past Aidan. "Ye doona wish to ken what they meant to do to ye and yer wife, or yer brother."

"Lachlan lives?"

"Aye, I—" Callum clamped his mouth shut. Several of the servants, their buckets empty, walked toward them.

"We're wastin' time," Aidan said and gestured to the stairs. He needed to find Syrena, to see for himself that no harm had come to her.

"I ken ye're anxious to reach yer brother, my laird, but if we doona rest before we head to Glastonbury, we'll be of no use to him."

Callum spoke the truth. Weakened from battling the fire and the blow to his head, Aidan could barely remain upright. If he thought he would put Lachlan in further danger by not setting out sooner, he'd damn the consequences, but Davina had said the ceremony would not take place until nightfall. And he wouldn't risk his brother's life by going to his rescue unprepared. "We'll set out at dawn's first light."

They met up with Samuel in the entryway. "Good job, lads, ye saved the place. The neighbors are mighty relieved. Lady Stanton took in yer wee wife, Laird MacLeod. 'Twas no' an easy task to convince her, but she was dead on her feet. I agreed to the Stantons' offer of lodgin' on yer behalf. I hope that's all right?"

"Aye, thank ye, Samuel. Do the Stantons have room fer Callum, Connor, Bess, and ye?"

"Aye, we've been given rooms in the servants' quarters."

"Good, we'll be leavin' at first light on the morrow. Do ye ken of any men who would ride with us?"

"Aye, there are a good many God-fearin' folks who didna condone the goin's-on in the house. They'll ride with ye as will Bess and I."

"Be sure they ken what we ride into, Samuel. 'Twill be dangerous."

"I ken that well enough. Doona fret, Laird MacLeod, we'll get yer brother and the Lady Davina back. The others can roast in hell fer all I care, and I'd like to be the one to send them there."

As would Aidan.

Bess walked beside Aidan along the corridor of the Stantons' town house to his chambers. "Poor wee thing," she said, quietly opening the heavy door. "She fell asleep by the fire and I didna have the heart to wake her."

Curled on top of a blanket by the hearth lay his wife with her sword clutched to her chest. Aidan was overcome with emotion. He would do whatever it took to protect her.

Bathed in firelight, her beauty was ethereal. She looked like an angel, but his desire for her at the moment was far from pure. The voluminous white night rail did little to conceal the heavy weight of her breasts, the dusky shadow of her nipples, and the sweet curve of her behind. He wanted to bury himself inside her, rid himself of the stench of death, the pervasive sense of evil that weighed him down.

Bess gave him a knowing smile and patted his arm. "I'll have some water sent up fer yer bath, my laird. I'll see to it that whoever comes is quiet so as not to disturb yer wife."

Although it did not speak well of him, Aidan planned on disturbin' his wee wife as soon as the door closed behind Bess.

"Thank ye, but I doona wish to trouble the household."

"As far as the Stantons are concerned, ye and the lads are heroes. Ye could ask fer whatever yer heart desired and they'd give it to ye." She winked. "But I'm thinkin' ye already have yer heart's desire, my laird."

His gaze strayed to Syrena. "Ye're a wise woman, Bess," he murmured.

"I'll tell my Samuel ye said so," she chuckled, the door clicking closed behind her.

Aidan crouched beside his sleeping beauty, her clean floral scent a fragrant balm to his senses. He reached out to touch her cheek. Noting his blackened fingers, he hastily pulled them away. He sat back on his heels and leisurely perused every glorious inch of her.

His gaze came to rest on her sword, glowing golden in the flame. Tentatively he touched the simmering jewels at its hilt. The blade heated and glowed red, a blazing hot, angry red. Bloody hell, 'twas like the thing was alive. And if it was, Aidan had the distinct impression it didna like him verra much.

Syrena shifted and, yawning, rubbed her eyes. "Aidan?"

"Aye, angel, were ye expectin' someone else?"

She sat up, her troubled eyes skimming over him as though she searched for some sign of injury. "That's not funny considering everything that's happened. Are you all right? No one else was hurt?"

"Nay, we managed to contain the blaze. None were injured."

A sigh of relief escaped her parted pink lips, and she leaned wearily against the embroidered chair at her back. The amber glow of the fire illuminated her body beneath the sheer night rail.

His fingers itched to cup the full globes in his hands, to press his lips to her nipples and suckle them through the delicate white fabric. To draw back and watch them push against the wet circle his mouth would leave. His gaze traveled to the hollow of her belly, and the soft shadow at the apex of her thighs.

"Aidan, what . . . oh," she gasped when he raised his gaze to hers.

A quiet rap on the door forced him to break the hypnotic heat that flared between them. "Give me a moment," he called, his cock as hot and hard as her sword. "And ye, get into bed."

She frowned. "Why? I like it by the fire."

"Aye, and if Bess sent lads up with my bathwater, I'm sure

they'd like seein' ye sittin' there as well. But I'll no' have them lookin' at my wife who might as well be naked fer all that gown covers," he said, pulling her to her feet.

"Honestly, Aidan, you're being foolish, you can't . . ." She pulled her hand from his and looked down. "Well, I'll just cover myself with—"

He grabbed the blanket before she could. "Nay, I'll be needin' that."

"Look what you've done." She brushed at the black hand-print on her snowy white night rail, making it worse.

"If ye doona get into bed, Syrena, ye're goin' to have one on yer bonny arse."

She muttered something under her breath, but did as he asked.

"Lord MacLeod, your water grows cold," a feminine voice called from the other side of the door.

"Come in," he said once he'd positioned himself in the chair. He tossed the blanket over his lap, bunching it in place to disguise his straining erection.

Syrena, with the covers drawn up to her neck, glowered at his lap pointedly. "I doubt they would even notice," she said as three maids, weighed down with steaming pails of water, sashayed into the room.

He angled his head and looked at his wife, all the while smiling in response to the lasses' beguiling greetings. "Shall I find out?"

"No," she grumbled. Arms crossed, she stared down the maids, who made certain to bend extra low while depositing the water in the tub they'd dragged closer to the fire and him. Making sure he got an eyeful of their bountiful charms.

He could have sworn Syrena growled when the pretty red-haired maid offered to bathe him. He bit back a grin. "Nay, my wife will see to my bath, but thank ye fer the offer."

As soon as the door closed behind the tittering maids, Aidan tossed the blanket aside and came to his feet. He watched Syrena as he tugged the tunic over his head. "Are ye no' goin' to help me? I'm afraid if I bend over to remove my boots, I'll land on my head." Not a complete untruth.

She scrambled from the bed. Her eyes full of remorse, she gently touched his arm and nudged him into the chair. "I'm sorry. It's just that you seemed so . . . so . . . You didn't appear to be in pain is what I mean to say."

Kneeling by his feet, she tugged on his doeskin boot. He was in pain, but not from the injury to his head. He would have shown her where he hurt, drawn her hand to his throbbing erection, if not for the glimmer of moisture in her eyes. She dipped her head, and he could've kicked himself for teasing her.

"Nay, look at me. Tell me what's wrong." With his fingers beneath her chin, he raised her gaze to his, and cursed inwardly. Why had he not noticed the tinge of blue beneath her eyes and the strained lines about her sweet mouth? She looked drawn and fragile, and he'd made it worse. 'Twas how he dealt with his anger and his fears, shutting them out, locking them away until he could release them in battle, but he should have known Syrena would need to talk. Even though it was the last thing he wished to do, he would do it for her.

"What isn't wrong? Lachlan is being held by a man who seeks to unleash the dark lords. And if that is not bad enough, a man who hates you and Lachlan above all else conspires with him. I . . . I thought you were dead, Aidan."

"It would take more than a blow to the head to kill me, angel. Davina told me the ceremony is on the morrow, close to the midnight hour. They'll keep Lachlan alive until then. We'll reach him in time, Syrena." A shadow had darkened her eyes at his mention of Davina. He could see she fought to keep her tears at bay. "What is it? Why are ye cryin'?"

She rubbed her cheek on the sleeve of her gown. "I'm not. Lachlan spoke to me tonight. His voice was little more than a whisper. He's given up, Aidan. He doesn't want us to come. He warned of the danger and said it was too late."

She laid her head in his lap. He closed his eyes, trying not to think of what Lan suffered. The memory of what Davina said they did to him. He couldn't tell Syrena, not now. It was bad enough she'd been alone when Lan contacted her. "Doona worry, angel, we'll no' be too late. Is that why ye knocked Connor out and tied him up, so ye could come lookin' fer me?"

She nodded into his lap, and he flexed his hand, stroking her hair to calm his rising frustration at the danger she'd put herself in. "Christ, Syrena, when I think what could have happened to ye searchin' on yer own. Ye should have—"

She raised her tear-swollen gaze to his. "I did. I came to the grand hall, but you were too busy with Davina to notice."

She rose to her feet, brushing away his hand when he tried to stop her. "I didn't think you'd wish to be disturbed when you followed her into her chambers."

"She was scared, Syrena, fer her and her bairn. I listened is all, and 'twas then I learned what their plans were. I never—"

"You were holding her. You touched her belly, the baby, as though . . ."

"As though what?" He pushed to his feet, wanting to comfort her, but she waved him off, and reluctantly he sat back down.

"As though the baby was yours, as if you wanted it to be." She wrapped her arms around her waist and her hand unconsciously slipped to her belly. Since the first time they'd made love and he'd spent his seed inside her, Aidan had been careful not to let it happen again. Knowing Syrena as well as he'd come to, he sensed it bothered her. She wanted bairns of her own, with him, but the fear he'd become like his father, a man who hated an innocent child because he was Fae, weighed heavily upon him.

"Syrena, it's almost four years since I last saw Davina. The bairn is no' mine. Come here," he coaxed, needing to hold her.

She hesitated then came to him. Kneeling between his legs, she rested her head on his thigh. "The bairn may no' even be John Henry's. Jarius, Ursula's brother, the man behind all this madness, forced himself upon her. She overheard Ursula speak of sacrificin' an innocent at their ceremony, and she's afraid they referred to her bairn. Ye must ken why I had to offer her my protection, my support."

"I do. I'm sorry, I should have trusted you." She raised her gaze to his, and he rubbed a smudge of soot from her cheek with his thumb. "But in truth, I have no right to expect you to be faithful, Aidan. You've made no commitment to me."

Her words were like a blade twisted deep in his belly. "Fer the love of Christ, we're married. What more of a commitment do ye want from me?" She held his gaze, the strained silence lengthening between them. He gritted his teeth and cupped her face between his hands. "I need ye. I want ye like I've never wanted another woman. Ye make me laugh. Ye make me smile. I can tell ye things I can tell no one else. Ye're my wife, Syrena, in every sense of the word," he ground out, furious at how vulnerable she'd made him feel. His feelings were laid bare to her, to him.

A soft smile played on her lips. She took his hand and pressed her lips tenderly to his palm, then shifted on her knees to face him and set about tugging off his other boot. Undoing his trews, her long, delicate fingers brushed over his cock. "Your bath is getting cold," she said as if it explained the slow torture she was putting him through.

He choked back a groan. "Are ye playin' at bein' a good wife, Syrena, now that ye ken our marriage is fer real?"

"You're hurt, Aidan, you can't do this by yourself," she said, urging him to his feet to tug his trews slowly over his thighs, to his knees. Sliding her hand down his leg, she lifted first one foot then the other, her pale pink lips tantalizingly close to his cock.

"I should have the maids bring you more hot water." With every word she spoke, her heated breath encircled his straining erection, tightening the painful noose of desire. Yet she acted as though nothing were amiss, as though his cock weren't brushing against her silky hair. Fer the love of God, she acted as though he was a bloody bairn needin' a bath!

"Nay," he rasped, wanting her mouth on him.

Instead, she rose to her feet and led him to the tub by the fire. He sank beneath the lukewarm water. It didn't matter—he was certain the heat of his desire would soon bring it to a boil.

She knelt beside the wooden rim, lifting her arms to wind her long thick hair into a loose knot. Her breasts strained against the thin fabric. Blissfully unaware of what she did to him, she gave him an innocent smile.

He gritted his teeth, fisting his hand beneath the water as he fought the temptation to drag her into the tub, to rip her delicate night rail from her lush curves and thrust into her.

Closing his eyes, he reminded himself that she wanted nothing more than to help him bathe. The last thing she needed was him foisting his attentions upon her. She'd been through enough this night.

Soft hands glided over his shoulders and down his arms, and he stifled a groan. The silky strands of her hair tickled his nose, and he inhaled her sweet scent. The intoxicating fragrance of the lavender soap she lathered his body with. "Am I hurting you?" she asked, her voice low and husky.

"Nay," he said between clenched teeth. He thought he heard her chuckle, and cracked one eye open, but she simply smiled and said, "Bend yer knees, Aidan, and slide a little lower so I can wash your hair."

"Mind the back of my head, it still pains me," he groused. He couldn't help it. He was frustrated beyond distraction, the ache in his head competing with the one in his cock. Bloody hell, she was drivin' him mad and didna even ken it.

"Poor baby," she crooned as though he were a bairn. The heavy weight of her breasts rested on his cheek as she bent over to gently wash his hair.

Bloody hell!

"Syrena, are ye almost done?" His lips brushed against her pebbled nipple.

"I'm sorry. It won't be much longer," she choked out her response.

Sweet Christ, he'd made her cry. "Nay. I'm sorry, angel, doona mind me."

Turning her back to him, she leaned over to wash his feet. Her hair came loose and the thick golden curtain shielded her face from him, but he saw the tremble of her slender shoulders.

Keep yer mouth shut, MacLeod, she's suffered enough fer one night.

Her hands stroked the insides of his thighs. He squeezed his lids shut and swallowed a frustrated oath.

Her fingers encircled his cock, and she glided them slowly over his shaft. His eyes shot open, and he saw the amusement in her gaze as she watched him. "Witch, ye kent all along what ye were doin'." Words failed him the moment she lowered her lips to his pulsating erection. He fisted his hand in her hair, guiding his cock into the heat of her mouth with the other.

With her mouth she brought him to the brink, and he couldn't hold back any longer. He hauled her into the tub with him, water sloshing over the side.

Dragging her night rail over her hips, she straddled him. Aidan fisted his hands in the drenched fabric and tore it in half. "I canna wait, angel." His face was buried between her breasts, muffling his voice.

She slid up and down his shaft. "I don't want you to." Raising her hips, she positioned the head of his cock at her tight opening. Aidan jerked his hips and thrust deep inside her, losing himself in her welcoming heat and letting go of his fear for his brother, of what tomorrow would bring.

Chapter 24

Through the thick fog of sleep, Syrena heard the muffled sounds of angry male voices. *It's only a dream*, she reassured herself, snuggling into the warmth of Aidan's embrace. The heavy weight of the blankets shifted to cover her bare shoulder.

"Get the hell out of my room, John Henry, ye're disturbin' my wife." Aidan's deep voice rumbled against her cheek.

With a concerted effort, she pried her heavy lids open. Three blurred figures stood at the side of the bed. "Aidan, what—"

"Go back to sleep, angel." He kissed the top of her head while he stroked her arm beneath the covers.

As she rubbed her eyes, the three men came into sharp relief. A tall thin man held a blade to Aidan's throat. "Oh," she gasped, her heart slamming into her chest.

Aidan held her firmly in place. "Doona move."

A lock of sandy hair fell over the man's forehead. A look of confusion creased his light blue eyes, and he lowered the blade. "I didna ken ye were wed."

"Aye, and I doona think this would be the time to be introducin' ye to my wife. Leave me to get dressed and then—"

"I want to ken where *my* wife is!"

Syrena slanted her gaze to Aidan's. He nodded at the silent

question in her eyes. After they'd made love, they had talked into the small hours of the morning. He'd told her about his cousin and Davina, and because she knew he was hiding something, in the end he told her how Lachlan was being bled for his Fae blood.

Davina's husband averted his gaze from Syrena, but a pained expression drew his handsome features taut with worry. Davina was wrong, she thought. Her husband did love her.

"Yer stepmother and her brother have taken her to Glastonbury."

John Henry lowered his lean frame onto the foot of the bed and waved the other men off. When the door clicked quietly behind them, he said, "So she's left me."

"Nay, ye bloody fool, they've taken her against her will, them and Lamont."

Syrena recognized the moment Aidan's words penetrated John Henry's initial relief. "What the hell is goin' on, Aidan? I come from Whitehall to find my home torched and my wife missin'. And who is this Lamont ye speak of?"

Aidan sighed wearily. "John Henry, as soon as Syrena and I have dressed, we leave fer Glastonbury. 'Tis where the bastard holds Lachlan, and now yer wife. Ye'll learn all ye need to ken then." Syrena didn't envy Aidan the task of telling his cousin what awaited them in Glastonbury. She felt a pang of pity for John Henry.

If not for what they would soon face, Syrena would have enjoyed the ride through the picturesque countryside. But even the late afternoon sun shining down upon them and the sweet musky fragrance of fall could not diminish her dread.

She glanced over her shoulder and Aidan offered her a reassuring smile. His cousin rode beside him in shocked silence. She could only imagine how difficult it was for him to absorb how so much had gone on without his knowledge. His guilt was palpable, but Syrena didn't think he could've stopped Jarius. If he'd tried, she felt certain he'd be dead.

And not that it made a difference now, but they'd learned how Lachlan had come to be in London. John Henry said his father knew he was dying and frantically searched for a cure. In his ramblings he'd spoken of Lachlan, how his brother by marriage, Alexander MacLeod, told him Lan was Fae. Lord Hamilton clung to the hope his nephew could somehow heal him.

John Henry, convinced it was only the ravings of an old man in the last throes of death, dismissed his pleas to contact his cousin. Ursula had not. But Syrena and Aidan both knew the reason for the woman's interest, and it had nothing to do with curing her dying husband.

Aidan believed Ursula had lured Lan to London with the threat of exposure. It had been a difficult conversation for Syrena to endure, learning her brother suffered because he was Fae. But it had been worse for Aidan—he held himself responsible.

As for Lamont, Aidan surmised once he'd healed from his injuries, he'd sat back and waited for an opportunity to get Lan on his own. Damaged in both body and soul, hell-bent on revenge, Ursula and her brother would have recognized Lamont's value to their sick plan.

Connor and Callum drew their mounts alongside her. She was glad of the distraction. "A precaution is all, my lady. We're several leagues from Glastonbury yet," Callum said.

She nodded, eyeing Connor, who held himself stiffly erect. They had journeyed all day, and the lad had yet to speak to her.

She blew out an exasperated breath. "Connor, I'm sorry you are angry with me, but I didn't know what else to do."

"Ye could've said somethin' instead of knockin' me on the head."

"I didn't knock you on the head. I just . . ." She reached over to demonstrate.

He slapped a hand to his neck. "Nay! Are ye mad?"

At Aidan's deep chuckle, Syrena shifted in the saddle. "What are ye doin' to the lad to make him shriek like a lass?"

Connor's head bobbed up and down. "Aye, why doona ye show the laird? See how he likes it when ye squeeze the life out of him."

Callum rolled his eyes. "Connor, lad, Lady Syrena saved yer fool life, now get over it."

"So ye say."

"If ye doona mind, I need to speak to my wife. Syrena." Aidan jerked his chin and galloped ahead.

Syrena had wondered if Aidan meant to share the plan of attack with her. She'd watched with growing frustration as he took small groups aside, knowing from the intent look upon his beautiful face, and the gestures of his big hands, he had set out a plan to the exclusion of her. Her husband had made his opinion of women in battle well known. But if he thought to keep her from this one, she would soon set him straight.

Guiding the black steed to the top of the hill, she reined in beside Aidan. His gaze focused on the emerald green valley below, and it took a moment for him to acknowledge her presence.

"Look there, Syrena," he said, pointing into the distance. "Do ye see the tower to yer left?"

Shielding her eyes, she spotted the tall spire and nodded.

"'Tis where they hold Lachlan and Davina."

She fisted her hands in the reins. The temptation not to wait until nightfall, to ride in and rescue Lan right then, overwhelmed her.

Aidan reached over and squeezed her hand. "I ken how ye feel, angel, I ken. But this night we'll have him back with us, and then we can put this nightmare behind us."

A suffocating ache built in her chest. She told herself it was fear for Lachlan's well-being, the success of their mission, but she knew better. She was simply afraid to delve too deep.

Her love for Aidan had never been in question. She'd loved

him from the beginning. But once they rescued Lachlan, her life would never be the same.

She would have to give up a part of who she was to remain in the Mortal realm, and today the reality of her situation struck home.

Aidan angled his head and studied her with concern. "Ye're quiet, are ye feelin' unwell?"

"No, I'll be fine." She forced a smile. "Now, would you like to share the plan with me since you have obviously shared it with everyone else?"

He grinned, the crescent moon deepening in his cheek. "I'm no' a fool. There's no one I trust more to have by my side in battle then ye."

Her throat swelled, aching with the attempt to contain the emotions his words drew from her.

"But I'd no' be honest if I didna tell ye 'tis the last place I want ye to be."

"Aidan, you can't—"

Pressing a finger to her lips, he stopped her protest. "I ken. I need ye and yer sword. None of us ken what we ride into. David gave us an idea of the numbers loyal to Jarius, those that would follow him here. And John Henry has a fair idea of those employed at the castle, but I'm no' certain we can depend upon them to come to our aid."

She scanned the small contingent that rode with them. David, the servant who had tried to force the drugged mead upon her, averted his gaze. He turned his attention to his companion, another of the men who'd served in the grand hall that night.

"Aidan, I'm not certain we should trust David. He makes me uneasy. I've caught him watching me and—"

Her husband quirked a brow. "What man doesna' watch ye? And ye're no helpin' matters insistin' on wearin' a pair of Connor's trews."

She allowed herself a moment of pleasure, enjoying the fact Aidan didn't like the idea other men found her attractive.

But instinct told her David had no interest in her in that way. "See how you like wearing a gown to sit astride a horse. Breeches are much more practical."

"Fer sittin' on a horse, aye, I'll give ye that. But they are verra hard on yer husband's concentration."

Syrena laughed. "I'll have to wear them more often."

The corner of his mouth twitched. "If ye keep it up, night-fall will be upon us before I lay the plan out fer ye."

"I promise to behave, now tell—"

He leaned over and silenced her with his mouth, seducing her with the slow slide of his lips over hers. He twined his fingers through her hair and deepened the kiss. And in that moment, she felt the love neither of them had the courage to admit out loud.

"I'll be sorely disappointed if ye behave all the time, angel," he murmured against her lips. "Last night ye—"

She gave an embarrassed squeak and covered his mouth with her palm. "Shhh, someone will hear you!"

Aidan laughed. "Doona pretend ye're angry. If ye were, yer sword would be glowing red."

She glanced at the yellow glow emitting through her fingers and frowned. "What do you mean?"

"Yer sword, it mirrors your emotions. When ye're angry, it glows red, and when ye're happy, 'tis yellow. What color is it when yer sad?"

"Blue," she murmured absently. Could Aidan be right? Did Nuie transmit her emotions and not the other way around?

No, it couldn't be.

"Doona look so troubled. At least ye'll no' be able to hide yer feelin's from me. I'll have ye carryin' yer sword all—"

"I won't have him much longer. Only the one who leads the Fae of the Enchanted Isles is entitled to carry the Sword of Nuada." The thought of giving up Nuie was more than she could deal with at the moment. In the last year he'd been her constant companion. Without Nuie, she never would have become the warrior she was now.

"It makes ye sad to think of losin' him?" The note of disquiet in Aidan's voice jolted Syrena from her thoughts. The last thing she wanted was for him to think she didn't wish to remain with him in the Mortal realm.

"No, I . . ." A blue light shone through her fingers, and she bowed her head. Aidan couldn't be right. Nuie found the thought of their separation as painful as she did; that was all it was. "I'll be fine."

For a long moment he held her gaze then nodded, but the teasing light in his eyes had dimmed. "We'd best go over the plan." He shifted in his saddle, gesturing to the castle. "Within twenty feet of the guardhouse there is a small copse of trees. John Henry says they check the area often.

"Callum, Samuel, and ten others will ride with me. We'll hide out in the woods until the time is right then pick the guards off one at a time. As soon as they've been taken care of, I'll signal ye and ye can bring the rest in. But considerin' how ye feel about David and his companion, mayhap I—"

"No, I shouldn't have said anything." He'd given her his trust, and she didn't want to disappoint him. She wouldn't have him question his faith in her simply because David and his companion unsettled her.

When they finished going over the plan, Aidan went over the layout of the castle. John Henry was certain they held Lachlan in the dungeon, and given their contempt for the Church, would hold their ceremony in the chapel. Syrena hoped he was right. Otherwise they'd waste precious time and lose the element of surprise.

She sensed there was an underlying tension between them now, and wanted to believe it was nothing more than battle nerves.

"Are ye certain ye're comfortable with the plan? Ye doona have any doubts or—"

"No, it's a good plan, Aidan."

"I'm glad ye approve." He smiled, and brushed his knuckles

across her cheek. "Watch fer my signal," he said before he rode down the backside of the hill.

Moisture gathered behind her eyes. The knot in her chest tightened. And her throat ached as she fought to keep the turbulent emotions at bay. She didn't realize Aidan had ridden back to her until he wrapped his arm around her and kissed her temple.

"Doona worry, Syrena. We'll make it through this. All will be well in the end." He stroked her hair.

It had to be. She couldn't bear the thought of losing him.

He leaned back and wiped a tear from her cheek. Framing her face with his big hands, he gave her a hard kiss. "Ye'll have me reconsiderin' my decision to leave ye in charge if ye doona stop yer cryin'."

His words had the desired effect—her tears dried up. He glanced at Nuie, who glowed red and grinned. "There's my lass."

Hidden on the side of a hill, not far from the castle, Syrena and those that remained huddled around a pitiful fire. The chill from the night air settled deep in her bones. She wrapped her arms around herself and scanned the shadows for Connor and the three others she'd set on the first watch. Syrena, John Henry, David, and his companion, Dirk, would take the next shift.

The full moon began its slow ascent over the peaks of the castle. David, on the opposite side of the fire, spoke with his companion. Every so often Syrena felt his gaze upon her. But she set aside her discomfort, certain her unease had more to do with the fact he'd followed Ursula's directives than with the man himself. After all, a servant was not given much choice in who they served—not with a family to feed.

All fell silent. Only the crackle and pop of the flames and the chirps and whistles of night creatures broke the quiet. Tension weighted her shoulders. This was the most difficult time of battle. The waiting—too much time to consider the outcome.

John Henry sat beside Syrena on a log. He snapped a twig and tossed it into the flames, and then another, and another. *Crack. Crack. Crack.*

Syrena's nerves were scraped raw, and she wanted to yell at him to stop, but she understood his fears and sympathized.

He shot to his feet. "I canna take it anymore. How much longer?" he asked Syrena. The light from the campfire softened the harsh lines of worry in his handsome face.

"Not long, Lord Hamilton. The moon has almost reached its apex." Across the dancing flame, David nudged his companion and nodded. Were they as relieved as the others that the long wait would soon be over, or was there another reason for his reaction?

"Doona worry about yer lady wife, my laird, she's a strong one. They willna break her," Bess said, as she attempted to reassure him.

John Henry stopped his pacing and pushed a sandy lock of hair from his face, his gaze seeking out the castle. "Aye, she is. If only I had told her I loved her, mayhap she wouldna . . ." His voice trailed off. His face pinched with sorrow, he strode in the direction of the horses.

"Poor mon," Bess murmured.

Distracted, Syrena watched David and Dirk follow after John Henry, and murmured an agreement to Bess's statement. She pitied the man his knowledge that the woman he loved might die without ever learning how he felt about her. Syrena decided she would not put herself in the same position. This night she would tell Aidan she loved him.

David ran out from the cover of the trees, his eyes wide and wild. "My lady, come quick, something has happened to Lord Hamilton!"

Syrena scrambled from the log and raced after him with a hundred scenarios running through her mind. As she pushed past the horses, the two men backed away to reveal John

Henry, lying on the ground, gasping for air. She dropped to his side and set Nuie on the ground. "Lord Hamilton, can—"

His red-rimmed eyes were glazed and bulging. Struggling to speak, he fisted his hands into her shirt and pulled her down to him. "Poi . . . poison." His voice was little more than a whisper.

Bess shrieked, "My lady, behind ye!"

Syrena whipped her head around. In the filtered light of the moon, David's face glowered with menace, and he raised Nuie over his head. "Prepare to die," he sneered.

On her knees, she twisted and lunged. Wrapping her arms around David's legs, she jerked them out from under him. Midway through his fall, he flung Nuie over his shoulder.

"Dirk! Take it . . ." David slammed into the ground, lying flat on his back.

Before she managed to untangle herself from his limbs, his companion had grabbed hold of Nuie and ran to the waiting black steed. He leapt onto the horse and galloped into the shadows of the night.

Connor rushed toward them, panting, unaware of what had transpired. "Lady Syrena, the signal."

Before she had a chance to respond, David struggled to sit up. A flash of silver glinted between his fingers. "You can't stop him. You can't stop any of it."

"My lady," Bess yelled and tossed her John Henry's sword.

Drawing the blade in a wide arc, Syrena slit his throat.

With a wet gurgle, he slumped over. Blood splattered his white shirt and the sword. She wiped the blade on the grass and met Connor's startled gaze. "Consider your friends' deaths avenged."

Mouth open, Connor gave her a jerky nod. "The . . . the signal . . ."

Everything was happening too fast, and the magnitude of Syrena's responsibilities threatened to overwhelm her. Aidan had entrusted her with the protection of his people, while the Fae had entrusted Nuie, their greatest treasure, to her care. She had failed on both counts.

Breathe. You are a warrior. You know what to do.

But how could she be a warrior without her sword? Without Nuie, she was simply Syrena, a Fae princess without magick, without power and strength.

As though he were with her now, Uscias's words echoed in her mind. "It comes from here, Syrena, your head and your heart. It's always been there. Look for it." An image of Aidan appeared before her, his beautiful smiling face when he told her Nuie mirrored her emotions, who she was, and not the other way around.

She took strength in their words and motioned for the two men who'd stood watch with Connor. "Go after Dirk. He's headed for the castle. He'll take the long way around."

She knelt beside John Henry. His weakened fingers encircled her wrist. "Tell Aidan . . . tell him there is a passage." He paused, gasping for air. "A passage from the crypt . . . from the crypt to the chapel."

"I'll tell him. Save your strength, John Henry," Syrena said as he struggled to speak, yet knowing he didn't have much time left.

"Leave me . . . save . . . save my wife. Tell her . . . tell her . . . I love her."

She held his gaze. "We'll save her, you have my word."

Syrena led what was left of her small party across the moors to the woods. In Nuie's stead, she carried John Henry's sword. She knew what the loss of her sword would cost her. Princess or no princess, she'd be brought before the Seelie court. Her defense, concern for a fallen Mortal, for her brother's life, would carry little weight. It would only serve to draw the Fae's derision. Having suffered their contempt in the past, she didn't care. It was only her promise to Nuie that mattered—her promise to protect him.

And there was only one way she knew how to do so.

Uscias. He would know she failed to fulfill her oath, be obligated to report her to the court, but none of that mattered.

They crossed the flat terrain that led to the copse of trees where they would rendezvous with Aidan. Syrena slowed her breathing and searched for the quiet in her mind. She had only ever communicated with Lachlan in this manner and hoped she would be able to do so with the wizard.

"Uscias," she called to him.

A low buzz vibrated inside her head. "Princess Syrena?"

Relief at reaching him rushed through her. "Yes, it's me. Uscias, I need your help. Nuie's been taken."

An ominous silence rang in her ears before he said, "I'll come, but first I must go to the Seelie court. Much has happened since you disappeared. Magnus and Dmitri attacked."

Syrena stifled a shocked cry with her hand. She hadn't been there to fight alongside them. Guilt and fear roiled inside her. How could she ever face the Fae? She'd failed them when they needed her most.

"We were victorious, princess. You trained your army well. Fallyn and her sisters are unharmed, but I'm afraid you . . ."

She knew what he was about to say. Even if she hadn't lost Nuie, she would have to face the Seelie court. "I know. It doesn't matter. Uscias, the Mortals have the Grimoire of Honorius."

Her mentor's curse startled Syrena. If she hadn't known how dire the situation was before, she did now.

"Are you certain?"

"Yes, we were told by a woman that they had the Grimoire in their possession."

"Where are you?"

"Glastonbury. They are attempting to release the dark lord. Uscias, they have my brother, and I'm certain the Fae that went missing."

"I've arrived at your uncle's palace, princess, I must break contact. The fate of both Mortal and Fae realms rests with you, Syrena. The Grimoire must be destroyed. It will sense your magick, your goodness, and try to destroy you by driving you mad. Fill yourself with light, and pray, pray to the angels for their protection. This has been your quest all along, my child. The angels chose you."

She heard Uscias grunt and in a quarrelsome voice say, "She needed to know. You cannot expect her to do this entirely on her own."

"Who are you speaking to?"

"It doesn't matter. I must go. I will come as soon as I'm able. May the angels walk with you, Syrena." The connection sputtered and silence filled her mind.

Angels. The angels had known all along where her father's quest would lead her. Once again, Syrena felt crushed under the weight of responsibility, the expectations of others.

"My lady, are ye all right?" Connor asked, holding up a bough for her to ride beneath.

"No . . . no, I'm not, but I have to be," she answered honestly.

"Doona worry, we'll get the laird's brother and Lady Davina back."

Connor was right. Nothing else mattered but saving Lachlan and Davina, and now, destroying the Grimoire.

A movement ahead captured her attention. Under the light of the moon, ghostly apparitions wove among the trees. Syrena held up her hand, and the others came to a halt. Connor whistled. Seconds later, a corresponding whistle came back in response.

"'Tis Laird MacLeod."

The shadows moved silently toward them, familiar faces coming into view as they drew near. Aidan stepped forward. His gaze scanned the riders then locked on to hers. "What happened?" he asked as he raised his arms to help her from her horse.

Syrena inhaled his warm, woodsy scent, allowing herself a moment in the comfort of his embrace before she stepped away. "Your cousin was poisoned."

Connor led the white steed toward them. They'd tied John Henry to his horse, and he lay slumped over the saddle.

"I'm sorry, Aidan, he's dead."

Connor asked if he wished him to remove the body and Aidan nodded, gesturing for Callum to help.

He didn't take his gaze from his cousin's body; a muscle pulsated in the hard set of his beard-stubbled jaw. "Who?"

"David and his companion, Dirk."

Aidan dragged his hand through the thick waves of his dark hair. "I should've listened to ye."

"No, I should've listened to myself. They were my responsibility. I should've been more vigilant. I promised him, Aidan. I promised John Henry that we would save Davina."

"Aye, and we will." He looked down at her and frowned. "Where's yer sword?"

"Dirk has it. I'm certain he means to give it to Jarius to be used in the ceremony. I sent two men after him, but he had a head start. He will alert them, Aidan. The element of surprise is lost."

"Nay, Jarius and Lamont ken well enough we'd come. The two of them are arrogant fools. We'll use it against them."

"Who . . . who . . . is . . . Uscias?"

Syrena started. *Lachlan.* "My mentor. Lan, we're here. We're coming. Where are you?"

"Dungeon . . . Coming to move, now . . . Where's Aidan?"

"He's here, with me."

"Tell him, sorry . . . sorry for everythin'."

Aidan watched her. "Lan?" he mouthed.

She nodded, and he drew her into his arms. Lachlan was saying good-bye, and she couldn't bear to hear it, didn't think her heart could take much more. "You tell him, when we see you."

"Syrena . . . thank ye . . . fer when I was a bairn. Ye . . ."

"No . . . no more, conserve your strength, we're . . ." The crackle of energy faded. Her head ached as much as her heart. She drew away from Aidan. "We have to go. They're moving him now." She closed her eyes for a moment, willing herself not to cry. "Aidan, he wanted me to tell you he was sorry."

He lifted his sword, drawing the men's attention. "Move in."

She didn't think he'd heard until he looked down at her, a telling sheen in his eyes. "If he comes to ye again, tell him . . . tell him he has nothin' to apologize fer. And tell him I'll kill every last one of the bastards."

Chapter 25

Even dying, his brother felt the need to apologize to him. Aidan cursed, his anger magnified with each bone-jarring step he took. He was no better than his father. With his bitter resentment, he'd pushed Lan away. It was as though Aidan himself had placed him in Jarius's hands.

If he hadn't blamed Lan for the debacle with the Lamonts, for every bloody thing that had gone wrong in their lives, Ursula wouldn't have been able to lure him to London with the threat of exposure. Aidan didn't need Lan to tell him he'd gone because of him.

He felt Syrena's presence behind him, running to keep up with him as his strides ate the ground beneath his feet. Christ, he'd done to her what he'd done to his brother—holding a part of himself back, blaming her for something she had no control over. And now, although he left it unspoken, he forced her to make a choice—him or the Fae. She'd willingly played the part, pretending to be something she wasn't. But he'd seen her face when she'd slip and mention her people, her home. The fear she'd make him angry, lose his love, simply because she was Fae.

Aye, he loved her, but he was no longer certain it was enough, at least not for her. Look what damage his hatred of the Fae had done to Lachlan.

"Aidan, I have to speak to you. Please, hold up, it's important," she panted.

He slowed his pace. "Is it Lan?"

"No." She took a deep breath before she said, "I . . . I contacted the Fae. I know how you feel about my people, Aidan, but I had to inform them I lost Nuie. They had to be made aware of Jarius's intentions and that he has the Grimoire." She searched his face as though waiting for him to explode. "Aidan, both Mortal and Fae are in danger."

It seemed Syrena had made her choice.

"Do ye think they will come?"

"Yes, but I don't know if it will be in time. Aidan, the Grimoire must be destroyed."

His brow furrowed. "Was that what ye sensed when we arrived at the town house?"

She nodded. "And now without Nuie, I'll have to fight its magick on my own."

"Nay." He reached for her hand and brought it to his lips, kissing the soft skin of her palm. He'd protect her with his life, even if it meant protecting her from him. "We'll fight it together. Come, Callum and Connor took out the two men manning the guardhouse. The chapel is on the ground floor."

She groaned. Closing her eyes, she shook her head. "Aidan, I'm sorry, I forgot, but when Lan—"

"What is it?"

"John Henry said there's a passageway from the crypt to the chapel."

"Doona worry about it. We still have time to use the information to our advantage." He whistled for his men. Within minutes they were headed for the low, whitewashed building at the back of the castle. The change of plans laid out, he welcomed the heated rush of blood through his limbs, the opportunity to make the bastards pay for what they'd done.

The closer they got to the crypt, the more Syrena stumbled. Aidan tightened his hold on her. "Ye're feelin' its magick, aren't ye?"

Her face a sickly white, she nodded.

Aidan cursed. He couldn't stand by and watch her suffer. "Go back, Syrena, and wait with Bess," he pleaded.

"No, I'll be fine. Don't worry about me. You need me, Aidan, and so does Lan." Her words were strained as though it was a fight just to get them out.

"Aye, but he wouldna want ye to suffer because of it and neither do I."

She didn't seem to hear him. Her mouth worked silently.

"Are ye doin' magick?" he asked, surprised to find he hoped she was.

She grimaced. "No, but if I was certain of its success, I would. I'm praying."

Aidan didn't think she looked very happy about it. "Prayin' is a good thing," he murmured as he shoved open the door to the crypt. The dank air enveloped them in its chilly embrace.

He motioned for the men to follow, cautioning them to silence. Syrena whimpered as they went farther into the room. Her fingers pressed to her temples. The last vestiges of his restraint all but stripped away from helplessly watching the agony she endured. His determination to kill Jarius intensified with each strangled breath she took.

Four well-fed rats scurried across the stone floor, taking refuge behind the elaborately carved wooden coffins. Cobwebs hung from curved stone arches, and he batted the sticky gossamer threads away before guiding her beneath them. "Fight it, angel, ye can do it," he said in an urgent whisper.

Rivulets of water streamed down the thick gray walls from the low ceiling, splashing onto the stone steps. He scooped her into his arms. She was in no condition to make the steep climb on her own.

Halfway up the stairs, the riotous whispers of the men behind him drew his attention. "Someone's comin'."

Aidan balanced Syrena on his thigh. Tucking her between him and the wall, he lifted his sword.

Through the muted light he saw Dirk round the corner, his eyes widening in fear as he took in the deadly intent of the men that surrounded him. A big hand muffled his terrified squeal. Beaten down by a flurry of fists, he disappeared from Aidan's line of sight. Moments later, Connor triumphantly pushed through the crush with Syrena's sword in hand. "I guess the bastard heard about the secret passageway." The lad grinned.

"What about the two men that were sent after him?"

Amusement faded from Connor's expression, and he glanced at the blood coating Syrena's sword. He wiped it clean on his trews and shook his head. "No sign of them."

Aidan cursed beneath his breath then dragged Syrena's hand from her head and wrapped it around her sword. Almost immediately, her breathing eased. Her eyelids fluttered open, and she pressed the golden blade to her chest. "Thank you."

"Nay, 'twould be Connor's doin', and I'm thinkin' whoever ye were prayin' to."

She smiled weakly at the lad when he said, "We're even."

"You can put me down, Aidan. I'll be all right."

Reluctantly, he did as she asked. He didn't think she was as well as she pretended to be, but he could not carry her and wield a sword at the same time. She touched the gleaming stones on the hilt with shaking fingers. Murmuring something to the sword, she raised it over her head. The blade sizzled, vibrating in the heavy, musty air. It turned a fiery red, illuminating Syrena in its heated glow. From the steps below, he heard the men's exclamations of awe.

"Ye're a wee bit fashed, are ye?" Aidan said as he allowed her to take the lead.

His concern for her well-being grew as he watched her struggle to climb the rest of the way. Her breath came in sharp, shallow gasps the closer they came to the top. He grabbed hold of her arm when she tripped and felt her violent trembling beneath his fingers. "Bloody hell, Syrena, I'll not put ye through this."

She placed a finger to his lips then climbed the last step to the narrow landing.

From behind the planked door came a low moan and a guttural grunt. "Ride him, Ursula, ride him hard. When he spills his seed in you, I'll slit his throat and you'll absorb his—"

Aidan lifted his foot at the same time as Syrena. Together they kicked down the door. The wooden planks splintered and crashed to the floor, sending up a cloud of dust. The air cleared, revealing his brother, naked, chained spread-eagle to a stone altar. Ursula, black satin gown hiked to her waist, straddled him. Her pendulous breasts spilled over the top of her gown, her head thrown back in ecstasy. Lan bucked, then moaned, spending himself inside her.

With his back to them, a man in coarse brown robes chanted. He raised his arm. Moonlight filtering through the stained glass window glinted off the lethal-looking blade he held.

Aidan swung his sword, severing the hand at its wrist. Blood sprayed in a wide arc over Lan and Ursula. The blade clattered to the floor still gripped within a closed fist. Ursula's blue eyes, glazed by drugs and lust, widened.

Aidan's men swarmed in from behind him and he lost sight of Syrena in the crush. The black-robed congregation frozen in place by the bloody tableau quickly roused themselves, and the din in the cavernous room rose to a frenzied pitch.

Lan slowly turned his head and fixed Aidan with a languid stare. "About . . . time," he slurred.

Aidan had no chance to respond. Jarius, his bloody stump cradled to his chest, raised his wild-eyed gaze to his. Letting out a bloodcurdling howl, the madman grabbed the tall, iron branch of candles at the foot of the stone altar and, ignoring the splash of hot wax, jabbed it at Aidan. Jerking back, Aidan positioned himself protectively in front of Lan. From behind him, Ursula shrieked then wrapped her arms around Aidan's neck, choking the breath from him. With a maniacal smile, her brother came at him again. With one hand Aidan tried to break her hold on his throat while defending himself against Jarius with his sword.

Aidan leaned against the altar and brought his foot up to kick away the flaming candles before Jarius could smash them into his chest. There was a flash of movement then Syrena was at his side. Reaching for Ursula, she broke the woman's death grip on him and dragged her from the altar. Jarius swung the iron branch at him, Aidan ducked and drove his blade up and into Jarius's heart. A wet gurgle rattled in his lungs. His eyes rolled back, and he crumpled to the floor.

"Jarius!" Ursula screamed, breaking free of Syrena to rush to her brother's side. She swiveled her head and snarled at Aidan. "I'll kill you for this." As she attempted to lunge for him, Syrena grabbed hold of her.

"Allow me to do the honors, Ursula," a man rasped from behind him.

Aidan whirled to face the man he knew was Lamont, raising his sword just in time to parry the first blow. Out of the corner of his eye he saw Syrena shove Ursula aside and take up her position in front of Lan. Lamont fought like a man possessed, and Aidan knew he would need to stay focused if he hoped to best him. He'd have to trust Syrena to protect herself and Lachlan.

Their swords locked and Lamont sneered. "I'd hoped to make ye watch yer wife and brother die in front of ye, but it seems like I'll have to kill ye first."

Aidan forced down his fury at the taunt, focusing instead on backing Lamont to the edge of the dais. Grunting and groaning, they struggled for supremacy, then Aidan broke his sword free and went after him with everything he had.

When they were less than a foot from the stairs, Aidan gripped his hilt with two hands and swung his blade at Lamont. The force of the blow was enough to weaken the other man's hold on his blade and Aidan lunged, throwing Lamont off balance. Lamont's arms windmilled as he tripped backward off the top step of the dais. His sword clattered to the floor and he landed on his back at the base of the platform.

Scrambling quickly to his feet, he backed away. Aidan prowled after him. Ripping off his black cape, Lamont swirled it in Aidan's face then grabbed a man from the crowd and shoved him in front of Aidan to make good his escape. Bloody hell. He pushed the man aside, about to go after Lamont when he heard Syrena's panicked cry.

"Aidan!"

He turned. One of Lamont's men closed in on her while she fought another. Having battled her himself, Aidan could see her strength was waning from fighting the magick. A wry man in black robes jumped in front of him before he could reach her. Cursing, Aidan blocked the smaller man's blade then drew back and slammed his fist into his face. Before the man had even crumpled at his feet, Aidan raced across the dais to the warrior that approached Syrena with murderous intent.

Knowing Syrena was too weak for him to waste time in a fight, Aidan stayed out of the man's line of sight and came up behind him. Wrapping his arm around the warrior's throat, he grabbed him forcibly by the chin and snapped his neck, shoving the dead warrior aside to reach Syrena. The man she fought caught sight of Aidan and took two steps back then turned and ran.

Syrena swayed and Aidan reached out for her, drawing her to him. "Are ye hurt?"

"No . . . it's the Grimoire," she said weakly, freeing herself from his embrace. "I have to destroy it."

"I'll help ye."

"No, you can't. Look after Lan." She took a steadying breath, her face pale as she took a wobbly step away from him.

Aidan hesitated, torn between seeing to his brother and protecting Syrena. As he tracked her unsteady progress toward the back of the dais, his decision was made.

"Callum." He motioned to the big man. The fight with the black-robed congregation was over, and he was rounding up prisoners. "I need ye to keep an eye on Lan."

With a quick nod, Callum signaled for Connor to relieve him of the two men he held by the scruff of their necks.

Aidan turned to follow Syrena then watched in horror as she flew through the air, landing on her back with a bone-jarring thud, cracking her head on the corner of a chair.

He ran to her. "Syrena!"

She raised dazed eyes to his. Blood streamed from a deep gash on her forehead. "Bloody hell, I'm no' lettin' ye do this."

"There's no other way." She leaned against him, then using his arm to hang on to, she rose slowly to her feet.

"Wait," he said, fighting the urge to drag her from the dais. He took her chin in his hand to examine her wound, gently dabbing the blood from her face with the edge of his tunic.

She took hold of his wrist to stop him. "Aidan, I have to do this now. Stay back."

"Ye think I can just stand by and watch while—"

She pressed a trembling finger to his lips. "Please. I will heal, you won't. I can't worry about you and battle the magick at the same time."

Everything inside him warred at the idea of releasing her. Never in his life had he done anything as difficult as letting her go. His chest tightened as he watched her square her slender shoulders and lift her sword. She turned and took a step toward the wood table where the leather-bound tome lay.

Within a foot of the Grimoire, she let out a pain-filled scream. Holding her head, she dropped to her knees.

"Syrena!" His heart wrenched in his chest and he lurched toward her.

"No!" She staggered to her feet. In a barely audible whisper she murmured words he could not make out then her voice grew stronger, more powerful. Gripping her sword with both hands, she raised it above her head. With lethal force she brought it down on the Grimoire. A blast of heat and flame threw Aidan off balance and he fought to remain upright.

Syrena stood within a cloud of black smoke. A disembodied voice filled the chapel, speaking words in an unknown language. The smoke along with the voice faded until all that was left was Syrena, standing before the ash-covered table with her head bowed.

Some of his panic eased. "Syrena?"

She turned slowly, a triumphant smile curving her blue-tinged lips. His own faded as he took in the singed tendrils that framed her blackened and bloodied face. The muscles low in his belly knotted painfully at the sight of her blood-spattered tunic, the fabric melted into her arms. What he could see of her flesh was seared to a fiery red, bubbling with weeping sores.

"I did it," she said, coming toward him.

"Aye, ye did." Trying to conceal his alarm, he carefully folded her in his arms, afraid to hurt her any more than she already had been. "Ye're badly burned, angel. Let me—"

As though she sensed his fear, she pulled back and touched his cheek. "I'll heal." Her gaze scanned the chapel, and she gasped.

"Did I hurt ye?"

"No . . . no, it's Davina," she said, looking in the direction of the altar.

Aidan turned. Naked, curled on her side with her hand clutched to her belly, Davina lay at the base of the altar chained to the stone. He released Syrena and strode from the dais to one of the men Connor held. Stripping the black robe from his bony white shoulders, he returned to Davina and draped it over her. Once he had her freed from the chains, she crawled into his arms and whimpered. He stroked her back, dreading the thought of telling her John Henry was dead.

He looked up to see Syrena watching him comfort Davina. "Callum, take her to Bess, but . . ."

Callum nodded. He understood what could not be said

aloud. He would make no mention of John Henry. Aidan would tell her himself. He disentangled from Davina and came to his feet, taking in his brother as he did so. Lachlan twitched in his drug-induced stupor, grimacing in pain.

He went to his brother's side and bowed his head. Aidan felt the warmth of Syrena's hand on his back, offering him comfort. "What have I done, Syrena?"

"You are not responsible for this, Aidan."

Aye, he was. He unlocked the chains that bound his brother. They fell away, clanging against the stone, but for each one Aidan released, another tightened around him. He would never be able to look at Lan again without seeing him like this, pale, emaciated, his flesh burnt, chunks of skin cut away, open sores raw and oozing. There was not an inch of his body unmarked. "How did he survive?"

"I know how bad it looks Aidan, but he will heal."

"On the outside, mayhap, but what about here?" He brushed the long, thick waves of matted blond hair from his brother's face and touched his head. "Or here?" He placed a palm over the shallow drum of Lachlan's heart.

Her hand fell away from his back. "I don't know."

"He will come to the Isles, where he belongs, where no Mortal shall ever harm him again," a deep voice intoned.

Chapter 26

Aidan reached for his sword and Syrena put out a hand to stop him. "It's King Rohan, Aidan. He's my uncle. They come in peace," she explained quietly, wishing somehow she could have put this moment off.

"My niece is right. Put your sword away, Mortal. I bring with me Uscias, the Wizard of the Enchanted Isles, Syrena's good friend Evangeline, and King Gabriel of England's Fae." He gestured to each of them in turn.

"I'm Aidan MacLeod, Lachlan's brother." Syrena waited for him to add "your niece's husband," but he didn't and a chill settled over her. She glanced at him but he stood stiffly erect, his attention focused on her uncle.

King Gabriel said, "I owe you a debt of gratitude, Mortal. With the help of your men, we have released mine from the dungeons."

Aidan nodded, keeping an eye on King Rohan, who stepped onto the platform and put a finger to Syrena's singed hair. "I see you retrieved your sword. The Grimoire?"

"Destroyed."

"You did well, Syrena. For your part in helping both Fae and Mortal avoid what in all likelihood would have been a catastrophe of great magnitude, the charges brought against you have been dropped."

"What the hell do ye mean by charges? Why—"

Syrena caught Aidan's eye and shook her head. "Thank you, Uncle."

King Rohan's gaze swept over her, and he arched a brow. With a flick of his wrist, he clothed her in shimmering robes of gold, her crown of precious gems coming to rest on top of her head. "There, more befitting your station, don't you think?"

Aidan stared at her as though seeing her for the first time. She clenched her hands, her nails biting into her palms, and forced herself to hold his gaze. Lachlan awakened and struggled to sit up. Aidan abruptly turned away from her, a muscle in his jaw twitching. He rested his hand on his brother's chest and gently ordered him to remain still.

"Who are ye?" Lan rasped, his heavy-lidded gaze on Syrena's uncle.

"King Rohan, your uncle." With another flick of his wrist, the black robe fell from Lachlan's broken body, to be replaced by robes the same as hers.

"You don't have much imagination when it comes to robes, Rohan." King Gabriel chuckled before he addressed them, "I must take my leave. My men are anxious to be gone from this realm."

"Gabriel is right. Let us leave here. The stench of evil lingers." Her uncle went to lift Lan from the stone slab, but Aidan held up a hand. "What do ye think ye're doin'?"

Rohan arched a brow. "I was going to carry him outside."

"I'll do it."

"As you wish."

Aidan gently lifted his brother into his arms, and Lan released an anguished moan. Her stomach lurched at Aidan's tortured wince. She took a step toward him but he gave an abrupt shake of his head, warning her off.

"Syrena." Her uncle offered her his arm.

"If you don't mind, Uncle, my wounds are painful, I'll

walk down on my own." She stepped out of the way so Aidan could go down first.

"Can ye no' do anythin' fer her?" he grated out angrily.

"If it was in my power, Lord MacLeod, I would, but it is not. Do not worry, Syrena will heal quickly."

"And my brother?"

"Will take time, I'm afraid."

Aidan grunted then walked ahead of them.

"The Mortal cares for you, Syrena," her uncle said.

"I thought he did," she murmured, not certain how he felt about her now that he was faced with exactly who she was. She swallowed the knot of emotion, assuring herself that he just needed time.

"Is there something I should know about your relationship?"

She bowed her head. She couldn't keep her marriage from her uncle, not if she wanted to have a life with Aidan. "He's my husband." She chanced a look at King Rohan to gauge his reaction. Noting the hard set of his mouth, she quickly added, "I love him."

"I see," he said as they stepped into the cool night air.

Evangeline came toward her with a blanket. "Here, your highness." She glanced over to where Aidan stood in the center of his men with Lachlan in his arms. "It might be less painful for your brother if he lies down."

"Thank you, Evangeline." She took the blanket and walked over to Aidan who was speaking to Lachlan. The two men were deep in conversation and she hesitated, not wanting to interrupt them.

"I heard him. They want me to return to the Fae realm with them. Do ye wish me to go?"

"Nay, but I was almost too late this time. And I doona ken how many have learned of yer Fae bloodline," Aidan answered Lachlan, keeping his voice low.

"I'll go. Mayhap if I do, ye can finally have the life ye wanted. No brother to protect. No brother to be ashamed of."

"Nay, 'tis never been that way,"Aidan protested, and the pain Lachlan's words caused him was etched on his face.

She wanted to intervene, but knew instinctively her interference would do more harm than good. Instead she knelt down and spread the thick blanket on the ground. "Aidan, perhaps you should put Lachlan down."

He nodded, but he didn't look at her. King Rohan motioned for everyone to stand back. Not knowing what to do, feeling like an outsider, she touched her brother's cheek then rose to her feet. She stepped away to give them some time alone together. She could only imagine how difficult it was for Aidan to let his brother go.

"Fer once be honest with yerself, Aidan. If it wasna fer me, ye'd be off with Iain, yer father would be alive, and so would Janet. Fer Christsakes, admit it. I canna do this anymore, pretend I'm someone' I'm no'. I'm half-Fae, and 'tis no' somethin' I had a say in. If our mother had no' been whorin' with a bloody faery, I wouldna exist, and I wouldna ruined yer life." Lachlan twisted his body to look beyond Aidan, grimacing with pain, sweat dotting his brow. "Get me out of here!"

Syrena covered her mouth with her palm, fighting to contain an anguished sob. She wanted to comfort them both. She knew how much pain Lachlan was in, but could only imagine how hurtful his words were for Aidan to hear.

Aidan crouched beside him and reached for his hand. "Lan, no, doona go like this."

Lachlan brushed his hand aside, and Aidan staggered to his feet. Syrena reached out to him, but he waved her off.

"Let me, princess," Uscias said gently.

He went to Aidan and laid a hand on his arm. "I'll look after him, Lord MacLeod. Do not let his words wound you. It is the drugs, the abuse that he has suffered making him say such things, but time heals all. When you are ready to see him, come to the Callanish Stones." He walked past Aidan and knelt beside Lan. Taking her brother's hand in his, they disappeared within a shower of twinkling lights.

Her uncle came to stand beside Syrena. He gave her shoulder a comforting squeeze before saying to Aidan, "Uscias is right, Lord MacLeod. Your brother will heal. And after what you've done this day, you will always be welcome in the Fae realm. Aidan, if I may call you, Aidan?"

Aidan scrubbed his hands over his face. "Aye."

"There's something I feel you must know. Especially after the disparaging comments your brother made about your mother. She does not deserve his contempt, nor yours if you harbor any. It is my brother who must be held accountable, and I'm afraid that is no longer possible. What I'm trying to say is my brother Arwan used magick to enchant your mother. It is against Fae law, but that never stopped Arwan before. Your mother would not have been able to resist—"

"He raped her?"

"Harsh, but yes."

Aidan took an angry step toward Syrena and she swallowed a startled cry. Heartsick at the rage she saw in his eyes when he looked at her, she was afraid that in that moment he'd forgotten everything they'd meant to one another. His nostrils flared, and he lacerated her with the contempt in his cold gaze. "Ye kent this all along and ye kept it from me?"

"No. I mean . . . yes I knew, Aidan, but I didn't keep it from you intentionally. I had no idea how you felt about your mother. If I ever thought—"

He balled his hands into fists, the muscles rippling in his arms as though he wanted to shake her. She almost wished he would. It would be less painful than the disgust she saw in his eyes.

"No idea! Yer father raped my mother! She bled to death hearing my father curse her! Died knowing she left a bairn no one wanted. A god-forsaken—"

Her uncle grabbed him by the arm. "That will be enough, Lord MacLeod. You've had a shock. And since I'm aware how well you know my niece, I'm certain when you've had time to think about it, you will recognize she's innocent of any wrongdoing."

Reeling from the ferocity of Aidan's attack, she barely noticed the high-pitched keening until Davina Hamilton burst through the stunned onlookers.

Throwing herself into Aidan's arms, she wailed, "John Henry's dead, Aidan. He's dead. What am I to do?"

Aidan held her. "It will be all right, Davina."

"But the bairn," she cried.

"Ye doona have to worry. I'll take care of everythin'."

Evangeline came to stand beside Syrena. She took her hand in hers and squeezed. Syrena nodded. Her chest ached from holding back tears. She should've known; she had seen it in his eyes earlier when he'd been confronted with who she was. She'd hoped she'd been wrong, but she wasn't.

"If we're through here, I have much that requires my attention," Aidan grated out.

"I can see that," King Rohan observed, his deep voice tinged with sarcasm. "But there is one more matter which requires your attention here."

Aidan narrowed his steely gaze on her uncle.

"No, Uncle, please don't," she pleaded desperately, certain she was the matter to which he referred.

"Quiet," Rohan ordered.

Aidan's mouth flattened. "What would that be?"

"The matter of your marriage to my niece. I—"

"It was a sham, nothing more."

Her legs buckled and if not for Evangeline's arm around her waist, she would have crumpled at his feet in a devastated heap. She'd lost him.

"So be it. I will tell you, though, that I would've been hard pressed to allow the marriage. I have never approved of a union between Mortal and Fae. But if I did, I certainly would not allow my niece to wed a man foolish enough not to recognize the treasure he throws away. A man not able to get past his pride and his misconceptions to fight for a woman whose value is beyond compare—"

"Uncle, please." She begged in a tortured whisper. She couldn't stand by while everyone watched the man she loved with all her heart denounce her.

"Are ye finished?"

"Yes," her uncle said then nodded when Evangeline leaned over to whisper in his ear. "Right. Thank you. Lord MacLeod, considering what has gone on this night, Evangeline has offered to wipe the minds of all those here." Noting Aidan's distrustful expression, her uncle added, "It is neither painful nor harmful, and is in some cases a benefit to a person suffering guilt or emotional distress. The one somewhat annoying side effect is that the person can lose several years of memories."

"I accept the offer. Thank ye," Aidan said to Evangeline, his gaze skipping past Syrena. "There are several people I will leave to make the decision on their own. But as to the rest, I'd ask ye to remove their memories of this night."

"Would that include yourself, Lord MacLeod?" her uncle asked, his tone silky.

"I'll have my memories wiped, if possible, the last two years." Aidan looked directly at Syrena when he said the words that shattered her heart. A muscle pulsated in his jaw, and he held her gaze, searching her face as though to memorize it, then he said, "Good-bye."

He turned and walked away, Davina clinging to his arm.

"I'm sorry, Syrena," her uncle said quietly.

She nodded. She couldn't speak. Her throat hurt too much from swallowing her sorrow.

Samuel and Bess wove their way through the crowd of curious onlookers to come to her. The older woman took her hand in hers. "I'm sorry, my lady, I doona ken what else to say. Samuel and I just wanted to tell ye we wouldna be havin' our memories wiped. They're too precious to lose. And . . . and we won't forget ye, we doona wish to." They hugged her then walked away.

Syrena hadn't said a word. Her tears were too close to the surface. And if she started to cry, she didn't think she would ever stop.

Callum came over and awkwardly patted her back. "I never thought Laird Aidan a fool until this night. Ye take care, my lady. Doona ferget yer promise to wee Alex and Jamie. They'll be expectin' a visit from ye, as will we all."

At Callum's mention of the twins, the thought of all she had lost came crashing down upon her. By the time Connor came to say good-bye, her fragile control over her emotions had snapped. Silent tears streamed down her face.

Connor shook his head. "I thought ye were a warrior, Lady Syrena. I'm sorely disappointed in ye."

"What do you mean?" She sniffed, wiping her eyes with the backs of her hands.

"'Tis obvious ye love the laird, and just as obvious he loves ye. Why doona ye fight fer him?"

"He's made his decision, Connor. He doesn't want me. I don't know how to fight that."

He jerked his head to where Aidan stood with Samuel, Bess, and Davina. "I think ye do. Besides, what harm could it do when he means to lose all memory of ye."

Syrena didn't know if Connor was right, or if she could do anything to stop Aidan from wiping her from his memories, but there was one thing she had to do. A promise she'd yet to fulfill.

She lifted her hand to her crown then let it drop before she removed it. She would no longer pretend she was anything other than who she was. Princess Syrena, a Fae princess, inept at magick, not as powerful or as strong as everyone imagined, but none of that mattered anymore. If she didn't accept who she was, how could she expect anyone else to? She'd heard every tortured word Lachlan said to Aidan. Her brother had done the same as she did and look where it got him.

"Lady Hamilton," she said quietly when she reached the edge of the woods.

The woman cowered beside Aidan. "I doona wish to speak to ye. Ye're Fae. Ye're responsible fer my husband's death."

"Davina," Aidan said sharply. "Syrena—"

"I can speak for myself, thank you. I wasn't responsible for your husband's death, Lady Hamilton. Two Mortals were. Nor was I responsible for what was done to you or Lachlan. Again, that would be Mortals. If this night has showed anything, it is that Mortals have a greater propensity for evil than the Fae. But that is not what I came to speak to you about. I made a promise to your husband. He wanted you to know that he loved you. With his dying breath, he sought to ensure your rescue." She wasn't certain the woman deserved John Henry's love, but it wasn't for her to judge. She'd done what she'd set out to.

She turned to walk away then bowed her head, swallowing her pride. She had made a promise to herself, and no matter how difficult it was to keep, she would. "Aidan, may I speak with you a moment?"

"Aye." He set Davina aside and took a wary step toward Syrena.

"Earlier today I made myself a promise. With everything that's gone on, it's not an easy one to keep, but as you have decided to wipe me from your memory, I thought . . . well, I thought you should know." She bit her bottom lip to keep it from quivering, blinking back tears before she raised her gaze to his. "I love you, Aidan. I love you with every fiber of my being, and I always will. I—"

He cursed and closed the distance between them in one powerful stride, crushing her to his chest. "Why, Syrena, why are ye doin' this to yerself?" he rasped in her hair. He drew back. Powerful fingers biting into her shoulders, he shook her. "I love ye. Do ye hear me? I love ye. I love ye too much to risk doin' to ye what I did to Lan."

"But—"

"Nay, I won't change my mind. Yer uncle is right. Ye deserve someone who will love ye without conditions. Someone who doesn't make ye feel as though ye're less than perfect just the way ye are. Take a good long look at Lachlan, Syrena, and see what I've done to him. Ask him if I'm the man fer ye. He'll tell ye I'm no'."

Aidan was right. She did deserve to be loved that way. And she held out hope that one day, after he'd had time to think things through, he would be able to. But if he had no memory of her, of them, he took away any chance of that happening.

Evangeline walked toward them. She took one look at Syrena and came to an abrupt halt.

Frantic at the thought of losing Aidan forever, she clutched his shirt. "Aidan, no, please don't do it. Don't take away your memories of us."

He cupped her face with his big hands and gently kissed her. "'Tis the only thing I can do."

Heavy hands came to rest on her shoulders. "Syrena, come away," her uncle said, taking her sobbing into his arms. "You truly love him, don't you?" he asked as he led her away.

She glanced over her shoulder, barely able to see Aidan through the cloud of her tears. He had his back to her now, talking to Evangeline. "Yes, I love him so much I don't know how I can go on without him."

"You're strong, you'll find a way. I'll help you. It is why he does what he does, Syrena. It's the only way he can think of going on without you." A fountain of sparkling light washed over them.

Chapter 27

Aidan folded his arms over his chest and leaned against a boulder on the rocky shores of Dunvegan. A brisk wind churned the azure waters, tossing the white-foamed swells against the rowboat Gavin lowered in the distance. Aidan was bone tired. He'd arrived at his cousin's keep the night before. Rory and Aileanna had urged him to remain, but he knew they'd harangue him about Syrena, and it was more then he could bear.

He found himself wishing, not for the first time, that he'd gone ahead and let Evangeline wipe his memory free of her. But in the end, he hadn't been able to go through with it. Not after Syrena, with strength and dignity, had bared her heart to him and begged him not to. No matter how painful the memories, he had to keep a part of her with him. To rip her from his mind would have been like severing a piece of his heart, his very soul.

Closing his eyes, he soaked up the watery rays, not strong enough to take the chill from the air, or his bones. A shadow blocked the sun. He raised heavy lids and groaned.

The wee demons.

"What do ye want?" He warily eyed the bundles they carried in their arms. The two of them sat their wee arses onto the stony shore, Alex on one side of him, Jamie on the other.

"We're comin' to Lewes with ye," Jamie informed him.

Like hell they were. "Ye're no' comin' to Lewes, so take yer bundles and head back to the keep."

"Aye, we are. We're goin' to fetch our auntie."

Aidan ignored Jamie's reference to Syrena. The last thing he wanted to do was talk about her, especially with the demons. "Yer da willna let ye come. Where is he?" Shooting a glance over his shoulder, he prayed he would catch a glimpse of his cousin.

"He sent us down to ye. He said he had to have a wee chat with our mam," Alex explained.

Aye, he could well imagine the kind of chat Rory was havin' with his bonny wife. Aidan would do the same in his place, with Syrena. He blew out a frustrated breath. Every thought led back to her.

"Yer Auntie Syrena had to go home. She's her people's princess. They need her."

"But you need her. She's yer wife. Go get her!" Jamie demanded with a belligerent thrust of his chin.

Aye, she'd been his wife, and he'd called their marriage a sham. It wasn't—it had been as close to perfect as he could ever have imagined, and he'd thrown it all away. He had to get rid of the bairns. They caused him to think too much, to question his reasons for giving up the only woman he'd ever love. "Yer auntie is no' like ye and me."

"Aye, she's a lass, like Mama," Jamie said, talking to him as though he were the bairn and not the other way around.

"Nay, I mean she's different, she's . . ." He didn't know what to say.

Jamie glanced furtively over his shoulder then whispered, "Special. She's Fae."

Sweet Christ!

"Who told ye that?"

"Mama. 'Tis our secret, but we can share with family. Families doona keep secrets. Mama says folks are silly and afraid of what they canna understand. She said there are some who might try to steal Auntie fer her magick if they found out she's Fae. 'Tis why only family can ken, but I think they'd want her 'cause she's bonny and loves bairns."

Aidan scrubbed his hands over his face. Aye, she was bonny, and he thought he might strangle Aileanna the next time he saw her. He didn't want to think about Syrena, didn't want to be reminded of what he'd lost.

"We're the same as Auntie," Alex announced proudly.

"Are no'," Jamie scoffed.

"Are, too. Our great, lots of greats, grandda was half-Fae. His mama was a Fae princess just like Auntie Syrena. She gave us the faery flag."

Christ, the bairn was right. Every one of them had Fae blood running in their veins, however diluted it may be. Aidan came to his feet, wondering why he hadn't thought of it before. But if he had, would it have made a difference?

"Oh, aye, I forgot." Jamie looked put out that his brother was right and him wrong, but quickly got over it when he jumped to his feet. Dropping his bundle, he excitedly waved his arms. "Look, Gavin and Donald are here to take us to Lewes."

"Jamie and Alex, where do you think you're going?" Aileanna called to her sons from the path leading down to the loch.

The demons tugged on Aidan's legs, moving him toward the rowboat approaching the shore. "Hurry, hurry, she's comin'," Jamie squealed.

"Ye're daft if ye think I'm takin' ye with me. Yer mother will have my head."

"Aye, she would. Boys, leave your Uncle Aidan be. He has to get back to Lewes," Aileanna said as she walked along the rocky shore toward them

"To bring Auntie home?" Alex asked.

"Aye, if he starts thinking with his heart instead of his head, he will."

Aidan dragged his hand through his hair and looked into Aileanna's shrewd blue gaze. "I doona think I can."

"Of course you can. You love her, and that's all that matters. Everything else you can deal with together, Aidan."

"I loved Lachlan and look—"

"Aye, you did, you do. It wasn't you or the Fae that hurt him, it was Jarius. You're not responsible for anyone else's actions, not even Lan's. He has his own demons to deal with, Aidan. You can't make it right for everyone."

He'd always known Lachlan was troubled, but he'd never known what to do about it. "Thank ye, Aileanna, I'll give it some thought."

She patted his cheek. "You do that. And, Aidan, you might want to remember the woman you love is a warrior, just like you. Together there is nothing the two of you can't overcome."

Aidan stood at the bow of the boat, the wind pushing the hair from his face, Aileanna's words ramming past his defenses. Gavin came to stand beside him and together they watched the stone walls of Lewes come into view—cold and austere. It hadn't always been that way. While his mother lived, the castle had been warm and inviting, the same as when Syrena had been there.

Thanks to Rohan's revelation, his memories of his mother were no longer tainted with bitterness and blame. His fury that night with Syrena had been uncalled for. Her uncle was right. He knew her too well to think she'd kept it from him on purpose. It wasn't her fault her father was a bastard, just as it wasn't his that Alexander had allowed drink to control his life and his actions.

"Are ye goin' after her?"

The closest thing to family Aidan had on Lewes, he had confided everything to Donald and Gavin. "Aye." He couldn't go on any longer without her in his life. And it didn't sit well with him that his wee wife showed more courage than he did. With his decision made, the resentment and anger that had consumed him for all those long years fell away.

Gavin clapped him on the back. "Good, now, do ye ken if she has some friends she'd like to bring back with her?"

Aidan snorted. "Ye may no' want to get ahead of yerself. I doona even ken if she'll return with me."

"Just be yer charmin' . . . Aye, ye're right, she may no'."

"Thanks fer yer confidence."

"Ye ken I'm playin' with ye. She loves ye, at least she did."

Aye, and now he had to convince her how badly he wanted her, needed her. And then there was her uncle. Aidan had an uneasy feeling King Rohan might be the hardest of all to convince.

Aidan slammed his sword against the Callanish Stones. He'd tried knocking on the bloody things, he'd tried whispering to them, and then yelling, feeling like a daft fool for doing so, but it was the only way he knew of reaching Syrena.

"You need to learn patience, Lord MacLeod," a craggy voice tsked from behind him.

"Uscias?" Aidan searched the circle.

"Yes, I wondered how long it would take for you to come." The old man stepped around a towering gray stone.

"So, ye're no' surprised to see me?"

"Why should I be? Our princess is the fairest of them all, is she not?"

"Aye, she is. Will ye take me to her?"

"Yes, but be prepared—circumstances in the Enchanted Isles are changing as we speak. And you will have to deal with the biggest change of all, Lord MacLeod."

Aidan grabbed the wizard's arm. "Has somethin' happened to Syrena?"

"It is not your wife to whom I refer." He held up his hand

when Aidan attempted to question him further. "All in good time, my lord, all in good time."

Syrena took her rightful place at the head of the table on the dais. She was now Queen of the Isles. Lachlan, whose wounds had slowly healed, took the chair to her right, while her stepmother, who'd finally agreed to the terms set out by her uncle, settled herself at Syrena's left. King Rohan, recently arrived, took a seat, making an appearance in honor of Syrena's coronation.

A little over a month had passed since the nightmare of Glastonbury. By tacit agreement, she and Lachlan did not mention Aidan. It was too painful for them both. She didn't tell her brother about Aidan's decision to wipe out the last several years of his life. Nor did she tell him about the circumstances of his birth. Lachlan had more than enough to deal with for now.

She squeezed his hand. "It's good to have you with us." It was the first night her brother had joined them in the hall, and Syrena was happy he'd picked this night to do so. It meant so very much to her.

It had taken time before she was able to experience any emotion other than sorrow. But with help from Fallyn and her sisters, Syrena had thrown herself into ruling the Enchanted Isles. Finding some balance between the rights of both men and women hadn't been easy. There was still room for improvement, but she thought circumstances for both had changed for the better.

Syrena formed one council for the women, and one for the men. When they reached a consensus within their group, they brought their issues to her. With Morgana at the helm of the women's council, the demands never ceased, but her stepmother seemed content with the arrangement.

"You must be feeling better," Syrena said to her brother, noting he no longer suffered from the sickly pallor he once had.

"He must be. He pleasures more women than yer father did on a daily basis." Morgana didn't bother to lower her voice. The men at the table snorted their amusement. Lord Bana and Lord Erwn were obviously pleased to hear of the king's son's prowess with the ladies. The women pretended disdain at Lachlan's behavior, all the while eyeing her beautiful brother with desire. Syrena wasn't blind to his dissolute conduct. Fallyn kept her informed whereas others would have shielded her from the information.

Lan sprawled on the gilded chair, raised a brow, then shrugged. He lifted the gold-encrusted chalice to his lips and wrinkled his nose in disgust.

Syrena laughed. "Here, take mine. I don't like it as sweet."

He snorted. "Since when?" His eyes shadowed at his reference to those long-ago days on Lewes.

"Oh, about a week ago." She smiled, trying to lighten the mood.

Syrena brought his goblet to her lips and wrinkled her nose as well. It was sweet.

"No," Morgana shrieked, "it's poisoned." She knocked the goblet from Syrena's hand. Crimson juice splattered the white linen tablecloth, and a circle of red bloomed in the center of Syrena's white robes.

Guards rushed to the table, but Lan already stood in front of Morgana with the tip of Nuie's blade at her throat. "A verra stupid move on yer part, Morgana."

"No, Lachlan, lower the sword."

He did as Syrena asked, setting Nuie at the side of her chair. She couldn't help but notice there was no glow of color when Lachlan held her sword. An icy chill skittered along her spine. She met Uscias's gaze across the long length of the table. He stroked his beard. "Time," he mouthed. He'd seen Nuie's lack of response.

Her uncle came to her side to examine the stain and the residue in her cup, sniffing its contents. "Rowan berries," he spat, pinning Morgana with a malevolent glare.

"It was not me. I saved her life." Her gaze shot to where the servants ringed the wall. She jumped to her feet and her chair skittered to the white marble floor. Pointing to the silver-haired woman attempting to escape the hall, she cried, "It was Nessa."

"Take them both to the throne room. We'll get to the bottom of this, now." Rohan cast an apologetic smile at Syrena. "I'm sorry, your highness. I overstepped my authority."

"No, you haven't," she said, placing her napkin at the side of the gold-rimmed porcelain plate. She rose to her feet. "Lan, are you coming?"

"Ye mean we're no' goin' to eat first?"

She rolled her eyes. His appetite for food, drink, and women was becoming legendary. "Lan, Nessa tried to kill you. Do you not wish to know why, or see her punished?"

He lifted world-weary eyes to her. "No' particularly."

"Lachlan, as the king's son, your presence is required," her uncle rebuked Lachlan, tempering his obvious anger.

"But no' necessary. My sister has it under control."

Their uncle blew out an aggravated breath. Syrena intervened before Rohan exploded. "Lan, please, I'd like you to be there."

Grunting, he threw down his napkin and came to his feet. "All right, but make it quick. I'm starvin'."

Rohan offered his arm to Syrena then glanced down at her gown. His brow furrowed. "Perhaps you'd like to change your robes, niece."

Fallyn, overhearing her uncle's remark, met Syrena's gaze and lifted a finger. Syrena shook her head. Since Glastonbury, she'd made a promise that the time for pretending was over. She would be true to herself. It had just taken her a little longer to come to the same place where her magick was concerned.

Syrena closed her eyes, murmured the incantation, and flicked her finger. She cracked an eye open and looked into the horrified faces of her entourage.

Oh, Hades.

Holding her breath, she glanced down. She'd clothed herself in a bronze gown that bared her arms and shoulders. The neckline was cut low to reveal the full swell of her breasts, a pleated sash wrapped at her waist.

She raised her gaze to Fallyn, who smothered a laugh with her hand.

"Lovely, my lady," Shayla said. "We wore gowns of a similar style at Dmitri's court, much more practical for our climate than these." She held out her heavy robe. With a flick of her wrist, she clothed herself in an amethyst gown like the one Syrena wore.

Fallyn did the same, as did Riana.

Syrena smiled at the three women. She didn't know what she'd do without them. With Evangeline busy at Rohan's court, and unwilling to come to the Isles with Morgana and Lachlan in residence, they rarely saw each other.

She understood Evangeline's issues with Morgana, but had yet to determine what was behind her friend's contempt of Lachlan. Surely his attempt at kissing her could not be the reason, but no matter how hard Syrena pressed the issue, Evangeline would not relent.

With a loud harrumph, her uncle guided her into the throne room. The Fae had already gathered, jostling for position. They were pressed tight against the white, gold-veined marble walls. Syrena made her way up the three steps to the curved dais and took her place on her golden throne. Lan prowled in behind her and sank into the matching throne at her left.

The guards held fast to Morgana and Nessa, who hurled angry accusations at one another. Uscias stood at the back of the room. He tipped his chin at Syrena, letting her know he'd cast a spell so that neither woman could use their magick to transport themselves from the room.

Syrena demanded silence and called the court to order. The charges were attempted murder of Lachlan, and accessory to the attempt. If the women were found guilty, the sentence for both charges was death.

"He has no right to sit on the throne. He's only half-Fae," Nessa spat out.

"As King Arwan's son, Lachlan has every right to hold the throne," Syrena said, worried now that she had pressed Lan to attend the proceedings. She knew how it felt to be made to feel unworthy and didn't want him to suffer for it. She stopped the thought—she had prevailed, and so would he.

"And that is what you want? You want one such as Arwan to lead the Fae? He was an abusive, lecherous murderer and his son will be no different!" Nessa twisted in the guards' grasp, her movements becoming more frenzied by the moment.

"Our father had his faults, but he brought prosperity to the Isles, and Nessa, outside of battle, he was no murderer."

The silver-haired woman's hysterical laugh raised the hairs on the back of Syrena's neck. "Yes, he did! He murdered your mother! No one would have believed me if I came forward, and if he knew what I'd seen, he would have killed me. But it's true, I saw him do it, and when he thought to name someone other than my lady as his successor, men as contemptible as he, I killed him," she shrieked triumphantly. "Great, powerful King Arwan, brought to his knees by a berry."

Pandemonium broke out in the room. The Fae shouted for the women's deaths, shaking their fists as they surged forward. The guards formed a defensive ring around the two women. The room wavered in front of Syrena, a gush of prickly heat flooding her body.

Lachlan took her hand in his. "If ye want me to, Syrena, I'll take over."

She squeezed his fingers. "I'll be fine, it's just a shock. All this time I thought my mother had faded." *I thought she'd abandoned me, didn't love me enough to stay, that I'd done something wrong.* Swallowing past the thick lump that constricted her throat, she asked her uncle, who now stood by her side, "Did you know?"

"No. If I had, I would have killed him myself. I . . ." Her uncle's amber eyes glistened, and his hand tightened on her shoulder.

She gathered her strength around her like a cloak. She was Queen. She needed her questions answered, a verdict rendered. "Why, Nessa? If my father no longer loved my mother, he simply would have cast her aside. He had no reason to kill her."

Eyes blazing with hatred, Nessa spat out, "Yes, he did. She was going to leave him. I tried to talk her out of it, but she said she could no longer stand by and let him treat you as he did." Pinning Syrena with a malevolent stare, she yelled, "You have no right to pass judgment over me, sitting up there as though you rule the Isles. You have no right to the throne. Helyna had an affair with King Rohan. He's your father, not Arwan."

Her uncle's hand slipped limply from Syrena's shoulder.

"I don't believe you. You've always hated me, Nessa. If what you say is true, why wouldn't you have said something before?"

"You're right, I do hate you. Because of you, Helyna died, but I loved her and made her a promise never to tell. But if you mean to condemn me, I condemn you with the knowledge she died because of you! You and Rohan!"

Lachlan came to his feet. "By yer own words, Nessa, you have sealed yer fate. The court finds ye guilty of murder and attempted murder. Yer sentence is death and will be carried out at sunrise on the morrow. Guards, take her away."

"Mark my words, Lachlan MacLeod, I'll haunt you from beyond," she shouted over her shoulder as the guards dragged her from the room.

"Ye're welcome to try."

In a daze, Syrena watched her brother take control of the proceedings. Her mind reeled with the thought she was to blame for her mother's death, and that the man standing silently beside her, a man she'd secretly wished was her father, truly was.

"Morgana, ye're charged with accessory to the attempted murder of myself and, as the evidence seems irrefutable, as an accessory to my father's murder. What say ye?" Lan said in a deep rumbling monotone.

"I am guilty of neither crime," she said defiantly.

Lachlan arched a brow. "Ye're sayin' ye didna ken my mead held poison?"

"Yes, but, I . . . I saved the Queen," she sputtered.

"And King Arwan?"

"No." She shook her head. "No, I only learned once the deed was done that Nessa had murdered him."

"Would ye have stopped her if ye kent what she planned to do?"

Morgana held Syrena's gaze. "No."

Syrena fought through her grief to come to her feet, placing a hand on Lachlan's arm. Morgana was not an evil woman. They'd had their differences, but her stepmother had suffered more than most at her father's hand. And over the years, she had done her best to protect Syrena.

"Morgana, would you have stopped Lachlan from drinking the mead?" she asked.

Her stepmother bowed her head. "I don't know."

"In good conscience, Morgana, I find I cannot condemn you to death. But neither can I allow you to remain in the Enchanted Isles. From this day forth, you are banished. I will see you escorted to wherever it is you wish to go."

Her stepmother nodded, a look of relief in her emerald eyes. "Thank you, your highness," she said before she was led away.

"Guards, clear the room," Lachlan ordered, leading Syrena to the throne. "Sit." He glanced at her . . . her father. "King Rohan, you might want to take a seat as well."

Rohan nodded and sat wearily on the throne. "She died because of me."

"No, she died because she tried to protect me."

"Don't, Syrena. I will not allow you to blame yourself for her death. The blame lies with my brother; leave it at that."

King Rohan was right. If Syrena had a child, she would've done the same as her mother. But the knowledge didn't make it any less painful. "Then you must do the same."

"I loved her, Syrena. We loved each other, but it was only that one night. Arwan, as you know, was not easy to live with and she came to me seeking comfort and . . ." He spread his hands. "I never knew you were my daughter. Helyna kept it from me. Most likely she was afraid I would force her to leave my brother and marry me. I would have, and she wouldn't have wanted to be the reason for a war."

Syrena leaned against the padded red velvet.

Rohan reached for her hand. "Promise me you won't blame your mother. Blame me, not her."

"I don't blame either of you."

He touched her cheek. "You're like her, you know. I've always thought of you more as a daughter than a niece. It will not be difficult getting used to the idea. I hope it will not be difficult for you either, Syrena."

"No, I always wished you were." She returned his smile.

Lachlan sighed. "If the two of ye are goin' to start greetin', I'm leavin'."

"I do not *greet*, nephew."

Syrena smothered a laugh then addressed Lan. "Thank you for taking over the proceedings. You handled yourself well."

He waved off her compliment. "'Twas nothin'. Ye would've dragged it on too long, and I am near to faintin' from hunger."

"You understand, Lachlan, that Syrena can no longer rule as Queen of the Isles. You must take your rightful place as king."

Syrena hadn't thought that far ahead, but her father was

right. A few months ago, it would've been difficult for her to hear. But no more. She knew who she was and no longer required anyone's approval, or her position as Queen, to validate her worth.

"Lachlan, I know it must seem a little overwhelming right now, but if I can do anything to make it easier for you, I will. And Uscias will continue to act as your mentor and . . ."

She stood and reached for Nuie. "Good-bye, my friend," she whispered, shards of blue glinting through her fingers. Her heart hurt. She hadn't been prepared for this, but Nuie now belonged to Lachlan. "Take care of him," she said as she brought the jeweled hilt to her lips. "He needs you as much as I once did, maybe more."

She blinked back tears and pressed the sword into Lachlan's hands.

He angled his head and regarded her with a baleful stare. "Are ye certain?"

"Yes, he belongs to you now."

"Well, I think he prefers ye. He doesna' make those pretty colors when I hold him."

Syrena couldn't tell him he had no feelings for Nuie to magnify. Lachlan was devoid of emotion, but he needed to discover those things on his own. She only hoped that one day he would find someone who could break through the barrier he had placed around his heart.

"'Twas nice havin' ye fer a sister, but I suppose I'll have to be satisfied that we are cousins."

"She's yer sister—sister-by-marriage mayhap, but yer sister all the same," the deep, familiar voice rumbled across the room from behind her.

Syrena closed her eyes, afraid she imagined him. Afraid if she turned around, he wouldn't be there and her slowly repairing heart would be shattered once again.

"Ye're no' dreamin'. He's here," Lachlan said quietly.

She opened her eyes and Lan nodded. Taking her by the shoulders, he turned her around.

"Aidan," she breathed his name. He towered over Uscias. Bigger, more beautiful than she remembered, his sensuous mouth curved in a gentle smile. She stumbled down the marble steps and flew into his outstretched arms. "You came."

"Aye, but ye kent I would, didna ye? Ye kent I'd never be able to stay away from ye."

She drew back and searched his silver-gray eyes. "You didn't have Evangeline wipe me from your memory, did you?"

He framed her face with his hands. "Nay, but I doona think it would have worked even if I did. Ye're no' just in my memories, Syrena. Ye're a part of me, my heart, my verra soul." He lifted his gaze from hers. "And I could no' risk forgettin' even one day with my brother, no matter our troubles."

Syrena looked over her shoulder to see what effect Aidan's words had on Lachlan.

Lan came slowly down the steps, holding his brother's gaze. "About time ye came to collect yer wife."

"Aye, it was. Ye look well. Are ye happy here?"

"Plenty of good food, wine, and women—what more could a mon ask fer? Speakin' of which, I'm starvin'. Come on, Uscias, let's leave my brother and his wife to get reacquainted. Ye, too, Uncle."

"Lord MacLeod has much to answer for before getting reacquainted with my *daughter*."

Before her father could say anything further, Lachlan admitted a guard carrying a missive for King Rohan. Her father grunted and looked over at her. "It seems I have matters to attend to. You are certain this is what you want, Syrena?"

"Yes." She smiled up at Aidan. "I love him, Father. As much as I'm sure you loved my mother. Please try and understand."

He closed the distance between them. "I do. But hear me well, MacLeod. I plan on spending as much time as I can with my daughter." He kissed Syrena on the forehead then strode from the room, garnet robes swirling about him.

Aidan groaned. "Ye could've warned me, Uscias."

"Yes, I suppose I could have, but what amusement would there be in that?"

Lachlan snorted. "Have fun, brother. He makes the MacDonald look like a mewling lamb."

"Thanks fer that, Lan," Aidan muttered.

Lachlan, hand poised on the door, took a deep breath then looked back at Aidan. "I wish ye wiped that night from yer mind, brother. What I said to ye. I didna mean it. 'Twas the drugs and—"

"I ken, 'tis forgotten." Before his brother left the room, Aidan called out to him, "Lan, we'll be expectin' ye to visit often."

Lachlan flung an arm around Uscias. "Aye, we'll be there, won't we, my wee wizard?"

"I am not yer wee wizard, King Lachlan," Uscias berated him as they closed the door behind them.

"My brother's a king—who would've thought it?" Aidan shook his head then looked down at her. "And I'm married to the most beautiful Queen in the land."

She rose up on the tips of her toes to kiss her husband. A man she loved with all her heart. "I'm no longer Queen of the Isles, Aidan. I'm only a princess now."

"Nay, ye're the Queen of my Isles, Syrena, and ye always will be. I love ye, angel," he murmured against her mouth.

"I love you, too, Aidan."

Epilogue

Isle of Lewis
December 25, 1605

Syrena stood over her sleeping husband and tugged on his hand. "Aidan, get up. Aileanna won't let Alex and Jamie open their presents until everyone is downstairs."

Aidan groaned and rolled onto his back. "What are ye talkin' about, Syrena?"

"They want to open their presents, the ones we were to put under the . . ." She bit her lip.

He arched a brow. "Tree," he finished for her. "The tree ye burnt down while ye were showin' off fer the bairns." He pulled her down on top of him then rolled her beneath him.

She slapped his broad chest. "I wasn't showing off. They wanted me to decorate the tree like Aileanna does and . . . I couldn't find any candles, so . . ."

"So, ye used yer magick and turned the bloody tree into one."

"I put it out."

"Aye, and ye flooded the hall while ye were at it."

"At least the presents weren't under it yet. Now come, we have to go down." She tried to wriggle out from beneath the weight of his powerful warrior's body.

"Nay, I'm thinkin' I'm goin' to open *my* present right now."

He encircled her wrists with his big hands and held her arms over her head. Nudging her gown aside with his stubbled chin, he bared her breast. His mouth closed over her pearled nipple, and he suckled, sending an arrow of desire deep into her belly.

Arching her back, she moaned at his expert attention. He released her hands and worked her night rail down to her waist, the heat of his bare chest rubbing against hers. Cupping her breasts with his work-roughened hands, he nuzzled her ear.

"Ye havena fed Ava yet, have ye." His voice was low and husky. Milk trickled from her nipples, and he lowered his mouth to lap it up.

She squirmed. "No, and she is not going to be very happy with you. She doesn't like to share."

"Uhmm, just a wee bit more." He gave his attention to her other breast. Sliding his hand beneath her night rail to nudge her thighs apart, he said, "Open fer me."

"Aidan," she moaned when he found the sensitive nub, rubbing his thick, hard erection against her thigh.

"I didna think ye could get any more beautiful, angel, but ye have," he said, looking deep into her eyes, his fingers stroking inside her.

Soft little whimpers emitting from the nursery that adjoined their chambers turned quickly to a hungry wail.

Aidan buried his face in her breasts. "Yer daughter is as demandin' as ye are."

With Ava's insistent cries putting a damper on their passionate interlude, Syrena struggled to get out from under him. "And she's as noisy as you."

Aidan pinned her on her back and gave her one last fierce, demanding kiss, devouring her with his mouth. "When Ava has her afternoon nap, we're havin' one, too."

Syrena laughed, pushing him off her. "You're only mad

because Rory and Aileanna *napped* when Olivia did yesterday and left you to look after Jamie and Alex."

"Aye." Aidan tucked his arm behind his head and watched while she adjusted her night rail. "And I'm tellin' ye again, Syrena, no' to let the wee demons play with Ava. I caught them tossin' her back and forth to each other like she was a wee toy."

"You did not." She laughed, entering Ava's room. "Oh, poor baby," she crooned, lifting her daughter into her arms, cradling her downy soft blond curls to her chest. "Papa is very naughty keeping Mama from her little angel."

Aidan had left the bed to wash, his muscular body displayed in all its naked glory. He glanced at Syrena and grinned. "And yer mama better no' keep lookin' at yer da that way or he's no' lettin' her out of this room." At the sound of her father's voice, Ava lifted her head from Syrena's chest and held out her hands.

"I don't think our guests will appreciate the host and hostess not making an appearance."

Wrapping his plaid around his hips, he took Ava from her and tickled their daughter's belly. Ava squealed and her father chuckled before he returned his narrowed gaze to Syrena. "And just who are we expectin' besides my brother and Uscias?"

"My father." Ignoring Aidan's groan, she went on, counting off their guests on her fingers. "Alasdair and Fiona, Iain, Callum, Connor, Evangeline, Fallyn, Shayla, Riana, Samuel, and Bess," she finished on a long, drawn-out breath.

"I hope ye warned Lachlan. Those four women have it in fer him, especially Evangeline."

Her husband had a point. The women of the Isles were not happy with Lan. Like his brother, Lachlan had a problem with women going to war. Which may have explained why Fallyn, Shayla, and Riana were unhappy with him, but Syrena had yet to discover the reason behind Evangeline's ongoing contempt for Lan. "I didn't, but perhaps we will be able to keep them far enough apart to avoid an all-out war."

Aidan snorted. "Good luck with that." He tossed Ava in the air, laughing at her delighted giggles. "Ah, Syrena, ye ken if Samuel and Bess are comin', Davina will be joinin' them?" He was smart enough not to look at her when he asked his question.

Syrena remained silent. Arms crossed over her chest, she waited for the coward to meet her gaze.

He shook his head and sighed before he turned to look at her. "What do ye want me to do, angel? She has no kin left and she was my cousin's wife."

"A fact she seems to have forgotten."

"'Tis no' my fault Evangeline's magick wiped out all her memories."

Syrena rolled her eyes and sat in the rocking chair beside the bed, holding out her hands for Ava. "It seems rather convenient your betrothal was the only thing she did remember."

Aidan grinned, settling their squirming daughter into her arms. He crouched beside the rocker and kissed the top of Ava's silky blond head as she latched on to Syrena's nipple. Drawing a finger along the curve of Syrena's breast, he said, "Ye're jealous."

"I am not." She gasped when his warm lips followed the path of his finger.

"Aye, ye are, and ye have no reason to be. Ouch." He pried his thick black hair from Ava's fingers then nibbled her little hand. Their daughter giggled, choking and sputtering on her milk. Bright violet eyes sparkled as she gazed lovingly at her father.

"Go below. All she wants to do is play when you're about."

"Uncle Aidan, Aunt Syrena." Alex and Jamie pounded on the door. "'Tis time to wake up."

Aidan stood. With his hands on his hips, he glared at the door. "How long are the demons stayin'?"

"Hogmanay." She smiled. "Uncle Aidan's coming," she called out to the boys.

"Ye owe me, princess." He pressed a hard kiss to her lips. "Remember what I said—ye'll be needin' a verra long nap today."

Syrena shifted Ava to her other breast and her daughter, noting her father about to leave, put out her arms. "Oh no you don't, finish breaking your fast."

Aidan laughed. "Ye love yer da, doona ye, my wee angel?"

"Go." Syrena pointed to the door. Feeding her daughter was one of the most pleasurable times of her day, but not when Aidan was around. She kissed Ava's forehead and blinked back tears of gratitude. Her life was perfect—she had a husband and a baby she adored, the love of friends and family. She could not have asked for anything more.

Pink and purple lights sparkled in front of Syrena's eyes. She blinked. And Ava disappeared.

From the other side of the door she heard her daughter's gurgle of joy.

"Syrena!" Aidan bellowed.

"How did she do that?" Jamie asked.

"Oh, no," Syrena groaned.

About the Author

Debbie Mazzuca thinks she has the best job in the world. She spends her days cavorting through the wilds of seventeenth-century Scotland with her sexy Highland heroes and her equally fabulous heroines. Back in the twenty-first century you can find her living in Ottawa, Ontario, with her very own hero, two of their three wonderful children, and a yappy Yorkie. You can visit Debbie on the Web at www.debbiemazzuca.com.

GREAT BOOKS, GREAT SAVINGS!

When You Visit Our Website:
www.kensingtonbooks.com
You Can Save Money Off The Retail Price
Of Any Book You Purchase!

- All Your Favorite Kensington Authors
- New Releases & Timeless Classics
- Overnight Shipping Available
- eBooks Available For Many Titles
- All Major Credit Cards Accepted

Visit Us Today To Start Saving!
www.kensingtonbooks.com

All Orders Are Subject To Availability.
Shipping and Handling Charges Apply.
Offers and Prices Subject To Change Without Notice.